NEWSWOF

NEWSWORTHY

Sara Burrell

MILL CITY PRESS

Mill City Press, Inc.
2301 Lucien Way #415
Maitland, FL 32751
407.339.4217
www.millcitypress.net

Paperback ISBN-13: 978-1-66288-300-2
Hard Cover ISBN-13: 978-1-66288-301-9
Ebook ISBN-13: 978-1-66288-302-6

For my parents~
Thank you for helping me to fall in love with reading and writing.
And for my husband and children~
Thank you for your support and love.

"Fair is foul and foul is fair."

~ Shakespeare, *Macbeth*

Prologue

How did this happen? How did she lose her entire family? Sunlight blinded Rita, obscuring her view from the doorway. Or perhaps it was the tears. They filled her vision, held back by some invisible wall keeping them from falling. One blink, and the dam burst, the reality of the scene before her sharp and clear once more. The blue and red lights flashed brightly, the siren silent, although it seemed she could still hear it, loudly wailing in her head.

This cannot be the end. She had tried to keep them together. She had tried so hard. Desperation clawed at Rita's chest, squeezing the breath from her lungs, but she dared not let the gasps escape her lips. If panic took over, she'd completely lose control. Did she ever really have control?

The door slammed shut, sealing the recent horrifying events into the obscenely cheerful, sunny day. This was definitely the end. *How did this happen?*

May 18, 1995

The back porch of the Walsh home was completely lit up, bathed in the last rays of the sun as it began its descent behind

ix

the horizon. Rita Walsh tilted her face toward the healing glow, continuing to rock the wiggly newborn that she held in her arms, making shushing, calming noises. She was trying her best to settle the baby, as well as herself, fighting to ignore the feeling of concern growing in her stomach. It was a gnawing ache that threatened to overtake any rational thought if she didn't tend to it carefully and immediately.

Frank was a good man, wasn't he? She'd always thought so. They hadn't dated long before becoming engaged, but she'd known him most of her life. Their families lived only a few blocks from each other when they were growing up, and she'd always known he had a thing for her.

Not to mention the fact that Frank was driven. He had goals and went after them. While she'd stayed near home, saving money to buy a car, Frank had moved away to college to Columbia University, which Rita found very impressive, and became a lawyer.

Neither of their families had much money for themselves, but Frank seemed determined to become well-off in order to live a life of comfort and means that his parents hadn't been able to provide. And didn't that say a lot about a person? Their sense of responsibility and determination?

Frank extended those qualities to include her as well, like a sword and shield, a knight coming to her rescue. Once he returned home after graduating, his first order of business was to ask Rita out. At least, that's what he claimed. But she had no reason to doubt him then.

She remembered how flattered and special she'd felt knowing that this handsome, intelligent, successful man had chosen to return to their small town with the express purpose of romancing her. Frank could've dated any girl in town. They all would've said yes to him, and he could've moved to a big city with more opportunities. But he picked Rita. He chose this life with her.

The diamond he put on her finger two months later was the largest she'd seen in real life, and it didn't take much convincing for her to begin imagining and planning their future together. The wedding itself was like a dream and Rita felt so smug and important showing off her new life and new husband. It had never been her intention to be a humble, gracious hostess. No, this was her chance to flaunt her good fortune and force everyone to look at her with fresh, hopefully envious, eyes.

She wanted all the guests to appreciate her worth, but most especially her mother, who was constantly reminding Rita that her beauty was only valuable to people who wanted something from her and would never ensure her long-term happiness. Even on that day, the greatest day of her life, her mom couldn't say anything positive.

She'd found Rita during the reception and said, "It's not going to last. You're just interested in his flashy life. After the honeymoon wears off, he's going to find out who he really married, a worthless, needy, push-over."

Well, she was wrong about that. Wasn't she? Her marriage to Frank had been romantic and smooth the entire first year. That's 365 days of bliss. Nothing is perfect forever for anyone.

She supposed, if she really reflected on everything, she could see that those first few times he'd accidentally hurt her had been more about his anger than her mistakes. Do other men really get that bent out of shape over their wives moving their shoes while cleaning up the house? It seemed a little over the top to Rita, but she hadn't grown up with a dad at home and she suspected there were plenty of people in the world who just got angrier more easily than she did.

In any case, he was always sorry and proved it by buying her the most wonderful gifts. Her husband had become her villain and her hero. Plus, she really had no other resources beyond what Frank provided, and he did give them a very comfortable existence with the money he made. She reckoned it was a good enough life and other people had it much worse than she did, and besides, she was going to prove her mother wrong if it killed her.

Frank had certainly not reacted well to the news of her first pregnancy. But, in just a few months, he'd come around to the idea of being a dad and even started to get excited with the possibility of raising a kid, in his words, "to become even more successful than I have!" Rita was pretty sure that he'd warm to his own child, giving him or her all the care and nurturing that a baby usually brought out in new parents. And he did. At first.

It'd only been recently that she'd started to worry about how Frank treated their sons. Rita watched as he ran around the backyard with Owen, Liam toddling in their wake. Her oldest tried so hard to please Frank, but the man really did have expectations that were too high for a four-year-old. Owen just wasn't as fast or as coordinated as Frank wanted him to be.

But still, Frank seemed to keep his patience, or at least he'd walk away from Owen when he got frustrated or perhaps throw some nearby object to vent his anger. Although, the look of rejection on her sweet boy's face whenever Frank left him out in the yard without an explanation, or the fear in his eyes as he watched his dad have a temper tantrum, was enough to break through her carefully created emotional wall. Lately, she'd learned to walk away, too. It was always better if she didn't witness what was happening.

Her concern came from watching the ease with which Liam, at only two years old, was able to grasp Frank's directions and commands in comparison with Owen's hesitation and confusion. Little Liam never seemed to evoke the same rage-filled reactions from Frank. But maybe she was just being paranoid. Surely, he would never treat his innocent children with the same disdain and violence that seemed to be reserved especially for her.

Rita looked down at Cara, whose eyes had finally shut in defeat, and switched the baby to her other arm. She had forgotten about the bruise on her bicep, and she'd let Cara lay against it long enough to make it throb. Cara sighed and made newborn dreaming sounds, soft mewing like a kitten. Rita admired the way babies had no knowledge of human nature, no nightmares or fears. They were just blank slates, full of possibilities and potential.

Rita had never had much control over parenting her boys. Maybe it was just being a new mother, overwrought and out of her element. Or maybe it was the fact that Frank had strong opinions about everything and never really wanted her input, even when it came to raising their babies.

But now, with a little girl, she thought perhaps she could be a better mom, more attentive and loving. Frank had no idea about raising a daughter. Girls were just different. Rita would never voice her desires to anyone, but her secret wish was that Cara would not turn out like the rest of her family. She could be better than all of them.

"I have so many hopes for you," she whispered into the tiny ear. "I hope you find a purpose for your life, and that you feel successful. I hope you'll always be safe and healthy."

Rita took a deep breath in through her nose and released it as slowly as she could, settling her jittery nerves. She watched Liam smile and pick up the ball that Frank had thrown. Frank applauded loudly and Owen seemed to still more with every clap, becoming immobile, his face wary and anxious.

"But mostly, I hope you're happy. I don't think I'm brave enough to find true happiness, but I hope you are."

PART 1:

OWEN

"Words have no power to impress the mind
without the exquisite horror of their reality."

~ Edgar Allan Poe, *The Fall of the House of Usher*

Chapter 1

I don't know why she insisted on seeing me this afternoon. I haven't spoken to my sister or seen her in person in five years, so I've been intensely curious of her motivations to meet ever since her early morning call to my hotel room.

Our relationship, if you could still qualify our tenuous connection as one, has been carefully built upon a series of predictable phone calls, formal politeness, and purposeful avoidance. She calls every year on May 18th. I don't call her. Ever.

In recent months, her behavior's been different. There's been a flurry of seemingly frantic phone calls from her every couple of weeks. I never pick up.

Even if it didn't feel dangerous to have a conversation with Cara, even if I wanted to talk to her, I probably wouldn't have acknowledged her calls. This entire year has been a whirlwind, an endless cycle of traveling, writing, researching, writing, traveling, writing.

Thoughts and memories have begun to blur at the edges, as one story of death fades into the next. My consciousness

3

is constantly slipping between the past and the present, and it's getting more difficult by the day to remain on this side of sanity. But when it comes to my sister, her presence, or even just the thought of her, brings every detail of my surroundings into sharp focus. My brain and body go on high alert, a fight or flight instinct. Cara's dangerous.

The last time I spoke to her, back in March, was quite by accident, as I would never do anything so careless on purpose. Actually, I answered the phone intending to tell her off for backing me into a corner and harassing me to the point of losing control, but I never should've allowed her to affect me like that. So maybe the word "accident" is an inaccurate description for why I picked up that day. I just wish there was a better explanation for the fact that she's the only person in my life that knocks me off balance, the only person that has the ability to completely wreck my self-restraint.

A cool breeze traveling through the park washed over my face, assuaging some anxiety. My eyes closed in sync with the deep breath filling my core and the memory of the last time I'd spoken to Cara on the phone flooded my brain.

I was sitting in the warm, quiet confines of the Other Brother Coffee Bar on Northern's campus, hoping to accomplish some writing. Still feeling unsure and a little insecure about the immediate success of my first series of articles, I was leaning on the current story to solidify my boss' positive opinion of my investigative skills, not to mention my unparalleled proficiency at telling an in-depth story.

My phone began buzzing on the table, tucked underneath my notebook and an untidy stack of papers. I ignored the noise and continued to type furiously, trying to get all of my jumbled thoughts out of my brain and into the article. The offending gadget was only quiet momentarily before it began to buzz and vibrate again, shaking the table and jangling my nerves. I continued to ignore it and the noise quieted for a second time, giving me a chance to take a deep breath and find my mental stride once more.

I had just recaptured a fleeting thought, when the barista at the counter called out, "Janet!", instantly startling me, this time completely destroying my concentration. I pushed back from the bar and shot an impatient glare at anyone who fell into my field of vision.

My current focus, Derrick Hoffman, was proving more elusive than my previous story. The evidence in the case pointed to an accidental death caused by Mr. Hoffman's own actions, but I knew someone else was to blame. If only I could concentrate on the details everything would become clearer. Irritation surged through me like intravenous fluid.

This used to be one of the few places that brought me any sense of productivity. It was always popular with the students when I attended college here, but never as crowded and noisy as Starbucks. But perhaps we all put too much stock in memories.

These days, it seemed to be all but impossible to find respite anywhere from my own raucous brain. Thoughts swirled and wrestled and twisted into something akin to a thickly woven curtain separating me from the bright light of reality, allowing me to spend my days hiding in the shadow of my ideas.

I can't stop thinking about these deaths, the mystery of them fuels me from the time I wake up until I restlessly search for sleep each night. And so, I research, and I write, sometimes putting pen to paper, and other times typing in circles, looking for a way to understand and explain. I am excellent at what I do, which is why I've become successful so quickly, but with the growing popularity of my article, and needing to travel so often, I am long on words and short on time.

The phone began to buzz again, breaking my reverie for the final time as I shoved the papers aside to find it. I looked at the screen and saw that it was my sister. The frequency in her calls had begun to increase in the last several months but she'd never called multiple times in a row before. I impulsively decided to answer and instantly regretted it.

"For heaven's sake, Cara! If I wanted to talk to you, I would've answered the first two times you called," I growled.

Some of the strain between us came from the natural progression of time and distance, causing us to interact more like strangers than siblings, but it's hard to remember the niceties when my concentration has been so severely disrupted. Maybe stranger is the wrong word. It would be unusual to feel such distinctive suspicion and particular distrust toward a person with whom you have no prior experiences with.

She was always closer to Liam, and once he was gone whatever tie we might have had as siblings was permanently severed. He was the link between us, as the middle child, although the three of us never actually grew up together.

By the time Cara came along, Liam and my roles had already been determined. He was the beloved, talented, charismatic son of a proud dad, while I was the strange, withdrawn, geek of an often belligerent, abusive father. As the youngest, and a girl, Cara fell into her own category, content to stay out of the way.

She ignored my rude greeting, as I knew she would, and spoke in a quick, soft voice. "Just listen, Owen. I'm calling because Dad's had a heart attack. A few days ago. I think Mom tried to call you... maybe left you a voicemail?"

This news surprised me, and I didn't respond immediately. I tried to recall if Mom had called, but I wasn't sure. It's possible. Even if I'd noticed her calling, I wouldn't have picked up. There are no reasons I can think of that would make me want to speak to my mother.

Before I could respond, Cara continued, "He's okay, though. He stayed in the hospital a few days, until yesterday, and then they let him go home. The doctor said that he's going to be tired for a while. At least Mom is there with him, handling his diet and medications. And you know she'll make him follow up with the cardiac rehabilitation..."

"Um, I'm not sure what to say... Well, what can I... I mean, what does he need?" I managed to sputter out. I bit down on my lip to control my voice and stop the grin attempting to bloom on my face. My German grandmother called

7

it "schadenfreude" and probably would've shamed me for finding joy in the troubles of someone else.

"What does he need? I mean, I don't think there's anything you can do."

As I listened to her voice, she didn't necessarily sound annoyed with me, but I always sense an undercurrent of disdain that she's holding back.

When I didn't respond again, Cara continued, "I know that you're busy these days, but I just think mom really wants you to come home and visit, to let her and Dad know you care."

This caught me off guard a bit. My mother had been trying to get me to talk to her for twelve years, but Cara's never attempted to forge that bridge between me and our parents. And why would she? She was present for the traumatic trainwreck that was our family life, so she's fully aware of the irreparable damage.

"Really? You say it's not serious, but they want me to come home and visit?" Frustration saturated my voice. I wasn't good enough to be their son until the day Liam died, and I still resented the shift in affection and attention that didn't come from a place of love, but a place of desperation.

"He's okay, I think. It wasn't bad. He spent a few days in the CCU, but nothing else happened and he seemed to recover pretty quickly. But mom mentioned wishing you'd come to the hospital. She sounded sad that you hadn't returned her call. It really does sound a little... indifferent, don't you think? I mean, I know you don't get along with Mom, and you and

Dad's relationship is... strained, at times, but you do care that he survived, right?"

There it is. The judgment. The disdain. The attempted guilt trip.

"Yeah, I care, I guess. Or maybe I don't. I'd probably be more interested if he hadn't been such a terrible father. But do any of you care that I'm finally on the road to big success? And I'm trying to remember when you called to congratulate me on my new job," I spat into the phone, my tone dripping with sarcasm.

"You know what, it doesn't matter," I said before she could try to blame me again. "To answer your question, I'll figure out a way to swing by and visit to check on him. Maybe once I wrap up my current story I'll head back south. But don't worry, you don't have to see me." My rant over, I held my breath a minute and listened to the silence on the other end of the phone. Two could play the guilt trip game.

I don't need her approval, or her loyalty. I pride myself on my understanding of human behavior, finding most people extremely easy to predict. But never Cara. I hate to admit that I never know what she's up to, which makes her difficult to manipulate, leaving my plans in disarray.

"Owen, I wish you wouldn't get so defensive. I haven't seen you in forever and I feel like I don't even know how to have a regular conversation with you anymore. I do want to see you. And I did try calling you back in December after I read your first article and realized you had been so close to home, but you never answered your phone!"

Now she was speaking too quickly for me to get a retort in.

"For real, though, if you'll let me know when you'll be around, we could get lunch together or something. I've been trying to get in touch with you. So we can talk," she finished lamely.

When we were younger, I'd wish that Cara would look up to me and worship me as she did Liam. As the years have gone by, however, I've realized I don't need her or anyone else to approve of me, or even like me.

The last twelve years have provided me with a thicker skin and a tougher heart. It's a consequence of working in journalism, possibly. Or maybe my newfound confidence and success has raised my chin and set my shoulders, physically and emotionally.

"We'll see. I'll try. I guess it just depends on Chelsey's schedule."

"Oh, okay. Well, let me know. And tell Chelsey it would be good to see her, too." She smothered a groan but was unable to completely cover her disappointment.

Cara was up to something. She has never liked my girlfriend, now fiancé, Chelsey. I've dated Chelsey for the last eight years and Cara made it clear seven years ago how she felt about her, which is why I included Chelsey's name in my response, to get my sister off my back.

"Alright. Well, I've got to get back to trying to make this deadline, so I've gotta let you go."

I knew what she'd say next.

"Alright, well, just remember that I'm always thinking about you."

The words themselves would be a loving sentiment said by anyone else, but her tone always has an obsessive, dark quality to it. It sounds suspicious and threatening all at once, and I remind myself once again that Cara has been socially awkward her whole life, solidifying at eleven years old when she became "the girl whose brother died."

After a slight inner eye roll, I responded, "You too," and hung up. I glanced at the screen and realized the date, March 19th. In two months, I'd have to endure another phone call on the anniversary of our brother's death. But next time, I wouldn't answer.

I was able to go visit my dad a few days later, successfully leaving Chelsey at home. It's not that I didn't want to be with her, but she is a pain to travel with. Nowadays, we go a few weeks at a time without seeing each other while I'm working on a story. That doesn't seem to bother her too badly. It did when I first began traveling, especially since we had just moved to a new city. But after that first successful series, and my sudden increase in notoriety, she seems more content to let me roam without much complaint.

Thankfully, I was able to avoid Cara during my visit. As predicted, she tried calling me several times while I was there, again a few weeks later, and even more since then. In her messages, she kept asking about my articles, wanting to get in touch, sounding concerned. I went back to ignoring the calls.

And now here we are, almost eight months later, standing together awkwardly, bracing against the wind whipping through the park and rustling the changing leaves. I haven't been to New York in years. Although this time of year can have beautiful weather and festive city sites, I have never enjoyed the large crowds or the overwhelming noise.

My brain is noisy enough without the chaotic sounds of the city dully playing on repeat in the background. All I can think about, louder than everything else, are the deaths, my stories, my success.

Standing in the middle of a busy park, meeting with my estranged sister for a reason that is not yet completely apparent to me, keeping an eye on my watch so I don't miss my ride to the airport for my flight, all while considering the strange circumstances of the most recent death that I've been writing about, is not even close to what I wanted to be doing right now.

My slippery thoughts bounced back to last night and I wonder what Detective Sanchez was hinting at when he said he suspected the rock near Johnny Rowe's body had been purposely placed there. It reminds me of something the police said after Liam died. But the passing thought is only momentarily within my grasp before it fades away again.

Maybe it's standing here with Cara that's bringing all these memories back now. Maybe she's the reason my flashbacks have intensified the last few months. Time is slipping away like never before. She reminds me of Liam. She's not like him in any perceivable way, but she is an immediate and constant reminder of my younger brother.

Afterall, she is the one who found him dead. It's one of the reasons we try not to see each other anymore. Whenever I look into her eyes, I see Liam's lifeless body, his face covered in her bloody handprints. She's never recovered, and I've never stopped being suspicious of my own sister.

Chapter 2

2007

*T*he late March afternoon was unseasonably hot and dry, even for Georgia. Every recent day had been stifling and smothering, causing my thick, cotton uniform polo to stick to my neck and back during the walks home from school.

Cara and I tramped loudly through the side screen door and dumped our heavy backpacks onto the floor of the kitchen on our way through to the living room. Cara collapsed onto the love seat angled in the corner and promptly switched on the rotating fan that stood at the ready for this time of year.

Weather in the south is predictably unpredictable. It's not unusual to have a week of uncomfortable temperatures, just before the air conditioning is switched on permanently, and just after the cool temperatures have come and gone when fresh breezes have ceased to exist. I settled on the floor in front of the couch, positioning myself in the path of the fan's blast.

"Owen?" Mom's call came from down the hall, probably from Liam's room or the laundry room. She was in a constant cycle of washing his dirty clothes and putting them away again; school uniforms, baseball uniforms, dress pants, and shirts left over from award ceremonies and school banquets.

"Yeah, Mom, we're in here."

"Homework already done?"

"Mom, we just walked in!" I huffed. I was never good at the "yes, ma'am" and "no, ma'am" responses that my parents tried to instill in me, especially to my mother, always ready instead to debate or get the last word. To be fair, my father is a lawyer, so I'd say I get it honestly, although I learned long ago never to debate with him.

"I think Cara said she finished all hers yesterday and I was just about to start mine anyway." I glanced at Cara for confirmation that she'd indeed completed her assignments, but she didn't seem to be paying attention and stared up at the ceiling, oblivious. *Why were my brother and sister always able to avoid Mom's overbearing scrutiny?*

"Are you gonna grill Liam about his homework when he finally graces us with his presence?" I had to throw one last jab.

"Owen! That's unkind. *He* usually gets it done without me having to prod him all the time."

That was a jab back at me, insinuating that I'm lazy or irresponsible, which is unquestionably untrue. Mom was never original with her snide remarks, insisting instead on imitating whatever insult Dad had been repeating most recently.

Mom was also delusional. Liam was either never assigned homework or got another kid at school to do it for him. Teachers generally went out of their way to make his life easier during any kind of sport season, which is year-round.

Conversely, I was a really good student, always completing my assignments early or on time, consistently making straight A's. Neither of my parents ever acknowledged that, never acknowledged me.

"Besides, his teachers are always understanding if he's running late," she reasoned lamely, probably feeling guilty because she knows what she's saying isn't even close to the truth.

"Must be nice," I grumbled under my breath. Debating with her was useless and never made me feel any better.

I don't mind a good argument, but there's no changing her mind about her precious golden child. I'm used to it by now- the constant comparisons, followed immediately by insults and declarations of me falling short of their expectations. When I'm lucky, taunting is all that happens.

My home life has been colored by guilt and shame, disappointment and resentment, pain and terror, for the last thirteen years, which coincidentally is how old my brother is. I've learned to take it in stride for the most part.

I may not be a talented baseball, basketball, or track phenom like Liam, but I can outwit and out-write anyone, even educated adults. One day, I'll make my mark on the world and I'll be remembered long after I'm dead because words, not sports, are what create history.

Cara seemed extra quiet this afternoon. She's usually reserved, really only speaking when spoken to, or adding awkward comments into an otherwise straightforward conversation. I wonder if perhaps she suffers from some level of social anxiety.

Although I am often her sounding board in the afternoons, there was none of her usual chattering as we walked home today. Cara spends so much of her time observing, watching, listening, and standing out of the way, that she saves up all the little morsels of information and fills my ears with them when we're alone on the days Liam stays for practice. It's really the only time we talk now.

I watched Cara again as she soaked up the cool air of the fan, lounging with her legs hanging over the arm of the couch. She continued to stare at the ceiling, daydreaming or lost in thought, hard to tell which. She's been more preoccupied lately, or maybe quietly frustrated. It seems like something's bothering her.

I got up and left to hide out in my room. It's better not to be hanging around whenever Liam does get home. On practice days, Mom leaves to pick Liam up before dinner, or Dad sometimes picks him up on his way home from the office if he left earlier than normal.

If it was Mom picking him up, they'd come in with her gushing and fawning all over him, waiting on him hand and foot. It's nauseating. If it was Dad, they'd burst through the door, loudly joking and laughing, bonding over Liam's latest conquests on the field. Either way, I prefer not to be around and not noticed than to be present and ignored.

That evening, there was no chance for me to escape the overflow of my father's pride. It barreled through the house as soon as the door opened, knocking my thoughts off track.

"Rita! Come here! You're not going to believe this!"

I cracked my bedroom door and peeked down the hall into the living room. Dad stood just inside the doorway to the living room, tall and proud, chest sticking out like a Silverback Gorilla, swollen with triumph. Liam stood just behind him grinning from ear to ear, basking in Dad's delight, as usual.

Mom shuffled past me down the hall, "What is it? What's happened?" Her voice had an unsure, anxious quality to it, coming out a bit breathless.

"Liam, you tell her." Dad turned to the side to let him slide past and take center stage.

"Coach Rogers invited me to come work out with the Varsity players starting tomorrow!"

My mother whooped and hollered and giddily congratulated him and petted him.

"That's so wonderful!" she gushed. "But wait a minute. Can a middle schooler play on the Varsity team?"

The octave of her voice was so high and her words so breathless with excitement that I thought she might pass out. I will never understand the obsession over physical prowess.

"Well, not exactly," he replied, "I can't play in actual games right now. At least not most of the time- but they're hoping to get me some playing time during certain games! I'll still technically be on the middle school team. But he said they can't afford to waste my talent! He said I'll be their best player before I'm even on the team! I'll definitely start on Varsity when I'm a freshman. I mean, that never happens. I bet Brett and those other jokers are gonna be so jealous!"

It's like a faucet has been turned on, the handle twisted until it popped off with no way to stop the flow of his words.

Growing up with a little brother who is revered by a dangerous, reactive father means that I'm constantly compared to him and always found to be lacking. I used to give Liam the benefit of the doubt, thinking that it's not really his fault that my dad values athletic skills over mental abilities. Or that my mom values anything and everything my dad says to value.

Cara wandered onto the scene from the kitchen, quietly excited, and hugged Liam from behind. I joined them to listen, and for a moment, it was a rare, joyful family time of congratulations and excitement. There was talk about what this could mean for Liam one day playing Pro ball, what kind of scholarships he could earn, or what college teams he might play for.

It all seemed far-fetched to me. I caught Cara's eyes and rolled mine in a mocking expression, mouthing the words "yeah, right." Not because he wasn't talented enough, but because the chances of that being his future were about one in two hundred. Still, it was nice to momentarily feel like I was part of a family who care about each other and celebrates successes together.

That is, until Dad said, "I'm just glad I have at least one son to be proud of. At least one son that's not a letdown," as he turned his back to me, placing his arm once again across Liam's shoulders, effectively shutting me out of the circle we'd been standing in together just seconds before.

He said it off-handedly, like I wouldn't take offense. Mom and Liam continued in their celebratory hugging, oblivious to the rude comment and the sudden change in my mood.

But Cara noticed. She gaped at Dad, then turned to see my reaction. She saw, or maybe felt, the shame and hatred behind my glare and turned away quickly, blushing as if she'd witnessed a public humiliation. Cara would never stand up to my dad to say anything about his constant commentary on the disappointments of having a non-athletic child, fearful of his reaction or the swing of his fist, but I would bet that it incensed her just as it did me.

In the past, we've discussed the downfalls of not being born Liam. Cara doesn't get the brunt of it like I do from Dad, maybe because she's a girl, maybe because she's younger, or maybe because she really does try to appease our parents.

I don't fully understand my father's moral compass. He doesn't bat an eye at breaking the bones of the woman he married, or battering and bruising his first-born son, but I've never seen him raise a hand to his youngest two children.

Unlike Cara, I'm not a people-pleaser, especially if the expectations are unreasonable or unattainable. I'm done trying to live up to that before I even start. I haven't always felt that way. Since I was the first-born, Dad poured all his encouragement and efforts to mold me into a superstar in those first few years of my life. And I did try.

From what I can remember, I enjoyed spending time with my dad, getting all his attention, at least whenever it was positive. I wasn't naturally coordinated, but Dad worked with me and tried to teach me, signing me up for any extra lessons or coaching when his schedule became so busy that he couldn't make the time to work with me himself anymore.

It was about the time I turned eight and Liam turned six, when I really found my groove in telling stories, that my father had the epiphany that he was wasting his time on the wrong son. I don't know if it was Liam's early success on the t-ball field, the fact that he was already shooting and making baskets, or the speed at which he could run.

Or maybe it had more to do with me leaving my hand-drawn comics all over Dad's home office, revealing that I had used up most of his printer paper, tape, staples, and good pens on "nonsense" and "trash". Perhaps it was the day Liam's little six-year-old legs caught up and passed me while running toward the football that Dad and I had been throwing together in the park.

However it happened, it was a relief. Dad's teaching methods often included corporal punishment, which could be motivating, but without natural skill, were often fruitless. I was grateful to be left alone to compose my stories. Words are my sanctuary, my place of safety and worship.

Dad continued to invite me to practice and play with the two of them, but I'd find an excuse and retreat to my room, thankful it wasn't one of his commands. The more I pulled away, the wider the chasm became. By the time Liam was ten, the distinction between his and my relationship with our father was unmistakable. I'd noticed long before that Dad coached Liam very differently than how he'd coached me.

Meanwhile, Cara skirted the line, staying somewhat active in sports and school clubs, able to remain just under the radar of any overly positive or negative attention. She saw how I was treated and didn't want any part of it.

She would sometimes ask me how I could stand it. I'd look into her big, brown, concerned eyes and lie to her. I'd tell her that I didn't really see it as all bad and that mostly I was glad not to be in the spotlight, always held to the ruler of Dad's expectations. I told her that she should probably worry more about what all that pressure would do to Liam.

Of course, that wasn't reality. In truth, every single mean remark and rude cut down from Dad or Liam burned within me. But the harsh words didn't hold a candle to the pain of the back of Dad's hand across my face, or his boot in my back. I just figured that one day Liam's success would eclipse my measly life in Dad's eyes, and then I could cease to even exist in their world, free to be myself.

Cara must've taken me at my word because soon after our first couple of conversations on the subject, when she was about five or six years old, she began to follow Liam around like a puppy. She was always concerned about what he was doing and how he was feeling. She would do anything he told her to do, and he took advantage of her naivety. It seemed to me a somewhat strange obsession, a kind of hero worship.

That was five years ago and lately things have been tense between my brother and sister. Moments like this afternoon when Cara was distracted or preoccupied with, what must be, internal revelations, were a lot more frequent.

Last week, I heard the two of them in a whispered argument across the hall in Liam's bedroom. Their urgent, harsh whispers weren't defined, but the tone was clear. Cara was upset and seemed to be admonishing him in some way. I've never heard her speak like that to anyone before and never would've thought she had it in her. Liam seemed equally agitated, and his voice rose and fell as he'd get frustrated and then rein it in again.

After Dad's comment, effectively ruining the nice, family moment, Cara and I simultaneously turned away from their happy scene. She stomped off down the hall and closed the door to her room just a tad louder than necessary, and I wandered off toward the kitchen, feigning hunger.

I glanced back before I rounded the corner into the kitchen and saw my brother, meeting my gaze and grinning wildly like a Cheshire cat, a broad, evil smile, full of teeth and superiority. And something inside me broke. It was a visual reminder of who Liam was at his core- conceited, smug, wicked. I felt whatever connection I had to him, whether it was blood, fear, or necessity, snap like cutting the string on a balloon and float soundlessly away.

Chapter 3

My thoughts of the past vanished on the sudden breeze. I've been standing here with Cara for close to ten minutes and so far, all we've accomplished is a few small talk comments about the chill in the air and the pitfalls of traveling anytime during the month of December.

She has had her body turned mostly away from me, not looking me in the eye, but off into the distance, watching runners and dog walkers make their way along the paths in the park.

I looked down at my watch for the dozenth time, willing the hands to move faster so I could have a good reason to leave. Unfortunately, Cara already knew what time my flight was leaving and would see through any attempt at excuses. I heaved a deep sigh and looked up to see that she had turned to face me and was staring at me intently, almost angrily.

"Are you even listening?" she huffed. Her eyes were watery. The wind circled our faces, ruffling our hair. She reached up to push some behind her ear and attempted to nonchalantly wipe at the tear threatening to fall.

"I'm sorry, what?"

"I said, have you finished writing the Rowe story? Have the police decided to classify it as an accidental death?"

I hadn't realized she had changed the subject. She was extra put-out having to repeat herself. The fact that she cares about this case, or any of my stories, has set me on edge and I feel out of sorts.

In fact, come to think of it, the times she's called me this year have all been after I began writing a new story about another death. Cara's called me after each one. I haven't answered, but she occasionally leaves a cryptic message. Now, her tone sounds suspicious and demanding, like she's interviewing me.

"Uh, well, I mean," I stammered and ran my hand through my hair as I tried to stay focused, "they've made a lot of progress and made an arrest recently. I'd like to think that some of it is thanks to my stories and my reporting. But I'm not convinced they've made the right decision in arresting McBride."

Cara turned away from me again, thinking, a deep breath shuddering through her.

Beginning to lose my patience, I asked, "Cara? What is this all about? You called me up this morning, saying you need to meet me before I leave town and that it can't wait. I didn't even know you were here in New York until a few hours ago. What's going on?"

That morning, the hotel phone rang like a screaming banshee, jolting me painfully awake. Rolling toward the sound and peeling my eyelids apart was like trying to pry open a bear trap. Six A.M. I had probably only been asleep for an hour and a half. It had been another long day, or late night depending on how you wanted to look at it, of finishing my piece on the Johnny Rowe mystery.

I'd already sent in the article for publishing today and was a few days ahead of what I was due to turn in for the series. Now, I had some time to travel home, catch up on a little sleep, and then head out to a new city in search of a new story. I didn't want there to be any long breaks in my articles being published. That's what kept the readers returning week after week.

My cases were mysteries in real time, unsolved and perplexing unexplained deaths or possible homicides, and my readers had the desire, and I felt the right, to be engaged in helping to solve the crime if there had indeed been one.

In my view, Johnny's death still needed more investigation, which is why I had been up so late meeting with Detective Sanchez, wanting to debate the new evidence found in their latest search of Rowe's home. I wanted to understand why they'd arrested his girlfriend because the timeline didn't fit, and it felt like a rushed, forced arrest.

However, the detective wasn't willing to give me any more information. Somewhere along the way, our relationship seemed to have soured, but I wasn't totally sure of the reason behind the estrangement.

The hotel phone rang loudly again, the red light blinking brightly in case I wasn't aware that the call needed my attention. I reached over and answered the phone lazily with a grunt, "hm?"

"Hello? Owen?"

It was my sister. This brought me into consciousness quickly. How did she know where I was staying? She sounded high-strung. I had been carefully avoiding her calls to my cell, but it seems she'd found a way to track me down.

"Cara? What is it? What's going on?" The words came out slowly and slurred together as I wrestled to throw off the heavy blanket of exhaustion.

"I'm in New York. I... I need to see you. Today. If possible. I mean, I definitely need to see you. It's... urgent. When, um, what time could we meet?"

Cara was acting flighty and maybe it was the lack of sleep, but it amused me a little.

"You know, you've really got a knack for ruining a nice, quiet moment. I was sleeping."

Silence.

"What's going on? Why do we need to meet?" I rubbed my eyes hard, projecting stars onto the black backdrop of my eyelids. "I've got a flight to catch this evening and I was hoping to be sleeping for the next several hours until then."

"You're leaving?"

Cara was ready with her question just as the last word left my lips. "I thought you were still working on the story here."

"Well, I think I've told Johnny's story as far as it's going to take me, so I'm going to head home for a few days to see Chelsey."

I tried to come across as easy-going about the whole thing. Hopefully, my voice didn't sound as perturbed as I felt. I'd been involved in this story from the beginning and the police and detectives had originally been very receptive to my role.

I thought back again to how Detective Sanchez seemed to be shutting me out recently, arguing with me, and avoiding me. It just feels like we're talking in circles, like maybe he's just looking for a good debate.

By the end of our conversation last night, the detective seemed ready to blame whoever crossed his path for Rowe's death, probably because the dead guy was rich. At one point, it felt like he was even interviewing me. I think he's lost his mind, overwhelmed with the pressure to close the case. He kept squeezing his eyes shut and rubbing his temples while we spoke. I left not long afterward, realizing we'd come to a stalemate.

While I was reflecting, Cara had been considering my change of plans and finally said, "Well, what time is your flight? I can come and meet you wherever it's convenient... Or maybe I can meet up with you when you get back to your house?" she suggested.

Now I sat up in bed and shook my head a few times, trying to knock out the cobwebs because I must have misheard her. She has never visited me in California before. *So for some unknown reason she's in New York at the same time I am, and is willing to travel to California just to meet up with me?*

Something was off, and all the old suspicions crashed into reality. There was an awkward silence in which I tried to come up with a response, but I had no idea what to say. I didn't want to see her or be delayed but was burning with intense curiosity at this sudden strange behavior.

After a long beat when I didn't respond, she seemed to recover herself a little and said, "I know that was random, I'm not trying to invite myself to your house. I just need to see you. I would've called sooner if I'd known you would be headed out of town so quickly. I'm here visiting a friend and realized after reading your article on Saturday that you were here too. But if you'll be home for a while, maybe I could take the opportunity to finally visit. What do you think?"

"I still think that sounds random. I don't know about a visit. Chelsey gets pissed off about last-minute guests, especially if I've been out of town for a while."

Not wanting to leave any room for her to talk me into letting her come to my house, I added "Besides, I'll be headed out again on Sunday, so that doesn't really leave much time for anything."

As an afterthought I asked, "You keep saying you need to see me... since when have you ever needed to see me? Is something going on?"

It occurred to me then that this was close to the longest conversation that we'd had in years. I do enjoy a good mystery and Cara was piquing my interest first thing this morning. Perhaps that was part of her strategy with calling me at the hotel. The sleep was long gone, and I was fully awake now.

"Wait a minute, you're leaving again on Sunday? Where are you going?"

I hesitated. I never like to tell anyone where I'm headed. I don't even tell my editor until I've arrived somewhere and found a new story to write.

Trying to divert her away from that topic, I said "Okay, you know what? I'm going back to sleep. I'll call you later when I'm on the way to the airport. My flight is leaving at six-fifteen. And we can plan a time to meet up in the next couple of months if it's so important to you. Maybe I'll even come down to Georgia to see you." I could probably put off a visit long enough to get her off my back.

"No, no, no, Owen, wait." Cara took a deep breath and released it slowly.

"I just need to talk to you about something. It won't take long. How about meeting me in the Park? Say three o'clock? You'll have plenty of time to make your flight." I caught a hint of desperation.

What was she up to? My suspicion and curiosity far outweighed both the exhaustion and the annoyance at this point. But I was kicking myself for telling her what time my flight was leaving.

"Fine. That's fine. I can meet you at three-thirty," I reluctantly agreed. "So, are you going to tell me what this is all about?"

She didn't speak for several long seconds. I laid back down as I waited, already anticipating going back to sleep, my eyelids feeling heavy once more. Cara cleared her throat before replying, "Um, well, I've just been thinking about you...

Actually, I'm always thinking about you. Always. I'll text you where to meet me. See you soon."

Chapter 4

As she probably expected it to, Cara's eerie comment at the end of our phone call made me irritated and jumpy. She knew it would cause this reaction, setting me ill at ease, which is why she'd hung up so quickly afterward. I attempted to fall back asleep, but my nerves were wrecked, and my brain was busy, like a hamster on a wheel. The sun was high in the sky and even the thick light-blocking curtains of my hotel room couldn't keep the rich, golden glow from seeping around the edges.

I got up, now feeling a bit manic, and began to wander around the room without real purpose. I thought about making coffee, but as soon as I reached the countertop where it sat, changed direction, and found myself back at the bedside table staring at the phone laying silently in its cradle.

Perhaps this is what sleep deprivation did to people, wrung out all their conscious thoughts until they were all tangled up in a confusing bundle, wrapped up with fidgety energy. I lowered myself to sit on the edge of the bed, stood again with a sudden thought to get dressed, then sat back down, unsure of how to make the next decision. *What was Cara up to?* Pieces began to fall into place in my mind as I pondered her actions.

I stared at the phone again and thought about the time after Liam's death. Everyone was concerned for my sister's sanity. She seemed out of control, living outside reality, falling to pieces regularly. Then, after months of therapy, she finally seemed to be settling into the steps of grief that were expected of us all.

Although she composed herself more each passing day, refining the image being projected, playing the part of someone who was healing, she also began to act differently toward me. I caught her listening to my phone calls, snooping through my room, and trying to follow me whenever I left the house. It was maddening.

My initial concern was fueled by my own state of shock after finding her with Liam's dead body. I was dying to know how she came to be in the woods with him that afternoon. Later, when her behavior toward me changed, I decided then that it would be best to avoid her altogether, or at least not find myself alone with her ever again.

I squeezed my eyes closed and rubbed at my temples. A throbbing had begun behind my eyelids. I felt exhausted and much older. The thought of meeting Cara this afternoon was making me anxious and causing the memories of her face and her stricken expression on that day when everything changed twelve years ago to engulf my brain.

The slightly uncomfortable humidity of late April 2007 had escalated into the stifling temperatures of mid-May. Spring was passing quickly in a blur of traveling and attending Liam's baseball games all over the state, late night dinners of leftovers or takeout after his practices, scrambling to finish homework after sleeping too late in the mornings, and endless studying and preparing for the end of the year school assessments.

Thankfully though, the busyness allowed me to mostly avoid interacting with my family. It seemed like we were always together, chained to the commitment of watching Liam play baseball. Everything revolved around it. But I found it was easy to be physically present and still block out anything going on around me. No one spoke to me directly or expected much out of me, so I was silent.

The new pace for our daily lives turned out to be a welcome distraction. The older I got, the less likely Dad was to punish me in public.

Once when I was eleven, we'd gone to one of Liam's games with his travel team. I'd begged Mom for money to get a slushie from the concession stand. Dad grew tired of my whining and begging, finally shoving a bill into my hands hard enough to also knock me in the stomach with the money grasped tightly in his fist. No one else noticed me double over or heard the breath escape in a rush of air between my teeth, but I didn't miss the fire in his eyes as I straightened up.

As I carefully carried the overfilled frozen treat back to my seat, Cara jumped up, throwing her hands in the air to cheer for something happening on the field, accidentally knocking the cup from my grasp. All I could do was watch in horror as the icy, blue slush poured down my father's leg. The flames in his eyes blazed. He reached out calmly, firmly taking my forearm in his hand, and used his thumb and middle finger to pinch my skin on the underside hidden from view.

It was the most painful pinch you can imagine as he rolled and twisted his fingers, using all his strength. I cried out and tears slid down my face. People turned to stare. Dad's face changed to a look of concern as he said sweetly, "It's okay Owen, it's just an accident. It's okay," all while squeezing the pinched skin so hard that it took a month to heal.

Those moments never happened in public anymore but being at home was a different story. I'd long been accustomed to the degrading and devaluing that came from my father, and he still managed to put me on the ground from time to time with a hard shove or well-placed punch to the gut.

But I never understood how this treatment from Dad gave my little brother license to bully me as well. Liam would go along with my father's abuse, smile and chuckle with appreciation of Dad's depravity, but not necessarily participate.

Over the last few years, in the moments of calm, during normal days filled with regular routines when he had nothing better to do, the battle between Liam and I raged on in the background. It's become a constant static, a continual dissonance woven throughout our relationship.

He'll stop by my room whenever he passes, and if I'm sitting at my desk, he'll stand in the doorway calling me names or making animal noises with the express purpose of goading me into a fight. If I react and attack him, I'm the one that gets Dad's wrath later. Sometimes, if Liam realizes I'm not in my room, he'll sneak in and steal things or move them around so I can't find anything. His favorite targets are usually my notebooks and journals, or anything related to my writing. Once, he stole my laptop and I didn't get it back for four long days.

Liam specializes in disguising his tormenting as juvenile, mean sibling tricks. Between his tactics at school and his pranks at home, there are no areas of my life left untouched by his wickedness.

It makes me feel small and ashamed that my little brother seems to have the upper hand in this war. Everyone likes him and agrees with whatever he says, even if, or sometimes it seems especially if, it's at the cost of my happiness. Mom and Dad have never believed the stories of his awful behavior, so I gave up trying to explain a long time ago. Anytime he catches a glimpse of me enjoying some aspect of my life, he sets out to ruin it.

Two months ago, Liam called a girl I liked and told her several embarrassing lies about my hygiene habits. I caught him using my phone, snatched it away, and heard the horrifying sounds of Jenna Millson, laughing hysterically on the other end of the line.

My revenge is usually more of a passive aggressive nature, but no matter what I try to do to get him into trouble or make his life miserable, my parents never get upset with him, or worse, they'll help him when things go wrong, completely nullifying my efforts.

I've grown to hate him. I mean, really hate him. I wish for the past, when he was still playing T-ball, a young prodigy that seemed just as surprised as everyone else at his successes. Now, he's almost worse than Dad.

And it's not just how Liam treats me. I've noticed Cara pulling away, spending less and less time with him, her interest and energy toward his activities visibly shrinking day by day. There have been many more whispered arguments, softly, harshly, spilling out into the hallway, rising and falling, and hard to hear exactly what was being said.

Many of the arguments have ended in slamming doors or objects being thrown. I was a little concerned at this escalation initially, but I know that Liam has started to treat Cara the same way that he treats me and everyone else, so I also feel a bit of pride that she seems to be standing up to him.

The day Liam died, I reached home first and alone. I was more glad than surprised that Mom wasn't home and that the house was empty. At first, I didn't pay much attention to the fact that it was vacant. It had been my general rule as of late to avoid every other Walsh at all times, so I'd become accustomed to seeking solitude and feeling grateful when I found it.

The walk had taken me longer than it normally does, and I'd gotten sidetracked a few times on my journey. Cara had stayed after school for a gardening club that she was a member of, so I wasn't responsible for accompanying her home. Usually, Mom would leave to pick her up about the time I arrived at the house, then bring her home before going back to pick up Liam after his practice.

I rushed in, hurriedly dropped my bag in the kitchen as I walked through to the living room, then to the bathroom. I was on a mission to clean up and take a shower before anyone saw me. It was a gloriously hot shower, the stream of water cleansing away the sins of the day, restoring me to a feeling of balance.

I emerged, resigned to dealing with my family and the impending drama of the evening. After getting dressed, I got a load of my dirty clothes started in the wash. As I went back down the hall to the kitchen for a snack, mid-step I realized that the house was still empty. The lights were on, there were drinking glasses sitting around on the table in the living room and the counter in the kitchen, and the TV was on, continuing mutely in the background, but the rooms felt distinctly uninhabited.

"Mom?" Silence echoed back to me.

I peeked at the clock on the wall in the kitchen: four-thirty. I'd only been home for about thirty minutes. I still wasn't worried, in fact, I was hopeful that everyone would be delayed a while longer, but I knew someone would be home soon, squashing my hopes. Visions of Kevin McCallister living his best life in Home Alone- one of my favorite childhood movies- flashed through my head and brought a smile to my face.

My daydreaming came to a screeching halt as my phone buzzed roughly in my hand. I glanced at the screen. I was shocked to see that it was Liam calling. Confused, I cautiously answered, but it was not Liam's voice coming through.

Before I could say "hello," Cara began shouting, "Owen? Owen! Something's happened! Liam's got blood all over him!"

I opened my eyes again to stare at the carpet of my hotel room, its dark, paisley pattern strangely comforting. There are times in our lives when we are willfully blind to the depth of destruction caused by the people around us who seem the most innocuous. Avoiding their toxic behavior seems the best solution when things feel the most out of our locus of control. But then there are moments when we step into the light and decide it would better serve our purposes to turn and fight.

There was no way I could go back to sleep now. Feeling in control once more, and fueled by the thrill of a new deadline, I opened my laptop and began to write.

Chapter 5

*A*fter I finally demanded to know why she wanted to meet me in the park this afternoon, I studied Cara's face, waiting for an explanation. She seemed frazzled, on the edge of something undefined. I remember Cara usually taking pride in dressing neatly, hair fixed in a certain way, tight smile playing at her lips, always attempting to mask her psychotic tendencies.

Years of therapy, addictions, and rehab have molded Cara into a more guarded person. She became so focused on smothering or camouflaging her emotions that if she was stressed, anxious, or angry in any way, it was not likely that those around her would know. Now, in stark contrast to that, she stood before me somewhat disheveled, antsy, worried.

I stared at her knuckles, white with tension as she clutched the hem of her shirt. The silence wore on longer than socially appropriate until finally, she spoke. Her voice began softly and then strengthened in volume.

"Well, um, I've been following along with all your stories. And, uh... you know, you're a really great writer?"

She stammered and paused, turning to smile at me like it was the punctuation at the end of her sentence. The smile didn't quite meet her eyes. *Why does it feel like she's stalling?*

"...Thanks," I said hesitantly, "I'm proud of what I've accomplished so far. I've been able to work with law enforcement and share people's tragedies in a way that hasn't been done before." I paused and smiled as well, pleased with the current direction of my life.

"But there's still so much that can be done," I continued. "I'm working on submitting my ideas for a book, or possibly some other publication focused solely on these kinds of stories."

Once the topic of my writing comes up, I have a hard time reining in my excitement. Cara's distracted me again. Realizing this, I stopped talking abruptly and stared at her, willing her to get to the point.

"Oh, okay, um, that's really great," as she spoke, her face faltered and she looked away from me, at some fixed point on the ground.

"Soooo," she dragged the word out awkwardly, "um, I wanted to see you because I've been having a hard time reading about the Rowe story. It's just, um, so similar, you know? I can't get it out of my head."

I continued to stare, still unsure what she thought I could do to ease her mind.

Hearing my silence, Cara snapped her head up to meet my eyes. "Do you not see it?" she asked, passionately. "Has it not bothered you at all?"

Seeing my angry expression in response to her obvious distrust somewhat mollified her outburst. Cara took a deep, shaky breath and tried again, calmer.

"Reading about how Johnny died has uncovered some painful memories for me and, um, I was just wondering if I was alone in that. Can you please talk to me about the case for a minute? I'm sure you know more of the details than I do and maybe it'll make me feel better."

Good grief. She was really losing it. I looked over her face again, while she searched mine, eyes roving back and forth like a dog following a scent. My annoyance and flash of rage subsided as I caught a glimpse of my little sister, worried and needy.

Cara has never been the same since that day twelve years ago. Truth be told, none of us have. The day Liam died was hard on everyone. But, as she got older, her reaction was to turn deeper inside herself, run from any conflict or hardship that might cause upset to her carefully ordered life, take on new vices every week, and to avoid any close relationships.

In contrast, I have grown and changed, strengthened and improved. I've become bolder, more charismatic, a free bird flying toward success. That day brought tragedy and mourning to our family, but it also brought me a newfound freedom.

Of course, I can't share those thoughts with anyone for fear of sounding callous. But liberation and relief ran parallel to, and eventually overtook, my grief following his death. I made decisions then on how my life would look and the kind of man I would be.

One thing I never intended was this distance that grew between my sister and me. That seemed to be a decision she made long ago when she started acting like a stalker. I had spent too many years feeling tortured by my father, neglected by my mother, and hated by my brother. I didn't need the only sibling I had left to turn on me as well, but when she did, I knew I needed to keep out of her reach.

Reluctantly, I gave in to Cara's pleading for a longer conversation about the Rowe case, mostly out of a need to get her off my back, but also with a deep curiosity to figure out the game she was playing. I knew she was lying and that I had to get away from her, sooner rather than later, regardless of whether I discovered her motives.

"Okay. Sure. I guess we can chat for a few minutes," I said, removing my hands from where they had been stowed deep in my pockets and spreading them out in front of me to indicate I was ready for her questions.

Relieved, her posture relaxed some. "Can we sit down?" she asked, gesturing to a bench a few steps behind where we were standing. I nodded, heading towards it.

The wind was still whipping around, and the bench was fully exposed to the sun, it did look inviting. I settled back on the seat, propped my foot on the opposite knee, rested my hands in my lap, and turned my face upward to soak in the warmth.

I glanced over at Cara, who seemed to be generally more composed, but when she sat, she perched on the edge, as if ready to flee at a moment's notice. Her entire body was toward me but she didn't immediately begin talking. Her hands wrung and fidgeted in her lap for a moment while she gathered her thoughts.

After another long, slow breath, Cara asked "How did you find out about Johnny Rowe's death?"

"Well, normally, I hear the initial report that someone has died, and if it sparks my interest as a death that seems suspicious or strange in some way, basically if it sounds like a good story, I begin contacting the officers and lead detectives and family members to find out if they'll allow me to follow the case closely with interviews and research..."

Cara shook her head as I finished speaking.

"That's not exactly what I meant," she sighed. "In the first article that you published about him, you seemed to be able to describe the scene of where he died in a lot of detail. Were you there? I mean, actually there when it happened?"

I looked at Cara skeptically. She already knew the answer to this question.

"Well, um, yeah. Sorta. I was in the area on a short hike, which you know is not normally something I'm into, but Chelsey has been on me recently to bring her on one of my trips soon. She said I've been working too hard. She wants me to plan something out though- an experience, she calls it." I rolled my eyes at Chelsey's choice of words.

I looked down at the sole of my shoe, running my finger over the edge of the tread as I spoke. "My impression is that she wishes I would fly her out to meet me, take her on some kind of adventure, like rafting or hiking- you know that's more her thing- take her to a nice dinner, stay in a nice hotel, then fly her back home. Something like that."

I shrugged and continued, "I don't know, it seems like a lot of hassle for a short weekend to me. But, now that I'm making more money, I can afford it. And she's right, I should plan something for her. I leave her alone a lot more now and she hasn't gotten to know very many people since we moved."

I glanced up again at Cara, who was staring blankly at me, listening.

"So anyway, Chelsey suggested that I check out Hudson Highlands, you know the state park, to check out Bull Hill and see if it's somewhere we might like to visit together. Of course, I wouldn't be able to bring her back until later in the spring because she hates to be cold. But she said it was worth a look." I chuckled at the ridiculousness of people hiking as a hobby.

Cara was unmoved and remained motionless, listening intently. She looked strained, as if she was concentrating.

"Anyway, I happened to arrive in the parking lot around the same time as Rowe. He had to pass my car to get on the trailhead and we were only a few feet apart, so I nodded to him. He seemed to be in a hurry, didn't nod or wave, just kind of blew me off even though he looked right at me. The man was probably just as much of an asshole as the media described him," I frowned, remembering my irritation that morning.

"I recognized him, of course, from seeing him on the news a couple of nights before. He didn't really look like he was dressed for hiking, but people that rich are weird, right? So what do I know about it?"

Cara nodded ever so slightly to say she understood my observation, encouraging me to continue.

"Well, then he immediately went off into the woods. I wasn't really ready, still had to switch my shoes, load up my water, and check the map a few times. I probably got started ten or fifteen minutes later."

I switched legs and propped on the opposite knee, rubbing where my foot had been. Reflexively, I checked my watch as I shifted, eager to catch my flight, but time seemed to have slowed to a snail's pace.

"After about ten minutes of hiking, I walked out of the trees into the abandoned quarry, which is a pretty cool place. Have you ever been there?"

I paused in my story again to see if she was still listening. Cara shook her head but didn't otherwise respond.

"The trail I was following took a hard right to continue uphill. And there was another trail going into the quarry that Chelsey had specifically mentioned, so I decided to check it out. It's a field, almost like Savannah grasslands. I walked out into the middle and there was a huge cliff with a rock face all around it in a semicircle." I smiled, remembering the beautiful scenery.

"When I got closer to the base of the cliff, that's when I saw him. He was laid out on his back, feet pointed toward the rock…"

I paused again, realizing I was getting carried away with my narrative. I needed to watch Cara's response because I wasn't sure what her reaction was going to be after being reminded of the eerie scene.

Cara's eyes were gathered up tightly, squinting, blocking tears. Her hands were still, but clenched around the hem of her shirt, knuckles white again.

"I should've just given you the short version. I was there. I found him. I called the police," I said.

"No," she said softly, then, more resigned, "No, I do want to talk about the details." Cara smoothed the hem that she had been wadding up over her lap and took a slow breath. "I'm okay, really. It's hard, but I need to hear what you think happened to him."

I glanced down at my watch again to check the time, wondering how long this pseudo therapy session might last. Noticing my distraction, she suddenly grew irritated. At this point, she was riding a full-on roller coaster of emotions, reminding me of the unstable teenage Cara.

"So what happened to him, Owen?" she snapped. My name sounded harsh; a provocation flung from the snarl on her face. It was the same question, asked in the same angry way twelve years before. Except that day, I was the one questioning Cara after finding her standing over Liam's lifeless body.

Chapter 6

The last time I reminisced about the day Liam died, I was working at the San Francisco Chronicle. It was a hectic day. Phones rang, keyboards clicked, people spoke in low voices all around me. The newsroom was busiest right before all the stories designated for the printed edition were due to the copy desk.

I'd been working on a dominant story for Sunday's front page, but the words for my lead felt stuck in the tangled mess inside my head. The story was written- a piece on the aftermath of Facebook executive Mark Zuckerberg's appearance before Congress to defend his company over data breaches- but I couldn't get the introduction quite right. The words were coming in fits and starts, but not solidifying into a tangible idea.

I don't like to write about the Zuckerbergs of the world, but it's always those in power making news and taking advantage of other people, so it's a necessity in my line of work. I'd rather tell the stories of regular people, those left behind, pushed aside, or forgotten.

Essentially, I began writing in order to heal. The human body is an amazing and confounding system. Rather than succumb to the psychosomatic distresses suffered by the rest of my family after Liam's death, I was strong enough to get out and move forward, to fulfill my purpose.

After I graduated high school, I moved to Evanston to attend Northern University for journalism. As if eight hundred miles away from home wasn't enough, I completed my degree there and promptly moved over two thousand miles away from my family to San Francisco.

After six years at the Chronicle, I finally felt like I'd found my niche in being a reporter. Reporting, investigating, digging into, and narrating the details of people's lives, that's where I've always shined. I'd already built strong connections with many of the local police and prosecutors, which afforded me more opportunities to be privy to stories as they were happening. But being in control of my life is still a new concept for me and it's hard to feel content. I'm always ready for more.

Growing up, my curiosity and entrepreneurial spirit were always touted by my father to be hindrances to logical thinking, or masks covering any "real talent." It wasn't until Liam's death, when he stopped beating me, and then my time away from home at Northern, that he finally began to show signs of appreciating my talent for writing. My parents frequently offered to visit me in Illinois during college, but they were the last people I wanted to see.

No, that's not right, Cara was the last person I wanted to see then, and it's still true now. In recent days, I've frequently found myself sitting, unproductive and impotent. I pin the blame for my recent setback entirely on thoughts of her.

After Liam's death, Cara became increasingly withdrawn. Her middle school years were highlighted by forced family therapy. I'm not sure that it helped much, she became angrier and reactive, especially towards me.

Shockingly, she actually attended college, even after her rocky high school years. It seems her depression and, I would say insanity, accompanied her on her collegiate journey, pushing her closer to the edge and into the embrace of new addictions.

Intuition tells me I can't trust her, and she certainly doesn't trust me. The further she retreated into herself, the more my parents began to reach out to me in exasperation, clinging to the only child left who kept a level head and worked hard to be successful.

The reason I found myself sitting at my desk, staring at my computer screen without a solid thought is because she had called the day before. There's only one day each year that she attempts to contact me without fail: the anniversary of Liam's death.

I don't answer the phone because I already know what she's going to say. When we were still at home together, she would leave me a note on my pillow or on my desk or even written in one of my notebooks. The same message, like a broken record. It always manages to rattle me for a few days afterward. It's creepy.

I was so close to getting the Facebook story completed before I listened to her voicemail. I'd successfully managed to forget that it was the anniversary of the day Liam died. The busier and more successful I've become, the more often I've been able to finally push thoughts of my brother aside and make progress in letting those old wounds heal. Cara seemed intent on ripping them open and exposing the pain to be fresh and raw each year.

I've learned to delete the message before listening to it. But for whatever reason, I guess I thought maybe it might be something different, that day I listened. After that, I couldn't seem to think about anything else.

The day Liam died floats on the periphery of my life as undefined memories, blurry and nonsensical. But hearing Cara's voice reminds me of her frantic call that day in 2007, bringing it all into picture-perfect recall.

After hearing her distress that May afternoon, I shoved some shoes on and ran out the door, leaving everything as it was- lights on, TV on, door wide open. I took off running toward the middle school, phone in hand. It had been difficult to understand her as she sobbed and shouted and choked in between her words, my feet pounded the pavement as loud as my heart pounded in my ears.

After a few tries, I deciphered that she had been walking toward home and had taken the route that cuts through the woods between school and her friend, Christine's house. She couldn't tell me anymore, she just continued sobbing.

Why was she walking home alone? Wasn't Mom supposed to be picking her up?

Christine's house was half of a mile from our house. I remember running through their front yard and into the back, dodging a couple of toys scattered on the lawn. Once I entered the woods, I'm not sure if I followed the worn walking path or not, my surroundings smeared and swirled into greens and browns.

"Why is Cara in the woods?" echoed in my head, my confusion outweighing my concern. I don't remember how long it took me to get to her, but I had an idea of where I was headed, and muscle memory took over.

I was staring at the ground, watching my feet move back and forth, one in front of the other, careful not to trip over roots and sticks. I looked up when I heard Cara's cries coming from the direction of the granite outcropping. Her pink pull-over peeked through the trees, and I took off running toward her again.

As I burst through the tree line, Cara stumbled back until she met the rock face behind her. Slowly, she slid down to the ground and sat crumpled, curled in on herself, laying her head down on her arms that she had folded across her knees. Then, I turned to look at Liam.

He was laid out, flat on his back, a peaceful look on his face. His head was pointed toward me, and his feet stretched away toward the rock wall peeking through the hillside. If it weren't for the large pool of blood spreading out from underneath the back of his head and the two child-size bloody handprints perfectly placed on either cheek, Liam would've appeared to be sleeping.

I walked over and knelt next to his head, looking closely. The blood was a deep red, almost black, thick and dull looking. It had begun to blend with the mud and dirt, and the creeping afternoon shadows. A gasping breath from Cara shook me from my observations and I turned to look at her. She remained with her head down, visibly shaking, gulping air.

I studied her for a moment. There was blood on her shoes, her pants, and on the sleeves of the hoodie. Her hands were the worst of it. As I stared at her, she slowly lifted her heavy head to look at me.

Tears streamed down Cara's face, forging paths on her skin through the dirt and smeared blood. When she spoke, it sounded strained and rough, "I don't understand what happened... I think he's dead. Is he dead? There's so much blood!"

I nodded carefully as I placed my fingers along the side of his throat, confirming what I already knew. Any sudden movements I made might further disturb her as she teetered on the edge of hysterics. She looked down at her hands and clothes and her eyes grew even wider in shock, as if noticing for the first time her gory appearance.

So many questions and emotions had been swimming in my head since her call, but now anger emerged, dominant above the rest.

"What are you doing out here, Cara?" I asked through clenched teeth.

"What..? Well, I...I...I didn't know...," she stopped and started.

"I've been so mad at him...why couldn't he...? I just wanted to... I don't understand."

I walked over and grabbed her by both shoulders, careful not to touch the blood, stared straight into her wild eyes and raised my voice, "What are you doing out here, Cara?"

"I had to go after him! I didn't know what else to do!"

Rage at her incoherence exploded from me as I shook her shoulders and shouted, "What happened to him, Cara?"

Chapter 7

Cara had lost her cool. Again. I could tell she hadn't intended on snapping at me because her expression testified to her surprise and regret. She pulled back and her eyes widened, then tightened. The hand that had quickly moved to cover her mouth, now slowly crept to her neck, and hovered there, shaking. She seemed unsure what to do next.

I continued to look at her calmly without responding, making sure my features were smooth and unreadable. Then, I grinned, hoping this was a look that would set Cara at ease again.

My smirk seemed to confuse her at first. But then, she glanced around and cleared her throat, obviously feeling awkward at the way I hadn't been ruffled by her sudden outburst.

I didn't think that she really wanted the details of Johnny's death, but I decided that I'd continue to push her until her motives became clear or she went over the edge, whichever came first. I'd been working on Rowe's story and debating with Detective Sanchez the night before, so every moment of finding his body was still very fresh in my thoughts.

After checking for Johnny's pulse, I took out my phone to call the police. I had to walk a little way back out of the quarry to get better reception. I made the call, gave them the best description of my location that I could, and sat down on a boulder on the side of the trail in the warm sunlight to wait.

I began to record some thoughts in a journal that I kept with me, logging the fresh details of what I'd witnessed. The snacks I'd brought along with me didn't last too long and I'd gone through all of them by the time the authorities arrived a short time later.

Various officers began to move quickly into the quarry. One of them, a large man, wide, but not very tall, named Officer Walls, stopped where I was sitting and stood over me, blocking the bright light streaming through the trees.

"Are you Mr..." he looked down at the small notebook he held in his chubby hand, "...Walsh?"

"Yes, sir, that's me." I brushed off my pants and reached out to shake his hand as I stood to greet him. Out of shape and overweight, he was still out of breath from his short hike and was sweating profusely even though the afternoon was brisk and cool. I tried to discreetly wipe my now damp palm off on my pants.

"I'd like to get a statement from you about what happened today," Officer Walls managed to huff out in between breaths. He flipped a page in the notebook and stood ready with his pen.

"Well, I was hiking, came into the quarry to check it out, and saw Mr. Rowe laying on the ground with a large pool of blood around his head."

"Did you touch him?"

"Well, yeah, I did check for a pulse."

"Did you touch him other than that?"

"No, why would I?"

"Just a question. When did you arrive at the park?"

I thought about that for a second. "I believe it was about 8:30, but I don't think I started hiking until closer to 8:45 or so."

"Did you see the decedent any time before that?"

"Yeah, I think I saw him getting out of his car."

"You called him Mr. Rowe. Did you know him?"

"I've never met him. But I recognized him from TV."

In fact, I recognized him from more than just seeing him on TV. Johnny Rowe, the CEO of a security company, had been a big focus in news stories since June due to an abundance of reports of sexist and belittling behavior towards female employees.

While the initial reports were being investigated, the board of directors discovered that Rowe had been taking unauthorized bonuses and loans in the amount of $10 million. He had paid for lavish parties, spent a lot of money on escorts, and bought his girlfriend, Motney Bride, expensive jewelry. He'd been brought up on charges of grand larceny and securities fraud, among others.

Johnny's trial was due to begin early next year, but the public just couldn't get enough of this rich bad boy and the closer the date crept toward his trial, the more popular he became. I'll never understand how anyone who treats other people like trash is listened to, liked, or respected. What makes a bad attitude and a mean spirit worth following?

I shook my head in bewilderment at these thoughts and checked my watch. Officer Walls tapped his pen on the notebook and looked up briefly at the movement going on around us.

"Did you see anyone else on the trail or in this area?"

"Well, I haven't passed anyone hiking at all. While I was in the quarry, and before I found his body, I thought I heard movement on this trail, but I never saw anyone. I guess it could've been an animal, it just sounded like footsteps in the leaves. I've sat here for at least thirty minutes waiting on y'all to arrive and no one else came by."

"I thought I caught an accent," he said as he wrote down my comments. "Where are you from?"

"I grew up in Georgia. Sometimes the south still slips out."

The officer grinned and seemed to be considering me for a moment.

"And do you live in this area now or are you visiting?" he asked as he took notes.

"My fiancé and I live in California. I'm just visiting the area right now."

"Do you often go on hikes alone?"

"No, not usually. The only reason I came on this hike was to see if it would be a place I could bring Chelsey, my fiancé, if we come back to visit."

"So you're planning a trip back to the Hudson Highlands sometime soon?" Officer Walls gestured around him with the notebook as we spoke. I was dying to take my own journal back out and record our conversation, but for the moment I was fighting the temptation.

"Well, I wasn't sure of the timing for the trip initially, but now I may be here for the next few weeks, so I might get her to fly out while I'm here. Although, I don't think I'll bring her on this particular hike now." I chuckled at that, but he just made notes and continued on formally.

"Did you not already have a set day for returning home? We will of course need your contact information, but you won't need to stay in town past today if it conflicts with your plans."

"Well, I'm a journalist. I'm a reporter for the Today Times and I travel to the stories. And I've found one, quite literally, that I can focus on for the next several weeks."

"Oh, yeah, I read the Today Times every evening." He glanced at his notes and asked, "What did you say your full name was?"

"I didn't. It's Owen Walsh. My column is all about unexplained or mysterious deaths, and..."

"You're the guy who writes the Newsworthy columns, right? I love your stuff!"

"Yeah, that's me. Thanks very much!"

Officer Walls reached out to shake my hand again as if we were just meeting for the first time.

"I heard your articles have actually assisted in some of the cases. Somewhat of a detective yourself, eh?" He approvingly jabbed me in the shoulder. The officer was more handsy than I preferred, but as long as he was passing out flattery, I decided to let it go.

"I do enjoy being somewhat involved in the cases and helping to dig out the details. My passion has always been helping the families of the victims to hopefully find a modicum of understanding, while also telling a good story."

He nodded in agreement but seemed to have stopped listening. "I think that's great! Well, you're really talented."

"Do you mind if I ask you some questions?"

Officer Walls suddenly looked uncomfortable. He pocketed his notebook and pen, while wiping his brow on the sleeve of his other arm. "No, I think you'll have to speak with my Lieutenant, Lieutenant Jeffries. Here, I'll write down the number for you."

He pulled the notebook back out and jotted it down quickly. "Someone may be contacting you soon if we have other questions. Thanks for your help so far, good to meet you."

I took the piece of paper and slipped it into my pocket as he turned to walk away into the quarry. Now that I was being left alone, I sat back down on the boulder and balanced my journal on my lap, getting back into reflection mode. I recorded the details of my conversation with Officer Walls and then stood again to put all my belongings back in the backpack, eager to return to my hotel and type a quick summary to send to my editor. But first, I'd need to give Lieutenant Jeffries a call.

I dialed the number and as it was ringing, I pictured my sister's eleven-year-old face as it looked when I had to call the police that day in the woods twelve years before, a mix of haunted, angry, devastated, and ashamed.

Even though Liam had turned into an unreasonable, unkind, and generally terrible person, Cara had mourned him fiercely. Would many people mourn Johnny? Hard to tell. Even without knowing the man, I can say with full certainty that the world is better off without him in existence.

While alive, people usually fawn over the wealthy, even if they are proven to be horrible humans. I was having a difficult time imagining the people that knew Rowe feeling anything other than relief. If the decision of whether we deserve to die is weighed on the scale of how we treat other people, justifying Johnny Rowe's death would be an easy case to make.

Sure, the people that knew him best would have to express sadness and a desire to have him back healthy and whole, but that would all be an act, just for appearances. No one would want to be the one that said they were glad he was dead. I had seen the same pattern of behavior in many of the cases that I had written about in the past year. And I'd experienced them firsthand. For me, it was all very familiar.

Chapter 8

2018

"I hate moving!" Chelsey said as she collapsed down heavily onto the couch that sat askew in the doorway to our new living room.

She hadn't been the one doing all the lifting and hauling and shifting and carrying, but she was sweaty and whiney, nonetheless. It was stiflingly hot. Everyone suggested we wait to move to Redmore during the fall months, when hopefully the hundred plus degree days would fade into cooler weather. But I had been unwilling to bend on the date. That would've meant that Chelsey stayed in San Francisco while I kept an apartment here, traveling on the weekends, and just generally spending money that I didn't yet have.

No, the best decision was to move together and get it over with. I was mentally predicting that with my new position at Today Times, I'd be able to double my current salary in the first year. The fact that this newspaper was a national publication, and extremely popular with the online community, also meant there was more room for me to grow.

I want to travel. I want to have the autonomy to find and report on my own stories. Chelsey didn't seem to be swayed by my excitement of personal growth, but her interest did increase when I mentioned greater opportunities to grow financially.

I've always known that Chelsey's out of my league. She's athletic, yet graceful. She's naturally blond and tan. Her hair always seems to hang in loose waves that look professional but take no effort on her part. Even when she's slouched on a couch, with a slightly sweaty upper lip, and a scowl on her face, she still manages to look like she just stepped off a runway.

I couldn't believe my luck when she agreed to go on that first date when I met her in our first year of college. I decided then that I would do whatever it took to keep her interested in me. Money wasn't what kept her by my side, which was good since I didn't have any. But I attended to her, complimented her, and showered her with affection, and it worked.

Recently, she seems more restless. But I won't lose her. I need her. Having a woman like Chelsey by my side when I walk into a room changes the entire atmosphere. When other people see her with me, I know their immediate reaction is respect and envy.

Plus, Chelsey is good at getting other people to do what she wants, which has also come in handy for me over the years. Also, luckily for me, she's not as smart as I am. I allow her to think she's got the upper hand and that I am her devoted, adoring boyfriend, but it's all part of a game to keep her content.

Her sudden collapse onto the couch has left me awkwardly wedged between it and the wall. I quickly hid my annoyance with a good-humored grin and said, "If you'll just help me get it across the room to the back wall, you can put your feet up while I finish unloading some things, okay?"

Chelsey's scowl melted into a cherubic smile of relief. She hopped up and walked around to the other arm to pick it up once again. We waddled across the hardwoods, barely gripping the large, solid piece of furniture. After finally placing it in its new spot, Chelsey did indeed lay down on the couch, prop her feet on the side, wedge a throw pillow underneath her head, and shut her eyes with a satisfied look on her face. It was actually a bit of a relief. She's no dainty princess, but when she has her mind set against doing something, she becomes quite the obstinate obstacle and purposely slows things down. It was better that she got out of the way for a while.

I continued unloading the moving truck until late in the afternoon. Every time I passed her lying on the couch, she would let out a breathy, deep sigh like one might if they were dreaming. It was a good act, but I knew she was faking it. Her eyes always twitched and followed my progress across the room underneath her eyelids.

I just let her little charade continue until I was on the last box. It was ridiculously heavy. I scanned the side to find how it was labeled, 'Bookshelf.' These were the books that went with me to every place I've ever lived. If there's one thing I can't live without, it's the power and majesty of the written word.

I groaned and heaved it into my arms, letting it sit heavily on my chest, as I slightly bent backwards under its weight. I carried the box into the living room to place it next to the bookshelves but decided once I got there to have a little bit of fun. I dropped it from chest height onto the wooden floors and the sound of it slamming into the ground sent Chelsey leaping off the cushions and then falling on the floor.

"I finally finished!"

Chelsey, who was now moving to her hands and knees, glared at me from between the curtain of hair hanging around her face.

I smiled sheepishly and said "I'm sorry! I didn't realize how loud that was going to be. I just couldn't hold it up anymore," while also shaking with a somewhat controlled laughter fighting to escape.

Walking over to give her a hand, I pulled her up to standing, and stretched my arm around her back pulling her into my sweaty embrace. At first, she seemed annoyed, but she probably felt guilty for faking her slumber, so she softened and leaned in to let me hold her close.

"I'm sorry I wasn't very helpful. I was just so tired! I couldn't keep my eyes open," she purred into my chest.

I held her away from me so I could look at her face. "That's okay, it went pretty quickly," I lied. "Now we just have to unpack all the boxes."

"Ugh," she pushed further away and leaned down to pick up the pillow that had fallen on the floor. "Maybe tomorrow. I'm not in the mood. I don't even want to look at another box.

And when does it ever cool off here? The sun's going down and I feel like the temperature hasn't budged at all!"

She had a point. But this was more of her pouting about having to move in the summertime. Chelsey had seemed all too eager to stay in San Francisco while I moved on my own. There was never any talk of breaking up, just a feeling of complacency about being separated by time and distance. This was another reason I had been determined that we would move at the same time. I couldn't allow her to come up with the notion that she could live happily without me.

"Well, there's always tomorrow, I guess." I sighed and sat down on the recently vacated couch. "I've got to go down to the office first thing in the morning to meet with my new editor and get my desk settled. You could do some unpacking while I'm gone."

It was immediately evident that Chelsey was not too keen about that idea. Although, I was impressed by her restraint.

She fixed a look on her face that was supposed to convey thinking it over and then smiled and said, "I might do a little bit. I feel like I've got plenty of time, though. I might just spend the hottest part of the day over at Whiskeytown."

Of course, she would. I knew when we moved here that Whiskeytown Lake would be an immediate draw for her. Sunshine and water were her only requirements to find her happy place. "Fine, fine," I sighed, and gave her a small kiss on the tip of her nose. Whatever it takes to keep her happy.

Over the course of the next couple of months, our pattern continued in much the same way. I worked, she sunbathed. I came home and unpacked boxes, she ordered take-out and "relaxed after a long day."

I realized after the first few days of working myself into a higher and higher level of irritation with Chelsey, that there hadn't been a period of time in our relationship before when only one of us was working.

She's a dental hygienist and is the very picture of a perfect, healthy smile. I was always suspicious of the last dentist she worked for. He seemed like a slimeball, always making too much effort to appear younger than he was. Dr. Davis had plastic surgery, spray tans, a personal trainer, and of course, a dazzling smile. Not to mention the fact that, as a journalist, I've never earned anywhere near the amount of money a dentist does.

I don't think I'll ever know if they were having an affair. As long as Chelsey stayed with me, I was okay living blissfully in the dark. It's once I'm aware of the overshadowing, the humiliation, the shame of falling short of expectations, that's when I'm at my worst.

She's never given me any reason to doubt her loyalty, but anyone who looks at us as a couple would probably assume that she's unfaithful. However, anyone who views us on the surface, wouldn't see how superior my intellect is to hers. She is entirely dependent on me and leans on me for most decisions.

Chelsey's not unintelligent, just easily manageable. I may appear to be her faithful puppy dog, but appearances can be deceiving. No, my writing is the most important aspect of my life. As far as I'm concerned, having a beautiful girl by my side is an added bonus.

Every day while at work, my goal is to be the new guy that no one can figure out how anything got done before he arrived. I aspire to be the helpful, indispensable, ask-Owen-he-probably-knows type of employee. It seems to be working and I feel like I'm finally getting into my groove. I think my boss appreciates my entrepreneurial mind and often labels my ideas as "new and exciting."

Then, I come home to my lazy fiancé, prattling on about how the heat is so oppressive and she just can't find the motivation to accomplish anything. Meanwhile, I often spy a small, day cooler turned over in the grass next to the garage, on top of a half-melted pile of ice cubes and a puddle of water.

Every evening since that first one, I've encouraged her to begin looking for open positions and submitting her resumé at a few dental practices. She hems and haws around the topic, dancing from excuse to excuse until I finally give up and change the subject.

One night, my short temper seemed to settle thickly in the kitchen like a dense fog. Chelsey walked gingerly into the room and came up behind me as I stood stirring the contents of the pan on the stove, putting her arms around me, and burying her face into my back in a long hug. I didn't stop stirring or make any comments.

"Owen?"

"Hm?" My short grunt response stilled the air even more.

She seemed to consider my mood and said, "If you wanted Chinese food, I could've picked some up. You don't have to cook this frozen stuff from the bag."

I turned to look at her in time to see her rearranging the disgusted look on her face. I angled back to the stove without commenting and resumed my stirring.

"I know I haven't been keeping up with going to the store recently, but maybe you can make me a list tonight and I can go for us tomorrow?"

I set the spoon down roughly on the counter and said, "I'll probably just pick myself something up and eat it at the office tomorrow. I've got a deadline coming up and I'll probably work late anyway. But yeah, it would be nice if you went by the store. Just make a list of whatever you think we need. You buy groceries this month and I'll buy next month."

I watched Chelsey's face fall. She was clearly hoping I'd continue to pay for everything. Or maybe she was already running out of money. Or both.

I had this growing desire to spend more time away from the house. If I traveled more, she'd have to get a job and start earning some money because I wouldn't be around to support her daily drinking habits. Also, her lazy disposition could become an out-of-sight, out-of-mind situation. If I could find a way to throw myself into work and put more time and distance between the two of us, perhaps our relationship would improve. At least she'd still be around for when I needed her.

Several weeks later, I sat alone at the worn, antique wooden bar of Malone's, happily enjoying a reprieve from my and Chelsey's now more frequent disagreements and celebrating my successful pitch to Roy for a new article. I've never been one to let anyone in power or authority intimidate me. Even though I've only been with the Today Times since the summer, my editor would have to be a total hack not to realize that I'm one of his best writers.

I set up a meeting with him and presented my idea about the new article. It will read like a mini-series for several weeks in a row, giving bits of information and clues one day at a time, building a story in order to engage the readers and ask for their help in solving a mysterious death.

He didn't spend much time mulling it over, calling me just an hour later to congratulate me on my 'fresh, creative angle on a topic that has intrigued human nature since the dawn of time.' Perhaps I'll borrow his description as a preface to a book I'm writing.

I raised my glass, the two fingers of Four Roses Single Barrel whiskey flowing around and over the ice like a caramel blanket, with a nod and a "cheers" to no one in particular. The sip warmed me from the inside out and brought a small, satisfied smile to my face. *Here's where it begins. This is the start of the success I deserve. Now, I just need someone to die.*

Chapter 9

*A*ll my rampant thoughts crashed back into the present conversation with my sister and the memories of the past were abruptly cut short. I sat unmoving and grinning at Cara in the midst of her outburst as she slowly calmed her features and rearranged her hands in her lap. She seemed to have surprised herself just as much as she did me with her sudden irritation.

"I'm sorry," she said softly, seemingly contrite, "I know you're just concerned about your flight. But I wish you'd stop checking your watch so often. We haven't sat down together in at least, like, five years."

My grin faded as I looked out into the park, gathering my thoughts. I watched Cara out of the corner of my eye. She did look to be settling down. A tight smile that didn't quite touch her eyes appeared on her face, then she bit at her bottom lip momentarily before releasing it again.

I sighed, resigned to my fate in this torturous discussion until I was able to get her to admit to the truth behind her questions. "Alright. Well, what else do you want to know?"

71

Cara seemed determined to drag herself into a pit of grief and regret, a morbid curiosity like slowing down for a car accident. As she studied me, her eyes searched my face, mouth open in a wordless reply, then closed again, varying emotions washed across her features.

"You asked what I think happened to Rowe, right?" I said, prompting her.

Her head nodded silently.

"One theory is that Johnny was climbing the cliff and lost his footing and fell, hitting his head when he reached the bottom. Or, maybe, he managed to reach the top of the wall somehow by following a trail and lost his footing while standing on top, falling, and hitting his head on the way down. It's hard to say. The evidence leads to conflicting conclusions. He didn't have other injuries that would indicate a fall from very high."

Pausing, my voice drifted off as I looked away from her again, toward the joggers' path. A woman who looked to be in her mid-forties ran by.

"But I think I agree with the detectives and that someone probably murdered him, perhaps not who they've arrested, but someone."

The jogger had her ear buds in and was staring down at her feet as she moved. She didn't seem to have anything in her hand and the phone playing whatever she was listening to was probably tucked away in a pocket somewhere. She smiled to herself, then softly sang a few words, never looking up at her surroundings or noticing the two of us sitting on the nearby bench. The woman moved away down the path toward a wooded section of the park and disappeared around the turn. *She's the perfect victim,* I thought.

After writing my column for over a year, I had developed a sixth sense for potential victims. People never seemed to have forethought about how their patterns of behavior left them open to the evil intentions of others. But, then again, sometimes fate didn't align with routines, instead choosing to ambush its victims at the rarest opportunities. Tomorrow is never guaranteed.

Cara broke that chain of thought. "Murdered?" She sounded surprised.

"And seeing someone who's died in that way doesn't bother you?"

I turned my attention back to her. "I never said that-"

"Honestly," she quickly replied before I had finished speaking, "I can't understand how you can write any of your articles. How are you able to follow these stories about death and speak to these families in the middle of their depression and sadness, and not let it faze you?"

Cara was increasing in volume and becoming agitated again. I should've known this would be her line of questioning.

She'd never given me the full details of how she ended up in the woods the day Liam died. I have been able to piece together what I think is the whole story over time, but I never came right out and demanded an explanation. Instead, I wanted to investigate, search for the truth, interview witnesses, and uncover clues. It seems predestined that it is precisely what I am doing for a living now.

I drifted into contemplation again as memories floated through my consciousness like dust on the wind. Sitting with Cara, it was getting harder and harder for my thoughts to remain in the present, as the past continued to fight for my attention. My mind was cluttered and bursting at the seams.

While waiting for the police to arrive that May afternoon in 2007, I sat near her against the rock wall, not touching her huddled, shaking body. It didn't seem right to console her. Something inside of me was angry and suspicious. I didn't touch her because I thought it might possibly contaminate the blood evidence. Even then I thought of it as evidence, although I wasn't sure what it was evidence of.

The timeline of that afternoon showed that the police arrived quickly after my call, only ten minutes later, but sitting in the afternoon heat, watching the blood covering her hands dry, it felt like much longer.

I asked her over and over "What happened to him, Cara?" I wasn't yelling, exactly. I spoke evenly, but sternly, raising my voice to a level I hoped would break the surface of her panic, earnestly wishing I could reach out and shake her to make her answer me.

As the sirens finally drew closer, and in between sporadic, gulping sobs, she told me that her and Liam's arguments had intensified that week. She wouldn't explain further, she just made vague statements like, "I can't believe he did that to me!" and "I was so angry!" and "How did this happen?"

Through listening to Mom and Dad's conversations I later learned that, according to Cara, Liam had done something to "ruin her life" and so she had it in her mind to try to ruin his. She told mom that she would be staying after school for a gardening club, but instead had used the time before being picked up to sneak into the locker room to find Liam's bat bag.

Those series of actions by my little sister were surprising in themselves, not to mention what came next. I had not known Cara to be a liar, much less a sneak and a thief.

Apparently, Cara had swiped Mom's prescription bottle of Prozac out of the cabinet in my parents' bathroom and saved it for the right moment. My mother had relentlessly searched for that bottle in the days before Liam's death. But, having never admitted that she was in any way depressed or needed such strong medication, the way she questioned her children was roundabout. She would ask us vague questions, trying for nonchalance, but falling short when her voice came out strained, her eyes tense and scrunched with worry.

Cara carried those pills around for a while, hidden in her backpack, waiting for the opportunity to exact her revenge. Knowing her, I can imagine how nervous and jumpy she would've been. It explains why she had seemed so distracted at the time. Her chance came on the day of the gardening club. Once she was sure that Liam's team had left the locker room to head out to the field, she snuck in and searched for his bag.

My father once wondered aloud what caused Liam to walk back into the locker room that afternoon. The boys were rarely allowed to leave the field for any reason. They were expected to emerge ready to practice, no excuses, forgetting nothing that was needed. Whatever the reason, he walked back in just in time to catch Cara in the act of hiding the bag of pills in his locker.

My stomach growled slightly, drawing attention to its empty cavern, and bringing my mind back to the present. I realized Cara was staring at me, eyes narrowed.

Feeling scrutinized and defensive, I finally said, "Look, I never said that being around similar situations hasn't bothered me. But you've got to realize that I've always dealt with it differently than you."

I took a deep breath calming my irritation and concentrated on keeping my thoughts on the immediate conversation. "I've never run away from reality. I've never tried to pretend that he didn't die or that everything was fine," I bit off.

Cara looked as if she'd been slapped. Another slight breeze ruffled through our hair and clothes. She turned slightly, angling herself away from me, frowning into the distance. The aroma of something fried drifted by, reminiscent of my southern childhood.

Following the hours I'd spent with Detective Sanchez and working on my article, I'd finally been able to get into bed in the early hours of the morning. Once Cara called, waking me to request this meeting, I'd spent a while pacing and worrying, and then restlessly trying to sleep without success.

My brain and body were wired from our brief conversation, so I eventually sat down with my laptop once again and put some of those jumbled thoughts and emotions about

Cara into another project I'd been working on for a while. Amid all that, I had completely forgotten to eat, which tended to happen from time to time when I was caught up in writing a story. Thankfully, Cara didn't notice the growl, or she chose to ignore it.

"You can't even imagine the guilt I've carried with me all these years," she spoke softly as she stared off to the side, not looking me in the eyes. "I wasn't running away. I was trying to get back to a point where I felt like I deserved to live. I've been trying to live."

One of Liam's coaches gave a eulogy at the funeral and used those exact words. Coach Andrews was a chunk of a man. I could never imagine how he could possibly model any athletic skill or encourage motivation to young, talented boys who are chomping at the bit with eagerness for the sport.

Steve Andrews was overweight, but only around the belt. His enormous belly hung over his waist like a pregnant woman in her ninth month. He kept a poorly trimmed, infrequently shaved beard and was often sweating or breathing heavily in uneventful situations. Not only was his physical appearance unsightly, but his personality was also lacking. I'm certain I caught him multiple times looking at me with a mix of pity and contempt. I had seen the look enough times on my father's face to recognize the emotions.

"I can't imagine how empty it will feel to spend time on the field without Liam and what he brought to the game of baseball. Our team will feel the empty space he's left behind. He brought so much life to ordinary days, and with his passing, Liam is leaving

behind a legacy of hard work and dedication. He had so much left to give. I think we should all resolve to bring more life to each day. We should go out and really live because he can't."

First of all, what thirteen-year-old has developed a legacy? And second of all, did Liam really bring any value to the relationships he built beyond his athletic talent? I hated that speech at the time it was given, and I hated to remember it.

My current reaction to those words is the same as it was so many years ago: an eye roll and a scoff. Cara's reaction had been inner reflection and self-deprecation. In the months following the funeral, burial, and various memorials, spending time around Cara consisted of long periods of silence, sullen glares, and far-away gazes. She would frequently run-away by hiding in friends' basements or under the neighbors' porch, just to be found in the evenings curled up and cloaked in shadows as the sun was dropping from the sky.

Mom tip-toed around her, speaking gently and trying to be understanding of her continued withdrawal. She insisted on family counseling, which is where I shined. I didn't let on to the extent of the relief I felt, no longer being constantly bullied and harassed by Liam, and set free from Dad's cold, hard violence. I carried that secret close, not wanting to alarm anyone with what was certain to come across as heartlessness.

During our sessions, I was the only member of my family to have the capacity to speak about our history or more recent events with any sense of decorum and purpose. They all leaned into my ability to remain calm, even Cara, for a while.

In those first days, she clung to me, emotionally and sometimes physically, to get her through the routines of daily life. Our parents were in pieces, shredded by their devotion to a now deceased son. I believe their marriage only remained intact because it had always been built on the foundation of the loyalty of my mother to my father.

Besides fearing the repercussions of leaving him, she has always and will always align herself with whatever ideas and decisions he makes. Dad lost his golden boy and his pension for abuse, at least toward me. Instead, he turned to me to fulfill his need for self-importance. His pride requires that he have a son to press all his hopes and dreams of a successful future onto.

Unfortunately for him, he was no longer going to have a famously athletic son, but over the years he became content to pin his hopes on my talent for writing. When Liam died, I was simultaneously released from my brother's and my father's torments.

It really wasn't until several months after Liam's passing that Cara's demeanor began to shift and her attitude toward me slowly morphed into suspicion and disdain. She resented my interest in the details and my questioning the facts of that day would send her into an enraged silence.

Once I graduated and moved away to Northern, we reverted to a somewhat amicable relationship, as long as it was from a distance. By all appearances, she was back to her socially awkward, mostly quiet personality, and she only interacted with me when absolutely necessary.

Except for the yearly phone calls. Those came like clockwork. Cara's sweet voice had developed a hard edge to it over the years. "I've been thinking about you, Owen. I'm always thinking about you, but especially on this day. One day soon, I hope we can talk about everything and get to the truth. Until then, just know that you never really leave my thoughts."

Every time I listened to the message, paranoia would spike my adrenaline and send my thoughts into a manic overdrive until I could remind myself that my little sister may be unhinged, but she's basically harmless. At least, that's what I'd always tried to tell myself, focusing on staying one step ahead of her delusions, or if that was impossible, avoiding her at all costs.

Now it seems that all her stalking has paid off and she's finally caught up to me. We've both been hoarding our own versions of the truth for twelve years. Mine has remained constant, my true north. Cara's has mutated and morphed, becoming ugly and black. She's been unable to live her own life, unable to separate herself from Liam's demise. It's her own fault. And now, she's trying to harness me with her warped version of reality.

Cara continued to stare off into space, trying to ignore my obvious aversion to the reminder of Coach Andrews' words. I needed to get her to admit to why she had drug me out to this park.

"How long are you going to hold on to your guilt? Don't you want to be happy? Maybe you should tell me the truth about what happened," I hissed.

Her head snapped up and her eyes ignited, burning me with her hatred.

"C'mon, Cara. You tell me yours, and I'll tell you mine."

Chapter 10

2018

*A*fter three weeks of being back in the south, I'm ready to wrap this story up and hit the road again. It's been a whirlwind of events and I'm running low on sleep, but filled with alcohol and caffeine, depending on the time of day. It is nice, however, to continue to be away from Chelsey's bad attitude and laziness. Not long after I left for this first assignment for my new article, she realized that if she wanted to have any money to play with, she'd have to go out and get a job. And not a moment too soon.

I left with a lot of excitement and a bit of trepidation. I'm not surprised that my boss went for my idea, but I was a little shocked that he trusted my intuition so much, allowing me to travel first, in search of the story, instead of waiting for news to happen and then going to report on it.

I really wasn't sure of the best place to start. From my experience of growing up in a small southern town, I figured if I could locate a story in this area that the details of the culture and social interactions would be more familiar and easier for me to sort through. I wanted to write about something I know.

I flew into Atlanta, arrived late in the morning, rented a car, and began driving toward my parents' house without much of a plan. I knew I wanted to be close to home in case I needed to reach out to old friends in law enforcement or media who could help me make connections and root out the juicy stories. I also knew that I didn't want my parents or Cara to be aware of my proximity to them. I decided on Mill City and arrived in town not long after lunchtime.

The downtown area was full of life due to the small college campus that sprawled across a large portion of the northwest corner of town. I drove down Hanes Street, admiring the beautiful, stately buildings that held various administrative offices and classrooms, as they eased slowly into the old, historic buildings of restaurants and businesses that continued down the main strip. I found a parking spot right in front of Orbital Coffee, one of my favorite places to sit and write.

Once I got my driver's license and needed to "get out of town," away from my family, away from scrutiny, I visited here often. As a high school student, the lure of this city, only twenty minutes away, with its bars and busy streets and college girls, drew me out of the shell I hid inside and clung to day to day, trying to avoid the stares and gossip of my own smaller town.

I spent the first couple days after I arrived in Mill City sitting in Orbital coffee shop, or outside Benedict's Café, or in the lobby of my hotel just outside of town. I made phone calls, asked questions, and read newspapers. I was hunting for the story. I began traveling to the surrounding cities, meeting people, and making connections.

You can expeditiously learn the gossip of a small town through a few long, rambling conversations. You just have to know how to listen and the right questions to ask. Southerners will turn a short story into an epic of Iliad proportions faster than you can blink. The harder part is following the family lines of who's related to who and how it weaves into the culture and spirit of the city itself.

After several evenings of eating take-out in my hotel room, I decided to venture out. I drove the couple of miles into town and parked in one of the first spots on the edge of the businesses. I wanted to walk for a bit and people-watch.

The December night was cool and there was a chilly breeze whipping between the buildings. I crammed my hands in my pockets and tucked my chin, walking faster, and staring at my shoes.

From the corner of my eyes, I could tell that a light from one of the doorways was illuminating more of the sidewalk up ahead. A sharp, angry voice pierced the night air, and I looked up in time to see a young man standing halfway out of the doorway, with his back to the street, talking to someone unseen just inside.

"... I mean, whatever. I just think you're a shit for thinkin' I wasn't going to call you out on it. You can't treat customers like that. You can't treat ME like that!"

I couldn't hear the other person's response, but it must've been apologetic, because the man said, "Nah, not a chance. I'm not paying for it. I didn't get what I ordered."

He turned to leave, then had another thought and abruptly spun around. "But you'll be paying for it- you might want to start looking for another job. You won't be working here much longer."

A middle-aged man dressed in the classic black and white uniform of a server in a nicer establishment, began to follow him out, pausing in the doorway to watch the irate customer leave. Glancing up at the sign hanging over us, I saw that it was "Gypsie's", a high-end tapas restaurant and bar.

I stopped a couple of feet away to stare at the exchange. The angry guy turned toward me. He was younger than I thought, maybe only twenty or twenty-one years old. He wore loafers, pressed khakis, a collared plaid shirt rolled to the elbows, and an expensive-looking watch glittered at his wrist. His hair was stylish in a way that was meant to not look styled. He looked like money.

He turned to see that I was standing there, but kept his quick, irate stride and slammed into my shoulder as he passed, not even slowing down.

"Well, fuck!" he practically yelled as he threw his arms into the air in exasperation after running into me.

Stumbling back, I caught myself after a step or two, watching him march to the Tesla parked at the curb a few spaces away, every step an exclamation point to his rage. He smoothly and quickly slid into the driver's seat, slammed the door, and peeled away, speeding off down the road.

From behind me I heard, "I hate that guy." The server stood glowering at the space the Tesla had just vacated.

"A friend of yours?" I joked.

The man didn't seem to hear me. "He thinks he can just treat people howeva' he wants," he mumbled, and then he practically spit "Asshole!"

"Who is he?" I asked, intrigued.

Looking up, the server finally realized I was standing there, blinked a few times, and said, "Oh, uh, nobody. I don't really know." He suddenly seemed fidgety and nervous, but then took a deep breath, smoothed his hair and the front of his shirt, then went back inside.

Fascinating. The waiter was uninterested in talking about him. *Was he scared? Definitely worth pursuing more information on this topic. Follow the drama.* I had reached my destination for the evening.

Entering through the ornate archway that housed the front door to Gypsie's, I had to blink a couple of times to encourage my eyes to adjust so I could look around. It was brighter than outside, but the lighting was low, coming from some candelabra-type chandeliers hanging over the bar that traveled the length of the room from the front door to the back of the restaurant. There were also strings of Edison bulb lights strung haphazardly across the tops of exposed pipes and beams in the ceiling.

In the center, a disco-ball hung down, not turning, but glittering, nonetheless. The back wall was brick and held shelves upon shelves of seemingly random objects: empty jars, pillows, antique lunch boxes, wooden picture frames and bowls, large white baking bowls, a toaster with a rooster painted on the side, and many worn books. Next to the shelves, a dress form stood on a rolling post, filled with antique, sparkling brooches and clips.

The tables that were scattered through the middle of the large room were just as eclectic- church pews pulled up to long dining tables, cafe-type high-tops, and farmhouse bench seating. There was something for everyone.

The right side of the room was even more of a jumble. The wall, which was covered with an expansive, colorful mural of concentric circles, peacock feathers, and elephant silhouettes, had pillows lining the bottom half to accommodate the lower tables where patrons could sit on the floor to eat.

The place was packed with customers, dressed in their finery, sitting on bar stools, church pews, and some sitting on the floor. I was perplexed and amused. A quick glance at the menu told me that I couldn't afford to eat here more than once.

I also took a quick survey of what I looked like, unsure about whether I was appropriately dressed. Luckily, I had changed into a pair of khakis and a collared shirt before I walked out of the hotel room. Also luckily, I wasn't wearing the old flip flops that had become part of my daily wardrobe recently, even with the cooler weather.

The hostess, although she had a bit of a skeptical expression, must've silently decided I would pass inspection, because her pursed mouth melted into a hospitable grin as she led me over to the only empty seat at the bar. It was filled with mostly men dressed in suits with ties or bow ties, or slacks and sport coats, but there were a few younger couples snuggled close.

As I climbed up in the chair, the guy to my right set his rocks glass down roughly and said in a gruff voice, "I hope you're just here to eat and leave the rest of us alone."

I was kind of taken aback, but recovered quickly and said, "Um, I might just have a drink if it's all the same to you." The man grunted in response and took another quick swig of his whiskey.

"Was there a problem with the last guy?"

The glass landed roughly on the bar top for a second time. "Warren Williams," he said with disgust. "Warren Wilson Williams, the third, if we're gonna be specific." He said in his deep, country drawl. "He goes by Trés. Like the Spanish word for three. You must be from out of town if you don't know who I'm talkin about."

"I used to be from around here, but I've been gone for a while."

I peeked more at the menu as I spoke, my stomach now growling in protest.

"Hmph. Well, just avoid anything to do with him- that's my tactic."

As the man spoke, a server appeared to his left and set three small, beautifully designed plates with steaming food in front of my neighbor. From the looks of their contents, and my short study of the menu, I guessed that he was having the Steak Tartare, Meloso de Cordero, and a couple of the Mini Burgers. The thought of so much meat made my priorly ravenous stomach turn a little.

I ended up only ordering one empanada and three fingers of Four Roses, neat. As I settled in and began to sip on my drink, I quizzed the stern, put-out man to my right, and the open, enthusiastic couple to my left, about Warren Williams.

Williams had returned home with a degree a little over a year ago after a college career at Dartmouth, which according to local gossip, was a feat secured by his father, Warren Williams, Jr., who goes by Junior and has been mayor for the last seven years. Junior has been a sometimes popular, but always intimidating public figure since Trés was a toddler. It seems Trés grew up modeling himself after a chauvinistic, angry, bully and became one himself.

Contrary to that father-son duo, Junior had another son, three years older than Trés, who was described as humble, altruistic, and low-key. He didn't parade around town in the most expensive vehicles, insulting and intimidating everyone who he deemed less than himself, or using his money to pressure people into bending to his whims.

Instead, he was often the target of Trés' rants and public humiliations, mistreated by his brother and father for being "less of a man." The brother's name was Jeffery, apparently after the grandfather on his mother's side. I found it interesting that the family name of Warren skipped him and fell to the younger brother.

Story after story flowed from the other patrons at the bar like they had been waiting for an invitation to spill the beans. The servers and bartenders that came and went and caught bits and pieces of our conversation, chose not to join in, but betrayed their opinions with poorly disguised grimaces and eye rolls whenever they passed.

It was clear to me that Warren was a guy who was disliked by everyone but was feared as someone who was influential to the point of having control over livelihoods and relationships.

"... Ohmygosh! I saw him do something like that just the other day!" the excitable young girlfriend of the couple to my left gushed.

"I was coming out of the Firefly, and he was walking with his brother- what's his name? Oh, right. Jeff," she said without so much as a breath. "Anyway, they were walking toward me. There was a woman standing there at that intersection. You know that one that always sells those paper roses?"

She continued without waiting for a response. "Well, when Jeff tried to give her money, Trés practically knocked the money right out of his hand! He called him an 'idiot' and a 'fool'. Jeff kept the cash from his reach but didn't really say anything back. He put the money back in his pocket and they kept walking. But can you imagine? His own brother!"

She swept her arms through the air with a lot of drama. "Trés cussed at him and made fun of him all the way down the street. I could hear them at the end of the block!"

As I listened, my sense of righteous indignation grew. It was all so familiar- the berating, the embarrassment, the bullying.

The girl broke into my introspection, "I know! I'd be pissed if I was him." The anger must've been showing on my face. I calmed my features, finished my whiskey, and shrugged.

"Yeah, I don't think I'd let my brother talk to me like that." I wiped my mouth and covered my plate with the cloth napkin. "Excuse me, I'll be right back."

I left my perch to search for the waiter I'd seen earlier, scanning the room as I walked toward the bathrooms and the kitchen. He wasn't coming in or out of the kitchen, or serving a table, or present anywhere else in the building. I stopped another server who was rushing by, described the man I had seen arguing with Trés, and asked if he was still around.

"Ah, no. He left," he said with a wild look around the room.

"Can you tell me the next time he's scheduled to work? I just want to ask him something."

There was a short pause. The kid seemed to be chewing on the inside of his cheek. He came to a decision and said, "Nah. I'm pretty sure he's not coming back. Uh, excuse me. I gotta get some drinks out. Sir."

The young man added the title as an afterthought, remembering that although he's only a few years younger than me, he's the employee of an establishment that's meant to treat their customers as the cream of the crop.

As he rushed away, I remembered that Trés had threatened the waiter's job and I wondered if he had preemptively quit, or if news had already reached his manager.

I left soon after, feeling frustrated at coming up short without my intended interview. My inclination toward investigating had kicked in and I was deeply intrigued at this discovery, determined to find out more about Trés and his family. First, I'd need to track him down and see for myself what kind of a person I'm dealing with.

Later that week, I awoke to the sound of a rolling suitcase bumping loudly down the hallway outside my hotel room, followed by the squeal of a small child, quick footsteps, and the stern admonishments of a motherly voice. Groaning, I rolled over and checked the time on the bed-side clock, 11:45AM. These people with kids really didn't understand how to get their little monsters to respect others' need for sleep.

Moving slowly, I inched off the mattress and rose enough to sit on the side. It had been an extremely late night for me. I probably only slept around six hours. Not enough.

I needed some coffee. After rummaging up some decent clothes, pulling a comb through my hair, and slipping the room key in my pocket, I made my way down to the lobby. They had cleaned up the complimentary breakfast since it was so close to lunchtime, but I was guessing coffee would still be available, hopefully all day.

I arrived in the lobby and discovered that the coffee had just been brewed. After pouring a steaming cup, I skipped over the sugar and cream, and found a comfy couch off to the side where I wouldn't be bothered.

The TV hanging in the corner of the room was set to channel 2 and the news at noon was just getting started. The reporter on the screen, an older, Hispanic gentleman with slicked back hair, was standing in front of a familiar looking scene. The title at the bottom of the screen said, 'Mill City, Georgia,' so I began to read the captions running across the bottom.

"...died late last night after his car went into the water at Chickasaw Greenway Park. The Barnes County Police said the driver was a young man in his early twenties. He died before rescuers could get to the vehicle on Thursday. The man's body has now been recovered from the mostly submerged vehicle, but his identity is yet to be determined. The cause of death is also still being determined..."

Finally, a story. My story. Here is where it would begin. This would be my path to infamy. I grabbed my jacket and rushed out the door, leaving my untouched coffee alone on the table.

Chapter 11

TODAY TIMES

THE NATIONAL AUTHORITY ON TODAY'S NEWS

Sunday, December 9, 2018   *Since 2012*

~*NEWSWORTHY*~
A Well-known Man Dies an Unknown Death
Mill City, Georgia
BY OWEN WALSH

Mayor Warren Williams' home was filled to the brim with family and friends early yesterday morning by the time Detective Wes Abernathy of the Barnes County police department called to deliver the news that every parent dreads. Warren Williams III, Mayor Williams' youngest son at just twenty-three years old, was found dead in his car several hours after the initial call came in to 911 on Friday morning.

The distinctive blue metallic, Tesla Model X, was spotted mostly submerged in the Chickasaw River, not far off the end of the Bubba Boat Ramp, by someone visiting Chickasaw River Greenway Park early Friday morning. At the time, it was hard to tell if there was a driver or any passengers inside the vehicle. By Friday afternoon, the Police Search and Recovery team had removed the approximately $80,000 Tesla from the river. Divers hooked cables through the front of the vehicle, and Allied Towing pulled it out of the water.

As the water drained and the inside of the car became more visible, it was apparent that there was someone in the driver's seat. The identification of the driver was unknown at the time, although the vehicle was registered to Warren Williams III. The Williams family was notified that his vehicle had been found and that there were human remains inside. The body was transported to the Barnes County coroner's office and after further identification efforts, was determined to be that of Warren Williams III, or Trés as he was known in the community.

The coroner determined Trés' cause of death to be drowning, and it was initially suspected that he may have been under the influence of alcohol due to the nature of the accident. However, after further tests, he was found to have a blood-alcohol level of zero. Police are unsure at this time why Mr. Williams would be driving in the area of the Chickasaw River Greenway after dark, and how his vehicle came to be in the water.

One of the first steps in this investigation will be to solidify Trés' movements Thursday evening into Friday morning, in order to understand the last hours of his life.

How did Warren Williams III, a young man just entering the most exciting times of life, son of a wealthy and influential figure, come to end up trapped in his car, underwater and alone? Anyone that knew Trés would describe him as social and indicated that he was frequently seen around the city entertaining friends.

If Williams was not under the influence of alcohol Thursday evening, what could distract him enough to drive off the end of the Bubba Boat Ramp going an estimated sixty miles per hour?

Was this a purposeful act, planned and carried out by Trés himself? Or was this instigated by parties unknown?

Follow me through this investigation as I hope to give our Today Times readers an opportunity to assist law enforcement in determining the reason for this tragic death. The next Newsworthy edition will focus on the details that have been uncovered by detectives so far, as well as my firsthand experience of visiting the scene of the accident.

If you have any information, please call 707-455-0102.

TODAY TIMES

THE NATIONAL AUTHORITY ON TODAY'S NEWS

Wednesday, December 12, 2018   *Since 2012*

~NEWSWORTHY~
The Brick That Changed Everything
Mill City, Georgia
BY OWEN WALSH

The sudden tragic death of twenty-three-year-old Warren Williams III, "Trés," has left the small community of Mill City, Georgia in a state of confusion and fear. The Bubba Boat Ramp that allows river access in the Chickasaw River Greenway Park where William's car crashed into the water early Friday morning, is located at the end of a parking lot off a road that is only traveled by park-goers. Authorities are stumped as to what could cause Williams to be driving through the area at a speed at least as high as sixty miles per hour.

It has been determined that there was no alcohol in Williams' system at the time of the accident. Adding to this mysterious situation, he suffered from an injury to his head that could explain why he was unable to escape from the car if it occurred beforehand or upon impact to the water. However, it doesn't explain why he was driving so fast toward the water. Trés' head wound was so severe that had he not drowned, doctors have concluded that he would suffer from a traumatic brain injury, and possible death.

I was able to sit down with Detective Abernathy, the lead on this case, to discuss the evidence recovered so far. "At this point, we suspect that there may have been foul play. Mr. Williams' skull was fractured in a way that suggests blunt force trauma beyond what impact with a steering wheel would do," said Detective Abernathy. "Also, a brick was found in the car, near the driver's side, and we believe it may have been used to hold down the gas pedal and increase the speed of the car. At this time, it is not clear whether it's the cause of his head injury."

Abernathy also expressed his concerns that Trés' whereabouts after midnight are unknown. "Friends and other witnesses have said that Mr. Williams was at House 727 for lunch on Thursday, but then left to go home about 2pm," Abernathy reported. "No one saw him leave his house again that afternoon, evening, or night, and no one had plans with him, that we know of."

Detective Abernathy went on to say that although Trés has security cameras installed around the perimeter of his home, they were not turned on that evening and didn't capture what time he left the residence. Abernathy and his team are now checking with business owners along the route Trés would've driven from *his home to the Greenway in order to find out if he's captured on anyone's cameras heading in that direction.*

After speaking with Detective Abernathy, as well as a few other officers assigned to the case, I was able to visit the scene of the accident. As I walked around the area, my first observation was that the parking lot does not provide much space for most vehicles to get up to sixty miles per hour before reaching the water, but Trés' Tesla Model X certainly would have handled that short distance. If the brick was used to hold down the pedal, I think it had to start near the entrance to the parking lot, and he must've already been unconscious at the time.

Noticeably absent from the scene was any other evidence as to what might have happened. There wasn't any type of tire marks in the parking lot from acceleration or sudden braking. The wooded area surrounding the parking lot was thoroughly searched by police and no further clues were found. There was no indication of a struggle of any kind, no blood, hairs, or any personal items have been discovered.

With the knowledge of the head injury and the presence of the brick, I do not believe that this was a plan concocted by Trés himself, but it does sound like it was a planned scenario by someone. Could he have been knocked out or injured elsewhere and then brought to the Greenway?

Who would want Warren Williams III to die, and in this way?

When did he leave his house, and with who?

The next Newsworthy edition will focus on my interview with Warren Williams III's family and friends. Who was he? Is there anything about his lifestyle or past that might explain why his life was cut short?

If you have any information, please call 707-455-0102.

TODAY TIMES

THE NATIONAL AUTHORITY ON TODAY'S NEWS

Sunday, December 16, 2018   Since 2012

~*NEWSWORTHY*~
Villain and Victim
Mill City, Georgia
BY OWEN WALSH

On Thursday, December 6, Warren Williams III left lunch with friends and was never seen alive again. Cameras installed at his house captured him arriving home at 2:25pm but were turned off at 5pm.

The time of death has been estimated to have occurred between 1am and 3am, early Friday morning. Williams' house has been searched carefully by the forensics unit, and there are no signs of a struggle, leading police to believe that he must've left his house before 1am. There is still disagreement among detectives as to whether he was knocked unconscious before being transported to the Chickasaw River Greenway, or if he acquired the head injury when the car went into the water at 60 mph.

Beginning to feel frustrated by the mysterious details of Trés' death, I decided to seek to better understand who he was. Mayor Warren Williams, Jr. and his wife, Charlotte, declined to speak with me at this time. But their oldest son, Trés' brother Jeffery, agreed and we sat down together yesterday, December 15.

"It's a tragedy that he's died, and in this terrible way," lamented Jeffery. "It's hard to fathom that he would take his own life, but I also don't want to think that he was murdered. There's just no way to get through something like this without a lot of questions, whatever the conclusion."

I asked Jeffery to describe Trés to me in a way that could help me to better understand who he was and what he was like. "Warren, I never really liked to call him by his nickname, was a little complicated. I think he had a hard time settling down after college, especially in this small town where we grew up, where everyone remembers everything that's ever happened in the history of everything."

Being from a small town myself, I can attest to his observation. He continued, "Warren had his own way of doing things and could be very particular about what he liked and didn't like. I'm telling you that just to say that not everybody got along with him, or maybe it's more fair to say that he didn't get along with everybody. I think most people just tried to make him happy."

Jeffery spoke to me at length about Trés' flamboyant lifestyle. "He always enjoyed being in the spotlight, being seen. He went out with friends pretty much every day, so it's unusual that he'd go anywhere by himself." According to Jeffery, the gap in the timeline of Trés' whereabouts Thursday night and early Friday morning is his biggest concern. "I'm not usually a betting man, but I'd be willing to bet that if we could figure out how his cameras got turned off and what happened right after that, that we'd have all the answers."

When I spoke with Sean Larmour, a close friend of Trés' and the rest of the Williams family, he stated, "There's absolutely no way that Trés killed himself. Impossible. No way. He was too rich and popular to be unhappy. Trés was always the life of the party! He was like the glue that held our crew together. It just feels like there's a big empty space now."

I wasn't successful in getting any of Trés' other friends to interview with me. However, I found a few members of the community that wished to comment and remain anonymous.

"That Warren Williams was just rude and nasty," said a wait-ress at one of his frequent hangout spots. "He thought he could just tell everyone what to do and we had to do it because he'd run to his daddy and tell on us. People lost jobs because of him. I personally know someone who was beat up by some thugs he knew! I can't remember the reason, but I wanna say it was over a parking space or a spilled drink or something silly like that," she went on to say.

A local shop owner, who was very concerned about not being identified, shared several stories with me about what he called Trés' "disturbing behavior" in which people who were strangers to him "got caught in his crosshairs" and "felt the pain of crossing his path on a bad day."

Another man refused to speak to me and walked away muttering, "I'm not putting myself in jeopardy by talking about that (exple-tive) and letting it get back to his father."

After hearing these personal accounts about Warren Williams III, along with the evidence collected by detectives, I remain con-vinced that he fell victim to an act of violence, pre-planned and carried out by unknown perpetrators, resulting in his drowning in the Chickasaw River.

Does Detective Abernathy have any suspects? Was Williams' car spotted on any of the camera footage in town along the route he would have driven? What are the next steps in the case?

The final Newsworthy edition of this series will focus on new leads and details uncovered during the investigation and the final report submitted by the medical examiner. Will the killer or killers be brought to justice? Will Mill City, Georgia and the Williams family ever be able to rest easy again?

If you have any information, please call 707-455-0102.

TODAY TIMES

THE NATIONAL AUTHORITY ON TODAY'S NEWS

Wednesday, December 19, 2018　　　　　　　　*Since 2012*

~*NEWSWORTHY*~
A Dead End
Mill City, Georgia
BY OWEN WALSH

As we conclude the story of what happened to Warren Williams III, it seems that we may not come to a very satisfying ending after all. In the almost two weeks since his death, detectives have interviewed thirty-five individuals, combed through several hours of security footage attempting to catch a glimpse of Trés' metallic blue Tesla headed toward the Chickasaw River Greenway, and carefully cataloged each and every detail of the scene of the accident, as well as his home. However, there have been no arrests made at this time.

"We are at a frustrating stand-still at this point," reports Detective Abernathy. "There is a definite cause of death, but how it occurred is still a mystery. We need the community to keep their eyes and ears open and contact us with any and all information that might lead to an arrest or an explanation."

"It's hard to move on and finish mourning Warren's death when it still feels so raw. It's so unfinished. It just plain sucks," said Jeffery Williams, Trés' older brother.

Here are the facts in the case so far:

Thursday, December 6, at approximately 2pm, Williams left House 727 after lunch with friends and drove home alone.

The security system and cameras installed around his house captured him arriving at exactly 2:25pm, parking his car in the garage.

At 5pm, the security cameras were turned off and the security system no longer recorded any activity.

Sometime between 5 pm and 1 am, Williams left his house. His car was driven into the Chickasaw River off of the Bubba Boat Ramp of the Chickasaw River Greenway Park before 1am. At this time, it has been determined that Williams was already unconscious due to blunt force trauma to his skull.

Williams was unable to escape from the car and drowned sometime between 1am and 3am Friday morning, December 7.

A jogger using the Greenway called 911 after spotting the car in the water at 5:38am.

Police arrived on the scene at 5:52am and began efforts to identify the owner of the vehicle.

It was quickly determined that the owner of the vehicle was Warren Williams III. When police could not locate Mr. Williams, they contacted Mayor Warren Williams, Jr. to notify him of their discovery.

By 12 pm Friday afternoon, the car had been removed from the water and human remains were discovered inside. The body was transported to the Barnes County coroner's office and an examination was conducted to confirm that it was that of Warren Williams III.

During the investigation that followed, a brick was found on the driver's side, seeming to indicate that it may have been used to hold down the gas pedal, explaining the acceleration of the vehicle toward the water.

Mr. Williams' head injury that rendered him unconscious prevented him from escaping the sinking car.

The head injury was determined to have been caused by the brick. According to the medical examiner, "the shape and severity of the wound is consistent with what we'd expect to find from blunt force trauma from a brick versus the steering wheel."

However, there was no forensic evidence found at the scene that would incriminate an attacker.

Police interviews focused on potential witnesses who may have information regarding Trés' movements and whereabouts Thursday evening, as well as individuals who may have had motive to harm or kill Trés. However, after countless hours of questioning, detectives have run out of people to question and leads to chase. The case will remain open indefinitely.

Warren Williams III's family and friends, as well as Detective Abernathy and the Barnes County police department implore the public to keep Trés' death fresh in their minds. "It's unsatisfying for sure," says Detective Abernathy. "And I'm not done or giving up. Not by a long shot."

If you have any information, please call 707-455-0102.

PART 2:

CARA

"Men have called me mad; but the question is not yet settled, whether madness is or is not the loftiest intelligence- whether much that is glorious- whether all that is profound- does not spring from disease of thought- from moods of mind exalted at the expense of the general intellect."

~ Edgar Allan Poe, *Eleonora*

Chapter 12

Sometimes I wonder why my parents even had me. I think I was an accident. For me, it's not a question about whether or not I'm loved, although it is true that no one in my family ever says they love each other. It's more that I don't feel seen. None of them ever really pay attention to me.

My friend Christina says it's a good thing, like my parents trust me to always do a good job. But I feel like it's more that I don't do as many newsworthy things as Liam. I don't want the kind of attention they give Owen, but I'd love to be treated like Liam.

Take today for example. My class had a social studies fair. I've been working for weeks on my project, all about the attack on Pearl Harbor. I've spent every afternoon for the last two weeks stuck in my bedroom, researching, cutting, gluing. Not once did my parents or brothers ask what I was up to or if I needed help. I created a masterpiece, complete with a model of the USS Arizona. I even wore a sailor suit that I used my own money to buy for my presentation during the fair!

So many classes walked through the library looking at all the projects and listening to the presentations, and mine was the most visited. A bunch of people seemed surprised. I guess they're not used to me speaking up, I'm pretty quiet most of the time. I just don't have a lot to say to most people. But that doesn't mean I'm not smart. I want good grades like Owen. I used to want to be like Liam, but he's so mean all the time now, and I don't really want to be the kind of person he is.

At the end of the fair, my teacher walked around giving out the awards from all the visitors' votes. I was shocked when she stopped at my table. I won first place! Everyone in my class gathered around to tell me "good job" and "awesome." It was really the first time most of them paid me any attention. I felt like I was riding on a cloud!

I didn't walk home with Owen like I do most of the time. On regular school days, he'll walk the few blocks between our schools to come and get me and then walk me home. Liam almost always stays for one practice or another and then gets picked up later.

But today I had gardening club after school and Mom came to pick me up. I go every Tuesday and Thursday. I practically jumped into the car to show her my ribbon.

She smiled and said, "Wow! Way to go, Cara!" and then in the very next breath said, "Okay, buckle up. We've got to hurry to pick up Liam. I'm running a little late and you know he hates to have to wait."

That's it. That's the only recognition I got. I mean, really? God forbid we make Liam wait an extra five minutes. I don't know what I was hoping for, maybe a special trip to get an ice cream, or my favorite dinner cooked for me, or for her to call Dad and brag to him.

But this is exactly what always happens. Me and Owen get overlooked. Maybe Liam wouldn't be so bad if they didn't give him everything he wants and do whatever he says. I rolled my eyes, but she didn't see me. Mom wasn't paying attention anymore. I was hopeful I could show Owen later when we got home. He'll listen to me. Plus, he's so smart and has really good ideas, so he'll probably be proud of me.

When Liam got in the car, Mom was all ears as he blabbered on and on about every stupid detail of his baseball practice. Coach said this and Coach said that. He used to play with me. Now he thinks he's so grown up and better than me even though we're both in middle school.

It feels like everything Liam does is on purpose to irritate me. He interrupts me when I'm talking to Dad and pulls his attention away from me. He takes food off my plate at dinner and when I get mad, he just grins and Mom says something like, "He needs to eat more so he has his energy. Don't be so selfish, Cara."

Everything is a contest, and he wins, especially with Mom and Dad. I know Owen has it worse than me, though. Liam isn't just a mean brother when it comes to Owen, it kinda seems like he's evil to him.

Usually, Owen just ignores what he can when it's coming from Liam, I guess. Especially since he can't ignore Dad's punishments. Owen doesn't really say much about any of it, but if I had it coming from every direction, I think I would've snapped by now. It's gotten worse since Dad brought Liam home and was freaking out about him being asked to practice with the high school varsity team.

We were all excited for a few minutes, until Dad cut Owen down. Even though he does things like that all the time, the hatred in Dad's voice always shocks me. Owen didn't deserve it, but I guess he never does. The rest of them didn't even notice that Owen and I had left the conversation. They don't really need us around.

But Owen has seemed even quieter and more distracted since then. He doesn't even talk to me as much as he used to. I know it's not the worst thing that Dad's ever said to him, but maybe it was the final straw.

When Mom finally pulled in the garage, I ran through the house straight to Owen's room to show him my medal. I busted open his door, trying to scare him. He was sitting at his desk by the window and his back was to me. He didn't move at all, and he didn't turn around, he just kept on typing something on his laptop.

"Hey, Owen!"

"Hey, Care. What's up?" he said, without looking at me. Annoyance saturated his clipped words. I don't even think he stopped typing.

I stared at his back for a minute, then asked, "What're you doing?"

Owen paused for a second, but still didn't turn around. Then, he let out a loud sigh.

"Just working on something for school. Do you need me?"

I thought about his question for a minute. *Do I need him? Maybe not.* I was already mad at Mom for what happened earlier, and Owen's mood was making it even worse.

I bet he's going to grow up and just be all about himself, just like Liam is now. They're both going to do their own thing and become successful. Mom and Dad will probably continue to be obsessed with everything Liam does and Owen will probably just ignore all of us the first chance he gets to escape.

Maybe I didn't need him after all. Maybe it's time for me to stop worrying about my family and do things for myself. Today, I just wanted someone to be proud of me and to be excited with me about my award. I didn't want another half-hearted response.

"Nah, just saying 'hey,'" I told him miserably. Then I closed the door, turned to leave, and ran straight into Liam's chest. I stumbled back and looked up at his face. Liam looked like he was laughing to himself. It wasn't a friendly smile.

"What're you doing, little sister?" The taunting began immediately.

"I was just talking to Owen. What're you doing?" I said, tucking the medal behind my back.

I don't know why I didn't want to show him. I hadn't brought it up on the car ride home and neither did Mom, so I didn't think Liam knew about it yet. His smirk grew and he bit his bottom lip, holding something back.

"Did you hear Mom calling for you? She said she wants you to get all the dirty laundry. I thought I'd help you out."

I looked down and realized he had something in his hands too. His socks. Liam suddenly shoved his dirty, smelly baseball socks into my face and rubbed them around so hard that it felt like he punched me in the nose. I fell back against the wall and pushed his hand away from my face. My eyes were filled with tears, but I could still see him leering through the blurriness.

Then, he looked down at my other hand and saw the medal no longer hidden behind my back. Although it didn't seem possible, his smile got even bigger. He reached down before I could stop him, and snatched my prize from me.

"What's this Care Bear? Did you win something?" he said, sounding surprised.

"Liam, you're sucha butt! Give that back!" I yelled.

This type of meanness from Liam was new to me. Owen had been dealing with it for a while, but he wasn't usually this mean to me, and I didn't really know how to handle it. It had gotten worse since school started back in the fall, and then it became almost unbearable after he joined the Varsity team.

Owen's door burst open, and he stood tall in the doorway, glaring at both of us.

"Can y'all do this somewhere else?" Owen grumbled. "I can't concentrate with all this noise out here."

Liam immediately puffed up, now standing a bit taller than Owen, and turned to face him. Even though Liam is a year and a half younger, he's a lot bigger since he works out pretty much constantly. He was still holding my medal firmly in his fist.

Liam reached out putting his empty hand on Owen's chest and shoved him backwards, hard. Owen stumbled back a couple of steps into his room and Liam reached down and grabbed the doorknob, slamming it closed.

"Freakin' loser," he mumbled as he stared at the closed door. I guess he was waiting to see if Owen was going to challenge him. Of course, he didn't.

I saw the medal hanging in Liam's left hand and reached down to try and grab it back while he wasn't paying attention. With much quicker reflexes than me, he anticipated my attack, pulling the medal up quickly, high above his head where it dangled way out of my reach.

"I don't think you know what to do with a medal. Maybe I should put it on *my* display where people might actually see it. You know, where they're used to seeing awards and medals and trophies..."

Liam had spun around and was marching off down the hallway with my medal held above his head. He reached his bedroom, went in, and shut the door. Then, I heard the lock click.

The whole five minutes was so surprising that I hadn't even moved from where I stood against the wall next to Owen's room. I snapped out of it and went to bang on his locked door.

"Liam! Liam! Give it back! Give it back!" I yelled. I could hear him laughing as he turned up The White Stripes loud enough to drown out my banging and yelling.

"Cara!" Mom shouted from the laundry room. "Stop that!"

"Mom, Liam stole my medal! He took it and won't give it back!" I whined.

"Cara, he's got enough of his own trophies, I'm sure he's not planning on keeping your school medal. Stop all that racket and bring me the laundry like I asked!" I kicked the door one last time.

When I got to the laundry room, crying, and carrying only Liam's dirty socks, Mom looked up with concern. "He took my medal from me and laughed at me, and he won't give it back!" She set down the shirt she was folding and hugged me to her, comforting me for once.

"I'll talk to him. I'm sure he's just teasing you," she said as she patted my back.

I sniffed and nodded. There was really no point in arguing with her. I knew Mom wouldn't help; she never did. I would either have to wait until Liam gave the medal back or I'd have to take it from his room when he wasn't home. I just hoped he wouldn't ruin it. Surely, he wasn't that mean.

After dinner, I was lying on my bed reading when Liam came in and sat down at the end of it. The medal was hanging around his neck and he was turning it back and forth, admiring it. I just watched him, waiting.

"This is pretty cool, I guess. Did you win it?"

"Yeah. First place in the social studies fair," I said.

"Hm," was all he said as he continued to turn and fiddle with the ribbon and medal around his neck. Then, he took it off and tossed it down next to me on my quilt as he said, "Here. I've got my own. I was just messing around anyway."

And then he got up and started to walk out. As he reached the doorway, Liam turned to my desk and looked down at whatever was lying on top. It was probably just some drawings that I'd done. He rifled through them for a second, touched a few other things, and said, "Better be careful. If you spend too much time stuck in your room by yourself, you might turn out like Owen, lame and alone, unloved and forgotten."

"Just get out!" I screamed as I threw my pillow at him, the closest thing that I could reach. The pillow bounced off Liam's shoulder and landed on the floor in the doorway. He turned fully to face me and leaned back on my desk with his hands behind him and grinned.

I bit my lip. I wish I'd kept my mouth shut and just let him walk out. Once Liam knew he'd gotten to me, it was going to be a lot harder to get rid of him. Deciding a little too late to try and ignore him, I laid back on my remaining pillow and pulled the book in front of my face so I wouldn't have to look at him.

I could feel him staring at me, but I didn't move an inch. I tried to keep my breathing calm and even through my nose, but I was so mad that it felt like I was having to hold my breath every few seconds to stop myself from crying.

After what felt like forever, sitting with the book held up like a statue, I lowered it to see what he was up to, but he was gone. I picked up the medal and crossed the room to hide it in the back of my desk drawer where I keep a few secret things. I didn't want him finding it again and doing something much worse with it the next time.

I slid the drawer closed and my eyes landed on my desk. Something was off. What was missing? I shuffled a few things around, arranging and straightening. Then, I realized what was different. My journal had been lying open where I'd been writing in it after fighting with Liam.

That journal was my best kept secret because no one knew that I even had one. I wrote everything in there; things I felt, things I'd seen and heard between Owen and Dad, things I'd done that I didn't tell anyone about, things I'd caught Owen or Liam doing, and things I dreamed of. And now it's in the hands of my awful brother.

Liam was definitely someone who would use what I wrote against me, maybe to torture me or maybe to get me in trouble. *When he reads what I've written about the things I've witnessed him getting away with, he will ruin my life. Or, if Dad ever found out what I said about the way he beats Owen, he might start beating me, too.* I'd do anything to get that journal back from him. Anything. I had to. But what could I do?

Chapter 13

The walk home from school today seemed to take forever. Maybe it just seemed like we were moving slower because of the heat. I wasn't expecting it to be so hot since it's only April. I heard Dad complaining last night about turning the air down again even though it was cold enough for long sleeves and blankets just last week. That's just how Spring goes sometimes, though.

Or maybe Owen and I were both dragging our feet, not wanting to get home and enter the gates of hell that hid our family drama from the outside world. Whatever the reason, we didn't talk much, and neither of us mentioned the incident with Liam in the hallway the evening before.

Owen's been so sullen lately anyway and keeping more to himself. Now I've got things on my mind, too, like how to get my journal back from Liam, and what I should do if he's already read it.

It seems to me I've got three options: ask Liam to give it back and hope for the best, tell on him to Mom or Dad and see if they'll make him give it back, or grab it from his room when he's not home. I mentally cross out the first option without even considering it. That would never work. The second option also gets disregarded quickly because it's not very likely, plus I don't want to draw other people's attention to the fact that I keep a journal full of secrets about everyone.

It seems my only option is to figure out where he hid it and steal it back. This would have been a lot easier if I had been in Liam's room recently. I haven't really been inside there at all in the last few years, plus he always keeps his door closed and it's usually locked.

Sometimes I catch glimpses when Mom is in there gathering laundry or tidying up and leaves the door open. I know the basic layout and where each piece of furniture sits. But I don't know his hiding spots. And I don't know if my journal is even in his room.

Owen and I almost always get home before Liam in the afternoons, but if his door is locked it'll take me longer to get in and Mom might catch me. I could wait until she leaves to go pick him up, but then she's only gone for thirty minutes. Is that enough time? Will I have to search in his room a bunch of times before I even figure out where to look?

As soon as we got home, I tossed my bookbag on my bed and continued down the hall toward Liam's room. I reached out and tried the knob as I passed by, not wanting to stop in case Owen or Mom saw me. Unlocked. I left it open a smidge and kept walking into the bathroom to divert suspicion. While on my detour, I tried to think about what my search process should be.

Opening the bathroom door a crack, I peeked into the hallway and listened carefully to the sounds of the house. Mom was on the other side of the house, moving around in the kitchen. I could hear her talking to someone. From the pauses in the conversation, I guessed she was on the phone.

I wasn't sure, but since Owen's door was closed, I figured that's where he'd gone. I walked carefully back to Liam's room, avoiding the familiar creaks in the floorboards, then softly shut the door behind me and looked around.

His bedroom was neat other than a few shirts laying around on the floor next to the hamper. The far wall had a large window with sheer, gray curtains halfway open, allowing the afternoon sunlight to shine through onto Liam's bed centered underneath.

He's a UGA fan, just like Dad, so his bed set was all red and black. To the left, between his bed and the closet, there was a large, floor to ceiling shelf and two display cases packed full of various medals, trophies, pennants, framed team pictures, and game balls showcasing his talents and triumphs.

On the other side of his bed, the wall was filled with his framed collection of Sports Illustrated covers featuring his favorite athletes. A low-sitting shelf ran the length of the rest of the wall over to the opposite corner and held his other collection of sports memorabilia: signed baseballs and footballs, a few jerseys, bobbleheads, several different UGA bulldog figures and statues, and other pieces he'd collected from stadiums he'd visited.

To the right of the doorway where I stood, there was an extremely organized desk area, set up with so many unused office supplies. Liam had probably never sat there to work on schoolwork or anything else. His large dresser sat to my left, next to the closet.

Looking around without much inspiration, I decided to start with the desk drawers. I pulled out each one quickly and jammed my hand inside, rummaging around to feel for my journal. No success. But I did find a piece of paper with Owen's handwriting on it. It sparked my curiosity, so I stuck it in my pocket to read later.

Next, I got down on my knees and peered underneath the bed. There were a few old, empty bat bags, a small stack of magazines, and individual socks missing their twin. I pulled the magazine stack towards me and brought the top copy out to look at.

The girl that stars in one of my favorite shows, "What I Like About You," smiled back at me. Her sheer, white shirt was pushed down around her waist and all she wore was a red, lacy bra and a lot of makeup. I gasped and closed my eyes quickly. I did not want to see that.

What's Liam doing with a magazine like Maxim that features articles about porn star secrets, best new beers, and Tiger's "texting temptress"? I slid the stack back under the bed and made a mental note to remember this for possible future blackmail ammo.

I groaned and stood up, feeling frustrated, when I suddenly caught the last syllable of Mom calling me from down the hall. Panic gripped me. I don't ever get in trouble, and I didn't want to start now. I couldn't face Dad's punishments.

Silently frozen in the middle of the room, I cocked my ear to listen. She called again, much closer this time. I felt her presence in the hallway, probably standing in between Liam and Owen's rooms.

After a second of indecision, I dashed to the closet and quietly slid the door mostly closed so I could peek out. Mom opened Liam's door, looked around, and closed it again.

"Cara?" she called for a third time.

"Owen?" she said louder.

"Yeah?" Owen responded from his room.

"Do you know where your sister is?" She headed back toward the kitchen again as she spoke.

"I don't know, Mom. Probably around here somewhere."

"Okay, well, I'm headed to pick up Liam. Will you please make sure Cara finished her homework? I'll be back soon, and we'll have dinner." I heard her carrying car keys and walking out to the garage without waiting for a response from Owen.

Crisis averted, I decided to continue my search while she was out of the house. I pushed the closet door open further and turned on the light. It wasn't a large closet and I'd been standing between some hanging shirts, so I could tell there wasn't anything else in the back of the small space.

I started to move things on the floor out of the way- shoes, cleats, a crate of Nerf guns and bullets, a remote-controlled truck, three different sport bags full of equipment, and a box of albums of baseball cards. I opened and checked inside the sports bags, just in case, rummaged through the box of albums, and even turned the crate of Nerf accessories upside down. No luck.

The top of the closet was more organized, but looked to be unmarked, cardboard boxes shoved onto the shelf however they would fit. I rolled the desk chair over and balanced myself on it. I couldn't reach the boxes on top, so I pulled a small, rectangular box from the middle quickly, hopeful that it wouldn't bring the rest of it down on my head in the process.

I set it down and pried it open. It was full of tapes, literal VHS tapes with labels like "1982 NFC Championship." It was Dad's handwriting. Dad must have recorded these when he was younger and passed them on to Liam.

I went through several other boxes, all seemingly harmless, full of memorabilia or old toys, pictures, or clothes that no longer fit. Feeling frustrated, I glanced at the clock next to Liam's bed. I probably only had a couple more minutes before I needed to put things back and get out of his room if I hoped not to get caught.

The last box I was able to coax off the shelf was much larger and heavier than the others and I had to lean it against my face and chest while carefully stepping off the rotating chair. When I couldn't hold on to it anymore, I dropped it to the floor and then held my breath at the sudden loud noise.

"Cara?" Owen called from his room.

Shoot. Would Owen tell on me? I couldn't be sure. I heard his footsteps headed to Liam's room and I just stood immobile. The door suddenly opened, and Owen stood staring at me. He looked at the large box at my feet, glanced around the rest of the room, and then met my eyes.

Neither of us said anything for a long minute before he finally broke the silence with "Are you okay?"

I nodded quickly. He looked down again at the box and I thought I saw a slight smile. It vanished before I could be certain I'd seen it, then he turned to leave and closed the door again.

That answered one question. I wasn't sure if he knew what I was up to, but it was clear that he either didn't want to know or didn't care. I let out the breath that I didn't realize I was holding and looked down at the box. It was different from the rest because it was sealed closed with duct tape. I decided to chance leaving evidence of my search and pulled slowly on one end of the tape until I could easily open the flaps.

There was a towel laid across the contents of the box. When I moved it aside, I was, at first, very confused. There seemed to be a random assortment of items, unrelated to Liam and to each other: a Diary of a Wimpy Kid book, a pair of sunglasses, a fidget spinner, a box of scented markers, a tiny baseball helmet like you might get a scoop of ice cream inside at a ballgame. I pulled item after item out of the box and set them on the floor, trying to figure out a connection. I'd never seen Liam with any of these things.

Then, towards the bottom, I found a worn copy of Bridge to Terabithia. The cover was frayed and bent at the edges. It looked very familiar. I opened it to find Owen's name scrawled in a much younger version of his handwriting in the top left corner right under my mother's name.

Now I remembered that he had loved this book. He would read it over and over again, and always had it handy in the living room whenever he didn't want to watch what was on TV. I remember him saying that it was his favorite book. He had been very distraught when it went missing.

Setting the book aside, I found a set of drawing pencils, a small, red UGA football that Owen had gotten when he went to a game with Dad when he was much younger, and a couple Reading certificates with his name on them that should've been used as a coupon to get free pizzas. All these things seemed like they were important to Owen at one time, did he give them to Liam? Surely not.

In digging further into this box of other people's treasures, I also found Dad's lost class ring, my mother's porcelain angel figurine that used to sit on the end of the mantle, and a Tom Petty record signed by Tom Petty that had been gifted to Owen by our grandfather several years earlier.

It occurred to me that I remembered each of these items going missing at some point. Liam was stealing my family's stuff, and maybe these things I didn't recognize were from other people. What was he going to do with it all, I wondered. It's not like they were all priceless or even expensive things, but they were emotionally valuable. That's when I noticed Baby.

Baby was a Beanie Baby koala that I got in my stocking from Santa when I was four. I used to carry Baby everywhere with me. She sat with me at the dinner table, traveled in my backpack to school, and slept next to me on my pillow. Baby soaked up my tears the night I sat waiting for Owen to wake up after he was punched in the gut so hard that he passed out.

Two years ago, I couldn't find her, and I searched everywhere I could think of. I never found her and eventually forgot about her. Here she was, stuffed down at the bottom of this box full of random stuff, her big, black nose covered in scuffs and dust.

Anger welled up inside and I thought I might explode like a volcano. I was outraged. *How dare he take my happiness?* Did he just take anything that brought someone else joy? Maybe Liam was evil, after all.

My hands were shaking as I put everything back in the box, except for Owen's book and my koala, and pulled the tape across the flaps once more. It wasn't sealed, but it would stick enough not to draw attention to the fact that it had been opened.

I wasn't sure how I'd get the heavy box back in the top of the closet, and stood there for a minute, trying to brainstorm through the red that clouded my vision and my logical thinking.

Suddenly, I heard the familiar rumble of the garage door opening. Thinking quickly, I pushed the box under the bed, hoping to find a way to get it back on the top shelf another afternoon before Liam noticed. I would need to come back to continue the search for my journal anyway. I closed the closet door, turned out the light, and looked around once more to make sure the room looked as I'd found it before closing the door and walking to my own bedroom.

Liam and Mom were chatting as they came in from the garage and then began moving around the kitchen, opening and closing cabinets. I stashed Owen's book inside my bedside table drawer, then collapsed on my bed and stared up at the ceiling fan, still holding Baby in my hand.

My thoughts focused on Liam. This new discovery changed everything. He wasn't just a malicious sibling. Liam was wicked, full of malice and spite, purposely hurting people's feelings just to witness their sadness. I wondered who all the other items belonged to, kids at school? And was he just a thief, or something more? And the worst part was, I couldn't think of a way to stop him. I had no idea what to do next.

Remembering the paper with Owen's writing that I'd put in my pocket, I pulled it out and smoothed it flat so I could read it. It was a story. It had clearly been ripped out of a binder and was torn at the holes. I didn't need to read past the title to know what it was.

"Newsworthy Nuisance: Is Fame All It's Cracked Up to Be?" Owen had written this back in the fall for a class at school. There had been a state-wide writing contest and all sophomores were required to submit an entry that would be counted as two grades.

Owen talked about this paper for a month while he was writing it. He never told us what he was writing about, just that it was the best thing he'd ever written, and he was sure it would win the contest. The day it was due, he told us what it was all about while we ate breakfast.

Owen never said that Liam was the subject, but after he explained the premise, we all knew. Mom and I were peeking over at Owen nervously, and Liam just sat there fuming. Dad had already left for work, which is probably why Owen waited until then to tell us.

I was surprised at the time that Liam didn't have a rude comeback or comment to say, but he just sat there, red-faced, and angry. When Owen got up from the table and left to brush his teeth, Liam left the table, too, saying he was going to grab his bookbag.

Later that day, when Owen got home, he went on a rampage, accusing Liam of taking the writing from his book bag, which Owen hadn't realized was missing until he'd gotten to school and was about to turn it in. He was throwing things and screaming. I've never seen him that irate before.

Mom was trying to soothe Owen and asked Liam if he took it, which of course he said he didn't. When Dad came home from work that evening, he heard Owen shouting at Mom as soon as he pulled into the garage. The door almost flew off its hinges as Dad burst through and slammed it shut.

For the first time that I've ever seen, Owen didn't back down or run to hide, he went toward Dad with his fists clenched. Dad started yelling at him about taking responsibility and blaming others for his mistakes, saying he never did anything right, and how did he expect for anyone to take him seriously if he couldn't act like a man. As soon as the question left Dad's mouth, Owen launched himself into his stomach, almost tackling him, sending them both backward to slam into the wall.

I watched from my doorway, horrified at my brother's bold reaction. Dad looked momentarily shocked, but then I saw the expression cross his face that I fear the most. Dad reached up, grabbed Owen by his hair, and half yanked, half threw him to the ground.

Owen landed hard on his shoulder, then rolled back, slamming into the nearby entertainment shelf. But Dad wasn't done yet. Tears had to fall, or blood had to spill before he was satisfied. There was barely a second in between Owen's back hitting hard on the shelf and Dad's foot kicking him hard in the stomach.

I put my hand over my mouth, gripping with all my strength, trying to smother my own crying. A slight movement down the hall drew my eyes away from the dreadful scene to see Liam slowly closing his bedroom door, shutting it out. His eyes met mine, he shrugged, and then he was gone.

Owen laid on the ground sobbing quietly, while Mom hovered in the kitchen doorway, waiting for her chance to check on him after Dad was finished. To my amazement, the episode ended as quickly as it had begun. Normally, it wasn't until I felt like I was the one being stomped on, that the abuse would finally subside. This time, Dad stared down at Owen writhing on the ground for several seconds, then stalked off down the hall, and slammed his bedroom door.

The silence in the house was the worst. I wouldn't find out until the next day if Owen was okay. We weren't allowed to tend to him after Dad had dealt out the punishment. Mom sometimes tried to when Dad wasn't looking, but as Owen's gotten older, he refuses her help, resents her for it. Too little, too late.

I hid out in my room, waiting. Dinner was never made. No one told me to take my shower or get ready for bed. That's the day Owen's sulky demeanor started.

And who could blame him? I don't know if I've ever felt an anger powerful enough to override my fear of Dad, but the more times I witness the injustice of his abuse, the more I question whether I can really claim that I'd never do what Owen did.

The two zeros that Owen was given for not completing the assignment ruined his average for that class and brought it down to a low C. So not only did he suffer a beating, but he also lost his status as an all A's kid, he couldn't compete in the writing contest, Dad gained new ammo to use as evidence for his failures, and Liam "won" in multiple ways the instant Owen lost his cool. I felt so bad for him.

My eyes had been opened. I never imagined that any kid could be so mean, much less my own brother. Panic seized me again as I thought about what Liam might do with the information he's read in my journal. I needed to get back into his room as soon as I could to try and find it, and I might just tear up his entire bedroom if I have to. It would be worth getting caught if I found it and got it away from Liam. Or, better yet, I decided I'd do just about anything to get revenge, to see him pay for all the pain he causes everyone else. Just about anything.

Chapter 14

I crumpled the slip of notebook paper roughly, squeezing it as hard as I could as if that would erase the words written on it. For two weeks, I'd been looking everywhere I could think of for my journal, searching every nook and cranny of Liam's room without anyone catching me, but also without any success. Unfortunately, a few days after I'd left the heavy box of stolen goods under Liam's bed, unable to lift it back into its spot, he'd discovered it and figured me out.

Liam stopped by my room that evening while I was reading. Leaning through the doorway, Liam gripped the doorframe tightly and scowled at me. It was a little unnerving, but I was determined not to let him get to me again. He continued to stand there, frowning, silently killing me with his eyes.

"Can I help you?" I quipped.

"No, I don't think so," Liam drawled acidly, "I got my closet put back together by myself, thanks."

My mouth went dry, and I stared at him, unsure what to say.

"That's what I thought. Stay out of my room and out of my business." And with that, Liam left and slammed the door closed so hard I jumped and dropped my book.

The next afternoon, when we got home, I went directly to his room, but it was locked. It's been locked every day since. I've searched the entire house. A few times, Liam's seen me rummaging in drawers or cabinets or looking under furniture, and when we make eye contact, he just grins and shakes his head.

Then, the notes started showing up. I have found pieces of notebook paper laying on my pillow, sitting next to my cereal bowl at breakfast, tucked into my pencil pouch, and even in my jeans' pockets, each one with sentences and phrases copied from my journal in the quick, messy handwriting that I recognized as Liam's.

The bits that he chose to copy were the things that I was the most worried about other people knowing. He was taunting me, letting me know that he held this power over me, mocking me with my own words.

I took the latest note and stomped up to Liam lounging in the living room. I stood in between him and the TV with my hands on my hips and stared him down, hoping my glare would burn a hole straight through his skull into his brain.

Liam looked up lazily and said, "What's wrong with you, Care Bear? Somebody pee in your Cheerios?"

I threw the paper ball as hard as I could at his face. It bounced off his forehead to the couch, and with hardly a flinch he said, "So, you want me to have this paper?"

Liam picked up the ball and held it up in front of him. I was suddenly regretting my actions and not feeling as brave as I had been five minutes before.

I lunged at his fist to grab the paper back from him, but he just squeezed his fingers shut tighter and held on. We began to tussle, me using all my strength, him frozen and unyielding. When he grew tired of me pulling at him, he stood up and dropped me onto the floor on my back.

Then, my evil brother looked down at me and in a hushed whisper said, "Don't mess with me, Cara," as he stepped over me and marched off down the hallway.

When I propped up onto my arms to watch him leave, I saw Owen looking on from the kitchen doorway. Our eyes met and his face was sympathetic.

"You should probably just avoid him," Owen said as I got up.

"Yeah, I know. He makes it really hard, though," I said glumly. I felt depressed and wasn't sure what to do next. Maybe I could gain an ally in Owen, and he'd know what to do.

"Um, I have something to show you," I told him as he turned back to the kitchen. "Can you come to my room for a minute?"

Owen followed wordlessly into my bedroom and I motioned for him to close the door. Then, I got his book out of my bedside table and held it out to him.

His eyes widened in surprise, and he reached out to take it from me. Owen ran his hand along the worn cover and then opened it to see his name written on the inside.

"Where did you find this?" his voice was almost a whisper.

I told him about searching in Liam's room, but didn't tell him what I was looking for, just that Liam had taken something of mine as well. As I recounted my discoveries, Owen's face began to darken. When I reached the part about Owen's paper, his jaw clenched and his grip on the book tightened, bleaching his knuckles.

After I finished, he looked back down at the book for a long moment before finally responding, "Thanks for this. Look, I know how you're feeling, but, Cara, I don't know if you're cut out to take on Liam."

"So, I should just give up?" This wasn't turning out the way I hoped at all.

"You'll never win. He'll never let up. He never stops. I mean, look at me. I used to put up a fight and he bested me every single time. He's still finding ways to make my life miserable..." Owen's voice faded away at the end and he looked up at the ceiling.

"One day he'll meet a dead end and there won't be anything else he can do to hurt other people," he said ominously as he glared down at the book again.

I gulped, realizing I'd never heard Owen sound so determined and angry.

"What do you mean?" I asked.

He snapped out of his shadowed mood and said, "Just that no one can treat everyone around them like he does and get away with it forever. It won't last. Just avoid him and ignore him."

Then he left, just like that. Owen left me standing there feeling abandoned again. I had no one on my side, no one I could trust.

Sometimes the hallways at school were just as lonely as being home, even though they were always packed with other kids. I felt like part of the scenery and would have to squeeze, unseen, between and around groups of friends who had stopped to have a conversation. I looked for my small group of friends where we'd usually meet, beside the 200 Hall water fountain.

As I wove my way through the crowd, I saw that only Christine was waiting for me. She looked anxious and was gripping her binder tightly across her chest.

"Hey!" I greeted her. "Where're Jacob and Avery?" The four of us had been friends since third grade. Lately, Jacob had spent less time with us and more time with other guys, which I've heard is pretty typical of middle school boys, so it wasn't so surprising that he was missing. But Avery, Christine, and I were always together.

Christine rolled her lips in and squeezed them shut, then glanced around quickly, grabbed me by the sleeve, and tugged me into the nearby girls' restroom.

"What is it? What's wrong?" I asked, suddenly feeling worried. Christine looked like she was afraid of something that was coming for her.

She took a deep breath and let it out slowly as she flipped open the binder and pulled out a piece of paper. It was white printer paper, but something that had been lined was copied onto it, making it look like the shadow of a piece of note-book paper.

"Cara, did you write this?" Christine asked me tentatively as she held the paper out for me to read.

I immediately recognized my own handwriting. It was a copy of something I'd written. As I began to read, all the blood drained from my face, replaced by the horrifying notion that anyone else had read these words.

It was an entry from my journal, something I had written around the time of Christmas break. The entry was a tear-stained rambling mess, very much a rant, about Avery and Jacob.

I had had a crush on Jacob ever since I first met him, but I had never let on to that fact. The beginning of my writing listed all the things I liked about him and how it would be so wonderful to one day try kissing him. Then it went into detail about our future wedding.

After this daydream scenario, I wrote about how Avery had shared with me that day that she too liked Jacob, not knowing that I liked him. I tore Avery down and listed all the things wrong with her and how she would never be right for Jacob.

The writing ended with my desperation and sadness that I'll never be brave enough to tell him or anyone else that I have feelings, and that I secretly hated Avery because I knew that she was the type of person who was brave enough.

Even though I knew every word, I reread the entire thing twice. I was trying to comprehend the fact that I was looking at an embarrassing, shameful piece of my heart on paper, and that Christine had also read it.

When I looked up at her, she was watching me silently, waiting for me to answer the question.

"I, uh... um... where did you get this?" I finally managed to say. My mouth had gone dry, making my words thick and sticky.

"Someone put it in my locker. I found it when we changed classes."

Liam.

I gulped and began to wad the paper up in my hand. "Look, Christine, it was just a bad day. I never meant for anyone else to read this." I hoped that I could explain the situation with Liam, and she'd feel sorry for me so that she'd keep all this information to herself.

"Well, I'm not the only one who read it."

"What?" My heart neared explosion, pounding in my chest.

"Yeah. Me and Avery and Jacob came from Mr. Johnson's class to swap out stuff at our lockers and wait for you. We all had a copy in our locker," she paused and then continued, "We all read it."

I grabbed my stomach. It felt like I might throw up. Luckily, the sink was nearby, and I held on to the edge to keep from falling.

"Ohmygodohmygodohmygod!" I was pretty sure I was having a panic attack, but Christine just continued to stand next to me and watch.

"What did they say?" I asked with barely contained terror.

"Welllllll..." she drew out the word like she could delay answering me. "We all looked at each other for a minute. I guess we were shocked. Then, Avery was so mad. She called you a few names. Then, um, well, she told Jacob that everything you'd written was a lie and she ran off toward the gym." She paused to take a breath.

All I could do was picture Avery's face. My friend was hurting, and it was my fault.

"Jacob, well, he was so mad too, but maybe more embarrassed? He didn't really say anything. He threw his copy away really quickly and went the other way down the hall."

I groaned and continued to hold on to the sink for dear life.

"There's more," she said before I could even catch my breath.

"There's more?!"

"So, well, um, I stuck the paper in my binder so I could ask you about it. And then I started waiting for you in our usual spot. And, um, while I was standing there, I saw Emily and Jessica both carrying the same paper down the hall. And I, uh, started looking around more, and, um, I saw Chase and Harry and Josh all had one, and..."

Thank goodness Christine stopped talking. She must've realized I was on the verge of fainting, as I sank to the bathroom floor and began to sob.

"So—what—you're- saying-is," I said in between gasps for breath, "that—every- body—I know—and even- the—ones—I don't,—have—read- this?" I held up the wad and started waving it around wildly.

Christine looked worried, but still didn't join me in my misery.

"Cara, I don't know what to say. I mean, I know you're upset, but so are Avery and Jacob. I just don't know what to do. It's out there, you know. I mean, I'm still your friend but I don't want Avery to hate me either if she hates you, so I don't know..."

I stared at her, unable to come up with a response.

"I'll, uh, call you later, k? I gotta go to class." Then, she left me sitting there, on the school bathroom floor, alone.

I'm not sure how much time passed, but eventually a couple of older girls came into the bathroom chattering loudly, then stopped abruptly when they saw me.

"Um. Are you okay?" one asked.

"I think she needs the nurse. She looks like she had, like, a heart attack or something," said another in a sing-song voice that sounded like she might be enjoying the show.

"Can you get up?" the third girl said loudly, as if my hearing had been affected. I guess I was just staring at them, crying, and not moving. Devastation had paralyzed me.

Someone touched my shoulder and I snapped out of it a little and wiped my face on my sleeve, sniffed and cleared my throat, and stood up. I tried to speak, but it came out like a squeak so that I had to clear my throat once more and start again.

"Yeah. I'm okay. I'm okay," saying it to myself as much as I was the girls hoovering over me. "I've gotta go to the nurse."

142

Rushing out the door, I was immediately deposited into a wall of people. I must've missed an entire class period because the halls were crowded again. Staring at the ground, not making eye contact with anyone, I began moving quickly. When I arrived in the nurse's office, I threw up in the trash can before I could even sign in or speak to her, so that sped up the process of getting picked up early.

Back at home, I laid curled up on my bed for the rest of the afternoon. Mom fussed over me, trying to get me to eat or take medicine. I didn't talk to her about what was going on, just soaked in the motherly comfort as much as I could.

Late in the afternoon, Owen came home and immediately went to his room and slammed the door.

"Owen?" Mom called down the hall.

"What?" he yelled back. His tone was so angry and impatient, it sounded more like Dad's voice.

"Excuse me?" came Mom's response. She was stomping down the hall toward his room, but before she knocked on his door, I heard it open, and she gasped.

"Yes, mother?" Owen's tone was now extremely sarcastic and overly sweet.

I crept over to the doorway to peer down the hallway.

"Do not speak to me that way!" Mom snapped at him. Owen was standing tall in his doorway, looming over her smaller frame. It looked like they were having some kind of silent stand-off.

"Why are you stomping around and slamming doors?"

143

There was another long pause in which he continued to stare her down.

Finally, Owen responded in a quiet, sharp voice, "Don't worry about me, Mom. I'm fine. I'm always fine. You've never worried about me before, no reason to start now." Then, he stepped back into his room and closed and locked his door.

Mom stood there staring at the door another second before she began to move away. I darted back to bed. She walked in and bent over me to speak softly in my ear.

"Honey, I'm going to pick up Liam and I'll be right back. Please drink some water." Then she left.

As soon as I heard the garage door closing, I decided to go snooping once more. Of course, Liam's room was locked. But then I wondered if I should check my parents' bedroom. That was the one room of the house that I hadn't searched yet.

I cautiously opened a few drawers in the dresser. It felt so wrong to be looking through my parents' things. My grandmother used to always say, "In for a penny, in for a pound." And that's exactly how I was feeling. Liam had ruined my life. There was no turning back.

I dug through drawers and looked under the bed. My parents' room was neat and organized and there wasn't much to find. Almost ready to give up, I went into the bathroom to look inside the only cabinets I hadn't opened. I went through the drawers and cabinets in the vanity one at a time, not really hopeful that I'd find what I was looking for.

I spotted a small prescription bottle nestled next to Mom's toothpaste and eye cream in one of the drawers. I didn't realize that either of my parents regularly took prescription medication.

The bottle said 'Prozac- Take one pill by mouth every morning.' I had no idea what it was or what it was for. It seemed our family had more secrets than I knew. I stared at the bottle another second before snapping out of my daydream and returning it to its place.

Continuing my search of the bathroom, I opened the linen closet, and there on the second shelf, on top of a stack of neatly folded navy-blue towels, sat my journal.

After all the searching and the stressing, I'd finally found it. It felt like a trick, and I was confused about finding it in the linen closet in my parents' bathroom, but relieved to have it back in my possession. When I pulled it down, a small slip of paper that had been resting on top of it drifted down to the floor.

It said, "I found this, and you need to read it. Cara's trying to get me into trouble, but it's really her that's the problem. ~ Liam"

I opened my journal and realized several pages were torn out and missing, but couldn't tell what he'd chosen to take out and what he'd left in. Liam had a purpose in the entries he wanted our parents to read. I wondered if Mom or Dad had read it yet or if Liam had put it there recently for them to discover.

The journal felt heavy, weighed down with my regret. Letting the cover fall open to a page that had a dog-eared corner, my eyes were drawn to the loops and swirls of the cursive handwriting I'd cultivated the last few years. I've always liked my penmanship, but now the letters on the pages in front of me seemed to have been written by another person, from another time. How could this have been written only four months ago?

Wait. Four months ago? The edge of a memory darkened my thoughts. I already knew what the entry was about, but I reread it anyway.

> "I can't believe what happened this morning. But I don't think anyone knows that it's my fault. My family never really pays attention to me, so I guess that's good this time. Last night, I was laying on the couch pretending to sleep so everyone would leave me alone. I heard a noise and opened one eye. Liam came out of Owen's room and ran into his room. I knew Owen was sitting out on the porch, so I went to peek and see if I could tell what Liam was up to. I found Dad's wallet laying open on Owen's desk. It was empty, but I know Dad always keeps some cash and usually has a few hundred-dollar bills. Dad was in the shower, so I figured Liam had grabbed Dad's wallet, taken the cash, and then left the wallet in Owen's room so he would get blamed. Liam knows Dad will beat Owen up. I can't believe he did that! I wonder how many times he's done something like that to Owen.

How many times has Owen gotten his butt kicked for something Liam set in motion?

I heard the water turn off in the shower, so I grabbed the wallet and ran. I didn't know what to do, so I shoved it into Mom's purse that was sitting on the table in the foyer. Owen came inside and saw me reaching into Mom's purse. He didn't say anything. He just pushed past me and went to his room.

Then, this morning, we were all sitting at breakfast and Liam kept grinning at Owen. Owen flicked him off. When his hand went back under the table, Liam kicked him hard. He must've caught Owen's hand between the chair because Owen screamed and fell backwards onto the floor. His hand was already bruising, and I saw him trying not to cry. Then Liam said, 'Good luck with your writing now' and then Owen jumped up and threw his Pop-Tart at Liam's face. I guess it was the only thing nearby. But right when he did that, Mom walked into the kitchen. She started yelling at Owen. He tried to tell her what happened and show his hurt hand, but she wouldn't listen. Then everything got worse. Dad came in, told Mom to shut her stupid face because the sound

147

of her voice was hurting his head. The rest of us froze and tried to act like everything was fine. Dad started looking for his wallet, couldn't find it, and was getting angrier and angrier.

When Mom was getting ready to take us to school, she picked up her purse then went looking for her keys. She pulled out Dad's wallet at the same moment he walked into the room. He snatched it out of her hand. Before she could say anything, he looked inside and found it empty. He screamed 'Where's my money? I give you everything! Is that not enough? Now you have to steal from me?' Then he grabbed her by the shoulder and shoved her. Mom stumbled into the coffee table and then fell and hit her head on the side table. All this is a pretty normal morning for us, but this time I knew what started everything. Liam is the cause of the chaos. After Dad walked out to the garage, Liam went to help Mom up. He glared at Owen like it was his fault, but maybe Owen didn't notice because he was staring at me. Maybe he thinks it's my fault since he saw me with my hand in Mom's purse. He has no idea that I helped him. I just can't stand it anymore. If Liam can cause all of this bad stuff to happen, maybe I can cause things to happen, too."

Something ripped inside of me. It seems that ruining my life at school wasn't enough for Liam, he intended to turn Mom and Dad against me, too. What had I done to him? I know Owen said I should avoid him and let it go, but I didn't feel strong enough to just walk away. I felt broken and angry. I wanted him to feel the way I felt. I wanted him to suffer the way Owen and I suffer. I wanted revenge.

With sudden clarity and determination, I tucked the journal under my shirt, took the Prozac bottle out of the cabinet, got rid of any evidence that I'd been there, and snuck back down the hall to my room. Owen was still holed up in his room as far as I could tell, and I vaguely wondered what Dad would do once Mom told him about the way Owen had treated her this afternoon.

I tucked the small bottle into the front zipper pocket on my backpack. At some point, I'd have to get rid of that bottle with Mom's name on it, but for now it just needed to be out of sight. Laying back on my bed, I heaved a deep sigh and grinned up at the ceiling.

"Liam thinks he's so smart, but I'm not going to let him mess with me anymore. I'm not helpless. I'll get back at him and he's going to regret ruining my life once I ruin his."

I knew it wouldn't fix what he had done to me, but maybe it would stop it from ever happening again. It felt good to have a plan.

Chapter 15

I sat staring at the rug that covered most of the therapist's office, following the blue paisley swirls through the gray and cream background with my eyes, trying to look anywhere except at Owen or Dr. Donner.

When we first started coming to these appointments, it felt like everyone was avoiding talking about Liam. I kinda thought that was the whole point of all this, but if I brought up his name, the conversation would get covertly steered in a different direction.

Until recently, Owen was the only person I really spent any time with or wanted to talk to. Every family therapy session, he was the only one who made me feel normal and calm. My parents were more condescending than helpful. And if they weren't crying, they were maintaining a fake composure, always on the verge of losing control.

Dr. Donner only wants to talk about "appropriate ways to express my grief," which means the way I'm acting is wrong. Apparently, I need to learn how to not make other people uncomfortable with my anger and sadness.

We spend a lot of time in these sessions modeling and practicing conversations with each other, deep breathing exercises, and discussing the kinds of hobbies I could "engage in, in order to bring a sense of peace to my daily life."

Once, Dr. Donner suggested journaling as a form of stress relief and I lost it. I'm sure I looked insane. But of course, she didn't know that the topic was off-limits because I never told anyone what Liam had done to me. I didn't feel like I could. If I had, I probably would've spent more time with the detective than a therapist.

During the sessions, my parents tried to play along and say things that appeared to be supportive, then we would go home, and Dad ignored me, and Mom talked to me like a fragile baby.

Luckily, most sessions only included Dr. Donner and me. But nothing ever got accomplished as I either sat silently or sobbed uncontrollably, only giving her the answers I knew she wanted to hear.

Opposite from my parents' behavior, Owen was always checking on me whenever we were home. He started talking to me more and spending time with me more than he had in a long time.

Owen would even stop by my room when he got home from school and check to see if I needed any help with my schoolwork because I'd been doing school at home with Mom since we only had a month left. Everyone felt it was better that I do not return yet, and truthfully, I would have been fine with never returning.

Then, a few weeks ago, even my renewed relationship with Owen went downhill. During our last family session with Dr. Donner, she was asking us how we felt our "family dinners," as she called them, were going in the evenings. Our very first homework assignment had been to sit down and have dinner together at least four nights each week and practice the conversational techniques she'd introduced us to. They hadn't been going well at all.

My mom would attempt to stick to the structure and get the rest of us on board to have a pleasant meal together, but it never worked out. Dad would sit sullenly and silently, that is, on the nights he came home on time. Owen continued to regard Mom with contempt and never responded the way he was supposed to, instead choosing to use sarcasm and rudeness.

To everyone's surprise, if Dad was around when Owen got like this, he would agree with him and snap at Mom, saying something like, "Geez, just let it go. Dr. Donner has lost her mind if she thinks we can exist in a reality of fake conversations. I'm not even sure why we're going to her. It's a waste of time and money."

Mom, still hurt by Owen's disrespect, would continue to needle, "I just don't understand why you're so angry with me, Owen! Frank, I really don't want him speaking to me that way."

"I'm telling you to let it go!" Dad would shout, and bang his fist on the table for emphasis, causing all the dishes to clatter loudly.

Mom wouldn't pursue it after that and everyone would just lapse into an uncomfortable silence, finishing the meal without another word. There's been several times after Dad's outburst that I'll look up to see Owen grinning at him, and Dad looking back with kind of a sad smile. They've never acted like this toward each other before. The world seems upside down.

When Dr. Donner asked her question about how our family dinners were going, Mom said, "I think it's going as well as can be expected."

"Does everyone participate in conversation?"

"...Well, mostly I think we do," Mom said hesitantly. She knew it was a lie, but she'd spent most of her adult years masking the reality of her tumultuous family life and the deception no longer felt wrong.

Dad sat quietly and just nodded along with whatever Mom said. The therapist's office is the only place I've ever seen Dad defer to Mom. He's probably just resentful for having to attend and hoping his agreement speeds along the appointment. It's also possible that he was just going along with the fabrication and reserving his frustrations until he had Mom alone.

But Owen scoffed, crossed his foot on top of his other knee, and began to jiggle it up and down quickly. Dr. Donner caught this change in attitude and turned to him.

"How do you think it's going, Owen? Do you feel connected to your mom, dad, and Cara?"

"Ummm, no. But that's not weird," he said, sitting forward again and rubbing the palms of his hands across his pants legs, smoothing the fabric.

"They," he gestured roughly to our parents with his chin as he spoke, "have never really made a big attempt to connect with Cara and me. That's the reason Liam's death has been so hard on Cara."

We all froze for different reasons. Mom gasped when she heard Liam's name. Dad's face crumpled into an anguished grimace. And I was holding my breath to see what their reactions would be to Owen calling them out in front of someone outside of our family.

"So," Dr. Donner continued obliviously, "are *you* not having any trouble grieving or continuing the family relationships you had previously?" I was thankful that she didn't utter Liam's name again.

Owen plowed on, "I grieved for Liam. And then I got over it. Cara's probably having more trouble because he made her so mad right before he died, and since she didn't feel like she could talk to Mom and Dad about any of it, we're here talking to you instead."

All eyes turned back to me.

"You were mad at Liam?" Dad had spoken up, his voice hoarse and clipped, choking on Liam's name.

"I, uh... um, well..." I hadn't told anyone how Liam had ended up in the woods that day. I'd just left that a mystery, claiming not to know. I looked at my dad's concerned, angry face and back at Owen's calm demeanor, and felt trapped.

Dr. Donner turned to Owen again and said, "How do you know Cara was mad at him?"

"Because they were arguing a whole bunch. And because when I found her, she kept saying that he ruined her life and that she was so mad with him."

Again, all eyes drifted back to me. I looked at each one quickly, trying to think of something to say. Owen just sat there smugly. I thought he'd been on my side. I thought he was taking care of me and being nice. But I realized that no one was on my side. He had been saving this information up to use it when it would sting the most. Owen was the one in control.

After that appointment, I had to go back and talk to the detective some more. We spent a lot of time going back through the events of the day. I admitted to putting the pills in Liam's locker and that he ran off after he caught me, but I never said anything about my journal. And I never told anyone about all the things Liam had done. It felt like that information would alert people to the fact that I had a reason to want to hurt my brother. I was in trouble with everyone for not giving the whole story. Life just got worse and worse.

Today, I had to sit in the same room with just Owen and Dr. Donner. Mom mentioned to her that Owen and I had not been talking recently and she scheduled us a therapy session to discuss it. Apparently, therapy is the answer to everything. I suspect Mom's lived with trauma for so long, avoiding real parenting, that she has no frame of reference for how to interact with us as a mother.

The entire session just fueled my indignation. I can't figure out what changed for Owen. I used to be able to talk to him and it felt like we were united against everyone else. Now, I resent him for telling everyone that Liam and I had been arguing, for trying to get me into trouble.

"Do you think seeing Cara with Liam after he died has made you distrustful toward her?" Dr. Donner asked. I hadn't really been listening, but this caught my attention, and I zoned back in to hear the answer.

"I mean, I've always thought it was weird that they were out there in the woods together. Now that Cara's admitted to trying to get Liam into trouble, it makes more sense for how she ended up out there. But he was supposed to be at practice, and I don't get why he left instead of just telling her off or telling Dad when he got home. And then, once he did run from the school, why did she follow him? It's like she wanted to get him alone out there. But that doesn't mean I blame her for his death if that's what you're asking. Nothing was normal about that afternoon, so maybe I'm just reading too much into it."

"How was the afternoon supposed to go?" Dr. Donner asked him.

"Well, usually I would get home and have some peace and quiet, time to write or read. Mom, Cara, and Liam would get home a little while later. We'd probably all avoid each other until dinner. Dad gets home right at dinner or a little after if he's not picking Liam up from practice. He'd probably look for ways to get on to me about something he thinks I've done wrong, while Mom and Cara go about their life like everything's perfect." Owen's voice had become loud and clipped.

"And what made it so irregular?" Dr. Donner asked.

"Well, just the fact that Cara lied about going to gardening club, Liam leaving practice..."

His voice faded out as he realized he had lost his calm composure and was ranting. Running his hand through his hair, his eyes fell on his watch, and he stared at it momentarily. The action seemed to calm and reset him.

Beginning again, he said, "I just think Cara wanted him to be out in the woods that day, so she could follow him. Why else would she lie about the club? She came up with something drastic enough to cause Liam to leave practice."

Dr. Donner was looking at him intently, sensing that she had another avenue to pursue with our messed-up family. I, however, was concentrating every ounce of restraint I had over my body not to vomit or faint. The primal part of me wanted nothing more than to dive across the open space between us and strangle my brother.

"I thought you said you didn't blame Cara for his death?" the doctor responded to his admission.

"Hmmm," he brought his hand to his chin as if considering new knowledge. "Perhaps I do blame her after all."

Owen's betrayal was complete, my visceral response a clear symptom of being stabbed in the back. I folded in on myself, unable to remain upright.

There were so many questions, so much confusion bouncing through my thoughts, it was hard to focus on one at a time. The house was never empty when Owen got home in the afternoons. If we didn't walk home together, Mom was always there until she left to pick up either me, or me and Liam, from school. Why was he lying about that?

It was unusual that Mom hadn't been home when he arrived that afternoon. We found out later it was because Liam's coach had called her to figure out why he'd left the field during practice.

No one from the gardening club had noticed I'd been skipping recently, and they certainly never tried contacting my parents in concern for my whereabouts. I hadn't realized that Owen had been told the newest information of my admission. Maybe he wasn't told anything. Maybe he already knew what happened and that's why he turned on me during the other session. But how would he know? I was mulling this over when I realized Owen was answering another one of Dr. Donner questions.

"...take care of her when I can. She's just a little kid, so I try to help her out. I've never really had a problem with Liam. I definitely don't get along with Dad, but it's actually been better recently. And Mom just drives me nuts, but mostly just because she's my mom and she's always griping about something, you know?"

The lies were just flowing from his mouth. He was completely misrepresenting the relationships we held with each other. I was used to Mom masking the truth of our disfunction, but Owen doesn't normally hold back. I doubted he would speak of the abuse but hiding his anger was unusual. There should have been a pile of ashes in his chair created by the force of my fiery glare. I had to figure out what he was up to and why he was trying to get me into trouble.

Later that afternoon, once we got home from Dr. Donner's office, I mostly shut my bedroom door and peered out the remaining crack, hoping to see Owen. He went into his room, then came back out carrying his laptop. I leaned out as he walked away from me down the hall and watched him go out to the porch. He often liked to sit outside and write.

I took the opportunity to sneak down the hall and into his room. I'm not sure what I was looking for, but I'd already been betrayed by a brother once, and I wasn't interested in waiting around for it to happen again. I stood in the center of the room and looked around, trying to decide what I was doing.

Then, I began haphazardly opening the drawers of his desk and the covers of various notebooks he had laying around. I had only been snooping for a few seconds before Owen came stalking back into the room. He stopped dead in his tracks, and we stared at each other.

"Get out," was all he said to me in a low, murderous voice.

I knew I was in the wrong, so I immediately left without another word, retreating to my room to wait. Once I heard him go back outside, I peeked out and saw that his bedroom door was closed this time. I tiptoed over and tried the knob. Locked. It was strange that he was being so secretive. As I turned to tiptoe away, I ran right into Owen's chest.

I hadn't heard him come back inside and walk up behind me. Startled, I looked up to see his face full of quiet fury. The expression seemed to be an echo of the one I'd given him in Dr. Donner's office.

"Should I worry about you sneaking around and going through my stuff, too, Cara?"

"I.. I'm sorry. I just wanted to... um, I don't know. I'm sorry," I said lamely. I couldn't come up with anything to say. I wasn't even sure what I was looking for, or doing, sneaking around. I hung my head and looked down at the floor, feeling ashamed. Owen scoffed and walked away.

At dinner, Mom called Owen to the table, and he called back, "I'm busy. I'll just make a sandwich later."

Mom's expression was disappointed again. She began collecting the plate and silverware that she'd just laid down for him to use and grumbled to herself, "He's always writing. There's never time for him to sit down with us...", which made me wonder again what he was writing. The time he spent on his laptop or with a pad of paper and pencil had increased immensely in the last several months since Liam's death.

As I pushed bites of food around on my plate with a fork, I allowed myself to do something that I hadn't since Liam died. I thought carefully about each detail. I had of course been talking about the events of that day over and over, but the story had become so repetitive, it was like talking about a movie I'd seen, and I'd never really reflected on my own feelings or focused on the details. So much for therapy.

Every night when I closed my eyes, all I could see was Liam's dead eyes and my handprints in his blood on each cheek. I didn't sleep as often as I could help it. And I didn't spend time thinking about what that afternoon had been like. I just repeat the story whenever I'm told, like a trained puppy.

Now, trying to remember everything clearly was confusing. Worse than the confusion was the guilt. And Owen was adding shame and fear to the list. I needed to figure out why he was lying and trying to get me in trouble, and what he was writing about. It couldn't be schoolwork; school would be over in three days.

In many ways, Owen was sneakier than Liam. I wasn't afraid of him, necessarily, just suspicious. Maybe he'd been spending time with me to find out information. I decided I'd have to figure out what he was up to if I wanted to finally be left alone, and to get back control over my life.

Just then, Owen came strolling through the kitchen with his laptop and a notebook tucked under one arm and his hoodie folded over the other. Without a word, he walked past Mom and me sitting at the table, grabbed keys from the hook, and left through the screen door, letting it slam behind him. Mom got up quickly, dropping her napkin on the floor, and rushed to follow calling his name. Outside, the car started and faded away as it pulled out of the driveway, then headed down the road.

When Mom came back inside, she had her phone to her ear.

"...I don't know. I can't get him to talk to me anymore."

She let the screen slam behind her and sighed as she leaned back against the counter. When she saw me looking at her, she turned to face the sink and dropped her voice lower as if we weren't in the same room and that action would give her some form of privacy.

"He probably went down to Mill City again," she said. "It's still early, I'm sure he won't be gone long. Maybe you can try calling him? I just don't know why he won't talk to me."

I didn't want to listen to her sad voice anymore, so I left my dinner, most of it uneaten, and headed toward my room. As I passed Owen's room, I made the sudden decision to go inside.

Standing there looking around at his somewhat disorderly room, except for his tidy desk where he spent most of his time, I had a clear sense that the next actions I took would determine which path my life would follow.

Did I really want to snoop in another brother's stuff and continue to fuel the disintegration of what little relationship we had left? Maybe not, but I did have questions that needed to be answered.

I decided that I wouldn't push Owen, but I would let him know that I wasn't going to be a push-over either, that I was watching and listening. I would let him know that he wasn't going to get anything by me, and that I wasn't some weepy middle-schooler that was just going to roll over and give in to everyone else treating me like a misbehaving child and trying to control me.

I found a pen and paper sitting on his desktop, so I sat down and wrote him a note.

Chapter 16

W hy was this so hard? I kept telling myself over and over that I needed to do this, I needed to get Owen to talk to me. I've spent months following his work, following him, just as I always had, reading his articles, and worrying about what he might know.

"I don't really want to talk about me right now, Owen," I said. He was staring off into the trees again. His stomach kept growling and I could tell he was preoccupied- with hunger, or something else? I couldn't be sure.

I decided to take another approach to the conversation. Up to this point I hadn't been doing a very good job with keeping my composure or setting him at ease. I probably shouldn't have let him know that I was keeping tabs on him all these years, then maybe he'd be more willing to talk with me now. The notes and phone calls may have been a mistake.

While Owen wasn't paying attention to me, I took another calming breath, let it out slowly, smoothed my shirt to sit up straighter and adjusted the contents of my pocket.

"Maybe we should take a break from Johnny Rowe. I've read your other articles, too."

At this remark, Owen turned back to face me. Leaning back on the bench, he propped his foot on top of his knee again, put his arm across the back of the seat and smiled. The change in subject seemed to relax him a little.

Feeling encouraged, I asked, "How about your first article? That seemed to catch on with people pretty quickly, huh? What was that guy's name? William something? The mayor's son, right?"

I was mostly just phishing to get him talking again. I had a crisp memory of all the details of Owen's life, including the murders he wrote about. This particular story was extremely familiar.

"War-ren Williams," Owen drew out his name when he said it, like greeting an old friend in the country. "Yeah, that's when I got my 'big break,' I guess you'd call it. The mayor's son. He was really such a jerk, if we're being honest." He was fully grinning now, but not at me, at a memory.

"Oh, did you meet him, too? Or just learn about him when you were researching?"

Owen cut his eyes back to me, then away again, suspicious. "Well, let's just say, I witnessed some of his aftermath. People generally hated him. Did you ever hear any stories about him up in Walton?" he asked.

I shook my head no and he continued, "Even after his death, there didn't seem to be a deep sense of sadness in the community. More like relief, I'd say."

"How did you convince the police to give you all that extra information you used?" I asked. "Your stories read like murder mysteries, but I know they're about real events. Is it hard to get people to trust you with their personal information?"

"Well, yes and no." He seemed to be genuinely considering my questions. "I wasn't really sure where to start with Trés..." At this, Owen rolled his eyes in response to the nickname.

"When I heard about his car wreck on the news it sounded like strange circumstances, and my intuition told me he might be the victim, so I decided to just show up at the scene with my press badge and go from there. Luckily, I had already spoken with the local sheriff on a few occasions earlier in the week, so he was at least familiar with who I was. When I got there, of course everything was in chaos."

I didn't need my imagination to understand what he was describing. A small-town murder incites a flurry of activity much like a fallen ice cream cone stirs up an ant hill.

"I had to stand around for a while before I got the chance to corner him. I stopped him on his way to his car and asked him a few general questions. That's when he told me that the case had already been turned over to a detective to determine if it was indeed a suspicious death."

I was physically squeezing my mouth closed to keep from speaking, pressing my lips tightly together. I already knew all this and was having a hard time not rushing him through this part of the story. *Calm, Cara. Calm.*

I mentally checked my expression to make sure it was neutral, but I didn't say anything. Owen always spoke more if I just sat quietly. He used to tell me that I'd probably make a good reporter because I could get people to share information with me easily.

Silence makes people uncomfortable, and they usually come up with ways to fill the voids with excess words. I made sure to refocus on Owen so I wouldn't miss what he was saying.

"Detective Abernathy wouldn't talk to me at first. But then I reminded him that he knows me." He paused in his storytelling to grin at me, but it wasn't a pleasant expression. It was the kind of smile people give you when they're anticipating a certain reaction.

"Don't you recognize that name?" he asked as I stared at him dumbly.

"You know," he continued, "Wes Abernathy. Jacob's dad?"

That name felt like a jolt of electricity. Now I was most likely staring at him with a look of horror as shock and regret raced through my veins.

Jacob Abernathy. I haven't thought about him in twelve years. Not since the day of Liam's death. I couldn't. It was all too intertwined. My heart sat tightly at the base of my throat, and I couldn't swallow. My skin began heating up and my mind was screaming.

"Cara? You okay?"

My eyes refocused and I realized Owen was staring at me, a look of concern on his face. Was it genuine? Did he really not remember? I couldn't recall at that moment if he and I had ever talked about exactly what happened with Liam and my journal.

I swallowed hard against the lump in my throat, and licked my lips that were suddenly dry with panic.

"Oh. Um, yeah. I'm good. I, um, haven't heard that name in a long time. I forgot that his dad was a detective," I managed to squeak out in between swallows. *Was I sweating?* I had read Owen's article and that name, Abernathy, but the connection to Jacob hadn't clicked in my mind.

"Yep. Remember? He used to be a police officer in Jefferson County, he worked Liam's case with Detective Mackie, but transferred to Barnes and then was promoted to lead detective about five years ago. Didn't you used to hang out with Jacob a lot? I thought you and he were the same age."

Was he grinning? He seemed pleased with my discomfort, but I couldn't be sure.

Owen's expression tugged at the shadow of a memory. This was beginning to remind me of those couple of months after Liam died, when our relationship became strained once he started lying to the counselor.

Our separation had suited me just fine, but in opposition to that, I needed to keep tabs on him. I needed to make sure he didn't learn the truth or set me up with more of his lies.

Two years after Liam's death, Owen graduated high school and left for Northern. Four years after that, he promptly moved to San Francisco for a job, and I attempted to keep up with him as best I could. It was harder back then, only catching the snippets of information he chose to share with Dad, never Mom.

Owen continued to ignore Mom and respond to her with hostility. I never did learn the source of the discord between them. Maybe it wasn't just one incident, but a build up over the course of his entire childhood. I guess everyone has their breaking point.

Since Owen was anchored in one place while he attended college, I was hopeful that my fears were contained, that the feelings of betrayal and suspicion would fade. But I just couldn't let it go, not this time. Not ever again. I knew he wouldn't respond to any phone calls from me, but I'd call anyway and leave him messages from time to time.

As I got older, during Owen's time with the Chronicle, I began to feel more secure, more at ease. I read his articles and tried to keep up with what he was researching and reporting on, just to make sure he was staying put.

I'd let him know that I was still there, in the background, never allowing him to forget that I was waiting and listening. For a while, it was good. I felt like I had the upper hand for once, like I was in control of my own destiny. But whispers of progress don't always lead to proclamations of success.

Owen cleared his throat, snapping me out of my reverie and I finally responded to his question about Jacob a beat too late, "Well, you know, we were in the same class a few years in a row, and we used to be friends, but I didn't hang out with Jacob or anyone else after Liam died."

"Yes, I remember," was all Owen said in that obnoxious, contemplative way that he had.

"Hmm. Well, anyway," he shook his head, clearing it, "I reminded Detective Abernathy of who I was, and we got to talking about the past." Owen looked my way briefly and then cut his eyes back to the trees again.

"I told him my idea about the article I wanted to write and assured him that we would be helping each other. I told him covering a story in this way could lead to more interest, which leads to more information, which leads to an arrest if there was a murder or any foul play."

"After he agreed to work with me," he continued, "I met with Detective Abernathy several times over the course of the following two weeks, and he allowed me to release certain details a little at a time. I was also able to speak with a few people in the community, although I wouldn't call them Trés' friends. The mayor and Trés' mother wouldn't talk to me, but the older brother did."

As Owen spoke about details of the case that I already knew, my mind faded into thoughts of the past again, when I'd learned that Owen had switched jobs, moving him from San Francisco to Redmore. I had just graduated, and Mom and Dad were helping me move my belongings from their house to my new apartment in Walton, just a short drive north.

At the end of the day, the three of us went to Angelo's to grab some pizza. As we sat in the dim light of the oversized worn, wooden booth, I decided to ask how Owen was doing and what he'd been up to.

Mom looked miserable and kept her eyes lowered, staring at the table. Anytime I did bring up my surviving brother, she reacted this way. Mom knew Owen hated her.

I wondered if mentioning Owen brought up memories of Liam. I suppose it probably did. I couldn't separate them either. It's like static cling, when you find a stray bit of fluff stuck to your pants leg, but every time you pull it away it clings to a new place, unwilling to relinquish its hold.

Dad answered my question, "Well, apparently, he's secured a new position at some online news source up in Redmore." He chewed loudly and took a swig of his beer as he continued. "What was it called, Rita? Something Times? Oh, yeah, it's called Today Times."

Dad was always a gruff, rushed eater. It goes back to all the years he spent as a lawyer, hurrying through meals. That combined with a commanding tone, didn't allow others to get much of a word in. Mom continued to pick at her salad as if he hadn't spoken to her, which I guess he really hadn't.

I was struck by this new information. Owen was moving.

I'd heard of the Today Times. It was a ludicrously popular, national newspaper, released solely online. It had millions of subscribers. People my age, all the way up to grandparents and retirees, and even some highschoolers, relied on it as their daily news source. If he was going to be writing for Today, his reachable audience would grow by five hundred percent.

I had fallen into a lackadaisical routine while Owen was writing for the Chronicle. After the first year, it felt familiar and consistent. We never spoke, but I knew it unnerved him whenever I'd reach out, and I was glad that Owen was now the one who would feel that pressure, that paranoia.

With news of him moving, I was enveloped by a feeling of dread. When it came to my big brother, I'd learned to fear change. Owen was extremely smart and manipulative, never wavering from the path he intended to take or allowing others to stand in his way.

Before Liam died, I would've also said Owen's predictable. That changed around the time he began to confine himself to his room and since then, I've known better than to assume what might come next. Without knowing what to expect, how can I protect myself? Until now, I'd kept my eyes open, watching him carefully, wary of any surprises. This loss of control, my fear of the unknown pulled me to the edge of sanity and all I could see was a dark, bottomless pit below.

Something had to give. This madness had to end. No more counselors and therapists. No more questions. No more medications. No more rehab. No more nightmares. No more self-doubt and self-inflicted guilt. No more awkward, unsure Cara.

My family became my bondage over the years. Drugs provided me with brief moments of escape while I lived with Mom and Dad and struggled to get through college. With all the abuse that my body and soul have been through in the last twelve years, it's surprising that I'm still alive.

Graduation seemed to be the light at the end of the tunnel, and I was hopeful that I could finally begin my own life, walking my own path instead of cowering in Liam's shadow, running from my parents, and stalking Owen. But here I was, still living close to Mom and Dad, and Owen was moving into a greater position of power to distribute information. I didn't want another brother with an over-inflated sense of self-importance and a desire to spread secrets. I didn't want to be lulled into a state of unawareness.

In the dim glow of the pizzeria booth, the air thick with Mom's depression and Dad's disgust, I began to formulate a plan. This story of death and betrayal had gone on for too long, but I would make it my job to find the ending. I would find my own happy ending, despite my brother's efforts to tear me down.

I couldn't believe my luck when I found out that he had come closer to me, to Mill City. Later, after reading the beginning of Owen's story about Warren Williams, I'd driven the hour south to seek him out and keep a careful watch on what he was up to.

I felt crazy for pursuing him, but this is what I'd been reduced to, what Owen reduced me to. In all fairness, I was first betrayed, belittled, and discarded by Liam, but as soon as he was gone, Owen picked right up where he'd left off.

But Owen was smarter and more underhanded than Liam. I'd already learned that trust and loyalty could never be assumed and any hint of them should be examined under the microscope of skepticism. There were too many thieves in disguise in my life.

Everyone has their own agenda and desires. Everyone has the potential to steal the joy and comfort that belongs to someone else and then convince themselves that their actions are justified in pursuit of their own needs. They're all guilty.

My father found redemption in Liam, his talented son, and neglected the rest of his family. He belittled and abused Owen and pushed me to the side. Dad used fear and intimidation to bully his children and his wife. No one's time was ever as important as his time. No one's feelings mattered if they caused him to question his own actions.

My mother was never brave enough to accomplish anything. She fought against her own children if they threatened to rock the fragile boat where she lived her life. There was nothing she could do to help anyone, and she was too afraid to really love us. Her hesitation was the choke hold on my childhood.

Liam. I never usually allow myself to think of him for too long. I've come to believe that he was broken when he was born. There was always something wrong that festered and then gained strength as he got older, until finally bursting forth once his level of pride had reached its max.

The short time I was tortured by his cruelty was also distorted by memories of love. However, once Liam realized he could manipulate others to get the things that he wanted, his sense of power and authority overpowered everything and everyone else.

Owen was the worst of all. My parents and Liam wore their sins like an outfit that gets put on daily. What you see is what you get. They weren't deceptive or sneaky, just unapologetic, obliviously terrible people. But Owen is the con artist, the one that will lull you into submission through good manners and false kindness.

At least with the rest of them, there was never any question of where I stood in their eyes. There was never any hope that I would earn greater affections. Owen makes you feel loved and listened to, and then he snatches it right out from under you when you're at your lowest.

I arrived in Mill City a little after noon and decided the best way to locate Owen quickly without driving around town all day was to park at the police station and wait for him to show up. I knew he'd been working closely with the police according to the interviews in his first article.

I sat in my car in the corner of the parking lot watching out the windshield toward the front entrance to the building. I stared at my fingers still gripping the steering wheel as I waited. My nails were chewed into short stubs. I released my grasp and curled my fingers into fists so I wouldn't have to look at the evidence of my self-destruction. It dawned on me that I was always hiding something, even from myself.

After a while, I caught movement as the front doors opened and glanced up to see an older man and woman leaving. They seemed to be fussing at each other. The woman was gesturing wildly and emphatically with her left arm, while putting all her weight on her other arm, which was linked through the man's. He was supporting her on one side, while managing a cane with the other hand, all the while shaking his head furiously. As the couple slowly meandered toward the parking deck next to the station, the doors opened again.

This time, it was Owen. He was walking quickly, head down. One hand was in his pocket and the other held his phone to his ear. Owen didn't look around, thank goodness, and never noticed me parked about thirty yards away. I don't even think he noticed the old couple as he cruised past them.

When Owen reached his car and opened the door, he stood there for a minute, the non-phone hand gripping the top of the door frame. He seemed to be listening and I couldn't tell, but it didn't appear like his lips were moving. After thirty more seconds, he climbed into the car, phone still to his ear, backed out of the spot, and turned right heading out of the lot.

I gave him a small lead, keeping his car in sight with a block or so between us. Following someone this way was easier in a small town where the traffic is thinner, and the streets are less crowded. However, for those same reasons, it's more difficult to stay out of range to be noticed.

I followed Owen out of the downtown area and up the rural highway for a few miles before he turned off the main road and onto a neighborhood street. I continued to leave ample space between us. Since there weren't many people driving this way, I fell back further and further, keeping him in sight, but feeling too exposed.

At the end of the street, in the cul-de-sac, he turned into the driveway of a stately ranch house, with four tall, white columns across the front. Even on this fall day, the lawn was crisp and green, and the beautiful brick exterior gave the impression of wealth and importance.

I pulled over before going any closer and parked on the curb, unsure what to do next. I thought that maybe I'd catch up to him when he was alone and have a conversation. I still hadn't come up with what I'd say, but I was beginning to piece it together in my head and rehearse it aloud as I sat waiting once again.

After an hour, Owen emerged from the house, got in his car, and began driving back toward me down the road. I had to suddenly dive into the floorboard to keep from being seen. I wasn't afraid that Owen would recognize my car. He hadn't been around me in years, so he had no idea what I drove.

As soon as he passed, I sat up and started the car. This time, he drove back toward town, but turned off right before reaching the main strip and the campus area. After a block, Owen turned again, following signs leading to the Chickasaw River Greenway.

There wasn't a soul on this dead-end road, and I decided to stop for a minute and allow Owen to get out of sight. If he didn't reappear soon, I'd drive further, park, and walk down one of the trails.

I wasn't patient enough to wait longer than about five minutes, so I walked along one of the trails that looped the area and fed into the parking lot. As the gray of the asphalt came into view, I spotted Owen moving around near the end of the boat ramp on the edge of the river. I left the trail and crept closer through the trees, but I was far enough away that he didn't seem to hear my footsteps in the leaves and pine straw.

There was still yellow police tape cordoning off the entire area, especially the entrance to the ramp. Owen was pacing back and forth on the other side of the tape, near the water. He stared down at the ground, stopping to rub his foot back and forth through the grass on the side of the ramp, then turning to walk back to the grass on the other side and repeating his rubbing. *Was he looking for something at the crime scene?*

As Owen paced and searched, he muttered softly to himself. Then, he suddenly stopped and shouted, "Shit!" and kicked a small rock near his feet. It flew from the bank and into the river where it immediately sank.

Owen clenched his fists and shook his head, then looked off to the side as he turned to walk away. Something must've caught his eye because he walked a few yards to his right, towards some sand and debris to the side of the ramp, and bent down, scrutinizing the ground. Before he stood up, he reached down and picked up an object, and when he straightened again, he was smiling widely.

There was something familiar about the shape of the object Owen was holding, but I was too far away to see with any real clarity. Whatever it was, he seemed relieved to be holding it. He began brushing it off, wiping it on his pants leg, then he pocketed it and looked around at his surroundings for the first time. I held still, barely leaning my head around the tree that I'd hid behind and tried not to breathe or make noises.

Owen seemed to come to some kind of decision and began walking quickly in my direction, back to his car. He reached down and pulled his phone out of his pocket to answer it.

"Hello, Detective," he said.

Then, after a pause, "Sure, I can head back. It'll take me about twenty minutes though. I just got back to the hotel a few minutes ago and I was about to jump in the shower." More listening. "Yeah, I spoke with him after I left the station." More listening. "Okay. Will you give me some more information on that? On the record?"

Owen reached the car, unlocked the door, and began to climb inside. Before the door shut, I heard him say, "Sounds good. One more thing, would you have time to take me over to the crime scene again today or tomorrow? I want to get some details on..." and then he closed the car door, and I couldn't hear anymore.

Owen was lying to the detective. I wasn't surprised. But I was afraid. I watched him drive away and thought back to the second article I'd read just the day before, documenting this story. Pieces began to fall into place in my mind and I realized what the object he'd picked up reminded me of.

Owen had picked up his watch right where Warren Williams' car went into the water.

Chapter 17

2019

I paced the small square-footage of the hotel room, biting firmly on my bottom lip, my phone held hard against my ear, as I anxiously listened to the shrill ringtone on the other end. He didn't pick up. Again. I glanced down at Owen's latest article about the Derrick Hoffman case pulled up on my laptop, then pressed redial again.

Finally, the ringing stopped, and I heard his familiar irritated voice come through, "For heaven's sake, Cara! If I wanted to talk to you, I would've answered the first two times you called." Owen sounded even more agitated than I expected. Although I had called him several times over the last few months, he'd never answered, so I hadn't been sure that he'd pick up.

"Just listen, Owen," I said. "I'm calling because Dad's had a heart attack." And then I added, "A few days ago. I think Mom tried to call you... maybe left you a voicemail?"

I wasn't sure of this fact at all. It was true that Dad had a heart attack, but since he's the only one that has any communication with Owen anymore, contacting Owen to let him know the situation wasn't the first thing on our list. But I needed a reason to call him now and Dad's sickness provided me with a good enough cover.

I took a minute to reassure Owen and ramble on about prognosis and treatments to fully immerse myself in the role of concerned sister. He interrupted me then, sounding unsure and uncharacteristically off-balance. Good, I wanted to disturb him. Then he asked, "What does he need?"

Owen seemed to be so removed from our lives that he assumed I was calling to get him to do something rather than just imparting the knowledge that something had happened to one of his parents. Not that I could blame him for wanting to put as much distance as possible between himself and Mom and Dad.

But I couldn't let Owen distract me from my objective. I knew he was in Evanston, near Northern. But I needed to figure out his next moves and I was going to have a really hard time doing that if I couldn't decipher his exact location or his next target.

I told Owen he should come home to visit Dad and his reaction was swift and strong, he was definitely annoyed. I tried laying on the guilt trip, thick and dramatic. I even called him "indifferent" to push him into proving me wrong.

I was more than a little surprised when it sounded as if my plan would work, and Owen said that he'd head south after finishing his current story. He was extra defensive and, realizing I may have pushed him too far, I tried smoothing over our brief quarrel by telling him how much I missed him and how we never talk. The needy little sister role was a bit rusty, but it seemed to calm him. Owen would be heading toward home within the week.

Now I only needed to get back there and catch sight of him in order to follow him again, or better yet speak with him and ask him a few leading questions to figure out what his next plans were. Ever since Mill City and the Warren Williams case, I'd been trying to get out in front, but felt like I was constantly three steps behind.

Unfortunately, it seems that Owen is very good at eluding me when he knows I'm trying to find him. Every time I tried to catch him at my parents' house during his visit home to check on Dad, he somehow slipped out before I arrived.

Once, I decided to stay at their house as long as it took until Owen came back, and he never did. He had left Dad a voicemail saying that he was working, but that he'd be around again to visit before he left town. A day and a half later, it became clear that he wasn't going to show up and I couldn't stick around waiting anymore.

He only left that message so I'd know that he knew I was there waiting for him, as convoluted as that idea sounds. Owen never calls Dad and he's not considerate enough to care whether Mom or anyone else was worried about him. In a way, I guess that shows I'm getting to him, that I've rattled him.

After I realized that Owen left town again, I looked back at his last article about Derrick Hoffman to find the name of the detective that he had been working with in Evanston. I found the phone number for Detective Miller easily and decided to call to get some information of my own, but not about Derrick, about Owen.

The phone rang a few more times after I was transferred to Detective Miller's desk, then I heard a rich, raspy, female voice answer, "This is Detective Miller."

"Yes, hello. My name is Cara Walsh. I know this may sound strange, but I wanted to ask you some questions about my brother. I believe you worked with him recently, Owen Walsh?" I tried not to sound as crazy as I felt.

"The journalist?" she asked, sounding a bit surprised.

"Yes, the one who was writing about Derrick Hoffman's death. Do you mind if I ask you some quick questions about the time you spent with him recently?" I kind of felt a bit like a journalist myself at that moment.

"Well, Ms. Walsh, I'll be as candid as I'm able." Detective Miller sounded wary, but something in her tone made me feel like I was on the right track. "May I ask why you're following up on your brother?"

I had no idea what to tell her. I decided that using part of the truth would probably be my best course.

"My parents and I are worried about his health and I'm trying to find out whether he's been behaving oddly. He won't allow us to help him, and he doesn't communicate with us anymore, so it kind of feels like I'm stalking him sometimes." I winced at my choice of words. I can't believe I used the word 'stalking' to a police officer.

"Um," I stumbled through an awkward chuckle and cleared my throat to get back on track. "I just mean, he had some childhood trauma when our brother died a strange death and we're all concerned about the fact that he's now thrown himself into this position of investigating and reporting on other people's deaths." I mentally crossed my fingers that what I was saying made sense to her.

"I see," she said. "Alright, how can I help?"

"When did Owen first contact you?"

"Oh, he showed up at the crime scene on the first morning of the investigation. We'd probably only been on North Kent for about an hour before he approached one of the officers. I'm not sure if he'd been among the crowd before that, but I'm doubtful. He would've stuck out."

The detective continued, "I didn't speak with him until the next day. But he was diligent with follow up phone calls and waiting for hours at a time for me to become available. It was... interesting. Frustrating, if I'm being honest."

"And when you spoke with him that next day, did he have any information for you?" I asked.

"For me? What kind of information would he be giving me?" she scoffed.

"Um, I'm not sure. Like I said, he's just odd. Somewhat of a loose cannon, so I'm never sure what to expect."

"Yeah. I've met him." Detective Miller mumbled. I wasn't entirely sure that she'd meant for me to hear her.

I thought for a moment, then asked, "I read all the articles about Mr. Hoffman, except for the last one that I guess comes out tomorrow. Can you tell me the outcome? I mean, was his death ruled a homicide or accidental?"

Detective Miller paused, then said, "Well, I can tell you that the case remains open, and we believe that Derrick Hoffman was murdered. I can't give you any details about the case. Do you have any other questions about your brother that I can help you with?"

"Did Owen act strangely during any of the time that you spent with him?" I asked.

"All reporters are strange, aren't they?" She laughed. "Mr. Walsh was a bit stranger than most I suppose, because he had the nosey tenacity of a reporter, but also seemed to be working through things logically like a detective. There were a few times when I had the distinct impression that he knew what I was going to say before I said it."

I mulled that over, forgetting that I was on the phone with someone. Detective Miller coughed lightly and broke my trance.

"And what was your personal opinion of him?" I asked.

She hesitated, "Well, I don't want to offend him or you..."

I assured her that whatever she had to say wouldn't phase me.

Detective Miller sighed loudly. "In our first few conversations, he seemed well-mannered and agreeable, and he was generally complimentary of my team. He was careful and considerate when he spoke to family members, we didn't have any complaints there. I was hesitant to speak with him at all, but to be honest, the details that he learned weren't any different than those we'd share with any other journalist. I guess the difference is that he went more in-depth, more personal, and told the story like an active timeline, instead of just reporting at the end. And, like I said, at first, he was very easy to work with and stuck to the boundaries we gave him."

"But later it changed?" I asked.

"Yeah, slowly, but yeah. After a few meetings, he became pushy and entitled, like we owed him the information. I don't think most people minded it so much, we're used to dealing with jerks in the day-to-day. But during one of our meetings, he started arguing with me about some facts in the case. THEN," she emphasized, "he started speaking down to me like I didn't know what I was doing, and that just did it for me. I cut him off and refused to work with him anymore. But at that point, he was wrapping up his coverage anyway and I didn't hear from him after that."

"Anything else, Ms. Walsh?" She sounded exasperated, wanting to wrap up our conversation.

Thinking quickly, I blurted out, "Did you notice if he was wearing a watch?"

There was a long pause, longer than is socially comfortable, then she said, "You know, I believe he was. He always seemed preoccupied with it when he was thinking. I remember him fidgeting with it often."

I ended the conversation and sat at the table in the kitchenette, lost in thought.

Derrick Hoffman had died in a strikingly different way than Warren Williams. Warren had driven his car right into the river and drowned. Derrick Hoffman had been found in a crime-ridden neighborhood behind the local food mart. His cause of death had been determined quickly as a drug overdose.

To an objective observer, neither death seemed to be related to the other in any way. There weren't any common details. In fact, I was positive that the only thing they had in common was that they were both covered by Owen.

I put my head in my hands and groaned. What was I doing to myself? Why couldn't I just move on and pretend he didn't exist anymore?

For a few minutes, I stared at the tabletop and pictured my life differently. The one thing I wish I could go back and re-do was taking Mom's pills. No, I would go even further back and remember to keep my journal hidden. Or maybe, keep my medal to myself and not try to get Owen's attention that afternoon after the social studies fair.

In a stunning ironic twist, Liam's death had divided us while simultaneously cementing our fates. I could not be around Owen because he was a constant reminder of my failures, a physical sign of the love I'll never have from my family.

But I also could not allow Owen to go unwatched, considering that at any moment he could ruin my tenuous hold on my peace of mind by sharing his suspicions or lies about me to my family or to the world.

I had come to this moment of indecision too many times to count over the course of the last twelve years. Each time I wrestle with the idea of how I could live differently, how I could let the past go and focus on my own future instead of Owen's. But I always come to the same conclusion: I can't. It's not who I am anymore. Maybe I never was. Maybe all three of us were broken from the beginning. And maybe I'm the worst one of all.

I got up and resigned myself to continuing along the same path. It was familiar to me now, like an old friend. It would seem counterproductive to anyone else to follow the very person I wished would get out of my life, but no one else has felt like I've felt and seen what I've seen.

No one else knew how evil Liam had been. It's inconceivable, but not impossible to think that my parents could've been aware of his enjoyment for torturing, hurting, and stealing from others. After all, depraved indifference seems to run in my family. Perhaps it's an inheritable trait, like blue eyes or a long nose.

I used to think that Owen didn't know the extent of Liam's behaviors like I did. Surely, he hadn't known how Liam acquired his collection of items that he kept hidden in his closet. It seemed mysterious to me when I first found them, but then took on a new meaning when I witnessed Liam's sins firsthand.

But Liam is dead.

So, more to the point, no one else knows how evil Owen is. It would be a mistake to try and live my life without knowing what he was up to or where he was going, like turning your back on a hungry alligator. Whether I like it or not, we are connected.

My next step would be to figure out where Owen went when he left my parents' house. So far, he'd traveled to Georgia, then three months later he showed up in Chicago.

In the time between wrapping up one article and beginning a new one, Owen had published several short series that focused on cold cases. He could write those articles from anywhere, but I would imagine he'd spent at least some of that time at home in Redmore.

Had Owen flown back to California immediately, and where would he go next to find a new story? The first story was near home and the second was near his college. It seemed like Owen was probably going to familiar places, which makes sense because then he'd be more comfortable with the people, businesses, press, and police.

But where else was personal to Owen? Where else would he feel confident enough to go? Maybe there was a way for me to manipulate where he'd show up next, to get back in control.

Chapter 18

*T*he tiny prescription bottle tucked into the pocket of my backpack was like a heavy weight pulling me down. It felt as if the straps were digging into my shoulders threatening to break me in half from the pressure. Part of me remained determined and strong, like a storm waiting to unleash its power. While another part of me had begun to whither in weakness and fear, trapped under the spell of revenge and retribution.

I had been floating through the last few weeks of school, trying my best to fade into the background of nonexistence that I once occupied in the minds of most of my peers. But ever since Liam passed out the copies of my journal pages, I hadn't been able to go unnoticed anymore.

Some would whisper when I walked by, but right out in the open, as if they wanted to appear to be secretive with their mouths behind their hands, but they also wanted me to know that they were talking about me. Others would cross the hall to walk on the other side away from me, or worse, narrow their eyes at me as if to say that what I'd done and said was unforgivable.

I decided to stop going to any function where I'd be required to participate in normal society. I was dead socially and some days I felt close to death physically.

I don't even go to the gardening club anymore. I told Mom I was still going every week, and she'd agreed to let me start walking home on my own. I'd sit down wherever I could to hide out and wait until the normal time the club would release us, then I'd start the short, lonely walk home. This little pill bottle and my plan to get back at Liam was my sword as well as my noose.

It wasn't a garden club day, but I trudged slowly along towards home, alone and depressed. Owen and I don't walk together after school anymore if he can avoid it. He doesn't spend time with any of us unless he must. I suppose he's trying to fade into the background in his own way.

Watching my feet move back and forth, never looking up, I was preoccupied thinking about how I could get the bottle into one of Liam's bags and who I'd want to discover it. It mattered who found the bottle. I didn't want it to be Mom or Dad. I wanted it to be someone who'd have to report it, or someone who could take away something important to him, someone like one of his coaches.

As soon as the screen door slammed behind me, I heard a scream of pain come from our next-door neighbor's house. I dropped my bag and ran back outside, looking toward where I'd heard the sound.

Our neighbor, Chris, was on the ground in the yard between our two houses, laying on his back, his left arm wrapped across his body clutching his right arm. He continued to scream like someone was stabbing him. His bike lay next to him on the ground, sticking out of a deep hole at an odd angle with the front tire almost entirely submerged.

I ran over to him, dropped to my knees, and yelled, "What happened?" so that he could hear me over his anguish.

With his eyes squeezed shut he wheezed, "Help!" and then began panting as he said, "It hurts so much!" over and over through clenched teeth.

I looked back at the arm he was clutching, and I could see a bone broken off and sticking out. Gagging, I turned away in horror. Then, I realized no one else was coming and I needed to get help.

I ran into his house and started calling out for his mom, who was usually home in the afternoons. She came walking quickly out of the back bedroom, confused but alert. She let me grab her by the hand and lead her outside. At the sight of Chris' injury, she burst into tears and called 911 with shaking fingers.

Chris Mays was a big kid, maybe even bigger than Liam. He played on Liam's basketball team and had begun to bulk up even more over the last school year while taking a weight training class in the off-season. There was no way the two of us could've lifted Chris off the ground and into the car and he was in too much pain to sit up on his own. I sat with them while we waited for the ambulance.

At first, Ms. Mays was rapidly firing questions, "What in the world is this giant hole doing here? Chris, did you not see this huge hole?"

Through pain and an air of exasperation, Chris managed to say, "No, why would I try to ride over something like that? There wasn't a hole. I didn't see a hole!"

He wasn't making much sense. I looked back at the bike. Clearly there was a hole about two feet wide and at least a foot deep. It was hard to miss. But Ms. Mays and I went back to calming Chris and comforting him and didn't ask any more about it.

The ambulance arrived within a few short minutes and loaded him up in the back. Ms. Mays climbed in, and they took off down the road. After they left, I sat momentarily bewildered from the whirlwind that had just occurred. When I realized I was still sitting on the ground next to Chris' blood, I shoved myself up to standing.

Chris' bike caught my attention, and I moved closer to it. For the first time, I noticed that there were broken sticks laying all around the perimeter of the hole. Inside the hole, there were more broken sticks, pine straw, and leaves lying along the bottom. It looked as if it had been covered with sticks and leaves, maybe to disguise it?

It was set up like a trap, like the ones you see in cartoons, where some unsuspecting character walks over the sticks and when they break, they fall in the hole, trapped. I took stock of the rest of the yard.

The hole was right in the middle of a well-worn bike trail that went between our houses and led down to the basement door of Chris' house. Every day, he would ride his bike home from school or practice and take that trail from the road to the basement entrance where he parked it.

There was a pile of fresh dirt next to the side of his house a couple of yards away. It appeared that someone had dug the hole and moved the dirt. Then, they covered it with sticks and pine straw and leaves in order to disguise it. But the only person who used that trail was Chris. So, this was a trap meant for Chris. *But who would do that?*

I pulled the bike from the hole. The front of the frame and the wheel were bent and would need to be repaired. Awkwardly, I guided it around the house and down to the Mays' backdoor where they could find it later. But when I got to the backdoor, it was open slightly. That seemed odd. Chris hadn't reached the door to open it and Ms. Mays had come out through the front door. I pulled it closed and walked back home.

Once inside, I grabbed my backpack from where I'd dropped it just inside the kitchen door and took it to my bedroom.

"Cara?" Owen's voice called from behind his closed door as I walked down the hallway.

I rolled my eyes. *How could he not have heard any of that commotion at all? Come to think of it, why hadn't Mom?* They'd both been home the entire time.

"What?" I called back while walking toward his doorway. I tried to turn the knob, but it was locked. I leaned my head against the door and spoke directly into the crack.

"Did you call me?"

Owen said, "Yeah, I was just wondering what took you so long to get home."

"I was here, but I went next door. Chris hurt himself! I had to go get his mom and she called 911! It was nuts! He wrecked his bike and broke his arm!" I was still worked up and a little freaked out about the whole thing.

"Oh. Well now it makes sense. I heard Liam looking for you and I thought it was weird that he didn't find you right away," he responded calmly. The news about Chris hadn't phased him at all.

"He must not have been looking very hard. I was basically in the front yard for the last thirty minutes," I mumbled back. I did not want Liam to be looking for me. I didn't want to see him at all.

"Wait a minute, why is he home already?" I asked Owen, sounding somewhat desperate even to my own ears.

Owen sighed loudly like he was getting tired of the conversation. He still hadn't bothered to open the door.

"I don't know. Something about repairs to the field so his practice was canceled for today. Mom brought him home a little while ago. Go ask him yourself."

"No thanks," I said to no one in particular.

Mom had come to our school and only picked up Liam. Of course, she did. She never remembers me. Mom probably hasn't even noticed that I'm walking home by myself every day and not just on the garden club days.

I realized how loudly Owen and I had been talking and looked around nervously expecting Liam to be waiting in the shadows to ambush me. Of course, he wasn't, but knowing he might be nearby put me on edge. I continued to my bedroom and stowed my backpack under my bed. I knew the pill bottle wasn't visible, but it felt like a burning, hot coal, shining as bright as a neon sign for all to see. I had to get rid of it, and soon.

On my way to get a snack, I happened to glance out the window on the other side of the kitchen. There was Liam, coming around the corner from the back of Chris' house, from the direction of his basement door. I felt like I was the one who'd been caught, and I darted to the wall beside the window to peer out from behind the curtain and watch what he was up to.

Liam looked around suspiciously as he glided up the bike path between the yards. When he reached the hole, he stopped and stared down at it for a few seconds, kicked at the ground a little where the blood had been, and a big smile appeared on his face. Liam was laughing.

Liam turned toward the house, and I saw that he had something inside his hoodie that he was holding up with his arm, trying not to let it slip out the bottom. He was walking toward the kitchen door, looking agitated, but excited. I sat down hastily in one of the chairs and grabbed a banana from the middle of the table, peeling it open in an attempt to look nonchalant.

He strolled smoothly through the door but came to an abrupt stop when he saw me. Smiling again, he said, "Oh, hey Care Bear. Afternoon snack?"

I just glared at him and kept my mouth closed tight. I wouldn't give Liam any fuel today.

"I don't know how you can eat after seeing Chris' nasty arm and all that blood. Weak little girls usually have weak little stomachs," he sneered.

I stared at him. *Had he watched the whole thing earlier?*

Liam seemed to consider me for a moment, drumming his fingers against whatever was underneath his hoodie, before adding, "But not you. You're hard core, right?"

Again, I didn't respond.

"So maybe you just needed a snack to get your writing strength up again? Getting ready to write some more juicy stories in your journal?"

I swallowed the acid rising in my throat. I couldn't take a bite of the banana, but I continued to hold it in front of me like it was my protection. Liam started to adjust the item he was hiding, but then suddenly pulled it out and set it roughly on the table.

It was a football, a red and black, UGA football with a signature written in Sharpie on the side. I looked at the football and looked up at Liam. He was smiling evilly, waiting for me to ask what he knew I wanted to ask.

"What's that?" I finally gave in.

"Well, genius, it's a football," he said. When I continued to stare at him, he said, "An autographed football that Chris was so proud of, to be exact. I don't know why he loved it so much, it's basically worthless."

"Did you steal it from him?"

He laughed a dry, abrasive chuckle. "It's not stealing when he owes me. I'm just collecting what I'm owed."

"But Chris is really hurt!" I cried.

Liam looked out the window and became serious once again. "I guess he's going to figure out that he shouldn't mess with me," then he looked back at me and said, "Isn't he?"

My expression must've been one of surprise or maybe disbelief because he began to grin again, feeding off my discomfort.

"Did you dig that hole?" I asked, not really wanting to know.

Liam leaned down into my face, close enough for me to feel his breath on my skin, and whispered, "I guess you'll never know." Then he stood up and walked out of the room, taking the football with him.

I let out the breath I didn't realize I was holding and sat there, mind blown. I had just come face to face with the true nature of Liam. He was getting worse. *Was this how he'd acquired all those things I'd found in that box? Was he hurting other people to collect the things they valued most? Was his sole purpose to break spirits like our father? Or was it just about getting what he wanted?*

Chris' pained expression floated into my thoughts. I couldn't let Liam do this to anyone else. I came to a decision for what felt like the hundredth time in the last few weeks. He had to pay. Liam had to lose what was most precious to him. He had to learn a lesson before he ruined anyone else's life, and before he ruined mine further. I would do whatever I had to do to survive.

Chapter 14

*A*s he spoke, Owen absent-mindedly adjusted the watch, pulling it forward toward his hand, sliding the face around to the inside of his wrist, then back to the top and pushing it higher up his arm, before reversing the maneuver and starting again. I'd seen him do this many times before. Maybe it was a nervous habit, or maybe just a peculiar compulsion. The rhythm of his movements mesmerized me as I tried to pay attention to what he was saying about the Warren Williams articles.

"... but in the end, I don't think Detective Abernathy really knew what he was doing. Poor guy. Big murder case with a high-profile victim and he didn't know if he was coming or going. I guess he was under a lot of pressure but was never able to make any arrests. I wonder if he still has a job?"

Owen's hands and watch grew still, breaking my trance, and I looked up to see a reflective expression settle on his face. I stole a glance at my phone, 3:55. *Just a little longer.* I slipped it back out of sight.

Before Owen took advantage of the lull in the conversation, I adjusted the contents of both pockets, and changed tactics.

"I'm not sure if I'd be very good at following clues like that and chasing down suspects. I'd like to think that most people are innocent," I said.

This time Owen's smile became fatherly and indulging. "Aw, come on, Cara. I know you. I know you figure things out quickly. And I know you learned to be suspicious of other people a long time ago."

I swallowed nervously, "I've done a lot of healing and growing up since then." Clearing my throat, I plowed on, unwilling to let him deter me again.

"Uh, so, how did you find out about the second case, the one near Northern? Were you already in the area?" I asked.

Owen rolled his lips in and out, and swapped feet to prop up on the other knee.

"Yeah, I went up to Evanston right after I left Mill City. Well, I did go home for a few weeks first. Chelsey was pissed that I didn't stay longer. But I was still feeling on top for once and I wasn't ready to take a break. I can't just stop writing. It doesn't work that way." He swept his arm at the park around us as if this meeting was also a disgraceful waste of time.

"I decided to head to another familiar place and use some of my connections," Owen continued. I stared at his hands while he spoke. He was still gesturing emphatically, seeming more agitated all the sudden.

"So, you found what you were looking for?" I encouraged, "A new story, right?"

Owen ran a hand through his hair and said, "Yeah, but not at first. A couple of people that I thought I'd be able to hook up with weren't there anymore. Last I'd heard, my buddy that I graduated with, Jackson, was a professor in their school of journalism, but it turns out he'd moved on."

"What did you do next?" I asked.

"Well, I contacted a few other people that I'd heard had stuck around the area, but I couldn't get in touch with any of them. It was frustrating."

He let out a loud huff as if he was describing something that had just happened. "After a few dead ends, I figured I'd try reacquainting myself with the area to see if I could meet some new people, maybe get some inspiration on a direction for my next story. I spent the next several weeks writing cold case stories and going out to spend time at bars and clubs."

A breeze blew through and ruffled our hair, diverting our attention to another bench several yards away where a young mother scrambled to collect the loose napkins that had blown from her child's hands. The little boy sat happily clutching his Wafel and Dinges sandwich, dripping with bananas, strawberries, and chocolate sauce, while the mom pawed at his sticky cheeks in vain.

I found myself smiling at her hovering and the child's obliviousness. In contrast, Owen's mouth was set in a grim line as he examined the scene. Was he thinking of our mother? She certainly was not the hovering, indulgent type.

After a slight head shake, Owen turned his attention back to our conversation and continued. "You know, you popped up in my thoughts a few times while I was in writing limbo."

"What? Why?"

"Well," Owen began as he absent-mindedly rubbed a hand across the back of his neck, "I know this will sound strange, but one time I was sitting in Other Brother, having coffee, making some phone calls, and I could've sworn I saw you out the window. I mean, it was just a glance, but it just felt like you were out there."

I stared at him, dumbfounded.

"So, I went out and around the corner to see if you'd walked by, but of course, you weren't there..." He paused, a questioning look in his eye, waiting for me to confirm this fact.

"Uh, nope. Not me. Weird, though." I laughed slightly and looked down at my hands in my lap, not wanting to look him in the eyes.

"Yeah, weird," he said flatly. "Well, anyway, when I got outside, there were a couple of girls, some students, who were sitting at those benches and one of them was really upset. I mean, like sobbing in public, upset. I saw she was drinking an Italian soda, so I went in and got her another and took it out to her. They were sweet and let me sit and chat with them a while. That was really the beginning of meeting people, after three weeks of nothing, just mingling and researching, and then finally getting some information about the area from some locals. So much has changed already in the six years since I lived there."

He smiled and said, "So, I guess you could say that you were the one that got me on the path to the next story. If I hadn't seen you, I mean, thought I'd seen you, then I wouldn't have gone outside."

I didn't know what to say to that. "Well, that's... um... good, I guess. Huh."

Owen straightened and stretched his back, pressing his hands into his hips. He glanced at his watch and said, "Do you mind if we walk around? I don't really want to sit here anymore."

"Oh, uh, I'd really like to just stay here. For a little while longer. Is that okay?" I needed him to keep talking to me. I took out my phone and swiped it to life, checking the time, 4:05.

Time seemed to be crawling by. This was becoming increasingly awkward and excruciatingly difficult to keep Owen's attention. He'd need to catch a ride to JFK for his flight very soon, he was already cutting it close, and I didn't want him to feel the need to leave suddenly.

"I just thought we could walk toward the exit while we wrap this up. It'll probably take me an hour just to get to the airport. I'm not missing my flight." Owen stood up and continued stretching as he spoke.

"No!" I half-shouted without thinking.

Owen stared at me for a second, questions in his eyes. He raised his eyebrows and tightened his mouth as if he'd tasted something bitter.

"Sorry. I just want to stay here for a few more minutes. That's all. I just feel like..." I searched for a reason, any reason. "...I just get distracted. By the city, I mean. I just feel like I can focus on the conversation if we just sit here and finish talking..." My voice trailed off under Owen's quelling look.

"Sure, Cara. Sure." He rolled his eyes dramatically and sighed as he sat back down. "I'm leaving at exactly 4:15. You've got ten minutes." He looked down at his watch again and said, "Nine, actually."

Feeling panicky once again, I blurted out, "Tell me more about Derrick Hoffman. Did you ever meet him?"

Owen tilted his head and regarded me with an amused expression, holding back a secret. But it seemed I'd hooked his attention once more. He settled back on the bench as he prepared to tell me his story.

"In fact, I did meet him. It was somewhat fortuitous, I guess. Of course, how could I have predicted that he'd be dead two weeks later? But it did give me a personal perspective on how to structure the articles," he said.

A shadow crossed Owen's face. "Have you ever met someone that you just knew was destructive? Someone who was an absolute typhoon of devastation and pain to everyone around them?"

He turned to face me with a knowing look. "I suppose that's a rhetorical question. Of course, you have," he grinned widely as my thoughts faded into the past, lost in memories.

I thought back to a time late in May 2009, when Owen had disappeared again the afternoon before, and this time he'd stayed away much longer than he ever had, not coming home until after midnight the following day. I don't think Mom slept at all. I awoke several times to hear her pacing in the hallway, not avoiding the creaky boards in the floor as she worried over his absence.

After she and I had almost finished eating a silent dinner the next night, steadfastly ignoring each other and most of the food on our plates, Dad arrived home in one of his common-place bad moods. As soon as the door opened, she pounced on him, begging him to tell her what they should do.

"Rita, he's eighteen. He's going to graduate next week and then he'll be moving and won't even live with us anymore. I hardly think we can expect him to check in all the time. He's probably been writing the whole time anyways," he responded, with an undisguised air of impatience, waving the thought away with his hand.

Mom followed behind him like a little terrier, nipping at his heels. "Yes, I know, but he was so rude to me before he left, and who knows..."

"Oh, for the love of..." Dad stopped short of swearing and looked up at the ceiling, searching for answers.

At this point, Mom's tears were freely flowing, and she dabbed at her swollen eyes with a tissue as she continued between sobs and deep breaths, "It's just that... how did I... when did I lose both of my sons? I've lost all my children!"

I averted my eyes back to the uneaten dinner laying cold on my plate. This was a frequent complaint from my mother. And how could I deny it?

Liam was dead. For the last two years, Owen's and Mom's relationship had continued to deteriorate. All that existed now were their daily arguments filled with words laced in hatred and hurt thrown from both sides. And when it came to her third child, me, I'm certain everyone saw exactly what I was, a hollow shell, withdrawn, depressed, and wasting away from the inside out.

Dad whipped around suddenly causing Mom to run into his chest as she spoke. He put both hands roughly around her upper arms, holding her in place, and spoke vehemently through clenched teeth.

"Do not push him. Do not continue to nag him. Do you hear me?" He shook her back and forth as he finished his question. "Let it go and leave him alone. Period."

Dad punctuated his point with a hard shove that made Mom stumble back a few steps before running into the wall, then he stalked off down the hall, loosening his tie as he went.

She did not respond again. She never did once she realized she'd pushed Dad as far as she could. My Mom was never brave enough to stand up for herself. I knew she wouldn't bring it up again. She'd continue to grieve, wallowing in her anguish. I was sure I'd encounter her on many nights to come, pacing, crying, fretting. But she would suffer in silence.

I gritted my teeth and closed my eyes to the anger that washed over me. My family had never been whole, but the last three years had been hell. Everything had worsened with Liam the year before he died, but it felt as if his disease had saturated into the rest of us after he was gone.

I wandered away from the kitchen, leaving Mom to clean up. I knew she wanted to be alone. I passed Owen's bedroom door and curiosity gripped me. I hadn't snooped in a long time, instead just keeping an eye on him as best I could without drawing any attention to myself. I had no desire to be caught again.

I inched Owen's door open slowly, half expecting him to leap out and stop me. His room was in chaos. Every inch was in disarray. Except for the desk. There was an empty space in the center, creating a perfect outline of where his laptop would sit. On either side lay sticky notes, pens and pencils, a rainbow of highlighters, stacks of papers, and a small clock, neatly organized and arranged.

I walked over, eyeing the layout without touching any of the items. Owen was always writing, whether it was here, out on the porch, or away from the house, he never seemed to stop. My curiosity increasing, I began pulling open the drawers on each side.

The largest drawer on the bottom left was packed full of file folders, each one labeled and hanging in alphabetical order. The first file said, "Anthony," and the last one said, "Westlake." I knew that Owen's best friend's name was Anthony.

I pulled out the folder and peeked inside. It appeared to be notes about his friend's life. There were several handwritten pages of facts, anecdotes, a couple of crude timelines, and even some printed pictures, all centered around Anthony.

"Wow. What a weirdo," I thought. *"What could he possibly need this information for?"* I supposed that this was the kind of

thing that a writer might do if he is preparing to write about a certain person or topic. Maybe this was like research. Then I wondered, was this research for a fictional character based on Anthony or was Owen going to write about Anthony. *"I sincerely hope he never told Owen any of his secrets,"* I thought ominously as I replaced the folder.

Looking over the rest of the folder tabs, I realized that each one was the name of a person in Owen's life, or the name of a place nearby. *"This must be why he's always writing in that notebook. He takes notes on everything!"*

Then, my eyes fell on a folder labeled "Cara." My breath caught in my throat and my mouth went dry as I impulsively snatched the folder from its metal cradle, ripping it open and almost dropping the contents on the floor. I steadied my hands and laid the bulging folder open on top of the desk.

The first page seemed to be a description of me: my likes and dislikes, preferences, favorites, and personality traits. There were many edits and additions. I could see erasure marks underneath some of the newer writing, comments written in a reckless, rushed manner, clearly penned in agitation. Some of the lines were etched deeply into the paper.

Three words at the bottom of the page, "unpredictable-sneaky- dangerous", flashed in my vision like a neon sign. A little too roughly, I flipped that page over to read the next. It did nothing to calm me down.

Rifling quicker through the pages, I found recounts of our visits to the counselor, in which I'm a sniveling, angry mess.

Owen's description wasn't too far outside reality, but his narration sounded accusatory.

I flipped back toward the front of the folder and came across several pages of stories regarding my arguments with Liam. Owen's writings contained surprisingly accurate details about my conversations with our middle brother, almost as if he was there.

I felt exposed and embarrassed, the old wounds fresh and raw once again. Anger and frustration shot through me, my fingers gripped and crinkled the edge of the paper. I slammed the offending sheet down on the desk. This was a bad idea. I knew how Owen felt about me, or at least I suspected as much. Reading his words, hearing his thoughts and opinions, a stone began to form at the base of my throat, and I couldn't swallow.

As I restacked the papers to replace the folder in the drawer, the edge of a sticky note protruding from the middle poked me in the palm and caught my eye. I turned to the page it was marking.

It was a story. It was a story about the day Liam died. I began to read and couldn't stop. I read line after line, sentence after sentence, simultaneously enraptured and outraged. Every word was an accusation. I don't know how long I stood there, pouring over the writing, analyzing the phrases. My fear held me hostage and I couldn't move until I reached the conclusion.

Finally, the last paragraphs floated into view.

"*Cara never recovered. And how could she? Seeing your brother die, watching his life slip quickly away, would send anyone into a depressive state. But to actually commit the crime? One would suffer a much greater trauma in causing the death. Cara planned, plotted, and carried out the perfect crime. After luring our brother into the woods and to the precipice created by the rock outcropping, Cara pushed Liam violently, causing him to fall and hit his head perfectly on the boulder at the base of the hill.*

Whether or not she intended for him to die is not the point. She intended harm. Cara wanted to hurt Liam. Perhaps it's not entirely her fault. I've suspected for some time that she suffers from antisocial personality disorder. Cara has a clear disregard for others, even members of her own family. Whatever the source of her anger and deceit, the fact remains that she is dangerous. I can no longer afford to allow her to get closer to me. I will not fall prey to her manipulation. I will not end up like Liam."

I stood breathless and stunned. How could Owen do this to me? How could he write this down? Had he shared it with anyone? Did he plan to?

I closed the folder quickly and cradled it against my chest. I suddenly became concerned that I'd spent too much time in Owen's bedroom and retreated to my own room, still clutching the folder to me. I held it out and stared at it, like it might catch fire any second, afraid to continue holding it, but also afraid to let it go.

Sitting next to Owen in the park, my eyes closed briefly, remembering. In the days following my discovery, I was able to get rid of the folder and destroy Owen's writing. But I was never able to let it go from my mind. I was never able to let go of Owen from then on.

Opening my eyes and seeing Owen's smug face brought my blood to boiling. With every ounce of willpower I had left, I shoved the indignation deep within me. *Breathe in. Breathe out. Keep your composure. There. I did it. I'm still here.*

I smoothed my hair, sat up straighter, and looked him in the eyes. Owen's confidence faltered under my gaze, and I watched the hesitation play across his features.

"So, you're saying that Derrick Hoffman was destructive? To who?" I was so proud to sound steady and in control.

"Er, yeah," he seemed disappointed with my reaction. "The guy was terrible."

Mentally patting myself on the back, I let out a soft, shaky breath while Owen continued. I didn't want to accidentally reveal how close I'd come to breaking down.

"But you read the article, right? I mentioned most of his bad behavior. You know, even after five different women reported him to the police, nothing was done? It's amazing what money can buy, how many sheep it can influence."

"He's the one who drugged the girls and raped them?" I asked.

"Rape. Assault. Whatever he was in the mood for. And the fact that he was so out in the open about it... It's a wonder that he was allowed to remain a student at Northern after the second report. Or for that matter, it's absolutely mind-blowing that women continued to talk to him. Apparently, everyone knew his reputation." Owen was visibly seething now, his hands clenched, knuckles white, eyes pulled together in a scowl.

I decided it was now or never. I just had to dive into the abyss and hope to survive. It was time to finally get to the point.

"And what do you know about how he died?" I blurted out. Owen opened his mouth to speak, but I held up a hand to stop him and clarified, "I mean, how he actually died. I want you to tell me what you know about the moment he died, not the details you reported afterwards."

Stunned, he gaped at me open-mouthed. I don't recall ever seeing him so thrown off balance. I was perched on the edge of the bench, legs bent, ready to bolt at a moment's notice if necessary because I couldn't predict what his reaction would be, and that scared me.

I watched Owen's face carefully. His eyes roved back and forth, searching his thoughts for what he should say, what he should reveal. Seeming to come to a decision, he got eerily still, staring down at his hands, or maybe his watch. He looked up then, his face composed, but shrouded in a darkness that sent my heart galloping.

When he spoke, his voice came out calm, but as hard as steel and as sharp as a knife. "Well, Care Bear, perhaps you should tell me what you know about how he died. I gather you could tell me how Warren Williams and Johnny Rowe died as well," he mused. "Maybe you know everything. Maybe you're just as dangerous as you've always been. And maybe this is the end of the road for you."

Chapter 20

TODAY TIMES

THE NATIONAL AUTHORITY ON TODAY'S NEWS

Sunday, March 10, 2019   *Since 2012*

~NEWSWORTHY~
Apparent overdose: First Time? Or Foul Play?
Evanston, Illinois
BY OWEN WALSH

A 22-year-old man found dead in an alleyway off of North Kent Avenue behind the Quick Food Mart was identified Friday by the Cook County medical examiner. Derrick Hoffman, of Trenton, New Jersey, died of a heroin overdose, according to a news release from the Cook County Medical Examiner's Office. Hoffman's death would not be an unusual story for the area, typically known for a high rate of drug use and crime, except for the fact that he is not a resident of the neighborhood where he was found, nor is he ever reported to have visited there.

Derrick Hoffman, a student in his senior year of the Kimber School of Management at Northern University in Evanston, maintained high grades in the challenging Kimber classes, and was also an active member in several of its notable clubs. His parents, Dr. Julius Hoffman and Mrs. Margaret Hoffman both hold prestigious positions in the community where they live in Trenton. Dr. Hoffman is the CEO of Robert Wood Johnson University Hospital Hamilton, and Mrs. Hoffman is the Executive Director of One Big Wish, a nonprofit that uses technology to raise awareness about adoption and connects donors to children who may be coming from difficult situations.

Gerald Brown, the night shift manager of the Quick Food Mart, called police around 4:00 AM last Thursday morning, after a customer reported seeing someone lying next to the back door of the building. "The guy was just laying there, kind of peaceful looking, like he was taking a nap. Except he had a needle hanging out of his arm and he didn't move or wake up when I shook his shoulder," said Brown.

Brown also went on to say that he wasn't surprised at first. This recent death came after a busy weekend when officers in Evanston responded to about twenty overdose calls, five of which were fatal. "But after I got a good look at him, saw his nice clothes, expensive watch and shoes and all that, I knew this was kinda weird," said Brown.

It has been reported that Hoffman died of acute intoxication from heroin and fentanyl. Although the cause of death has been determined through autopsy, Detective Miller has declared this to be an open and on-going investigation.

I was able to speak with Detective Miller and inquire as to why this overdose death was not a straightforward case. "There hasn't been any evidence recovered yet to suggest that the deceased went through any type of trauma or struggle. However, at the request of his family we are hoping to figure out how someone with no known drug habit, and no history of ever visiting the area where he was found, died in this seemingly sudden way."

Investigators will begin working to determine how Derrick Hoffman arrived at the Quick Food Mart. His car remained in his parking spot at the apartment complex where he lived. Did Hoffman travel here alone without his car, or was he brought here? They will check store, bus, and street camera footage, as well as interview family and friends, and any possible witnesses in the area.

The attorney and spokesperson for the Hoffman family, Debra Winship, said, "This case is painfully tragic, and Mr. and Mrs. Hoffman are devastated over the sudden loss of their beloved son. Substance use disorder is an issue that countless families *suffer from each year. However, we ask the public to refrain from making any rash judgment and to respect the family's privacy at this difficult time. We are hopeful for some answers soon and the family will be offering a $10,000 reward to anyone having information pertinent to solving this case [as determined by the detectives and police in charge]."*

Did Derrick Hoffman use heroin or fentanyl regularly? If so, how was he able to hide his use and where did he get the drugs? If not, why did he use them this time? How would someone else force Hoffman into injecting heroin without also injuring him in other ways?

If Hoffman did not drive his own car to North Kent Avenue, did he walk the hour distance, take the bus, or ride with an unknown person?

Follow me through this investigation as I hope to give our Today Times readers an opportunity to assist law enforcement in determining the reason for this tragic death. The next Newsworthy edition will focus on the details that have been uncovered by detectives so far, as well as my firsthand experience of visiting the scene.

If you have any information, please call 847-212-6634.

TODAY TIMES

THE NATIONAL AUTHORITY ON TODAY'S NEWS

Wednesday, March 13, 2019   *Since 2012*

~NEWSWORTHY~
Missing Evidence, Mysterious Crime
Evanston, Illinois
BY OWEN WALSH

In a city where your chance of being a victim of a drug-related crime may be as high as 1 in 131 in its central neighborhoods, why would a well-known, successful, and affluent student attending Northern University be found dead in one such neighborhood? The death of Derrick Hoffman last week has brought Evanston, Illinois under the microscope of the public eye. The mysterious circumstances have left many wondering how this could happen to someone like Hoffman.

Derrick was last seen Wednesday afternoon leaving a study group that was meeting at the University Library. He told friends that he'd see them at the Gamma Sigma Kappa fraternity house on Sheridan Road at 7PM for the Spring Formal. Friends reported that he did not intend on bringing a date to the event, so his absence wasn't noticed right away. "He never showed up. We weren't freaked out at first but then later on when no one had seen him all night, we started to worry," said Tony Goodroe, the Vice President of Gamma Sigma Kappa, of which Hoffman was a member.

Police found a Starbucks receipt in Hoffman's apartment indicating that he stopped there around 3:45 PM on his way home from the study session. There is video footage of him arriving home alone at 4:10 PM, parking his Lexus GX in the parking lot, and going inside the apartment, but no evidence that he left after that. His cell phone was found sitting on his kitchen counter and police will be unable to track his movements through its signal.

Although he didn't show up to the party that he was expected to attend, no one called the police to report him missing. It seems no one was aware that anything was wrong until the 4:00 AM 911 call reporting the discovery of a dead body in the alleyway behind the Quick Food Mart.

Hoffman died of acute intoxication from heroin and fentanyl. He was found lying on his back, one arm draped across his chest and the other next to his side, with a tourniquet wrapped tightly around his bicep and a needle still inserted in his vein. The customer and manager who reported finding the body said that Mr. Hoffman appeared to be sleeping, his face calm and his eyes closed. He had his wallet in his pocket, an expensive watch on his wrist, and designer shoes on his feet, so he does not appear to have been robbed, and he has no injuries.

I was able to speak with Detective Kristin Miller, the lead investigator for this case, and she said, "We have uncovered evidence that Mr. Hoffman may have been brought to this area against his will, but I cannot give you those details at this time. What I can tell you is that we will not rest until we find who committed this terrible crime."

Detective Miller and her team allowed me to visit the scene on Monday. Derrick's body was found near the rear door of the Quick Food Mart, on an alley road where cars do not drive. "The only people that walk back there or come that way live nearby and it's like their shortcut," said manager Gerald Brown. "No one would go back there unless they was coming to my store or maybe if they was meeting someone back there, you know, for buying drugs or something."

There was no blood anywhere along the alley road. There were no suspicious items found that appear to be related to Hoffman's death. There are no recent tire tracks or footprints. The Quick Food Mart does not have working cameras in the back of the store. The camera posted at the front entrance captured a dark-colored vehicle driving past, toward the back alley, around the same time the police estimate Hoffman to have died. In the video, the license plate is not visible, so the owner of the car has not been identified. However, it is still unclear at this time whether Hoffman died at the scene or beforehand, so investigators are unable to say with certainty if the vehicle in question was involved.

It seems the police have been left with a complex mystery. The cause of death has been determined, but not the manner. It is still unclear if the scene where Mr. Hoffman was found is also the place where he died. No one has been able to ascertain whether Hoffman was with anyone, or how he arrived on North Kent Avenue. His car and phone were not with him when he was found.

With the knowledge that detectives believe that Derrick Hoffman was brought to this location against his will, I do not believe that he was a regular user of heroin or fentanyl. How was he coerced, or perhaps, forced to inject the drugs?

Who would want Derrick Hoffman to die, and in this way?

When did Hoffman leave his apartment, and with who? Or was someone meeting him? If he left home on his own volition, why would he leave his phone behind?

The next Newsworthy edition will focus on my interview with Derrick Hoffman's family and friends. Who was he? Is there any-thing about Mr. Hoffman's lifestyle or past that might explain why his life was cut short? I will also report on any other evidence that has been recovered.

If you have any information, please call 847-212-6634.

TODAY TIMES

THE NATIONAL AUTHORITY ON TODAY'S NEWS

Sunday, March 17, 2019   *Since 2012*

~*NEWSWORTHY*~
Victimizer Turned Victim
Evanston, Illinois
BY OWEN WALSH

On Wednesday, March 7, Derrick Hoffman walked away from the Northern University Library and was not seen alive by friends again. The circumstances of his death are extremely mysterious and have left investigators without much to go on.

So far, we know Hoffman arrived alone at his apartment on Ingleside Place. Cameras recorded Hoffman pulling into and parking in the lot, entering his apartment, but not exiting again. It is possible that he left through a back door, but if this is the case, he was most likely not alone since he left his car behind. He also left his phone behind, which is uncharacteristic of Mr. Hoffman's normal behavior.

None of the cameras around the Quick Food Mart on North Kent Avenue have any incriminating footage to help police determine

222

when and how Hoffman arrived on the scene. Derrick Hoffman died of acute intoxication at 2:30 AM but was not found next to the Quick Food's back entrance until around 4:00 AM.

I spent some time with Detective Miller and her team recently, as they amped up their investigation into Hoffman's death. I was able to hear more about the evidence recovered that has persuaded the investigators to think that this mystery may well prove the result of foul play.

"Both of Mr. Hoffman's wrists had a sticky residue on the skin left from duct tape, indicating that his hands were bound a short time before his body was found," said Miller. "The medical examiner found a puncture mark in Mr. Hoffman's neck, made by a medical-grade needle. Pending a further toxicology report to determine what he was injected with, this discovery tells us that someone may have given him some kind of sedative, which would explain either how he arrived on North Kent or how someone could forcibly inject drugs into his system without harming him any other way."

This new evidence is shocking. It's difficult to imagine a scenario that would prompt anyone to commit this type of crime. Does this mean that the case is a homicide? Do detectives have any suspects?

I wanted to know more about Derrick in order to figure out how this came to be his fate, so I interviewed a few of his friends and acquaintances. *"Derrick was the life of every party. He knew how to get people to talk to him. And he definitely knew how to get things done. If you put Derrick on the job, things just started happening,"* said Mario Bautista, a fellow Gamma Sigma Kappa and former roommate. *"Well, he just had his ways. I've never really known him to not get what he wants,"* said another friend, Georgia Evans.

The perspective I heard from some of his acquaintances- his class-mates- shed a different light on the 22-year-old business major student. "I never trusted him. I heard a bunch of messed up stuff about him a few years ago. I don't know, but I heard it more than once. I can't say what," said one student, who asked to remain anonymous.

"Derrick was troubled. We all knew that" said Shirley Rountree, Hoffman's aunt. *"His mama and daddy never wanted to open their eyes to it, but it's always been there. I wish we could've helped him. I wouldn't be surprised if he'd finally gone too far."* I tried to contact Derrick's parents and sister to get their reaction to these quotes, but they declined to comment.

I started looking into Northern's campus crime and incident reports. I was not able to access many of the campus police records. However, I was surprised to learn through various sources that Derrick Hoffman had been named in eight different "incidents". Five of the reports were made by female students and accused him of adding Rohypnol (more commonly called "Ruffies") into their drinks. All five women were raped. Two of the victims also suffered brutal beatings, another was choked and fractured a finger, and a fourth suffered some internal injuries.

In three of the five cases, Hoffman was suspected, but no proof could be found on his person or in his car or residence, and no DNA evidence has been recovered. In the fourth case, a witness came forward to confirm the accusation, saying that he saw Hoffman put something in the glass of the victim, but still Derrick was not charged with the crime.

The most shocking case, in my opinion, was the most recent report. The situation was very different in that the scene of the crime was not a party or a bar with a large group of people. The victim, a freshman attending Northern, stated that she was house-sitting for a friend and was there alone. She says Mr. Hoffman came to visit her and brought a bottle of wine. The young lady became unconscious at some point during the evening. When she awoke, she was alone and sensed that something was wrong. She immediately went to the ER where they performed a rape kit, as well as a drug screener on her. The victim was found to have been drugged and raped.

Charges were pressed against Hoffman. He was arrested but made bail quickly after spending only one night in jail. Once the family lawyer, Debra Winship, intervened, charges were soon dropped. Ms. Winship claimed that "the woman who filed this report has a personal vendetta against Derrick Hoffman, and police have no evidence, no witnesses, and no basis to pursue him as a suspect for this terrible crime."

It seems that there was much more to Derrick Hoffman than just the image that he wanted the world to see. The fact that he was accused of drugging women and then forcibly controlling them, adds an extra layer of intrigue to his mysterious death.

Although Hoffman didn't have his phone or car with him, could searching each of them shed more light on his movements the night he died? What will the toxicology report reveal about what he may have been drugged with?

The next Newsworthy edition will focus on Derrick Hoffman's phone records, the results of searching his vehicle, as well as the final report from the medical examiner. Will Detective Miller and her team be able to solve this mysterious death?

If you have any information, please call 847-212-6634.

TODAY TIMES

THE NATIONAL AUTHORITY ON TODAY'S NEWS

Wednesday March 20, 2019   *Since 2012*

~NEWSWORTHY~
A Life Interrupted
Evanston, Illinois
BY OWEN WALSH

"Mr. Hoffman should still be alive. Whoever perpetrated this crime had no right to take his life," said Detective Kristin Miller, lead investigator in Derrick Hoffman's death. "Whether or not he's a sympathetic victim, it's still a life interrupted. It's still a crime, a heinous crime." Detective Miller seems especially agitated after almost two weeks on the case without much progress.

Miller has worked many hours to create a timeline of Mr. Hoffman's movements on the day of his death. At 3:45 PM, he left a study session held at the University Library and went to the Starbucks on Sherman Avenue. Friends say that although there was another Starbucks closer to the library, the one on Sherman was his preferred spot, and so this out of the way route home was not unusual. Hoffman arrived at the coffee shop at

4:02 PM, picked up his mobile order from the drive-thru, and pulled into his apartment complex parking lot at 4:10 PM.

Phone records show that Hoffman made three phone calls between 4:30 PM and 10:00 PM: one to his sister, another to Robbie Johnson, a friend attending the Spring Formal at the Gamma Sigma Kappa house where Hoffman was supposed to be, and the third to his apartment complex's front office. The phone call to his sister at 4:56 PM lasted only twenty seconds because she did not pick up. Hoffman did not leave a message.

At 8:00 PM, an hour after Hoffman should've arrived at the social event, a call was placed from his phone to Robbie Johnson. Johnson picked up but claims he couldn't hear whether Derrick was saying anything because the music in the house was too loud. Johnson hung up, assuming he'd see Derrick later on that evening.

The third call to the apartment complex's front office was made at 9:52 PM. The office closes at 9:00 PM and all calls are transferred to the company's answering service. The call from Hoffman's phone was cut off as soon as the representative answered.

Hoffman did not drive his car again after arriving home that afternoon. Detective Miller and her team performed a thorough search of his vehicle earlier this week. Several fingerprints were lifted and identified, those individuals were questioned and ruled out as suspects.

Detective Miller shared with me that they also found several unidentified fingerprints on Hoffman's backdoor and in several rooms inside the apartment that seem to belong to one individual. She stated that the person is a suspect, but they have no other comparisons to use to determine who the prints belong to at this time.

No one spoke to Hoffman again or saw him until 4:00 AM when he was found next to the Quick Food Mart rear entrance. Investigators have combed carefully through the video footage of the apartment complex where he lived. The manager of Ingleside Place admits that the cameras are only focused on the parking lot and front entrances to the apartments, but that there are several paths and entrances along the sides and the back of the buildings that are not monitored.

Detective Kristin Miller explained her theory of the crime in our last interview together. She believes that someone Hoffman knew showed up at his backdoor sometime between 6:00 PM and 1:00 AM because there are no signs of a break-in or struggle. Death from Opioid overdose usually occurs 1 to 3 hours after injection, rather than suddenly. Since Hoffman's time of death was 2:30 AM, Miller believes that whoever visited him incapacitated him through sedation using Ketamine injected into a vein in his neck. After about ten minutes, he would've been easily injected a second time with a lethal combination of heroin and fentanyl, especially once his hands and feet were bound with duct tape.

Once Hoffman was in a drugged state, he could've been moved to a vehicle, driven to the Quick Food Mart alley, and left there sometime before 4:00 AM when he was found. It's also possible that Hoffman was led to a waiting car after the Ketamine was injected, rendering him more susceptible to suggestion and more easily manipulated. Once in the car, the perpetrator could then inject the lethal combination. No fingerprints were found on the needle left at the scene.

Regardless of the order of the events that led to Hoffman being dumped in the alleyway, Detective Miller is adamant that there is a witness to this crime that hasn't come forward yet. "It doesn't seem likely that this homicide, with this level of planning and premeditation, could be pulled off without a witness, or someone with prior knowledge, or any kind of evidence trail. There's always another clue and we'll find it."

The case will remain open, and investigators are hopeful in finding the person or persons responsible for the death of Derrick Hoffman. His family and friends, as well as Detective Miller and the Cook County police department, implore the public to keep Derrick's death fresh in their minds. "It's a travesty of justice," says Detective Miller. Tony Goodroe, Hoffman's friend and fraternity brother, shares Miller's sentiment and added "Derrick deserves justice. It's not about who's a good person or not. Murder is murder."

If you have any information, please call 847-212-6634.

PART 3:

THE CONCLUSION

"The boundaries which divide Life from Death are at best shadowy and vague. Who shall say where one ends, and where the other begins?"

~ Edgar Allan Poe, *The Premature Burial*

Chapter 21

I hate these cases, thought Detective Donald Mackie, or Mac, as his colleagues called him. *Why did it have to be a kid?* He'd worked scenes with juvenile victims before, but they made his heart ache every time. No matter the age, it always reminded Mac of his son, Joseph. The first time, the little boy had been the same age as Joseph. The first time, had almost changed his mind about being a cop.

The two-year-old's tiny body and still-baby features were mangled and distorted in such disturbing ways it made his stomach churn. Mac rushed outside of the tiny trailer they'd filed into that morning, into the blindingly beautiful sunny day, and barely got his face over the porch railings before he started vomiting. The sounds of his retching were in stark contrast to the peaceful gurgling of a nearby, crude water feature set up in the neighbor's yard.

A few of the more veteran officers smiled grimly as they passed by, but no one commented. They had all experienced that first time at some point in their careers. "Don't worry about it, Mac. You never get used to it really," his lieutenant had lamented as he roughly patted him on the shoulder. Mac glanced up to see the ghost of some terrible memory slide from the older man's face.

Still, he didn't want to appear weak, never wanted to be seen as a rookie, even when he was so green, he practically ran to murder scenes in his eagerness to prove himself. Mac had wiped his face, downed a bottle of water, and took a couple of deep breaths in preparation for returning to the dark trailer. How could he, or anyone really, steady themselves enough to go back and objectively view the body of the small, dead boy?

In his defense, Mac didn't expect the toddler to look so much like raw meat. He hadn't stopped to think about what it might look like for skin to be peeled away from muscle, or for bones to be sticking out of places that they're not supposed to be.

An hour earlier, the two-year-old hadn't been strapped into a car seat and was instead sitting in his six-year-old sister's lap in the backseat while the father smoked a blunt on their way home from his dealer's house. The sister either lost control of holding him or lost interest, the boy managed to open the door while the car was moving, fell out, and was run over by his dad's car as well as the one behind it.

After being dragged along the asphalt for a few feet, the boy's face and chest were almost unrecognizable. The panicked father quickly grabbed the child off the pavement, got back in the car, and drove the last few miles home, clutching the boy to his chest, before calling 911.

Mac shook the thoughts from his head as he focused on the current tragedy. This scene was not nearly as bad as that. But still. A child. And another victim that's the same age as Joseph, now thirteen. Absolutely too young to die.

The young man looked peaceful, lying still, eyes closed. There was a large amount of blood puddled around the back of his head that had started to congeal and darken. Immediately noticeable were the two bloody, child-size handprints on either cheek. They were obscene and out of place.

As Mac took in the surrounding area, he felt trapped in a dichotomy. Nature remained pure and untouched by death, a visible contrast to the lifeless boy laying at the base of the rock wall. The sun was still shining brightly, just beginning its descent toward the horizon, trees swaying in a gentle breeze. He even heard a bird chirping in the distance during lulls in the hushed conversations around him.

"Detective," his thoughts were interrupted by Officer Abernathy. "The body has been identified as Liam Walsh, thirteen years old. When we arrived, his younger sister and older brother were here. The brother, Owen Walsh, fifteen years old, called 911. The sister, Cara Walsh, eleven years old, was hysterical and covered in blood. Rameriz drove them both to the station and their parents are meeting them there. We were able to contact the mother first and I believe she called the father. Where do you want to start?"

Mac took a deep breath and let it out with a huff. "Anything in his pockets?"

Abernathy rolled his lips in and out, sighed, and said, "yeah, a plastic bag of Prozac and one batting glove. According to the brother and sister, his phone was in his hand. The sister removed it to call the other brother, Owen. He ran here, their house is less than half a mile, that direction."

"Who touched the body?" Mac asked as he walked around the deceased, trying to look at every angle.

"Those are the sister's handprints," Abernathy said as he pointed to the bloody marks on the dead boy's face. "And we know she pulled Liam's phone from his hand, but we didn't get much from her..." he looked uncomfortable. "She just kept screaming and crying. There was a bunch of snot and blood and nonsense coming out." He rubbed the back of his neck and up to the top of his head, cleared his throat, and continued, "The older brother, Owen, said he only touched the neck, checking for a pulse."

Mac wrote some thoughts in his pocket notebook, tapped the pen on the edge of it, then said, "Well, how far out is the ME?"

"Ten minutes."

"Alright. Let's tape off this area, even though I doubt anyone's gonna show up in the middle of the woods. Make sure the crew is collecting any and every item, trash, whatever. Tell them to be looking for any and all signs of disturbance and blood. Let's bag everything possible to bag, better to have too much, than not enough. Oh, and please make sure that the other family members are already at the station. I'm headed there next."

Officer Abernathy trotted off to relay the orders and keep the scene running smoothly. Mac stared at the victim's face. *How did he get out here in the woods? Was he with anyone? Why is he wearing a baseball uniform? Did he fall off this ridge?*

Questions buzzed through Mac's head as he paced around. Looking at the granite outcropping again and the position of Liam's body, it seemed odd that the boy could fall from the top and land in this position with his feet facing the rocks, lying on his back. It's more likely that he may have been trying to climb up the rocks, fell backwards, and hit his head.

Mac noticed a brick-sized rock near Liam's head, smeared with blood. The rock wasn't embedded in the soil and seemed to Mac to have been dislodged from another location. He made a note to try and locate where the rock may have originated. A fly buzzed by his face and brought him abruptly back to the body. *It doesn't take long in the heat, does it?*

Mac felt so bad for the boy's parents. It was a small mercy that they'd never have to have this image of Liam lying here in their memories. The same couldn't be said for his siblings.

After a few more conversations with officers and giving them some directives for the remaining afternoon light, he decided it was time to face the family members and begin the interviews. Mac would never admit it to anyone, but he was procrastinating. Talking to a parent about the death of their child was the number one thing on his list of 'Things I Never Want to Do Again.'

The station sat nestled in the middle of the downtown area of their small city, a short distance from the scene. Mac drove in silence, slowly winding down a few extra roads he didn't really need to take so he could consider the facts in the case so far. After parking in his usual spot, then calmly strolling to the entrance, he began gathering his thoughts as he approached the front doors. His hand on the door handle, Mac could hear a loud wailing coming from inside.

The girl seemed so small in her temporary clothes. The loaned disposable coveralls were swallowing her, especially as she burrowed as much of herself as she could into her mother's arms. Mac could see the dried blood on the backs of the little hands that tightly gripped Rita Walsh's sleeves.

As the door to the interview room shut behind him, the girl jolted upright and continued silent-scream-crying as she stared at him. Her mouth gaped open as she seemed to emit a low wale, eyes teary and wild, sending streams down her blood and mud-stained cheeks.

That was the toughest interview Mac's ever conducted. By far. The brother and father were much easier in comparison. The father, Frank, in his mid-forties, hair graying at the temples, sat still, visibly composed, but clearly clinging to the edges of a shattered heart.

Mac could tell his middle son had meant the world to him. There were several times that Frank Walsh started a sentence, only to begin stuttering, cut himself off abruptly, and clamp his lips closed. He appeared to be in physical discomfort from holding in all his emotions.

Owen sat beside his father, poised and confident. Mac couldn't explain it, but the way this teenager conducted himself reminded him of his granddad. Grandad Mackie was a difficult man, impersonal and too clever for his own good, and always in control.

The young man sat rigidly, alternating his stare from Mac to his dad like at a tennis match. Throughout the conversation, Frank looked to Owen for confirmation and reassurance. This father was so broken, he needed someone to save him from drowning in sorrow, someone to pull him to shore, and he was relying on a child to handle it all.

How is this fifteen-year-old maintaining such a steady head in all this trauma and confusion? Mac wondered to himself. It was strange, but still, he'd seen stranger things.

Owen recounted the details of the afternoon with perfect clarity, unemotional, and succinct. He never had to search for an answer or think back to remember any part of the day. Mac was a little creeped out by both kids. In fact, the entire family's dynamic was off-putting. Mac made a note to have them all speak with one of the department's contracted psychologists to get a better read on how they interacted with each other, and their level of trauma.

Later, while sitting at his desk sorting through the photos taken at the scene and his interview notes, Mac tried to summarize for himself a logical sequence of the events that lead to Liam's death. He needed a timeline to work from. It was still a mystery as to why the boy left the field during baseball practice.

The coach stated that it had never happened with Liam before, and no one realized for at least ten minutes that he was gone. Once he left the field, it seems Liam stopped by his locker, only took out the bag of pills and his cell phone, then left the school campus on foot. He hadn't called his mother to pick him up and he didn't take the rest of his bat bag and other belongings with him.

Neither could anyone explain why Liam had walked home through the woods without changing out of his uniform. He still had one of his batting gloves in his pocket, which was an indication to Mac that he'd left in a hurry, or at least sooner than he'd intended to, stuffing them into his pocket on the way out.

And if he left in such a hurry, why stop to rock climb? But if he'd left unexpectedly, how would anyone know how to find him on that path in the woods? Maybe someone chased him?

There were no visible signs of assault or injuries other than the head wound. The ME said that Liam Walsh had died due to blunt force trauma to the back of his skull. He also stated that the blow to the head could have come from falling onto the rock from a great height, or from the rock bashing against the skull with purposeful force, as if someone hit him with it. *But if Liam had fallen onto the rock, why wasn't it under his head? It was more likely that someone smashed the rock into his head from behind.*

There were no other clues left behind at the scene. It seems that Liam was alone before his sister arrived that afternoon, yet Mac knew that someone else had been there. The evidence was contradictory.

Liam's death and the circumstances surrounding it pointed to it being a homicide, but there was nothing concrete to confirm his suspicions. He also didn't have a reason or physical evidence to suspect that one of the family members hurt Liam, just a feeling, an instinct. It's always odd when people coincidentally change their routines on the day a loved one dies. Mac did not trust coincidence.

Oh, you've never driven that route home from work before, but today you'd thought you'd try it?

So, you usually rush home to relieve the babysitter, but today you decided to stop at the dollar store for no particular reason?

You always call your husband after lunch, every day except today?

Even being in the type of profession that Mac was in, the business of death, he had come to believe that most humans were inherently good. This was why the accused had such a hard time sufficiently covering up a crime or lying about a murder. Deep down, they know they should be punished, that they've done something wrong.

One detail casting an alien light on the Walsh family's normal routine, was that Owen hadn't arrived home at the time Rita expected him to. But she explained this away with a motherly swipe of her hand, dismissing the detail as unimportant. She said Owen had been staying at school later and later, so she wasn't surprised.

Another troubling detail was that the younger sister, Cara, had lied to her mother. Cara originally said that she always stayed later at school on Tuesday afternoons due to a gardening club that she was a member of. Rita would some-times come to pick Cara up and they would watch the end of Liam's practice before they all headed home.

Recently, Rita Walsh had allowed Cara to walk home by herself after the club once she found out that Cara had been doing it anyway on other school days without permission. That was the plan for the afternoon in question, the day Cara finds her brother, who, by the way, is supposed to be surrounded by people on a baseball field, but instead is alone and dead in the middle of the woods.

The mother stated that she'd learned just a few hours ago that Cara hadn't been going to her gardening club for the last couple of weeks. Apparently, she would just wait around the school campus until the time when the club would usually finish, and then walk home alone, as if everything was normal. The only reason Rita Walsh had driven to the school suddenly that afternoon, was because one of Liam's coaches had called to try and locate him after it was discovered that he was missing.

When Mac contacted the school administrators, they said that Cara had left to walk home that day, just as she had every other recent afternoon. *Another instance of oblivious parents neglecting to follow up with what their kids were up to after school,* Mac thought.

For most of that first interview, Cara sat silently, staring at the wall behind Mac's head. Then, at the mention of how she'd been reported to have left school, heading for home, Cara turned to them and said in a soft voice, "I... um... did. I wanted to... walk home. So, I cut through the woods... near... um, Christine's house. I go that way. Most of the time."

Mac wanted to take advantage of her willingness to speak, so he asked, "So, is that not the path you always take through the woods?"

Cara's eyes refocused on Mac like she was looking at him clearly for the first time, a look of revelation passing over her features before fading away again.

"Well, yeah...I guess so. We all do, me, Owen, and... It's really the only way through the woods, and the fastest way home if you're walking."

The mother confirmed this with a nod of her head.

But neither of them, nor the father or brother, could figure out why and how Liam had left practice and was on that path, too.

"How did you come to find Liam?" Mac had pressed.

"I just... I just, well, I... um..." more stuttering and crying, but he waited and gave her time.

"I just did. He was just there... I.. I.. didn't know he'd be there. He just was." Rita Walsh had pulled Cara into her again and cradled her face against her in a protective gesture.

Mac decided to shift attention to the mother again, hoping to figure out why Liam had the bag of Prozac with him. Rita stuttered and stammered all the way through her explanation.

"Well, I... don't know exactly why... I'm prescribed that, but... it, it, it went missing... a while back. And I couldn't...

find it or, or, or get a refill yet... I mean, I've been looking for it... And he's never done anything like that before!"

Mac ended the interview soon after, as both mother and daughter erupted once more into a series of sobbing and rocking.

Mac and his team spent the next several days interviewing coaches, teachers, friends, and neighbors, and not one person could think of a reason for why the boy would be in the woods. Not one person saw him leave the field or the school that day. Everyone they spoke with liked the kid and didn't have a bad thing to say about him.

In fact, Mac had a hard time getting the people he asked about Liam to shut up once they got started. Apparently, he was some kind of sports phenom and was talented at many things, but mainly baseball. He got the impression that Liam's coaches and most especially, his father, had big plans for him to go pro one day.

Mac didn't want to be judgmental about the depth of the parents' attachment to Liam, of course, he was their son, one of their babies, who was way too young to die, and met with a surprising and untimely end. But... the thoughts kept resurfacing in the back of his brain.

This is another level of attachment. This is an obsession. There are some kind of strange expectations in this household. I wonder if any of them are really good enough in the eyes of the others. There's something wrong here.

The weirdest thing that happened that first week of the case, was when Frank Walsh brought Owen back to the station to speak to Mac. Owen said he didn't want his father to come into the interview room and Frank hadn't put up a fight about it.

Sitting across the table from this highly confident fifteen-year-old was something new for Mac. His own son, Joseph was still very awkward and self-conscious, toeing that teenage line between rebellion and wanting to please his dad.

"So, Owen," Mac began after Officer Abernathy pushed the record button on his phone, "tell us what this is all about." The two men sat across from the teen, Mac relaxed, and Abernathy formal, sitting straight and attentive.

The young man looked at Mac with an air of superiority and said, "Well, I know my family was a bit of a wreck the last time you saw us, understandably, but still."

Mac thought he'd caught a bit of an eye roll there.

Owen paused and pulled at the watch on his wrist. "I just wanted to see if you needed any other information or maybe you need me to clarify something." Owen tugged the watch in a circle around his arm and played with its band as he spoke. Mac waited to see if he would explain further.

Owen looked up from his watch, face smooth once again, but didn't say anything else.

Okay. This kid is super weird. Mac felt as if Owen was trying to use his own interview tactics against him. The watch made another circle around Owen's wrist during the pregnant pause.

Mac broke the silence, "That's a nice watch, Owen."

The young man looked back at it and a smile spread across his face. "It is, isn't it," he said, pride filling his voice. "Dad gave it to me. He said that I've been so solid and responsible and he told me that if our family survives this, that it'd probably be thanks to me." Owen continued to smile down at the time piece. "It used to be his, and I think maybe my grandfather's, too. You know, I think Dad was planning on giving it to Liam someday." He heaved a deep sigh as he said this.

Mac supposed that losing a son might cause a father to lean into his remaining children, to hold onto them however he could. Joseph was Mac's only son. If he lost him, he'd probably just want to die. But Frank Walsh had two other children and a wife to take care of. If he and his wife and daughter were falling to pieces as one would expect, then Mac could imagine that having Owen's calming influence, ready to speak reasonably and help with plans would be an asset.

"So, what more can you tell us? What's brought you here today?" Mac tried to direct them back on topic.

"Well, Detective Mackie, I was more interested in what you could tell me. Do you have any new details about what happened to Liam? Have you figured out why he left practice?"

"Nothing new. Nothing worth sharing. But Officer Abernathy will contact your mom and dad on Monday to update them," Mac said. He wasn't willing to talk to this teenager about anything and he felt as if he'd been tricked into meeting with him.

"I see," Owen responded slowly, carefully. "It all seems rather odd, though, don't you think... Cara and him being out there when they weren't supposed to be?" Owen's speech pattern and phrasing sounded like a much older man to Mac. It distracted him momentarily and he answered a beat too late.

"I mean, yeah. It's odd. Look, I appreciate you taking the initiative and interest in helping your family through this difficult time. But you need healing, too. Has your mom or dad called any of the counselors that were recommended?"

A look of annoyance crossed Owen's face. He clearly rolled his eyes this time and crossed his arms. Now that looked more like a teenager.

"Yeah, yeah. Mom called them. We're supposed to start that next week."

Mac began gathering his notepad and phone in his hands and said, "I really do appreciate you coming by Owen. I think it's great that you want to help, but my team is on top of it. We'll update y'all soon. In the meantime, if you think of anything specific, please give me a call."

Abernathy stopped the recording and picked up his phone as well, taking his cues from Mac.

Mac could've sworn he saw the kid narrow his eyes at him, but then the moment passed. Owen stood up, grabbed the water bottle he'd been offered, and sauntered from the room.

Officer Abernathy watched him leave, then turned to Mac, "Weird. Did that conversation give you anything helpful at all?"

"No, nothing," *except the willies*, thought Mac. "Didn't you mention something earlier about knowing the Walsh's?"

"Uh, well, not exactly. Jacob has been friends with Cara for several years. But I'm not sure if they still hang out. And of course, we've seen... uh... saw Liam play ball a couple times this spring. That kid was fun to watch!" Abernathy sounded just like the people Mac had interviewed.

"Did you meet any of the Walsh family before this case?"

"Well, I've been around Cara several times, and I've had conversations with Frank and Rita. I don't think I ever spoke with or met Liam."

Abernathy thought for a minute, rubbing his hand across the top of his head. "I've met Owen a couple of times, too. You know, at birthday party drop-offs and such. One of the parents would bring Cara, and the other would be with Liam at whatever practice or game he was playing in. But Owen was always kinda tagging along. I don't think I've ever really spoken to him, though. He mostly just stood around looking sullen."

Hmm, it sure seems like he's talkative now, certainly not just standing around and letting people talk for him.

Both siblings saw their brother lying dead in a pool of his own blood. One seems to be shattered, finding it difficult to function normally. Cara's grief is deep and overwhelming. The other doesn't seem to be suffering at all. Owen may be grieving differently, but Mac questioned if he was grieving at all.

There was just so much that didn't fit. It was an unsettling, disturbing feeling. Mac couldn't straighten out his tangled thoughts about Liam's strange death. And he couldn't put his suspicions into words.

Did the eleven-year-old cause her brother's death? Is Cara clever enough to completely cover up her guilt? Most criminals give themselves away with their words, some purposefully, some accidentally, or leave behind some piece of evidence. It was hard to imagine this small girl acting in such a sinister way and doing so successfully.

Mac also got the feeling that Owen knew more than he was letting on. And perhaps his guilty conscience led him there that day. Who would he be covering for? Who was guilty? The sister? The father? Himself?

Or was this another case of unexpected teenage depression? The more Mac learned about Liam, the less likely that theory seemed. Liam didn't appear to suffer from the usual issues that lead to or triggered teen depression, such as obesity or peer problems or bullying or trouble in school.

But Mac had seen over the years that depression manifests differently, more complexly, in young people, and it knows no limitations to who it affects. Many teens hide it well. Maybe this act of leaving practice was the first, the only, and unfortunately the final sign that something was wrong.

No, that theory didn't fit well. It was like a pair of socks that didn't dry completely and were just damp enough to begin a blister. Mac needed a theory that felt more like slipping on a pair of warm, dry socks on a cold night, comforting, a relief.

In most cases, he's able to work quickly and smoothly, the next clues and answers coming to him easily. But this was different. With so many questions, Mac wondered if he'd ever have the answers.

He clicked off the lamp that sat on the corner of his well-worn, much-used desk, and headed for the door, calling it a night. It had been a long week. Grief, even someone else's, was draining. It sucks the life right out of everyone it touches, and Mac would never get used to it. A fog had settled over his thoughts and vague images of death seemed to float in and out of his vision.

Soon morning would come, and dawn would break. He would go home to see Joseph and greet him before he left for school. Mac pictured his teenager with his socked feet, wandering downstairs for cereal, not in the mood for a hug and definitely not wanting to spend time with his dad.

But Mac was grateful anyway. He was grateful to start every new day knowing his boy was still alive. For the Walsh family, every new day would be the first day of the rest of their lives. Every day they would awaken remembering their boy was dead.

Chapter 22

2018

"*S*hit, *shit, shit,*" Detective Wes Abernathy swore under his breath as he wrestled with bed sheets that were twisted and knotted around his torso, effectively confining his arms from reaching out to the ringing phone. Still wrapped like a mummy, he made a full body hop toward the bedside table, lost his balance, and slid head-first over the side of the mattress, pulling the sheets along with him. The charging cord caught on Wes' shoulder and brought his cell slamming into the side of his face as he hit the ground.

"Shit!" How in the world had he managed that? The phone stopped ringing while he roughly tore the sheets away from his body. Rubbing his cheek, Wes glanced down at the ID of the missed call. Lieutenant Lane. *What time is it?*

As he stared at the time, calculating how much sleep he'd actually gotten after his very successful third date with Charlotte, it began to ring once more. Lieutenant Lane again. Must be a case.

As soon as Mac pressed the answer button, and before he could say hello, he heard, "Abernathy? You awake?"

Still rubbing the sleep from his eyes, he'd barely mumbled, "Yeah, I'm just..." before Lane started in again, "Meet me down at the Greenway, near the boat ramp. Trés' car is submerged in the river. I don't know if he's in it, but whether he is or isn't, there's gonna be hell to pay."

That knocked consciousness into Wes like running into a glass door that you didn't see until it was too late. Trés' car? There was no mistaking that car. No one else around here has one, the color is some special hue that can only be custom ordered. And if the car was in the river and Trés wasn't the one to report it stolen or damaged, if no one had heard from him about it, Wes knew the odds were it was because Trés had sunk along with his beloved Tesla.

Their mayor, Warren Williams, Jr., was a polarizing personality, people either loved him or hated him. His son, Warren Williams, III, Trés, was a lot like his father, but worse. In Wes' mind, the kid was a prick, but it always seemed inconceivable when someone who was young and wealthy died, no matter what their personality was like. Lane was right, his death would shake their small town to its core. Maybe even divide it down the center.

After several assurances that he'd be headed that way in five minutes, running the toothbrush quickly through his mouth, and throwing on his only clean suit, Wes started his car exactly seven minutes later.

There was no reason to turn on his lights, but Wes drove at the speed of someone rushing to an emergency. And maybe it was. It was essential for him to get the scene under his management and organized before the chaos began.

Wes lived close to downtown and the drive to the River Greenway only took eight minutes, especially early on a Friday morning with little to no traffic slowing him down. The sun was beginning to peak over the horizon in his rearview mirror.

It seemed like it would be a beautiful, albeit crisp, December day. Since it was still early in the month, the temperatures had remained pleasantly hovering around fifty-six degrees. The dashboard thermometer said it was currently only forty-two degrees. Wes was glad he'd grabbed his jacket.

"Thank goodness," he said aloud as he entered the parking lot, relieved to only see two squad cars as he pulled closer to the boat ramp. "Time to get this circus started."

He grabbed his phone, his notebook and pen, and the granola bar he'd snatched while running through the kitchen just ten minutes earlier, then got out to speak with the concerned-looking officers.

Wes had known Officers Jenkins and Mallory for years. They'd both joined the Barnes County department a few years after he had. Jenkins, who was rarely serious, one of the biggest jokesters Wes knew, had a worried look on his face and an anxiousness emanating from his stance. Mallory, who was always calm and easy-going, mirrored Jenkins' mood. She pulled at her ponytail absent-mindedly as she walked toward Wes.

"Good morning, Charlotte," he said as a greeting since Jenkins was out of earshot. He wanted to say more about last night, but it didn't feel appropriate, and he could tell she would have none of it. Charlotte Mallory gave him a tight-lipped smile and then became all-business.

"I'm surprised you beat Lane here," she said.

"What do we got?" He'd be professional, too. They walked together toward the boat ramp. Jenkins joined them as they passed and handed Wes a coffee. Bless him.

"2018 Tesla Model X. Blue metallic paint. A jogger called it in about 30 minutes ago," Jenkins recited. "He waited until we got here. We got his info and sent him home."

"I responded first. As soon as I saw the back of the car, I knew it was Trés'. I recognized it immediately." Charlotte's voice tightened as she spoke.

Wes remembered that her older sister, Virginia, had been dating Jeffery Williams for the last few years. He wondered how often Charlotte had been around Trés during that time. Surely, she hadn't spent much time with him since he'd been at Dartmouth until recently.

Jenkins spoke over Wes' thoughts, "I ran the license plate and confirmed that the vehicle is registered to Warren Williams III."

The group had reached the end of the ramp and simultaneously peered down into the river at the rear edge of the submerged car as the water lapped at their shoes. No one spoke for a long minute.

With a deep sigh of resignation, Wes asked, "Have either of y'all contacted SAR yet?" Both officers shook their heads but didn't speak. "Alright, I'll give them a call. Jenkins, contact the station and find out if anyone knows Warren's whereabouts. Oh, and for the love of everything holy, please do not talk to Amy. That woman has no regard for delicate matters," he added as an afterthought.

Amy was a dispatcher who had a knack for knowing everything and a bad habit of sharing everything. Jenkins was sweet on her and probably couldn't help himself, but Wes stared him down to let him know he was serious. Wes gave him the 'don't mess this up' look. Jenkins momentarily broke out of his grim facade to give Wes a sarcastic thumbs up and jokingly said, "That woman don't own me!"

Wes had a hard time keeping a straight face as Officer Jenkins strode back to his car and got out his phone. He glanced over at Charlotte, but her face remained creased with worry, her bottom lip caught under her teeth.

Wes cleared his throat and turned to her to ask, "You alright?" That seemed to snap her out of it. She looked up at him, her face cleared and calm, and said, "Of course. Why wouldn't I be?"

Ignoring the question, Wes said, "I want you to tape off the ramp, then set up a block at the end of the road. No one gets down here unless they've been cleared by me or Lane."

Charlotte nodded once and turned quickly to get started on her tasks. He watched her walk away and thought wistfully about how, with the current situation and new case looming, it would be longer than he'd prefer before he could see Charlotte away from work again. This was going to be a long day.

A few hours later, Search and Rescue had finally pulled the water-logged vehicle from the river, revealing the corpse within. Water poured out from every crevice and flooded the asphalt. Wes felt like he was watching a movie. This didn't seem real, certainly not like anything he'd ever dealt with before.

Charlotte and a couple other officers had done their best to keep all media and unwanted spectators from seeping into the small parking area, but the way word spread in this town was proving more formidable than their somewhat puny attempt to remain secretive. At this point, Wes' team had to set up a secondary taped-off area to create a buffer of space for them to work and continue the investigation.

The body was pulled from the car once the vehicle had drained and was laid out on a tarp beneath a small tent erected to shield their tasks from the onlookers. The coroner had begun a preliminary examination to try to make an initial determination of the time since death.

It would've been better to have a forensic pathologist and not this know-nothing, elected hack, Wes thought to himself. He'd never liked Ben Craine, didn't trust him. Regardless of his personal feelings, this was already turning out to be a unique situation and Craine lacked the specialized medical training for conducting an autopsy. He used to be an EMT, but that certainly didn't qualify him as an expert, and Wes needed everything to be done exactly right.

As he stood in the middle of what felt like a busy beehive, Wes' team swarmed around the area taking photographs and measurements and searching for any forensic evidence. Their department was not equipped to handle something like this, and he worried about possible issues with everyone following the proper chain of custody. Wes had seen a few of the officers in a conversation, laughing and joking like they would on a normal day. It made him feel like their attitude was too casual, too flippant.

Lieutenant Lane showed up soon after Wes' phone call to SAR. Lane had been angry at everyone, snapping off orders and shouting at anyone who entered his vicinity. Wes knew he was under a lot of pressure, and therefore, Wes was under a lot of pressure.

The mayor had been alerted that Trés' vehicle had been found with a body inside, but they hadn't made any speculations during the notification and neither had the mayor. Everyone involved was holding their collective breath, waiting for the other shoe to drop.

"Whelp, De-tec-tive," Craine always spoke to him in a mocking-type tone, "You got yer work cut out for ya today! I'd put my money on this being Trés, but I can't officially say that until there's a dental, fingerprint, or a family identification…?" He trailed off in a questioning manner and looked up at Wes to hear his reply.

But Wes didn't answer him. He was thinking about how long it was going to take to finally confirm what everyone already knew but couldn't say. Then, there'd be an autopsy.

Trés had some kind of large wound across the top of his head, just past his hairline. Would that be what killed him?

Or had he drowned? It seemed unlikely that he wouldn't have had enough time to get out of the slowly sinking vehicle had he been conscious.

Wes glanced over his shoulder, peering at where the car must've come from, driving toward the boat ramp. Were there tire marks? Had Trés tried to stop?

He walked away from Craine, who was still staring at him with a look of irritation and began searching the ground for clues to what might've happened. He passed several familiar faces; the editor of the local newspaper, a few council women he recognized, and a smattering of other journalists and media personalities that he'd met before, but purposely avoided- and then he spotted a very different familiar face.

It was a young man, maybe in his late twenties, standing about fifteen feet away off to the side of the crowd, watching Wes and boring holes through him with eyes so intense it made him shiver, causing him to zip his jacket up a little more to keep the chill out. The face was ringing bells- were they alarm bells?—in his head, but he couldn't place where he knew the guy from.

Realizing he'd held the stare much too long to pretend it had been a casual glance, Wes gave one curt nod, hoping to break the trance. The guy's face remained motionless in an unrelenting glare. Wes saw that he had a press badge hanging on the end of a lanyard around his neck. Maybe that was the connection. Reluctantly tearing his eyes away from the young man, he resumed his careful inspection of the ground along the path it appears the Tesla had traveled.

Where were the skid marks? Surely, if this was a way for Trés to kill himself, he'd have stomped on the gas hard and fast to prevent any time to change his mind. The way the car had entered the water was not at the right angle for him to have come from the road leading into the parking lot.

No, Trés would've had to have been stopped near the perimeter, then accelerate quickly straight at the ramp, which the Tesla was more than capable of, in order to drive the car into the water as far as he had, in the direction that he had, and with the impact that matches the evidence they'd collected so far.

Wes scratched his head. It probably seemed like a gesture of confusion to anyone watching him, but he'd always found it to be comforting. He'd rub his hand up the back of his neck, across his head and run his fingers through his hair, scratching, massaging, thinking.

"You're Officer Abernathy, right?"

Mid-scratch, Wes looked up to find that the creepy journalist had moved much closer to him and was now only a few feet away, still staring. And waiting for a reply.

Hoping his face remained passive while also conveying an impatient irritation, Wes finally responded after an awkwardly long pause. "*Detective* Abernathy," was all he said, emphasizing his title. He did not move closer or make any further introductions.

"Hm, yes, I see that now." The trance broken, a slight smirk crossed his young face. He glanced back toward the tent that the body was under, trying to hide the smile blooming on his face, shoved his hands in his pockets, and shuffled his feet a little. The change in his stance felt contrived, a poor attempt at an ease that didn't exist. Perhaps it was just the actions of an ambitious, young journalist trying to hide his obvious excitement about reporting on a notable death. Maybe it's his first story. But what was it about that smirk that tugged at Wes' memory?

"It all seems rather odd, doesn't it?" he remarked.

The phrase tickled the back of Wes' brain. His thoughts felt loose and wired at the same time. Maybe he was too tired. There were so many things to get done and to think about, but he wanted to do them all at once and think about everything immediately, which was resulting in a complete lack of attention to anything.

"Detective Abernathy?"

The journalist was staring at him again, casually this time, but willing him into a conversation with his intense eyes. The emotions were off, distorted. His strangeness was too strange. He seemed to be walking a precarious line, but Wes wasn't sure between what. Was it desperation or professional interest, friendliness, or dislike? Wes could not read him, and that scared him. Maybe his coffee had worn off.

The man suddenly extended his hand, perhaps sensing Wes wasn't much in the mood for a friendly dialogue, and said, "I'm sorry, I should've started with telling you my name."

Wes' upbringing and his ingrained southern manners caused him to automatically embrace the handshake before he'd realized what he was doing. It was an impulse.

"Owen Walsh. You may remember me, though it's been quite some time since we last spoke."

Wes stopped shaking hands abruptly, surprised. He looked closer at the face in front of him, trying to focus. It was that of a grown man now, but he could still see the boy's face from- when? Eleven, twelve years ago? He would never forget that name or what that family went through.

There was the younger brother's mysterious death, of course, but there was also somewhat of a public trial by scrutiny and gossip. It had reminded Wes of the witch hunts he'd always read about. Something was wrong, improper or inhuman, and the more proof of innocence that was found, the more it confirmed the validity of the accusations, not the acquittal of those involved.

As an officer involved in the case, he'd had a front row seat to their destruction. The perfect family, crumbling and breaking apart.

Wes ran his hand through his hair again, noticed Owen's eyes following his movements and let it fall limply back to his side.

"I remember you," was all he finally responded.

"Are you in charge of this scene, *Detective* Abernathy?"

Was that a mocking tone?

Wes regarded him once more, taking in the small notebook just visible sticking out of his back pocket, the press badge hanging at his chest, and the hand that was still in his front pants pocket, possibly using his phone to record the conversation.

"I'm sorry to cut this short, but we'll be releasing a statement to the press within the next hour. This isn't just a car accident. Some of the details require delicacy and we will follow all the proper procedures to get the information to the media. If you have questions, stick around. Me or my Lieutenant will speak with you then."

He decided to get some distance and turned to leave as he spoke. Before Wes could take more than a step, he heard Owen rushing to say, "I don't write for a local news source, and I don't publish case details or quotes from the department until you agree that I can. Just hear me out."

Wes hesitated and didn't move away as quickly as he'd intended. Owen must've sensed the waver in his resolve and continued, "My articles aim to help investigations, to work alongside law enforcement and to give the deceased a voice. I want to make sure their stories are heard, to keep the case from running cold."

Wes had now turned back to face Owen and was listening, but not reacting. Although, it was hard to feign disinterest. Owen continued, his volume and excitement growing as he spoke.

"It's all too often that journalists are being kept in the dark about crimes that the public should be told about. They have a right to know what's happening in their community. And you stand a better chance of catching the culprit if you use the media to appeal for witnesses!"

Now feeling irritated more than intrigued, Wes asked, "What crimes? What culprit?"

Owen grinned, spread his hands out, palms up in an appeasing gesture and said, "Well, now, I didn't mean to imply that for this situation. I just get a little worked up- passionate- about my vocation from time to time." He spoke calmly, as if talking to a worried child. "I'd just really like a chance to speak with you personally, to find out more about what's happened, and get my facts straight."

This was an interesting turn of events. Wes stood stock-still, appraising Owen, and considering his options. He'd need to get approval from Lane. But there was also his morbid curiosity to consider.

Whatever happened to the little sister, what was her name? She had the toughest time of any of the family members- finding the body, sitting through interview after interview with seasoned, unrelenting investigators, being demonized at school, in the community, and possibly at home. She was a ticking time bomb of explosive, angry behavior, when before she had always seemed a mild, sweet, quiet girl.

Her parents shut her away from the world- for protection, or from shame? Then, after years of speculation and questions, she was gone- sent away or finally free?

As he stood thinking, Wes saw Owen's grin widen. It was a poor attempt at a normal smile, meant to come across as patience as he waited for an answer, but it still sent chills running up Wes' spine again.

A memory of sitting across the table from Owen popped into Wes' head. He remembered the unsettling feeling of interviewing this quick-witted teenager who was sizing him up, too. Owen would align his movements and responses to be similar enough to Mac's, the lead detective for the case, or his own, to create a feeling of agreement and familiarity. It was slight enough that only someone trained to scrutinize body language might notice.

Owen would ask probing questions and check in with the police department often, more often than even the parents, to inquire about updates in the investigation or to make suggestions.

Mac had always said he thought the teen knew some detail or pertinent information that he wasn't sharing, that maybe he was hiding something.

But Wes thought it more likely that Owen wasn't even aware of what he knew, not consciously. He may have been fifteen, but still just a kid for God's sake. He reasoned that maybe Owen had seen or heard something that was buried in his memory and because he couldn't verbalize it, he hovered in the background, trying to understand what was going on.

There was no reason for him to be suspicious of Owen, or the sister, or anyone else in the family for Liam's death. He knew Mac hadn't felt the same way. They never had any official suspects because they'd never found concrete evidence of foul play. The death was determined to be an accident, although a few pieces of evidence hadn't really lined up with that theory, it was the most plausible. There were those who thought the boy had killed himself, but not Wes, or Mac for that matter. It just didn't fit.

Feeling the weight of exhaustion once more, Wes shook his head to break from the flashback and glanced down at his watch to check the time, then looked back up at Owen.

"Look, Mr. Walsh," he began.

Owen cut across him once more, saying, "You know, my brother never had anyone to speak up for him, not really. It's the curse of a small town. Everyone believes that they're safer, that nothing truly evil can happen when everyone knows everyone. His mysterious death was laid to rest as an accident, which we both know never made sense."

Owen paused and cast his eyes down at the ground for a moment. His right hand reached over to encircle his left wrist. He appeared to be momentarily startled, having a sudden realization, then he dropped the wrist and looked back up at Wes with sad eyes and continued.

"When Liam died, I knew my purpose for this life. I need to tell these types of stories. Please. Let me set up a time to meet with you and we can make a plan for dispersing the information relevant to what's happened here... to what's happened to him."

Owen pointed back at the tent concealing the slightly bloated body they both knew to be laid out on a tarp underneath. Wes took a deep breath and looked around at the rest of the scene. How long had he stood here? Surely only five minutes, but this reminder of the past had caused everything to blur at the edges, making it feel like he hadn't slept in years. His head ached and pounded.

The chaos that had permeated the small parking lot for the last several hours seemed to have softened into a dull roar. Officers, emergency personnel, and other investigators all had their marching orders and were calmly, but seriously carrying out the tasks. Wes suddenly felt proud of the way he'd managed everything so far. This may be a small town, with a low to nonexistent rate of violent crime, but it didn't mean they were bumbling idiots. And he certainly was no Barney Fife.

The moment of pride was punctuated with a moment of worry. He was still anxious about everything being done correctly, every protocol and procedure being followed to the letter. His career was riding on this, and they couldn't mess this up. He really wanted to believe his team was capable of putting together a flawless investigation, but knew it was unlikely.

"Alright, Mr. Walsh," he finally said. "Here's my card." He pulled it out of his wallet and handed it to Owen. "You can call and leave me your information and we'll set up a time to meet."

As Wes stepped back to walk away, Owen said, "Thanks very much, Offic...that is, Detective Abernathy. You won't regret it." That strange grin crossed his face once more. Wes left and walked back toward the tent intending to speak with Craine and then maybe give Lane a call to update him.

Wes felt confident that speaking with Owen would be a good thing. Plus, he thought he could finally ask Owen some questions about his brother's death that had been plaguing him ever since that case. It appeared as if the witty teen had grown into an even more clever and well-spoken young man. And Wes felt bad for him. He'd seemed the most grounded of his grieving family, but had it messed him up in some irreversible way? How would any child recover from trauma like that?

Wes' strides lengthened and he began walking faster. He was too tired to consider if he was motivated by urgency, or if he was seeking the safety and familiarity of taking charge again. Maybe both. The wind picked up and rushed past him, blowing his hair back and causing him to shiver once more. He pulled his jacket zipper all the way up and tucked his chin, like a turtle, hiding from danger. What was creeping him out so much?

Chapter 23

2019

"I've already watched that video. Twice."

Kristin rolled her eyes to herself and clicked the mouse to replay the scene once more from the beginning. She was hoping Detective White would get bored and wander back over to his desk. There had to be at least half a bag of Doritos waiting for him, and she was sure he wouldn't leave them for long.

At the thought, she glanced down at his pants leg and saw the tell-tale sign of the red, cheesy dust smeared where he'd wiped his fingers recently. Disgusting.

"You should be rewatching that one with the car driving past the front of the store," he said matter-of-factly.

Kristin continued to watch and rewind the video from the apartment complex parking lot, ignoring White completely. She started rhythmically tapping her long, fake fingernails on the metal desk as she sat in silent protest to his meddling.

"Stubborn woman," White mumbled to himself, before turning back toward his station. "Let me know when you

267

need me, Miller," he said louder. "I'm going to make some phone calls."

Greg White wasn't a bad guy, and he was a good cop, but he was a guy all the same. They'd been partners or worked on the same team for the last five years and Kristin had grown accustomed to his mannerisms, and she was certain he'd gotten used to her as well. She knew she could be difficult, but that's what helped her rise to her current position.

The video from the apartment complex was grainy but was from a distance and a position that would normally be a great recording, full of helpful information, if only it showed anything. Anything at all.

In this case, Miller was convinced that the absence of evidence was itself a piece of evidence. How was Derrick Hoffman able to enter his apartment, not leave any time after that, and end up dead in a completely different part of the city several hours later?

Kristin had watched the footage several times, but now had the feeling they were looking for the wrong thing. They had been watching for Derrick's car to leave the lot, which it did not, or they had been hoping to at least see him coming out the front door of the apartment, which he didn't. But this meant that they'd been watching for larger movements, big changes to the scene.

For the last several hours, Kristin had been watching the videos of that night in shorter segments, slowly and method-ically. She was looking for small movements near the edges of the frame. Would she be able to tell if someone had arrived and driven around to the back of the building?

She'd concluded that Hoffman must've left or been taken out through his backdoor. There's a chance that someone could drive around the perimeter of the parking lot to the back and not be seen by the cameras if they'd stuck closely to the edge of the pavement, almost in the grass. If so, the perpetrator knew there was a camera and where it was posted and then purposely avoided it.

There! She hit the mouse harder than she'd intended to stop the video. *What was that? A shadow?* She backed it up and watched the part again, slowing it down some. It was a movement across the bottom left corner of the screen, so slight that someone might assume it came from another person's shadow walking behind them as they watched the video. Kristin paused it at just the right moment and yelped with excitement.

"What're you so excited about over there?" came White's voice.

Kristin smiled to herself as she opened a new note on her phone. She needed to record the timestamp. Greg had already trotted back to his spot behind her chair and was now leaning over her shoulder, squinting at the image on the screen.

"What am I looking at, Miller?" he asked.

"A tire and part of a door panel, White," she replied.

He eyed the screen doubtfully. "You mean this rock and this shadow?" He started to point one of his Dorito fingers at the corner of the screen, then, noticing, quickly switched hands.

"Look. Watch right there. I'll press play. Don't take your eyes off that spot!"

She let it play for a split second as they stared at the bottom corner. A quick change in the lighting and a dark object flashed momentarily in the space before disappearing again.

White didn't say anything, just turned to her with an eyebrow raised high and his lips pulled tightly together. She hated it when he made that condescending face. He caught the look she'd given him in response, glaring out of the corner of her eye, and threw up both his hands in a gesture of surrender.

"Here, watch it again." Kristin played the clip back once more and was able to stop it perfectly this time. "There! Do you see it now?"

"I think I did see something that time. But there's no way to really tell what it is or use it to prove anything, is there?"

Kristin pushed back from the desk and stood up for the first time in... well, too long. Clasping her hands above her head, she heard her back pop as she stretched toward the ceiling.

"It's definitely a vehicle and it's definitely heading toward the back of the building."

White looked at her expectantly waiting for her to continue.

She sighed, a little exasperated with his slow comprehension. They had been working long hours recently, trying to solve what happened to Hoffman before the dreaded forty-eight hours mark, so maybe she couldn't really blame him too much.

"It means that it's possible someone came to Derrick's apartment, drove around back, and either incapacitated him in some way, or he willingly got in the car and left with whoever it was. I'm assuming they left the same way, driving around the edge of the lot so they could avoid the camera."

"Okay, I'm with you so far," White looked as if he was thinking deeply, but then his mouth stretched into a huge yawn and the effect was ruined.

They really did need to take a break and come back with fresh eyes and fresh energy. Kristin checked her phone and saw that it was already midnight again.

Later, as she walked through the parking garage to her car, she considered who Derrick might allow into his apartment. None of the friends or acquaintances they'd spoken to had any guesses or information about who he'd leave with or why.

The interviews they'd conducted so far had been thorough and she'd felt confident with their believability. Every one of them had been eliminated as a suspect. That's when she began to obsessively view the video footage again, looking for any leads or a new angle.

Rounding a corner, she ran straight into Meeks. She huffed out an irritated breath and stepped back to see him better. He grinned, friendly, but a little creepy, too. Kristin had never really liked Officer Tim Meeks. He'd asked her out a few years ago when they'd first met. She turned him down immediately, not her type.

But he's one of those guys who still holds out hope long past the point of being complimentary. She didn't like the way he smiled at her. And his comments were always worded mildly, sounding innocent, but said with what she felt was an intense edge to them.

"Hey, Miller, did you miss me?"

Kristin half-laughed, somewhat smiled, then decided it wasn't worth the energy because she was dead-tired. She dropped the fake friendliness almost instantly and said, "See you later," walking quickly away before he started a conversation.

"Sure, later tonight or later tomorrow? My place or yours? Or you just wanna give me a call when you're ready? C'mon, Miller! Stop actin' like you're not into me!" He continued to shout after her as she walked quickly away. *Geez, were all guys the same?*

Even though she outranked Meeks and boasted a near-perfect case record that should garner respect, he and several of the other men Kristin worked with still felt entitled to flirt with and harass her. Then again, they'd continued without ramifications because she never took the time to file a report, it seemed easier not to.

A woman! The idea popped into her head like it had just been waiting for an invitation. Who would Derrick Hoffman willingly let into his apartment or leave quickly with on short notice? A woman!

From what she knew about the young man, it seemed that any woman that crossed his path was liable to fall victim to his advances. If one just walked into his presence with an open invitation, she doubted that Hoffman would turn it down. That thought led her down a variety of rabbit holes, chasing so many questions, essentially leading to dead ends with still so many unknown variables and no suspects.

Almost a week later, but still not much further in the case, and still feeling preoccupied, Kristin didn't immediately notice the journalist sitting in the lobby, in one of the well-worn chairs, predictably sitting alert and confident, and waiting for her.

He seemed even more eager than he had the day before if that was possible. Kristin realized too late that she'd made eye contact and tried to avert her gaze back toward the elevator, but he'd already spotted her and jumped up anticipating a greeting. She kept walking, on a mission to get her day started.

"Detective Miller!"

He was just a couple steps behind her, trying to catch up to her fast pace. She didn't slow. The first two conversations she'd had with this Mr. Walsh had been okay, straightforward and productive, but there was something about his manner that made her wary. Not exactly cautious in the same way Meeks made her feel, just unsure of herself. And Kristin never felt unsure of herself. In this line of work, it was good insurance to trust your gut.

"Good morning, Detective!" He tried again, louder.

She had just reached the elevator, but now was forced into the dreaded waiting-while-staring-at-the-floor-numbers-changing purgatory that tends to catapult people into unwanted, awkward moments. Reseting her face into a less annoyed expression, she turned to address him.

"Good morning, Mr. Walsh," Kristin said in her most pleasant, business tone. "I didn't think we'd set up another interview today. I thought you were going to come by at the end of the week to let me read through your next draft for approval to publish. Didn't the last article just come out yesterday?"

He patted the laptop bag that was slung over his shoulder and then with a deep air of satisfaction said, "Well, I finished the next one earlier than expected, so I thought I'd go ahead and bring it by. Do you have a few minutes you can spare me? It would probably be faster for us both if you were able to read through it while I was here so I can make immediate changes."

He flashed her a grin letting her know he'd probably hound her until he got what he wanted so she might as well cooperate now and get it over with. Kristin sighed and motioned for him to follow her just as the elevator arrived and opened.

Once they reached her station, Walsh sat in the chair that was set up next to the desk and immediately began pulling out and booting up his laptop.

"Listen, it might be better if you emailed it next time, Mr. Walsh. These impromptu meetings don't really work for me, and I..."

He broke in and interrupted her to say, "This really will be quick. And worth the couple of minutes it might take. Here." He thrust the computer over to her, setting it on top of a loose

274

pile of paper she had in front of her. Kristin took a couple of extra seconds to give him a scathing look before turning her eyes to the screen to begin reading.

After a minute she said, "I don't want you to include this part about the vehicle that may have been seen on the apartment video footage. Take it out."

Walsh looked at her, confused. "I thought that was a great clue!"

She was shaking her head at him.

"Well, what about your theory that a woman may have been involved in the abduction? Any further evidence of that? Maybe one of those girls that he's assaulted, out for revenge?" He asked the question as if it were the perfect piece of drama to add to a fictitious story, waggling his eyebrows in a knowing way.

"No. Do not include it," she replied.

Walsh looked disappointed but pulled the laptop back toward himself to begin the editing.

"And I want to remind you that we do not want to treat anyone like a suspect until we've sufficient reasoning to do so." As she said this, Kristin raised one of her perfectly shaped eyebrows at him in question.

Pausing in his typing, he looked up at her, clearly affronted.

"*Miss* Miller, I intend to do no such thing."

She did not miss his intentional use of the casual title when he'd dropped the 'Detective' that usually preceded her name. It was not unlike the reaction that many men have when they're trying to save face by hoping to make her feel inferior. She internally rolled her eyes.

After a couple of seconds, Walsh asked, "Can you tell me about the other evidence found on the body?"

How had he known that they'd found additional evidence? Reading the question in her eyes, he quickly said, "I'm just making an assumption!" and threw up both hands in a "don't shoot me gesture".

Kristin weighed the pros and cons of divulging the new information and decided it wouldn't hurt. Her supervisor would be sharing the same information with the media in the next two days and Walsh wasn't quite ready to publish yet, so he only had a little bit of an advantage.

Walsh didn't miss her glancing down at her watch to check the time.

"Five more minutes. Please give me a few more quotes or a bit more information that I can use to rewrite the paragraph about the video footage," he pleaded.

Kristin spent precisely seven more minutes with him, explaining the residue on the victim's wrists that had been left by duct tape binding them together, as well as the puncture mark in Hoffman's neck.

"So, he was probably sedated? Hopefully, once you get the toxicology report back, we'll know what was used. Maybe that information will finally lead you to a plausible suspect."

Walsh was right in step with her thinking, as usual. It was annoying. She liked to keep her theories and facts close and not reveal her thoughts on a case until she had a complete picture.

By the end of their short discussion, she was already exhausted and realized once again that this case still had more questions than answers. The journalist thanked her for her candor and was packing up his laptop and notebook when she stopped him.

"I'm not so sure it's a good idea to report on those incidents at Northern..." She trailed off at the end. She didn't like feeling unsure and worked hard never to show it. But Owen Walsh seemed like he was ambitious enough to print as much as he could get away with, no matter who got hurt or upset, just to make a name for himself, and she didn't feel right about it. Her name would be mentioned in the articles and the connection to this other scurrilous information made Kristin feel dirty.

Walsh seemed unaffected and unconvinced, saying, "Don't worry about it. You come off as competent and thorough. I don't write to blame the victim, but I do provide all the facts. If Derek was sedated, then his destructive behavior and penchant for drugging women are obviously relevant. Plus, I have permission. Your problem is that you can't control me, and you don't like it."

He said it without heat in his voice, without anger or malice, just matter of fact. And it slapped Kristin in the face. Before she'd formed a response, he grinned that unnerving smile, turned, and walked away.

Monday morning came quickly, after another weekend of little sleep, too much coffee and reheated food, and little-to-no progress in the puzzling Hoffman case. They'd received the toxicology report from the ME, which had provided a better understanding of how the crime may have taken place.

However, the suspect list remained empty. Kristin felt wrung out. She couldn't stand the thought of the trails running cold, leaving the case open and unsolved.

Rushing through the front doors, out of the near-torrential rainfall outside and sliding a little on the slick tiles, she ran straight into Owen Walsh who, this time, was standing near the hallway's entrance, almost blocking her way to the elevator. Kristin had pulled off her dripping jacket hood a split second before barreling into his chest.

"Oh!" she exclaimed, skidding to a stop.

"Good morning, Detective." This morning his expression was less friendly. He was still emanating confidence and a barely contained eagerness, but there was a hint of impatience as well.

"Morning, Mr. Walsh. I'm guessing you'd like to speak with me?"

His answering nod was slow as he raised his eyebrows in a sarcastic expression that read "Obviously."

She started to apologize and tell him she truly didn't have time at that moment, but he anticipated her reaction and said, "I will only be writing one more article in this series, so this could be our last meeting. If you would please indulge me for about fifteen minutes, you might just be done with me for good." He turned as he spoke and was already walking toward the elevator.

Kristin caught up to him and agreed to meet with him once more, if only to take control back. This was her job, her desk, her time. How dare he continue to show up uninvited and entitled?

Remembering his last words to her the week before, she swallowed her growing irritation in an effort to prove him wrong. More than losing control, more than being unsure, she hated being wrong.

The floor was unusually quiet. No one had shown up as early as Kristin. Everyone else seemed to have a life, yesterday was St. Patrick's Day, after all. She'd never been able to let loose and have fun when she was working a case. It felt wrong.

The pair settled at her desk for, hopefully, the last time. Kristin began booting up her computer, shuffling her papers out of Walsh's sight, and just generally busying herself to keep from making eye contact with him. His last article still had her feeling a little uncomfortable. The accusatory comments about Hoffman's lifestyle caused a lot of extra phone calls from both sides.

Unable to hold her tongue any longer, she blurted out, "Mr. Hoffman should still be alive. Whoever perpetrated this crime had no right to take his life, whether or not he's a sympathetic victim, it's still a life interrupted. It's still a crime, a heinous crime. And you should treat it that way!"

Walsh had just finished setting his phone on the desk between them and she realized it was set to record.

"Can I use that as a quote?"

Walsh seemed unperturbed as he continued unpacking his notebook and pen, like a student poised for class to begin. Without waiting for her answer, he continued, "Have you had any witnesses with additional information come forward yet?"

Kristin filled him in, somewhat reluctantly, on a few of the callers they'd had over the weekend, claiming that they, too, had been victimized or had a run in with Derrick Hoffman.

"No one had anything to say about the day he died, or his abduction, or anything else that we haven't already heard. Your comments stirred people's emotions, but not their memories it seems." She wanted him to feel insignificant. There was a strong urge to smother his over-inflated sense of self-worth.

"Valid point."

What was wrong with this guy? Did nothing ruffle his feathers?

"Tell me what you found out from the toxicology report," he commanded.

Kristin gritted her teeth. Only a few more minutes and he'd be gone. It wasn't sharing the information with him that was bothering her. It was his attitude and the way he spoke to her.

As she filled him in on the contents of the report, he listened intently, taking notes, until she named Ketamine as the sedative injected into Hoffman's neck. He stopped her, his head snapping up suddenly.

"Wait. You found Ketamine in his system? Um, is that something you've seen in this area recently?"

"No. I checked. We haven't had any cases involving Ketamine used in this way. There were a few instances back in September of last year that the drug had been obtained illegally and confiscated during another crime, but the perpetrators had it for personal use and there doesn't seem to be a connection there other than maybe having the same source. My partner tracked down the seller and, as far as we can determine, they haven't sold any since last year. It's unlikely that it's the same stuff."

Damn. Why did she tell him all that? She bit her bottom lip, unnaturally out of sorts. But Walsh didn't seem focused anymore. He looked deep in thought.

"So, you think that the person who sedated six-foot Derrick Hoffman, hauled him into a car, and transported him to the backdoor of that Quick Mart might be a woman who had access to Ketamine?" Walsh didn't sound like he was wanting her to answer, more like he was talking to himself, but she replied anyway.

"It sounds far-fetched, but that's what the evidence is telling me so far. I think it's likely that she talked him into getting in the car before or soon after she sedated him."

Shaking his head slowly as if clearing his mind, he asked, "Can you walk me through your theory of the crime one last time? Summarize the facts?"

Kristin sighed deeply and loudly but agreed. Walsh's demeanor remained off-beat from his usual mood. He was angry and distracted, but she wasn't sure why.

"So, in a nutshell, you've got a lot of evidence, but no idea how it all fits together. You're no closer to solving the crime. You don't have any suspects," he summarized, interrupting her mid-sentence, and ticking each accusation off on his fingers. Taken aback, she just stared at him.

"Look, what's your problem? I'm helping you out, remember? I don't need you; you need me." Kristin felt her face flush with the burning rage that was close to exploding out of her, but she kept her voice controlled and even.

"It sounds to me like you're giving up. I think you've run out of ideas and you're moving in circles, like a dog chasing its tail. Derek Hoffman was a terrible human being and clearly there were dozens of people waiting in line to get rid of him, but I bet you couldn't follow good evidence even if it was lit with a neon sign." He met her gaze without blinking or looking away.

"You've got some nerve judging me or this investigation!" Now she was getting worked up. Walsh had pushed her last button and her volume increased.

"It doesn't seem likely that this homicide, with this level of planning and premeditation, could be pulled off without a witness, or someone who has prior knowledge, or any kind of evidence trail. And you don't know anything about me! You don't know anything about how I run this or any other case! There's always another clue and we'll find it!" Now she was shouting.

Stopping to take a breath and gather herself once more, Kristin said, "It's time you left." Then, she stood abruptly and silently dared him to argue with her.

After listening intently, staring through her as she ranted, Walsh packed his notebook and laptop back in his case. He seemed to be taking extra time, going slower to force her to remain in his presence longer than necessary. Once he'd gotten the last of his items packed away, and pocketed his phone, he stood.

"We may see each other again, Detective," Walsh said. His sudden shift in moods unnerved Kristin, his demeanor sliding seamlessly back to cool and in control. He extended his hand as if he wanted to shake hers to say 'goodbye', as if they hadn't just been in an argument. *Had she reacted exactly like Walsh had wanted her to?*

Kristin suspected that she had played right into his hands. She ignored his attempt at a formal farewell, wishing with every fiber of her being that she could slap the grin from his face. On the edge of lashing out, she turned her back on him and walked away.

Walsh called out from behind her, "It's not wise to burn your bridge with me. One day soon you might decide you need me and the information I can give you. You might regret walking away."

Kristin didn't turn around, but she could hear the edge in his voice, and it sent a jolt of adrenaline through her veins. She felt like she was escaping, but from what?

Chapter 24

TODAY TIMES

THE NATIONAL AUTHORITY ON TODAY'S NEWS

Sunday, November 24, 2019   *Since 2012*

~NEWSWORTHY~
Rich Playboy Found Dead: Criminal or Victim?
New York, New York
BY OWEN WALSH

Forty-two-year-old Johnny Rowe, the Founder, Executive Chairman, and Chief Executive Officer of Systech, was found dead in Hudson Highlands State Park yesterday morning under strange circumstances. Rowe's body was discovered by another hiker at the base of a steep cliff near Bull Hill. The Putnam County medical examiner's initial report states that Mr. Rowe died from a head injury that caused blunt force trauma to his brain. Now the police are scrambling to figure out if the injury was due to Johnny Rowe falling from the top of the cliff, or possibly, something more sinister.

The anonymous hiker called the Putnam County sheriff's department at 9:23 AM on Saturday morning, and the NYS Park Police, firefighters from Putnam Fire-Rescue, as well as members of the Greater Appalachian Rescue Group all arrived between 10:05 and 10:15 AM. Soon after identifying the deceased as Johnny Rowe, the area became a crime scene and an investigation into his cause of death began. The medical examiner puts his time of death around 8:45 or 9:00 AM.

According to the hiker, Mr. Rowe was lying at the base of the steep side of a quarry along the Bull Hill trail. He was found on his back, with a "large pool of blood around his head, but otherwise looked fine." The hiker checked for a pulse, found none, then immediately contacted the authorities.

Adding to these mysterious circumstances, the young millionaire has been in the news frequently over the last two years, due to over two dozen accusations of sexual harassment against Mr. Rowe, as well as the recent charges of grand larceny and securities fraud that were sending him to trial early next year. It doesn't seem too much of a stretch to imagine that there are many people who might have a motive to harm Johnny Rowe.

Detective Roberto Sanchez, lead investigator in this case, stated on Saturday that his department is "eager and ready to find the truth about what may have happened to Johnny Rowe." The initial police report indicates that Johnny had his wallet, high-end sunglasses, and some loose cash in his pockets, and that he was wearing expensive shoes and jewelry, so robbery doesn't appear to be a motive if he was attacked.

Those closest to Rowe have expressed confusion as to why he would have traveled to the park alone. He wasn't known to be a hiker. The trip wasn't marked on Mr. Rowe's extensive and detailed calendar. Friends say that Johnny always spent the weekend before Thanksgiving with them, celebrating Friendsgiving, as well as attending Systech's "Feed Your Mind, Feed the World" annual ball and fundraiser, which has been held the Saturday before the holiday for the last eight years.

I met with Detective Sanchez for the first time on Saturday evening, and he stated that, "It would be extremely unlikely and out of character for Mr. Rowe to go hiking, especially on the morning of his company's biggest event of the year." He went on to reveal that Rowe wasn't dressed to go hiking and that he didn't have any of the usual accessories that someone venturing into the wilderness might need.

Investigators will start working to determine why Johnny Rowe was in Hudson Highlands State Park. Today, they plan to begin interviewing those that knew Johnny, hoping to find out the reason for his solitary visit. Was it his intention to be alone? Perhaps all the media attention drove him to seek respite in the woods?

Rowe's current girlfriend, twenty-seven-year-old actress, Motney Bride, as well as Trenton Black, his personal assistant, have helped authorities with locating his calendars, gaining access to his online accounts, and attempting to fill in blanks in the timeline leading up to his death. "I'm absolutely gutted. People always tried to take advantage of Johnny, but I know the truth about him. He was strong, but gentle, and I'll never love anyone as much as I loved him!" said Bride.

I asked Black whether he knew that Rowe was going out to the park, and if he knew why. Black responded that "It's bizarre and I don't really get it. I'm supposed to know every single move he makes. As far as I know, he's never been there, and had no reason to go there. He should've been at the Crystal Towers downtown by 11:00 AM."

I also questioned whether making an unscheduled trip was something he'd ever done.

Black said that a last-minute change of plans wasn't unusual for his employer. "Johnny does what Johnny does. When he changes his mind about something, which can and does happen at any moment, I have to just figure it out and keep up. So, I guess, yeah, he might just decide that he wants to go out into the middle of the woods for no reason other than to mess with people."

Did Johnny Rowe enter Hudson Highlands State Park alone? If so, what was his motivation to do so? If not, who was with him or convinced him to go? Did he die from an accident or an assault?

If Rowe was meeting someone there, did they talk about meeting up ahead of time, maybe by phone, email, or text? Did Rowe's controversial lifestyle and criminal charges lead to his death? Or was it something else?

Follow me through this investigation as I hope to give our Today Times readers an opportunity to assist law enforcement in determining the reason for this sudden death. The next Newsworthy edition will focus on the details that have been uncovered by detectives so far, as well as my firsthand experience of visiting the scene.

If you have any information, please call 845-235-7174.

TODAY TIMES

THE NATIONAL AUTHORITY ON TODAY'S NEWS

Wednesday, November 27, 2019   *Since 2012*

~*NEWSWORTHY*~
Quandary in the Quarry
New York, New York
BY OWEN WALSH

Billy Joel said, "Only the good die young," but there are many who knew Johnny Rowe who might dispute that description. Millionaire playboy, Rowe, the Founder, Executive Chairman, and Chief Executive Officer of Systech was involved in the current investigation of over two dozen accusations of sexual harassment, as well as the recent charges of grand larceny and securities fraud that were sending him to trial early next year. There are many people at Systech who might use different terms to describe Mr. Rowe, such as, exploiter, intimidator, victimizer, or abuser.

Rowe was last seen at his home Friday evening by his girlfriend, actress, Motney Bride. Bride says that she went to sleep earlier than Rowe, but when she woke in the middle of the night, around 3:00 AM, he was in the bed next to her. She woke again at 8:15 AM and he was gone. The security system, including the cameras, was turned off at the time. Bride states that Rowe "turned the system turned off a while back, maybe in August, but I'm not sure why. I wish he hadn't done that."

Police discovered on Sunday that Rowe's phone was missing. It wasn't found on his person, in his car, or in his home. "It appears that Mr. Rowe was still in possession of all of his important and valuable items, except for his cell phone, which is another reason we believe there to be foul play involved in his death," said Detective Roberto Sanchez. Investigators hope to quickly procure the phone records from Rowe's phone, so that they can begin to set up a timeline for his movements the morning of the 23rd.

Detective Sanchez also informed me that none of Rowe's credit cards have been used since November 22nd and will not assist in plotting his route to Hudson Highlands State Park. Investigators have been unable to locate any witnesses that may have seen him traveling that morning. They are now focusing on the highway and business cameras posted along the path Rowe would've driven.

Rowe died of blunt force trauma to the back of his skull. His body was found lying face-up at the base of a steep cliff and first indications were that he'd fallen either while climbing or from the top of the quarry wall. Detective Sanchez and his team have now ruled out the theory that he may have fallen while climbing. "Due to his attire, the position of his body, and especially what we know about Mr. Rowe personally, it is not plausible that he would've

hiked to the quarry and then decided to go rock climbing," said
Sanchez when I spoke with him on Tuesday.

The quarry, which has now been officially designated a crime
scene, is truly a beautiful place. There are multiple trails and
paths for hikers to choose from. The eastern trail splits off after
about a half mile from the trailhead, one path leading into the
quarry, and the other to the top of the cliffside. Standing on
top of the wall of the quarry puts even experienced hikers in a
precarious position, and the potential for falling over the edge
is heightened.

Crime scene investigators have performed a series of tests, hoping
to determine if Rowe's injuries would be consistent with a fall.
Their final report states that had Mr. Rowe fallen from the peak,
1,000 feet to the valley floor below, his injuries would have been
much more extensive than just blunt force trauma to the back
of the head.

According to Detective Sanchez, the evidence tells him that Rowe
died where his body was found, which means that someone else
must have used an object, most likely a rock, to cause his injuries. There was a large rock found near his head, but Sanchez
says it appears to have been placed there and Rowe falling onto
it is not likely to be the cause of death. "If Mr. Rowe had tripped
and hit his head on that rock, he would be injured, but probably not dead." No other pertinent evidence has been recovered
from the scene.

As we continue to lay out the evidence and sort through the facts, it's become clear to me that Johnny Rowe was a victim of homicide. Someone else was present on the trail and in the quarry that day. Someone moved that rock to make it appear as if he'd hit his head or fallen onto it and died. Someone took his cell phone with them when they left. How was the perpetrator able to kill Johnny, then leave the area quickly enough to not be seen by other hikers?

Did Johnny Rowe's recent charges cause someone to be angry enough to kill him? What caused him to leave his house that morning? Why was he in Hudson Highlands State Park and on that particular trail?

The next Newsworthy edition will focus on my interview with Johnny Rowe's family and friends. Who was he really? Has the news media unfairly portrayed him as a monster? Is there anything about his current lifestyle or past that might explain why his life was cut short? I also hope to report on any new evidence or theories of this mysterious crime.

If you have any information, please call 845-235-7174.

TODAY TIMES

THE NATIONAL AUTHORITY ON TODAY'S NEWS

Sunday, December 1, 2019　　　　　　　　　*Since 2012*

~NEWSWORTHY~
The Unforgiving Timeline
New York, New York
BY OWEN WALSH

It's clear that Johnson William Rowe was made for the spotlight, as it has followed him in life and in death. During the news coverage of his recent charges and seemingly bad behavior, his social media followings nearly doubled. Many people, particularly women, who have never met Rowe, set up websites, Facebook pages, and GoFundMe pages intended to support and defend him against the accusations and impending trial. In the nine days since his sudden death, Rowe's social media followings have almost doubled once again.

As I walked into Systech's offices last week, I was amazed at the crowd gathered along the sidewalk. Some were there to profess their adoration and unwavering loyalty to Johnny Rowe, and some were there to scream hatred and obscenities at his supporters.

One thing that cannot be disputed: Rowe has become, or perhaps has always been, a divisive personality among those that interacted with him in daily life.

Trenton Black, Rowe's personal assistant, said in another recent interview, "You either love him or hate him. There is no in between with Johnny. And if you hated him, he could sniff that out a mile away. That's never good- to get on Johnny's bad side." I asked Black to elaborate on what he meant by that statement. "Well, he's got a lot of power, doesn't he? Johnny would take care of everything and do anything for people he knew respected him, or at least pretended to. But if he knew that someone didn't like him, it's like being cut off from a rich daddy bent on teaching you a lesson," he responded.

I decided to test his point and went in search of a variety of Rowe's friends and acquaintances to find out people's perspectives on the young bigwig. I discovered that there's a lot of truth to Black's observation. Everyone I spoke to about Rowe had a strong opinion of like or dislike. Most people who expressed their dislike for him were unwilling to interview with me or be identified. However, I was able to get a few anonymous quotes.

"Mr. Rowe was disgusting. He abused the power of his position. He treated people like pawns and toys. His only concern was the profitability of his business, and I don't think he cared who got in his way."

"I really think he thought nothing could touch him, like, take him down. I don't know how anyone can do all the things he's done, and still remain in the position he was in. I mean, I guess he was going to be held accountable, maybe. But how long did it take to get to that point? And why wasn't he held accountable after the first woman reported being assaulted or harassed?"

Police have an extensive list of potential suspects with motivation to harm Johnny Rowe. Detective Sanchez and his team have been methodically working through the list and interviewing, and most have been eliminated.

Rowe's long-time girlfriend, Motney Bride, was brought in for questioning on Saturday, for the third time since the investigation began. She was interviewed for six hours before being arrested and charged with Rowe's murder.

Is Motney Bride guilty? Here's what we know about Rowe's last hours.

On Friday, November 22nd, Rowe had dinner at his home with Bride. Bride has stated that the couple finished dinner around 8:30 PM and began drinking together. She now claims that she doesn't know exactly what time Rowe went into the bedroom, while she stayed awake. Initially, she stated that she had been the one to go to bed early but has now changed her story. Bride is certain that he didn't leave the house and states that he was in bed asleep when she laid down around 1:00 AM. At 3:00

AM, Bride says she woke up and saw that Rowe was still next to her, asleep in the bed.

Bride's alarm went off at 8:00 AM, then again at 8:15 AM. Bride says Rowe was no longer in the bed at that point. She claims she looked for him all around the house and property but couldn't find him anywhere. It was then that she discovered one of his vehicles was also missing. She told police she assumed he'd gone out for breakfast, or maybe to the park for a jog. Bride called Rowe's cell phone at 9:00 AM, which went straight to his voicemail.

The security system at Rowe's home was not in use at the time. Investigators have combed through video footage along the route that he would've taken to get to Hudson Highlands State Park. On Friday, November 29, Rowe's vehicle was identified in traffic camera footage along I-95 at 7:16 AM heading in the direction of the park where he was found. It is unclear in the footage if Rowe is alone in the vehicle. However, the hiker who discovered Rowe's body reported seeing Rowe arrive in the parking area around 8:30 AM, alone. The phone call to the police occurred at 9:23 AM. The medical examiner in this case has reported Rowe's time of death to be between 8:45 and 9:00 AM.

Investigators have not been able to locate Rowe's cell phone, but they have received his phone records. The movement of his phone supports the timeline of evidence and witnesses so far. The phone was turned off at 9:08 AM, which is more evidence to the theory that the phone was taken after Rowe had already died.

There were no phone calls to or from Rowe's phone after 12:00 AM on November 22nd, other than Ms. Bride's call around 9:00 AM on the morning of the 23rd. Detective Sanchez suspects that there are text messages that the perpetrator is hoping to hide. Police are unable to confirm this without being in possession of the phone. His last iCloud backup was from November 20th and will not be useful in collecting stored or deleted data.

Rowe's home was searched again yesterday morning while Bride was being interviewed. Detective Sanchez was unwilling to update me on any evidence found from that search.

What could investigators have found that might implicate Motney Bride in this terrible crime? What were her motives? This reporter finds it difficult to believe that Ms. Bride would be able to commit this murder, unseen, in the narrow timeline that police have determined.

The next Newsworthy edition will focus more on Motney Bride and her relationship with Rowe, the results of searching Rowe's home, as well as the final report from the medical examiner, and any additional evidence. Will Detective Sanchez and his team be able to solve this strange death?

If you have any information, please call 845-235-7174.

TODAY TIMES

THE NATIONAL AUTHORITY ON TODAY'S NEWS

Wednesday, December 4, 2019   *Since 2012*

~NEWSWORTHY~
Bride is Charged with First Degree Murder
New York, New York
BY OWEN WALSH

Twenty-seven-year-old actress Motney Bride has been formally charged with first degree murder in the November 23rd death of her forty-two-year-old boyfriend, millionaire Johnny Rowe.

Bride was questioned on three different occasions during the investigation before her arrest on Saturday, November 30. Detective Roberto Sanchez said investigators were able to uncover more information, and some of Bride's statements left them with questions.

"Some of the things she was saying were not lining up with the evidence. We have to rely on the physical evidence, which doesn't change," Detective Sanchez said on Monday. "Her details changed more than once, and in my experience, is usually an indication of someone being deceitful."

First degree murder is typically defined as the unlawful killing
of a human that is premeditated, deliberate, and willful. In the
state of New York, like aggravated murder and murder in the
second degree, murder in the first degree is one of the few crimes
that is a class A-1 felony. If Bride is convicted, she could spend
the rest of her life in prison. The minimum sentence would be
15-40 years.

"We believe there was some kind of altercation between the two,
but we do not know exactly what led to this," said Detective
Sanchez. I asked the Putnam County Sheriff if his office had previously responded to any calls, domestic or otherwise, involving
the couple. He confirmed that there had been frequent calls of
disturbance and domestic altercations involving Rowe and
Bride at Rowe's home. "Those two have a history of being vola-
tile, but they hid it well," Sanchez said, agreeing with the Sheriff.

At this time, the investigators are unable to share whatever evidence may have been found in Rowe's home during their search
on Saturday. However, I have been able to interview more
friends and acquaintances that knew the couple to get their
opinion on the recent developments in the case.

"I think Johnny met his match with Motney. She really just gave
back whatever he dished out. I think they really did love each
other. But they probably weren't good for each other," said Bride's
sister, Jessica Helmly. "Motney would never do this. She would

never kill Johnny. I think she thrived off of confrontation, but she also thrived off of being with him. She just couldn't have done it."

Rowe's assistant, Trenton Black, said, "I don't know how to explain it. Sometimes they made me a little nervous because you never knew what might happen. But I was never afraid of either of them or of them together. Plus, I don't see Motney planning something like this. She's all passion. If she was going to kill him, and I'm not saying I think she did, she'd do it in the moment."

Bride's attorney, Danielle Hill, made a statement on Saturday after Bride was formally charged. "Ms. Bride has been cooperative and honest with the police. She has provided them with any and every single thing that they have needed from her. These are completely outrageous and unreasonable charges against her. Added to her grief over Mr. Rowe's death, she will now have to fight for her life and freedom."

According to the timeline of evidence that Detective Sanchez and his team have put together so far, there doesn't seem to be enough pieces of the puzzle that point to Bride being culpable in this homicide. Whatever new evidence has been found, it is being held tightly, and somewhat secretly by investigators.

Johnny Rowe died from blunt force trauma to the head, according to the Putnam County New York medical examiner. The full autopsy report lists the following injuries: abrasion of the posterior scalp, subgaleal hemorrhage, multiple linear fractures of the base of the skull, comminuted fractures, a hinge fracture, sub-dural hematoma, subarachnoid hemorrhage, and contusions.

The M.E. described Rowe's injuries in layman's terms, "It appears he was struck with a large, heavy object, without much of a distinct shape, to the back of his head. Also, this may have happened while his head was against another surface, like a wall, or if he was laying on the ground face-down. The injuries are not consistent with a fall. We've also determined that Mr. Rowe died quickly after the injury. With the size of the wounds he incurred, it wouldn't have taken long for him to bleed-out, possibly within five minutes or less."

The questions that I've posed to the police have gone mostly unanswered. Is there camera footage of Bride driving the same path to Hudson Highlands State Park, either before or after Rowe? Do her phone records show that she traveled to the park that morning? Was there any physical evidence of the crime found in Rowe's home? Has Rowe's cell phone been found? If Bride premeditated this murder, what weapon did she use?

The case isn't closed yet, and I remain hopeful that investigators will find the right person or persons responsible for the death of Johnny Rowe. Motney Bride's family and friends are also hoping that justice will be served appropriately. "This just cannot stand," said Motney's sister, Jessica. "It should be pretty easy to rule her out, since she didn't do it." Detective Sanchez commented, "My team is confident in our findings so far, but it's not over yet. One way or another, we will solve this case."

If you have any information, please call 845-235-7174.

Chapter 25

DECEMBER 2, 2019

*N*o matter how hard he pressed into his temples with his thumbs, the throbbing ache continued. Roberto lifted his head from the cradle of his hands and opened his eyes, catching another glimpse of the newspaper article centered on his laptop screen. The headache raged in his eye sockets again and he hastily shut the laptop, causing a loud snap.

At the sound, Ben's head swiveled around to face him with a questioning look. "Don't let it get to you, Rob," he croaked in that deep tone that he had.

Why do people always feel the need to spout off useless advice? Give me solutions, or keep your mouth shut- that was Roberto's motto. He swatted away Ben's comment and turned his chair toward the window.

There was something going on with this journalist. It hadn't seemed particularly wrong to speak with Mr. Walsh about the case and the details that are soon to be released to the public anyway, but it still wasn't sitting well with him.

Naturally suspicious, Roberto was always wondering what people's motivations were, and how they might try to take advantage of him. Just the thought of being manipulated, squeezed against his heart, beating faster in his chest.

Deep breaths. There was no point in getting fired up about a self-created, and most likely incorrect, scenario. His worries swirled around in his mind and his thoughts became segmented and choppy. Attempting to focus on reality, he thought back to the beginning.

It had surprised him to discover that the witness at the scene was a reporter, but it was definitely a lucky break for the guy. What are the odds that a journalist who reports on mysterious deaths happens upon a mysterious death? It was immediately clear that there was no way he'd be able to keep Walsh from becoming overly interested in the details of the case. Roberto figured he would interview Walsh as a witness, maybe give him a few tidbits and stray promises for more information in the future, and then shut him out at a safe distance, as he does most reporters.

After their initial meeting, Roberto's impression was that the younger man was well-mannered and intelligent, well-spoken, and enthusiastic. But there'd been a feeling gnawing at him. It was as if Walsh was adapting himself, like a chameleon, to fit whatever image Roberto needed to see to be comfortable and let down his guard. It felt more like a job interview than a witness interview. He'd given away more details than he intended and hadn't successfully shut Walsh out.

This was probably what was eating at him the most. Roberto was known for successfully extracting relevant information from any witness. He'd found early on in his investigative career that he had a knack for effective interrogation techniques, they just came naturally to him.

He shook the memories away, cleared the foggy thoughts, and stood up to stretch. In the first article, Walsh had certainly asked all the right questions. But Roberto found himself feeling uncomfortable and somewhat wary of the way Walsh had referred to the background and criminal charges of Johnny Rowe. It's true, they're probably relevant, but it seemed to be off to a negative start in the court of public opinion.

Or maybe not. Hell, he couldn't really tell these days, what with the way everyone lived their lives on social media, got offended over everything, and decided to start defending some very real monsters. Roberto had to keep up with how society was changing, but it didn't mean he had to like it.

His cell phone buzzed and rang loudly, breaking his reverie. Ben's head whipped toward him again, clearly trying to listen in to the conversation.

"This is Sanchez," he answered, turning his back once more on his nosy neighbor. The conversation was not what he was expecting. His partner, John, was calling to relay a message that a woman, claiming to be the journalist's sister, had contacted the department, asking for Roberto. She had made it clear to John that she felt it was an emergency to speak with them as soon as possible.

"What is this all about?" Roberto asked when John finally paused. "This doesn't make any sense."

Nothing about this case has made sense. Usually, the path of an investigation begins to smooth and straighten during the first twelve hours, after Roberto and his team had time to put together a timeline and gather a list of suspects. This case had done the exact opposite. It had more twists, turns, and roadblocks than any he'd worked in his career so far.

"I don't know, but she was adamant. Said if you didn't call her back today, that she'd just call again tomorrow, or just show up if she never heard from anyone."

Roberto chewed on the end of his pen while he thought about what this meant. Ever since he'd quit smoking, all sorts of things, but especially pens, were drawn to his mouth like a magnetic force pulled them there.

"Is she a reporter, too?" he asked.

"No, I don't think so." John fell silent for a moment, then said, "But she did say that it was relevant to the Rowe case." He spoke slowly, sounding skeptical. Roberto could hear the silence of Ben's paused typing. *Nosy asshole.*

"What in the world?" Roberto was practically whispering now.

"I know. It's not anything I've ever heard before."

The pen's top was almost chewed to a pulp before Roberto pulled it out of his mouth and threw it away. This just wasn't what he needed. Or was it? His head was spinning with why the sister of the journalist reporting on his biggest case would need to speak with them about, well, anything.

"Do you think this is something?" he asked John.

John could be straight with him; he trusted his instincts. Ever since they'd become partners, their closure rate was ninety-two percent, higher than any other investigator or team

in the department. The others often tried betting against
them, but quickly regretted it. Which is why someone like
Ben would love to have inside information about a possible problem with the Dream Team. No one actually called
them the Dream Team, but that was the name they used at
Wednesday night trivia down at the pub.

"I don't know... But there's something about it that's bothering me. It's just so weird. I think you should talk to her; she
wouldn't speak to me over the phone and insisted that you
be present. I guess because you're the one that her brother has
been communicating with, maybe. You're the one quoted in
his articles. Do you want me to call her back?"

"Yeah. See how quickly she can get here. I don't want to
waste my time with this if it's just some rabbit hole. And if it's
not, and she's got something real to say, then I want to know
before I waste my time talking to the other Walsh again."

When they hung up, Roberto felt the throbbing in his
head again. *Coffee. That's what I need.* Twisting in his chair,
and rubbing at his temples, he met eyes with Ben again.
Jesus, help me.

"You got something, Rob?"

Roberto stood, grabbed his jacket, and turned his back
on his jackass coworker, ignoring the question.

It had been a long, exhausting week full of interviews,
most of which led to dead ends and negative reports that left
them literally clueless, and he felt the need to escape. His most
recent interview with Motney Bride, the second one in just a

matter of days, had been especially frustrating. Her timeline seemed to fluctuate a little each time they spoke.

There was pressure coming from his Lieutenant, and who knows where else, to bring this case to a conclusion quickly. It was clear that the protestors who were currently lined up on both sides of the street outside of his building were beginning to take their toll.

Lieutenant Jeffries had called him just a few hours ago to suggest that he and John interview Ms. Bride a third time and get a warrant to search Rowe's home for the second time. Roberto saw the logic in these steps but didn't have a lot of confidence that they'd yield the desired result. He didn't think Ms. Bride was guilty.

Jesus, he thought again but this time added to his desperate prayer, *please just let something good happen. I just need some good news, or some answers.*

Roberto stepped out of the building into the crisp, evening air and took a few deep breaths. He realized immediately that he'd made a mistake coming out the front door. Protestors surrounded him on all sides, some hurling questions, and some insults. It took every ounce of self-control that he didn't even realize he had to refrain from punching each one in the face.

Stuffing his hands deep into his jacket pockets, he barreled through the crowd toward the parking deck without saying a word or using his fists. He continued to bury the rage and frustration bubbling near the surface, deeper and deeper, attempting to smother the dangerous thoughts. *Geez.*

If he wasn't killed in the line of duty, stress just might be the death of him.

Two days later, after little sleep and a too-early, exhausting conversation about their upcoming family vacation with his wife, Roberto found himself stirring another cup of coffee before sitting down at his desk across from a peculiar young woman.

Cara Walsh, although very attractive, seemed slight and wispy, like she might blow away in a strong breeze. But there was a fire behind her eyes that hinted at some kind of inner strength. She seemed the type of person who'd been through trauma and fought her way to the other side. Or maybe he just sensed that because he'd googled her the night before and found out about the death of her other brother. An ordeal like that was sure to mess up a little kid and cause some deep-seated damage.

Roberto wished John could've been present for this, too, especially if it turned out to be the babbling of a lunatic. However, his partner was currently conducting the interview with Motney, while the rest of their team served the search warrant at Rowe's home.

Ms. Walsh sat straight in the chair and watched Roberto warily as he set up his notepad, found his favorite, non-chewed pen, and woke up his laptop. He was creating tension, looking for signs of her impatience, trying to force emotions to break the surface of her serene mask.

Pushing someone to their point of frustration was usually an effective shortcut, getting quicker to the heart of the issue. But Cara Walsh sat, unmoving, watchful, and remained silent until the detective was ready to start.

Roberto cleared his throat and asked, "Well, Miss Walsh, what's this all about?"

The girl, she seemed so young, it was hard to think of her as a woman, dropped her shoulders down and back to sit up even straighter, if that was possible.

"I'm trying to do the right thing. And for the first time, I think I might know what that is," she sniffed.

When she didn't say anything else, Roberto motioned with his hand for her to continue. The girl looked down at her lap, thoughtfully twisting a tissue that she was clutching in both hands.

Damn it, he thought, *just spit it out!*

When she remained staring down at her lap, Roberto again cleared his throat and squirmed in his seat. "Great. Do you mind sharing that with the class, Miss Walsh? I really do not have all day for this meeting."

He was not usually so impatient and rude, but Roberto just didn't care at this point. He was tired of being jerked around, tired of talking to people and getting nowhere.

Cara Walsh slowly looked up at him with watery, doe eyes, and he had a moment of regret. His face softened and his mouth opened to apologize for his sarcasm, but then, she smiled. It wasn't reassuring. The sudden change of expression was unsettling.

She'd used his own trick against him. Roberto's mouth closed quickly, forcing his lips into a straight line, muffling the worthless apology. He had to get control of his irritation.

"I'm glad you agreed to meet with me, Detective Sanchez, because I can tell your investigation is headed in the wrong direction. My guess is that you don't even have any idea where to look next. But I do."

The comment hung heavy in the air between them. Roberto waited a beat to find out if she'd repeat herself or elaborate to fill the silence. In the lingering stillness, he watched for a change in body language, such as rapid blinking, shifting, or fidgeting. Was she deluded, possibly only out to get attention?

Cara Walsh kept her gaze steady, but he remained silent, hoping to break her focus. For a second, it was a staring contest between kids on a playground. The tactic didn't work. With a sigh, he turned from her stare to look down at his blank notepad and gather his thoughts.

"Alright, please tell me what you think I need to know." Roberto picked up the pen, determined to get something useful out of the situation.

A shadow fell over her face when she said, "My brother is not who you think he is." She paused, looked out the window to Roberto's left, and sighed. "He's a killer."

Caught off guard by the calm confession, Detective Sanchez almost fell out of his chair, but instead, his body tensed, and he didn't breathe for what felt like several minutes. It was a good thing he didn't have any coffee in his mouth, or he might've choked. Cara sat unmoving, gazing out the window.

"What?"

"I believe my brother killed Johnny Rowe," she said, matter-of-factly, turning back to look him in the eyes. A statement. A fact. No waver in her voice. No hesitation or hint of doubt.

Incredulous, anger crawled up Roberto's spine, and throbbed in his neck. Letting the pen fall, he pushed away from the desk roughly and leaned back in his chair. The ceiling didn't hold any of the answers to the questions buzzing around in his mind. Closing his eyes tightly, Roberto pinched the bridge of his nose, hoping to relieve the building pressure.

Finally, he said, "Let me see if I have this right. You think your brother, Owen Walsh, murdered someone he's never met, then stuck around the crime scene to be a witness, and is now interviewing the investigators working the case so he can write a story about it?"

"Yes."

He had to do something with his hands. He needed a cigarette. Instead, Roberto sipped his coffee slowly, holding on tightly to his mug with two hands, giving space for his disbelief to solidify, then said in a huff, "And he did all this without leaving behind any evidence?"

"Are you quite sure he didn't?" Cara Walsh looked at him as if he had no capacity for intelligent thought, her voice sharp and accusatory.

"I'm *quite sure* we haven't found any DNA evidence on the body or at the scene..."

"That's not the kind of evidence you're going to find," she cut him off mid-sentence, pursing her lips and shaking her head.

"Oh really? Then what should I be looking for?"

"A puncture wound. From a needle."

Roberto regarded Cara Walsh carefully. She seemed sane, but he felt like he was floundering, frantically trying to keep from drowning in this sudden flood of ridiculousness.

"Look," she said, before he found the words to speak again, "I know this whole thing is really random and hard to believe. Just check it out. Find out if there's a puncture mark anywhere on your victim. And look up 'Derek Hoffman.'" Cara stood up as she spoke and gathered her purse over her shoulder.

"I'll wait for your call," she said as she turned to go. "But don't wait too long. This has to stop." Then she walked away without waiting for a reply.

Roberto sat with his mouth hanging open, watching her retreat down the hallway toward the elevators. As the doors slid closed behind her, he snapped out of his shock with a jolt and grabbed his phone.

"John, you're not going to believe this."

Sunday morning, Roberto sat across from John at their desks, both men practically vibrating with anticipation and the adrenaline that comes with discovering a breakthrough in a case.

"Doctor Shaw said that he'd put a rush on that tox report, but even then, it's going to take at least three weeks," John said as he dug through one of his bottom desk drawers.

"Yeah, I know. We can't wait on that. The fact that there were two hypodermic needle puncture marks on Rowe's body, makes me wonder if this looney sister is in on it with the brother. I mean, how would she know that? Maybe she's just trying to lay the blame on him."

John found the recording device he was looking for and sat up. "But then why even come in and tell us about it? I mean, who knows if we would've ever thought to look for needle marks. And if they'd been discovered at some point during the examination, I don't think we would've necessarily thought they had anything to do with anything since his cause of death was blunt force trauma."

Their thoughtful silence was only broken by the squeak of John's chair as he pushed back from the desk. "Alright, she'll be here in a couple of hours. And Detective Miller agreed to call at nine. I'm going down to see Peyton about this thing," he said, gesturing with the device.

Roberto nodded but was still lost in thought as John left. *What was he missing?* It seemed unlikely that this strange case was about to be wrapped up with a neat, little bow.

The Walsh siblings had lost their brother at a young age... Did either of them witness his death? According to the articles he'd read, Cara Walsh was the one found with him that day.

Roberto was anxious to speak with Detective Miller. The information about the Derrick Hoffman case was puzzling. There weren't any similarities between Rowe and Hoffman when they were alive. Nothing was the same about the area where the deaths occurred, either. The only parallel was the puncture wounds, which were found in the same location on both bodies. Hoffman had Ketamine in his system. Would they find it in Rowe's as well?

Wait, no. That wasn't the only thing the two cases had in common. Both deaths were written about by Owen Walsh.

And if Cara Walsh's accusation was correct, did her brother also murder Derrick Hoffman? The question that bothered him the most was, how many articles has this deranged journalist written?

Chapter 26

*C*ara sat nervously in the small interview room, looking around at the worn, gray carpet, the beat-up table, and the far wall that had a fist-sized hole through it. *This is where criminals sit, in this same wobbly chair that has one leg shorter than the other three.* As if cued by her thoughts, the chair tilted forward and back once more.

She'd have to remember to be as still as possible once the detectives came in. *Deep breaths.* This was not about her. It was about Owen. That was why she was here, to finally tell her story.

Uncrossing her arms, Cara stretched her hands out flat on the tabletop and looked at her nails. All she had to do was distract herself with insignificant details and her pulse would slow, her breathing would even out.

She focused on her nails. She'd had them done recently, at a place not far from the station. The shop had been clean and well-run, but it wasn't really the type of place Cara would normally visit. Of course, if you have a nail emergency when you're out of town, you really don't have the benefit of knowing which places are the best. Cara felt agitated again at the thought and decided that her nails were not the right topic to focus on at that moment.

She didn't have time to think about anything else because in the next second, as she was placing her hands in her jacket pockets, Detectives Sanchez and Lenderman came striding purposefully into the room.

Detective Lenderman was holding his hand out to her, saying, "Good morning, Ms. Walsh, I'm John Lenderman, Detective Sanchez's partner. We spoke on the phone. We appreciate you coming back in to speak with us today."

Cara shook his hand and smiled. Detective Lenderman had a kind face and she sensed that he really did appreciate the information she was offering. Looking over at Detective Sanchez, she got the impression that he wanted the information, but was extremely agitated that he was having to get it from her. Was this going to be good cop, bad cop?

Sanchez set a small stack of manilla folders beside him on the corner of the table, then laid a blank notepad and a pen on top. Cara eyed the stack questioningly, but he made no attempt to give her an explanation. She remained still and poised, waiting for them to begin. Body language was everything.

They took turns adding to a preamble of why they'd called her to come speak with them again. Cara listened quietly, only nodding from time to time, but they weren't telling her anything she didn't already know.

She knew they'd found a puncture wound in Johnny Rowe's neck. She also knew that they'd discovered from a conversation with Detective Miller that Derek Hoffman had the same marks on his body when he was found.

Sanchez opened one of the folders, his eyes roaming the pages as he spoke, "… and Hoffman's toxicology report found Ketamine in his system, along with the illegal drugs that killed him. Miller's team believes that whoever killed Hoffman, sedated him first, then tied a tourniquet on his arm and injected lethal amounts of heroin and fentanyl." He closed the folder and placed it back down on the table, looking up at her as he did so.

Cara waited.

Sanchez shifted in his chair, then leaned forward. "If your brother killed both of these men, one would have to assume that the puncture marks on Rowe's body indicate that he was also sedated with Ketamine, just like Hoffman."

She waited for the question.

"Does Mr. Walsh have access to Ketamine?" Detective Lenderman asked.

"Well, I'm sorry to say that his access may have accidentally come from me." Cara could feel her face screwing up in a sardonic smile. She hated this connection to herself.

"How's that?"

Cara removed one of her hands from its warm pocket and used it to prop up her head, a gesture of distress or anxiety.

"A couple of years ago, I was seeing a doctor about my severe depression. She would give me Ketamine by IV

318

infusion a few times per week." She bit her lip nervously as she continued. "I was suicidal at that point in my life."

Cara could remember how the antidepressant pills never even touched the edges of her despair. Then there was the esketamine nasal spray that did manage to make a difference, but not enough. Dr. Laskey seemed hesitant to begin the IV regimen, but quickly changed her tune after seeing the positive transformation it brought to Cara's life.

"I was taking it legally, under my doctor's care... but then, I became addicted to it." At this admission, she hung her head for a moment, remembering the shame and desperation, mixed with elation. It gave Cara the best feeling she'd ever felt, made her calmer and more normal than anything else she'd experienced.

Detective Lenderman slid a box of tissues closer to Cara on the table. She smiled thankfully at him, pulled one from the box and dabbed at her barely damp cheeks.

"So, anyway," Cara continued, "I found ways to get it through friends I'd met at college. We always called it Vitamin K. And honestly, it really felt like I was helping myself, taking my vitamins. I mean, that's how I always rationalized my behavior to myself."

Lenderman was watching her with interest but had not changed his posture or facial expression. Sanchez, on the other hand, had a look of judgment on his face. Cara knew that he'd be like that. After she met him the first time a few days ago, she knew he was the type to be suspicious and judgmental of everyone. She turned away from him and gave all her attention to Detective Lenderman.

"How did Owen end up with it?" he asked.

"I'm not exactly sure, but I think he must've taken it from my parents' house. I got clean a little over fifteen months ago. I had been staying with them for a while so I could finish classes online and graduate on time. When I moved to Walton, I still had some K left over. I don't know why I kept it. But I know it was there when I moved. My dad had a heart attack and Owen came down to see him, so he could've taken it then. Or maybe he took it before that last fall when he was nearby in Mill City writing that first article."

Cara kind of felt like she was rambling. She stopped abruptly to see their reaction.

Detective Sanchez asked, "But how did Owen know where you'd left it? And when did you notice it was gone?"

Cara steeled herself for the next part of the conversation. She'd known that they'd have to dig this deep, but it was never easy to explain her relationship with her brother.

"What you have to understand is that Owen and I have a long history of avoiding each other, as well as spying on each other."

The detectives glanced at each other with raised eyebrows. Cara could understand their exchange. She was the one living this strange life.

"I was trying to speak to him when he came home on that trip last December, and then again when he came home to check on Dad, but he kept avoiding me. When I got to Mom and Dad's house and realized he'd gone, I went straight to my old bedroom to take inventory. I just don't trust him. And I was right. I kept it in a small Tupperware box in the back of one of my dresser drawers, and it was gone."

"That was when I started to suspect him."

Cara waved a hand in the air in front of her as if to erase that last statement. "No, that's not right. I've suspected him ever since Liam died. I'm pretty sure that's the first person he killed. Our brother."

Detective Lenderman took a deep breath, folded his hands behind his head, leaned back in his chair, and let the breath out slowly. Detective Sanchez was nodding thoughtfully and looking down at his notepad where he'd already taken copious amounts of notes. Neither man acted surprised. Cara decided she wanted to trust them with the rest of the story.

"Owen was never charged in his death," Sanchez said, opening a different folder. "Liam Walsh's death was ruled accidental. Blunt force trauma?" he asked as he read the information in front of him. He seemed lost in thought for a second before he added, "Owen wasn't found at the scene, but you were."

Cara explained why she'd gone to Liam's school that day and what happened after he caught her trying to plant their mom's prescription drugs in his belongings. She didn't follow him immediately because she was frozen with fear, unsure of what would happen next. She was afraid to go home and face their father, but really had no other plan. Waiting it out didn't seem to be a realistic solution, so after a while, Cara finally headed home.

"Our house is so close to Christine's, to that spot in the woods, it wouldn't have taken Owen but just a few minutes to run home afterward, get cleaned up, then run back when I called him from Liam's phone. I still don't know if Owen was following me, or Liam, or if it was just an accident that he ran into him that day. He didn't have classes the last two periods of the day that semester, so he had time to get over there." Cara knew she sounded as if she was pleading with the detectives to understand her accusations.

"But why do you think your brother would kill these men that he doesn't know?" Lenderman leaned forward in his chair again and placed both forearms on the table, eager to hear her opinion.

"For the story. I mean, I guess it would be more obvious to you if you knew Owen, if you'd grown up with him. Owen's stories were always the most important things to him. But that's where he retreated to," she said softly.

Cara was feeling more uncomfortable with this part of the conversation. Discussing their childhood was almost like a slow torture. Every memory recounted was like a fresh feeling of shame and sadness. A wound torn open and exposed for everyone to see.

"Owen hated Liam. Well, they hated each other. But Liam was the rising star in our family, the golden boy who could do no wrong, which meant that Owen couldn't do anything right, especially in our dad's eyes. Liam was spoiled and did whatever he wanted, taking advantage of others, never suffering consequences. He took whatever he wanted, and some of the ways he got what he wanted were, um, less than savory, I guess you could say. Think about those men that died, Derrek Hoffman and Johnny Rowe, what kind of men were they? From what I read they sounded exactly like what I would've expected our brother's future to be like had he lived long enough."

Cara took a deep breath and a sip of water. This was getting a little easier and she felt invigorated by finally letting her thoughts into the open.

Sanchez had opened a third folder from the stack and was scrutinizing whatever he'd found on those pages. The silence continued while he read, and Cara felt as though she might jump up and scream at any second. Luckily, she remained in her seat, hoping she looked calmer than she felt. It probably helped that she was gripping the seat with both hands now, her fingers curled tightly around the plastic edges.

Finally, the detective closed the folder and said, "So, we know that you contacted Detective Miller. But in your brief conversation with her, you never implicated your brother or shared your suspicions, and you never asked to meet with her. What made you want to reach out to us?"

Cara thought back to reading Owen's articles about Derrick Hoffman. The Ketamine connection was important, but she hadn't been sure that anything else would tie him to the murders. "Did you read the details of my brother's death? I mean, what the scene was like?" she asked.

Sanchez said, "Yeah, we saw that Liam and Johnny Rowe's deaths were very similar, in the position of the bodies, the type of area they were found, and the cause of death."

"Yeah, that's what I noticed, too. As soon as I read the way Owen described how Johnny Rowe's body was laying…"

Cara paused and took another sip of water. It was getting hard to breathe again. "…I mean, it was like a carbon-copy of Liam. The ME's reports from both deaths sounded almost exactly the same. When Liam died, the detective at the time, Mackie I think, maybe, he kept getting stuck on a piece of evidence that he said didn't make sense. There was a rock that was lying near Liam's head with blood on it that Liam could've hit his head on, except it wasn't close enough to his body. Plus, the rock was loose on the ground, not embedded, so he said he thought it had been moved, and possibly used to cause Liam's head injury."

As she spoke, Detective Sanchez opened the folder once more, reading and nodding as he listened.

"He could never make sense of it because they didn't have any evidence to prove that anyone was there when Liam died, but it appeared that another person could've hit him in the back of the head with the rock so hard that it only took one time to knock him out and kill him."

"And with Rowe…?" Detective Lenderman slowly swiped his hand through the air, palm up, in a questioning gesture.

"And with Rowe, I think Owen tricked him into meeting him out there, maybe some kind of lie a journalist would tell, I mean, Rowe was having legal trouble, right? Then snuck up on him, sedated him, and hit him with the rock while he was already lying on the ground, maybe."

Closing the folder with a snap, Sanchez said, "Do you have any other information to tell us that could lead to the discovery of physical evidence?"

Cara bit her lip and considered the question. "Mostly, it just *feels* like he's guilty. I know it in my gut."

"That's not evidence."

"I know." She hung her head momentarily, feeling defeated, like a fool who's not going to win an argument. For so long, Cara had been sure that Owen killed Liam. But she knew it was true the same way a person might know it's going to rain. Meteorologists find nothing on the radar, but there's been a change in the atmosphere, and you know in your bones that a storm is coming. There was never any physical evidence to use to prove that Owen killed Liam, but Cara knew it to be true in her very core.

There must be a way to prove what I know is true, she thought.

"What if I can get him to confess?" she asked, suddenly excited.

"What are you going to get him to confess to, exactly?"

Now Cara was allowing the chair to totter back and forth freely as she bounced around, unable to contain her enthusiasm for this new idea.

"Does it matter? One of the murders? All of them?" There was a confidence in her voice, an edge of excitement. She knew this would work, that this was the answer they needed.

"I'll do whatever it takes. Just tell me what I need to get him to admit to."

Twenty-four hours later, Cara sat nervously on the worn, wooden bench, looking around at all the parkgoers carrying out their daily routines in what must be very mundane lives. She was physically and metaphorically wired. The anxiety surrounding the task she'd agreed to, actually, the idea she'd come up with, had her wound as tight as a drum.

Detective Lenderman had helped to tape the wire to her skin. It stretched from the middle of her sternum just below the neckline of her shirt, across her chest to her armpit, and down the side of her ribcage and waist to the small box that Cara imagined must be some kind of transmitter. The box was in her pocket and was a similar shape to a phone, so she figured it was inconspicuous.

She rearranged herself again, trying to relax and get comfortable. The detectives were setting up their team and testing the equipment. Currently, they just needed her in place and wearing the device, but Cara found that the waiting involved with this part of the plan was turning out to be excruciating. Her thoughts swirled rampantly around in her mind as she tried to piece together exactly what she'd say to Owen. There was only one chance for her to get this right.

Detective Sanchez met with Owen last night under the guise of one last interview for his article series on Johnny Rowe. Sanchez wanted to find out if he could get Owen to reveal any other clues or information that might help them bust him. They were probably hoping they could get him to slip up, so they didn't have to agree to her wearing a wire today.

Cara knew he wouldn't be successful. Owen doesn't slip up. He only tells you exactly what he wants you to know.

Her plan for their conversation today mostly involved her pushing and prying at him until she made him angry enough to admit to what he'd done. And she was sure he would. Owen would want to hurt her, to flaunt his power and scare her into submission. He was just like their father.

Thoughts of Owen caused her mouth to go dry. *Deep breaths.* Cara closed her eyes and let the light breeze blow across her face. Imagining this nightmare coming to an end, made her smile. Her heart rate slowed once more.

Patting the device in her pocket, Cara remembered her last conversation with Owen. Fueling his curiosity on the phone this morning had been a good idea. She knew he couldn't resist a good story, even if, or maybe especially if, it was about him.

The detectives had encouraged Cara to use all emotional weaponry she had at her disposal to get him talking.

"And once he's talking, keep asking him questions. You can insinuate ideas and make suggestions, but he has to say that he killed Johnny. It has to come from his own mouth in his own words," Detective Sanchez had said.

"But what if he doesn't admit to killing Johnny Rowe? What if he admits to Derrick Hoffman, or maybe even Warren Williams? I'm pretty sure he killed him, too."

"We'll be listening and watching. There'll be officers posted in plain sight in disguise, as well as some out of view. If he acts like he's going to get physical or be violent toward you in any way, we're going to come out and stop the entire thing. But if he confesses to one or several of the murders and doesn't make a move to hurt you, just let him keep talking. We'll apprehend him once he walks away from you."

This must be what hope feels like, Cara thought. She'd never really experienced the sensation, but the end seemed so close now, her body was tingling with the anticipation of it.

Whatever happens next, only one of us is leaving here with our freedom intact. I don't care about the other deaths, but he has to pay for killing Liam. Either he's going to have to kill me, confess to what he's done, or I'll hunt him for the rest of his life— forever a slave to bringing Owen to justice.

Chapter 27

When he was younger, Owen's father used to always make grand statements meant as bits of wise advice, such as, "Honesty is not always the best policy. If you're going to lose, lie until it's the truth."

As a lawyer mostly dealing with divorce, Frank Walsh was often unethical, and consistently unapologetic. There never seemed to be a ceiling on how far he thought he could push people. Owen had grown up being needled, insulted, and squeezed into submission by his father's position as the ruling, god-like entity of their family.

Owen's current conversation with Cara had him feeling like a wounded animal, backed into a corner. The words that were coming out of his mouth sounded like Frank Walsh, riding high on the victory of another case won. Owen's voice didn't even sound like his own, so complete was his transformation into the worst monster he'd ever known.

This was Cara's fault. How dare she look so scared? How dare she push his back against the wall and then make him feel like he's the one who should be ashamed of himself?

Owen was done feeling ashamed of himself. That feeling died the day Liam died. He no longer lived to please anyone else. Never again would he let anyone, even his father, make him feel like he had something to prove. Now, here was his little sister, his conniving, sneaky, untrustworthy sister, cajoling him into this current waterfall of words. How did she always seem to put him on the defensive?

"Is this the end of the road, Cara?" he spat his question at her as she stared at him wide-eyed. "Did you call me here to confess?"

Suspicions finally boiling over, he couldn't maintain his brotherly facade any longer. The breeze stirred around them in the pause that followed his question. Leaves blew past on the ground and thoughts of Mill City last fall floated through his head. Slippery memories that he couldn't quite grasp back then had begun to settle and become visible this morning after Cara's phone call, solidifying the truth in his question.

"What? Me? What am I gonna confess?" Cara began to raise her voice and leaned away from him on the bench, a movement of disbelief and confusion.

"This is bullshit. I'm not sitting here with you any longer. You need help."

Owen stood abruptly and stared down at her. His sister. A stranger. He knew they were both damaged, never to be whole again. But Owen had grown, changed, become something more. He didn't need to be complete as other people defined the word. All he needed were his stories. How dare she try to take them from him! How dare she try to manipulate his life!

Outrage filled him and spread all the way to the tips of his fingers. He felt himself flexing them and squeezing them into fists at his sides. His arms hung stiffly, barely holding back the intense energy pulsing in his veins.

Now Cara was on her feet, too. She faced him and mirrored his body language, hands in tight fists, an anger burning so brightly that she seemed to be turning red before his eyes.

"I need help?" She half-shouted the rhetorical question at him. Then she bit her bottom lip, holding back a laugh. "That's how you've wanted me to feel for the last twelve years! You have literally ruined my life! First Liam was out to get me, and then you. I didn't need your help! I was taking care of my problem with Liam, and it would've been fine if you hadn't turned against me. Everything that's happened is your fault!"

Several passersby had slowed in their activities to turn and watch the two of them arguing. The mother and her little boy sitting not too far away were not even trying to hide their stares. They looked as though someone had told them to freeze and caught them in awkward positions, her hand mid-air holding a napkin, the little boy's mouth hanging open with the sandwich perched on the edge of his bottom lip. It would be comical were Owen not so worked up.

He knew he shouldn't have come, shouldn't have met her here. This was never going to end any other way. Cara was like a dog with a bone. Ever since Liam's death, she'd followed him, spied on him, and looted through his belongings. Owen never could seem to get far enough away from her. And then there were the notes, then the phone calls. What was she hoping to accomplish? What could she possibly get out of harassing him?

Maybe, he thought cynically, she was always broken. Just like Liam. Just like Mom. Their father was at the heart of the dysfunction, the abuse. Owen wondered if Frank Walsh made them all who they are by the way he lived his life, or was it something in his DNA? The age-old question of nature versus nurture.

Maybe neither he nor his siblings ever really had a chance to be normal. Sanity was probably overrated, but he did often long for a happier story. *Ah, well.* It was never in the cards for a Walsh to become a good person. The thought occurred to him that perhaps Cara was finally living up to her full potential of being a monster, just like him, just like Liam, just like Dad. *Of course, she blamed him. Everything was always Owen's fault.*

Suddenly, Owen was eight years old again, kneeling in the backyard of their childhood home, fiercely clutching the baseball in his hand. He continued to stare down at the dirt, his vision blurry through the tears drowning his eyes. Wiping his face on his shoulder sleeve, Owen noticed the dark streak of blood that was left behind. The baseball had a smear as well.

He crawled around a little where he was kneeling to further the facade that he was still looking for the ball that had rolled behind a bush. Scraping the ball on the ground as he moved, Owen was hoping to get rid of the evidence of his injury. Injuries were failures. Bleeding was a weakness. Crying was what babies did.

"Get up! Where's the ball?" His dad's booming voice carried across the lawn and caused Owen's shoulders to tense. There hadn't been any warning before the back of his father's hand had collided with the side of his face, the knuckles catching his bottom lip and smashing it into his teeth. That was probably where the blood was coming from.

Owen knew it was his fault. He should have caught the ball. That was his first mistake. Then, to make matters worse, Liam had beat him to pick up the ball, flying past Owen as he jogged to where it had landed. He should've been faster. That was his second mistake.

Liam had snatched the baseball up, just as Owen was reaching for it. By the time he'd gotten back to his dad, Liam was standing nearby, basking in the glow of their father's pride. The approval was literally shining on his face. Determined not to let another afternoon go by without getting some kind of compliment from his dad, but also intent on avoiding the repercussions of allowing his little brother to beat him, Owen tried to mask his frustrations.

He picked up the bat and said, "Dad, will you pitch to me?"

"Sure, sure," was the uninterested response. Their dad lovingly patted Liam on the head, guiding him toward where Owen was standing. "Go catch, Little Champ." That was the nickname he'd begun to call Liam in recent months.

He came to stand behind Owen, glove held up, ready to catch. The first pitch sped by Owen before he had a chance to think about swinging. Liam's stifled giggle sounded thunderous in his ears. It steeled his nerves, and he zeroed in on the next pitch. He shouldn't have let his little brother get to him like that. This time, he smashed the ball. It flew over Dad's head, landing in the field behind their house, and rolling under the shrubs planted along the edge on the other side.

Victoriously, Owen threw the bat behind him, pumped his fists into the air, and began an elated jog around their make-shift bases. He was so excited that he'd finally managed to show up Liam in front of his dad, that he didn't notice the fury on his dad's face until he was heading for home plate. He stopped in front of where they were standing, Dad's large frame shadowing the spot where Owen now stood.

Liam peeked out from behind Frank Walsh, a scrape next to his eye, slightly bleeding. He wasn't crying, but Owen could tell that he was holding it in. It was very satisfying to see his little brother upset and hurt. The smile slid from his face, however, as he looked up to see his father's angry glare.

"Look what you did, you little shit! Don't you know, you never throw the bat? You drop it!" That was when Owen was backhanded. It sent him stumbling and then falling backward. To hide his surprise and disappointment, he jumped up quickly and turned to run into the field where he'd hit the ball.

After making sure the bleeding had stopped, and wiping his tears away, Owen trotted back to where they'd been playing the game. Liam was sitting on the porch with an ice pack held to his cheek, and their mother was stooped over him pawing at his hair and making shushing sounds. She looked up at Owen as he approached and noticed the look on his face.

"Owen! What happened?" She sounded concerned, but she didn't leave Liam's side as she spoke, her only movement was a sideways glance at her husband. "I guess I'll go get you an ice pack, too."

As she turned to go inside, Frank grabbed her arm and held her still.

"Nah, he's fine," he said, in that short way he had that brokered no argument.

She seemed unsure, looking back at Owen's face, probably noticing the dried tears, blood, and mud smeared across his skin, or perhaps the swollen lip.

"Well..." she started to say but was immediately silenced by Frank squeezing the arm he still held tightly.

"I said he's fine. It's his own fault anyway, right Owen?" His dad looked down at him, expecting a swift agreement. Owen nodded once but didn't speak. Everything was always his fault.

But that was then, and this was now. He was done being blamed.

He had to get out of here.

"Fine, Cara, fine. I ruined your life, so you're trying to ruin mine. Good for you," he spoke loudly over his shoulder as he turned and quickly began to stride away from her. He was pretty sure he wasn't headed in the right direction, but at that point, he just needed to be away from her before he said or did anything he might regret.

Cara caught up to Owen quickly, practically jogging next to him.

"Owen. Just admit it. Just say you've always hated me. Just say you've always tried to turn Liam's death back on me. That you wanted everyone to think that I killed him!" She was still speaking too loudly, half-shouting at him as she kept up with his fast pace.

Where was the exit? Owen switched directions and strode quickly down a different path. Cara followed close to his heels.

"Where are you going?" Cara managed to ask in between huffs. She was getting out of breath.

Owen came to a stop abruptly and swung around to face her. She suddenly looked around and back over her shoulder like she was in the middle of a war zone. His sister seemed paranoid, or maybe anxious. Or maybe she reminded him of a person searching for a friend in a crowd.

"I haven't always hated you. But I learned to after all the years of you hunting me like an animal!" He was angry again. Resentful. "The truth is, Cara, everything that's happened has been your fault. Yours." He turned on the spot, pacing a few steps to the side, growing more agitated.

For once, Cara stood there, silent. Owen knew she was waiting for him to speak, to fill the silence, and he didn't really care anymore. Pacing back toward her, the sorrowful look on her face pushed him over the edge he didn't realize he was clinging to.

Owen got inches from her face and whispered menacingly, "You almost messed everything up. Everyone assuming you had something to do with Liam's death was your own fault. If you weren't so wrapped up in your little pre-teen drama, you would've noticed that some of us were actually suffering!" To his horror, his voice had grown thick, and he choked on the last word.

Masking the emotion, he turned on the spot once more and began walking. There she was, beside him within seconds. Was it his imagination or was she still looking behind them? He had the sensation that they were being followed and he turned to look back. Suddenly, Cara grabbed his sleeve and yanked him to a standstill.

"So, you thought you'd share that suffering with me? My life has never been normal! You could've helped me. You could've saved me! But you chose not to. Instead, you pushed people to be suspicious of me! But I didn't kill him! And you know it!"

Cara was still shouting. This time, though, it felt as if they were all alone in the park. There were no bicyclists or joggers passing by any longer, no conversations to be heard nearby.

This struck Owen as odd, but he was too wrapped up in his rage to care where they'd stopped to scream at each other.

"Why were you out there? Why were you in the woods that day?" He looked at her, boring his eyes into hers, willing her to answer.

Cara hesitated, biting down on her lip, her eyes darted back and forth. Finally, seeming to come to a decision, she said, "I really did find him by accident! I went there, to the field, trying to frame him, I guess. But he came back to the locker room. I don't know why." The memories poured out of her now. She spoke urgently, her voice saturated with regret.

337

"He caught me trying to put that bag of pills in his bat bag. I wanted him to get in trouble, maybe get kicked off the team, or fall from grace, or whatever."

She took a deep, ragged breath and continued, "He snatched the bag from me, grabbed his phone, and took off running. He didn't even say anything! I didn't know what to do. I didn't know where he'd gone. I left and wandered around in the halls for a little while. I don't know how long."

Owen had never heard this part of her story, not from Cara. He'd assumed some of the details, figured out a few others, and he was quite satisfied to know how close to the truth he'd been.

"I was freaking out. I figured Liam was going to call Mom to come get him and then he'd tell her what I was up to, about what I tried to do." Cara stood wringing her hands, inching closer to her own destruction.

"Why were you in the woods, Cara?" Owen repeated his question, calmer now, more in control. He knew where this conversation was headed, and he realized he was ready for it. Ready for the truth. Finally.

Cara's eyes met his, pleading for his understanding, while at the same time clearly conveying her disdain.

"I didn't know what else to do," she hung her head. "I just thought I'd walk home and meet with whatever consequences came after that. But then..." she paused, holding her head up, tears flowing down her cheeks now.

"But then, I found him. I came around the turn in the path where the rocks are, and he was just lying there... I couldn't...

I mean, he didn't..." She lapsed into a silent sob, leaving her sentences unfinished.

Owen couldn't stand this. His sister had always been too fragile, too weak.

"I'm done with this, done with you."

Before he could move, she'd reached out and grabbed hold of his sleeve once more.

"You lied!" Cara yelled at him.

He stared at her.

"What, nothing to say for once?" she taunted him. Owen was a little intrigued by how furious she suddenly seemed to be. It almost made him forget his own outrage. Almost.

"And what did I lie about?"

"Everything! You lied about where you were that day! You lied about the watch! You lied about me, over and over again to the police and the doctors!"

Owen felt a bubble of laughter rise in his throat. This wasn't funny, so why was he having a hard time keeping a straight face? Maybe it was the irony of it all. Maybe it was her righteous indignation when he knew the truth. Whatever was causing it, Owen was glad for it. He felt back in control of his emotions and thoughts. He felt powerful.

"Like I said," he spoke calmly, a smile spreading across his features, "you can only blame yourself. Or maybe you can blame it on being in the wrong place, at the wrong time? You shouldn't have been in the woods that day. You almost ruined everything."

Chapter 28

When Cara was eight years old, she used to squat at the edge of the backyard, in between the dark pink azaleas blooming, and wait to retrieve any of the balls Liam hit while practicing. He'd use the pitching machine for hours, and she would faithfully run around and fetch for hours.

Owen was always baffled by her commitment to be Liam's obedient assistant on these occasions. They'd arrive home from school in the afternoons and Owen would retreat to his room to stay out of sight and have the privacy to write and create without scrutiny. Meanwhile, his little sister would wait at the living room window like a lonely puppy, watching for Liam to come home after practice.

It was sickening, really. Even back then, he should have seen the dangerous devotion that she was developing for him. Even before Liam was unbearable and egotistical in the worst ways, Owen sensed his true nature. He could tell that the tension was building in the Walsh family, a perfect storm was accumulating within each of them.

One spring evening, before he'd learned not to interfere or retaliate, Owen decided that his younger brother didn't deserve the attention of their sweet, innocent sister. He didn't like the way Liam would take advantage of her willingness to help, or the way she yearned for his compliments and love, but never received them.

Owen walked by the window that faced into the back-yard and watched the scene for a few minutes. Liam wasn't using the pitching machine. He was pulling baseballs from the bucket, tossing up one at a time, and hitting it straight at Cara. She was running back and forth, dodging the balls, like a game of Duck Hunt on the Nintendo. Cara's smile seemed forced as she narrowly avoided baseball after baseball, while reaching her small, gloved hand out every once in a while, to try and catch one.

Liam's laugh was mean and taunting, "C'mon, Care Bear! Catch the ball! What are you doing out there? You look like a dog chasing its tail!"

Owen stepped out onto the back porch so he could see Cara better. She turned to run from a ball coming at her head and unknowingly stepped right on top of one lying next to her on the ground.

In the next second, her feet slipped out from under her, and she landed flat on her back, hard. With the wind knocked out of her, Cara rolled to her side and curled up, clutching her stomach, and gasping for breath. Tears streamed down her tiny cheeks, and she squeezed her eyes shut to stop the flow.

Outrage burst into Owen's chest at the sight of her lying hurt on the ground. The laughter coming from Liam sounded like drumming as his pulse beat uncontrollably in his ears, an idiosyncratic march. Brushing past him, Owen stomped out to where Cara laid and kneeled down to check on her.

"Why do you let him do this to you?"

She opened her eyes, squinted up at him and said in a whisper in between breaths, "He didn't mean to... I fell down... We were just playing a game."

Owen looked back over his shoulder to where Liam stood, slowly recovering from his doubled-over with laughter fit. Without a second thought, he left Cara lying on the ground, made it to his younger brother in a few quick strides, and shoved him with all his strength.

Liam, who was caught off guard by the sudden outburst, fell backward, landing roughly on his backside with a shocked look on his face. Owen stood over him, momentarily satisfied, feeling vindicated for this instance and every other slight and misdeed that had come before.

The feeling was fleeting, however, because in the next moment their father, who Owen hadn't even realized was home already, came striding out the backdoor of their house, letting the door slam loudly behind him.

"What's going on?" he demanded.

The three siblings stared at him, saying nothing, collectively holding their breath. They all knew what was coming next.

Frank Walsh's eyes passed over each child, hesitated on Liam, and landed on Owen. His face was not a question, but a demand for an explanation.

Owen spoke up quickly, pleadingly, "Liam was hitting balls right at Cara's head! On purpose! Trying to hit her! And then she fell and hurt herself and he's laughing at her!"

His dad stared at him for an eternity before turning his head to look down at Liam. "Is that so? And why are you on the ground?"

Liam's lip revealed a slight tremor before he was able to smooth his lips into a straight line. "Cara wanted me to hit some balls so she could try catching them. Which is what I was doing. And then she slipped on a ball. But before I could even see if she was okay," he continued, volume increasing, "Owen just pushed me down! I don't know what he's so mad about!"

"That's not what happened!"

"Is so!"

"Liar!"

"Enough!" Their dad's deep, booming voice cut them off. He looked over to Cara, who had walked closer to the group. "Are you okay?"

She nodded solemnly.

"Did you come out here to catch balls for him?" He pointed at Liam who was still sitting unceremoniously sprawled on the ground.

She nodded again.

Frank looked out of the corner of his eye at Owen. "And did Owen push Liam down?"

Cara hesitated, then glanced down to see her father flexing his left fist, while his right hand jiggled with agitation against his pant leg. Owen followed her eyes. He was standing too close to those hands.

Cara nodded again.

SMACK!

Owen felt the wind of the fist before the impact against his nose. He stumbled a few steps back but stayed on his feet. Blood dripped down his face.

Frank looked at Owen, still standing, still facing him. It must have seemed like an insult or a challenge. Owen was sure he saw a slight smirk on his father's face, effectively canceling out the courage he'd felt moments before. In two quick steps, Frank's smile and arms widened as he reached out to shove Owen, the violent push forcing Owen to his back, slamming his skull into the ground.

His father stood over him with a grim face and said, "You still feeling like a big man? Like you can push around people smaller than you?"

Apparently, the irony was lost on Frank Walsh. Owen would've been crazy to laugh. Life was too unfair for it to actually be funny. But when he thinks of that day, the question makes him laugh.

That was the night their dad gave Liam his prized, antique watch that he'd received from his own father. After a silent, sullen dinner, where no one said a single word during the meal, Frank told Liam to come into his office. He never let any of the children come into his office, so Owen was envious and curious, and decided to spy on them.

He watched and listened through the crack where the door had been left slightly ajar, while his father gave Liam the watch he'd been telling Owen was meant for him since he was five years old.

The promised treasure, a valuable family heirloom supposedly, was to be given to him when he turned 18. Now, here was his dad, passing the watch to Liam at the age of ten, in secret. Owen had held out hope of earning back his dad's favor, but he knew at that moment that it was a wasted wish.

That night, Owen laid on his bed, on top of the sheets, lights on, lost in despair, not really making any attempts to get up or get in the bed. That's when Cara walked into his room. He ignored her. She slowly walked around his room, running her hand along the books lining his shelves, obviously wanting him to acknowledge her, but he couldn't.

"I wished you woulda just left us alone," she said sadly as she arrived next to the bed.

Owen rolled on his side to look at her. His nose was aching, and his back hurt every time he moved. As he scrutinized his little sister's face, he decided he didn't like her sad eyes.

Cara can't blame him! She's the reason it all went wrong! If she would just stop trying to please Liam all the time like everyone else, maybe they could help each other! She should wake up and pay attention to who's really on her side.

Anger rose up in him. "You know what? Don't count on me helping you next time! This is all your fault!" he whisper-shouted as he gestured to his face.

He huffily rolled onto his other side, facing away from her, his spine aching and sending shooting pains down his legs as he moved. "Just go away. First, Liam ruined my life. Now, you. You both ruined everything!"

Grown-up Cara's eyes grew large and round, wide and wild. "What did I almost ruin?" she whispered.

Owen knew it was time. He'd give her what she wanted, what she'd haunted him for. Maybe then he could finally be rid of her.

"Liam had to go. None of us could continue the way we were while he lived."

The color drained from Cara's face and her shocked expression excited him, satisfied him.

"So you killed him? You killed your own brother?"

"Oh, please, Cara. Don't act like you didn't have thoughts of what it would be like if he was dead. We both know you hated him, that you were scared of him. If I hadn't killed him, you probably would've."

Tears flowed steadily down Cara's cheeks. Owen wrenched his sleeve, which he just realized she was still holding onto, out of her grasp, getting ready to walk away again.

"Please! Tell me what happened!"

With an exasperated sigh, and a quick look around himself to see who else was within earshot, but finding no one, Owen resigned himself to share the whole story.

346

"I didn't know what you were going to do that day, but I knew Liam had been torturing you for weeks and you'd started snooping around the house all the time. That part worked out better than I could've planned because it put everything into motion. I wasn't sure exactly how I'd get him away from the school after practice and before Mom showed up. I was there, waiting, sitting on that brick wall outside of the gym, when I saw him running from the fieldhouse."

Owen took a breath and a step back. Cara was in silent mode again and he knew he didn't have to tell her every little detail, but he couldn't help himself. The words were tumbling from his lips now.

"I started following him immediately, but far enough back where he didn't notice. Or maybe he was just too wrapped up in whatever he was thinking about to get back at you. He started walking and then stopped at the rock outcrop. The whole thing just kept lining up with the perfect situation for me. When I got closer, I realized he'd sat down at the top, with his legs dangling over, not facing me."

Owen noticed that Cara had taken a step toward him to make up for the distance he'd tried to create. As he continued, he shuffled his feet, like he was pacing or swaying, but beginning to create more space between them. Cara still said nothing.

"I walked slowly, not making any sounds and found a rock. It was big, but I could still hold it in one hand. I gripped it and used my other hand to grab Liam by the collar. I yanked him backward and swung the rock as hard as I could into his head. I heard a loud crack, and his skull gave way when I hit him. It was intense." Owen mimed the actions, reliving the final release of all his outrage and desperation.

He looked down at Cara, who was now trembling, and realized he needed to get out of there.

"Well, you know the rest..." he continued hurriedly, "...I only hit him once, but it was enough. Then I dropped him over the side of the rock wall so that he landed on his back. I put the rock down by his head, but apparently not close enough. Yada, yada. Then I ran home to clean up."

Owen paused, looking at Cara significantly, while continuing to move away from her, but she reached out and grabbed him around the wrist this time.

"But before you left, you took his watch, didn't you?" she asked as she gripped the object in question beneath her hand.

"This is not his watch! It was never his! It's mine! It was always supposed to be mine!" Owen knew he was shouting now, but anyone listening be damned.

"That little bastard started keeping it with him all the time because he knew it should be mine and that I would get it back, so when hiding it in his room stopped working, he started wearing it all the time!" he ranted. "It's an antique, family heirloom watch, you think he wore it for fashion? He wasn't even supposed to have it on while he played baseball, but he did whatever he wanted just so I couldn't get what was mine!"

"I saw you pick it up next to the boat ramp where Warren Williams died," Cara said as she continued to hold him by the wrist, keeping him still.

"You what?"

"I was watching you. You were sneaking around at the crime scene by yourself, and you were looking for something. Then I saw you pick it up. You lied to the detective."

"Well, I..." Owen hadn't expected her to know that.

"You know," she continued, "I always knew that you'd taken it from Liam the day he died. You told Mom and Dad that he had tried to throw it out, but that you found it. Owen, the hero. That's why Dad gave it to you, I mean, let you keep it. We both know that Liam never tried to throw it out. Like you said, Liam never left that watch behind and he definitely wouldn't have tried to get rid of it. He'd keep or take anything that held power over someone."

Owen's conviction that Cara was aware of, and probably even a victim of, Liam's pension for theft and assault slid another piece of the puzzle into place. But further proof of her knowledge of his movements over the last year enraged him. If he let her slow his momentum, the power he'd held over her moments before would slip away. It was dangerous to be out of control, to be at the mercy of someone else when they knew your secrets.

And then suddenly, clarity. Cara had been watching him on the boat ramp. This last bit of enlightenment steadied his resolve, and his objective became clear. But before he could act on it, she continued in her rant, wholly unapologetic.

"So, you murdered Liam and Warren Williams. Does that mean you killed Derrick Hoffman and Johnny Rowe, too? Are there any others?" she asked as the tears began to dry on her skin.

"What are you talking about?"

"You've already admitted that you're a killer. I know you've been murdering these men, these philanderers and con artists."

"Ridiculous! I didn't kill any of them! You know I didn't!" Owen roared in response.

How dare she! How dare she accuse him of manipulating his stories! She was the manipulator. Owen was very aware of his hands throbbing with agitation. Cara's small hand still encircled his left wrist. His right hand felt hot and twitchy hanging at his side.

Then, Cara surprised him again. She released her grip, turned, and began to walk briskly away from him.

"Yes, you did!" she called back over her shoulder as she retreated in the direction they'd just come from.

Jolted back into awareness, Owen rushed to catch up to her. She couldn't just accuse him and stroll away like she'd won the argument, like she was better than him. His resentment was boiling near the surface now. This had to end. Cara had to be stopped.

Reaching out, he grabbed the back of her collar and pulled her to the ground in front of him, her feet rising above her head as she fell onto her back. Visions of Liam's face in his last moments of life flashed in Owen's mind at the sight of her tumbling backward.

Something small and square fell out of one of her pockets. It landed next to her but didn't bounce any further, seeming to be attached in some way.

Cara choked and reached up to pull the collar away from her throat. As she did so, Owen noticed something long and black taped to her chest. His eyes followed its ghostly path beneath her shirt to the object dangling from her hip and he understood. Recognition dawned on him, and all the pieces clicked into place- a complete picture of everything leading up to this moment.

"You're recording me?!" He leaned over and screamed down into her face.

In the next second, Owen's hand was wrapped around Cara's throat, and he was pressing with all his strength and rage, with all his pain and fury. Leaning his body weight into her thin frame was easy, it continued to give way as he pushed down to crush her.

Cara's face turned a deep purple with red splotches adorning the edges of her contorted, agonized expression. He could feel the air and the life leaving her body, and he was glad.

Chapter 29

*T*here's never been a pain like this. *Is excruciating an adequate word?* Maybe. Partnered with the gagging, gasping, wrenching agony throbbing in her throat, was the confusion and surprise that someone was hurting her.

Cara knew Owen had reached for her, but it felt as if the scene had changed completely. She was sure they were now barreling through a tunnel on a train, hanging precariously onto the outside of it, like in the movies. She felt off balance, like she was falling, although somewhere in her mind she was certain she was already lying down. And what was that popping sound? It was shocking that she could even hear the noise over the loud shouting permeating her brain.

"Cara," her name sounded like a growl. "This is how you die," Owen's voice was harsh, forced out through gritted teeth. "This is what you deserve." His breath felt hot on her cheek, his grunts sour and poisonous.

Suddenly, the pressure on her neck stopped and Cara instinctively began moving her arms and legs, fighting to break the surface of the water, because surely, she'd been drowning.

The choking sound seemed to be coming from her, but there wasn't any air filling her lungs, at least not quickly enough.

"Miss Walsh? I'm going to give you some oxygen. You'll need to calm down and try to take some slower breaths."

That didn't make any sense. How does someone take slower breaths if they're not taking any breaths at all? Something soft, but firm covered her nose and mouth and there was a clinical smell. The air was sweet, and it felt so comforting going into her nose and mouth.

"That's it, slow breaths."

"Her heart rate is beginning to come down. Breathing is stabilizing."

"She's ready to move."

"Miss Walsh? We're going to be transporting you to the hospital and one of the police officers will meet you there."

Cara felt her body lift off the ground in one movement. A second later, there was a firm surface underneath her, but she could tell she was moving through the air.

Her thoughts were beginning to solidify, but it was like waking up from a dream after taking a sleeping pill, fighting through a thick fog of confusion. Glimpses of paramedics, police officers, trees, and blue sky popped in and out of her narrowed vision.

Oh, yeah. Owen. The meeting. He figured out I was taping him. He tried to strangle me!

She remembered. The relief of knowing she wasn't going to die made her very, very tired. Cara closed her eyes again as they loaded her into the ambulance and the sounds of police radios and low conversations were abruptly cut off, replaced by a rhythmic beeping and the rumble of an engine.

When she woke up, a bright light was piercing her still closed eyelids. She opened them slowly, blinking to adjust her vision, gradually becoming aware that she was lying in a bed and two people were standing next to her. A nurse with a kind, motherly face smiled back at her, checked her watch, then patted Cara on the shoulder gently before moving away to the end of the bed.

Detective Sanchez's storm gray eyes were squinty and creased with either irritation or worry, she wasn't sure which. They appeared cold, guarded. Cara knew she wouldn't get all the information from him that she wanted, and it filled her with trepidation.

"Well, that didn't go exactly like we hoped," the detective said sarcastically, as a greeting.

Cara opened her mouth to respond and a wheeze that should've been a word came out. It was like she'd been walking through a desert. She licked her lips and tried again.

This time, her voice came out in a rasping whisper. "What happened?"

She knew what had occurred, but wondered what events followed her becoming unconscious. Was Owen arrested? Did they get the information they needed? Was it enough? But she couldn't get all those words together into complete sentences yet.

"It seems you pushed your brother a little too far."

The detective took a deep breath but relaxed his shoulders as he did so. "But we've got his confession for killing Liam." He paused, giving space for the grief and relief that he must've seen flood Cara's face.

"Owen was pulled off of you after just ten to fifteen seconds of contact."

That was mind-blowing. Mere seconds? Her brother almost squeezed the life out of her in a few seconds?

"But still a lot of damage done, huh?" Sanchez summed up her thoughts succinctly, with a slight grimace meant to convey the regret he was feeling for allowing her to become involved.

"And... the others?" She managed to breathe the words loud enough for him to hear.

Detective Sanchez shifted his weight and began fidgeting with his belt loop before he answered. He seemed uncomfortable.

"Well, you know he didn't admit to being involved in the other deaths in his conversation with you. He's down at the station right now in an interview room. Once I get over there, Detective Lenderman and I will see what he has to say."

Cara's eyes became blurry, filling with tears. At least they had him for killing Liam. She knew it. She'd always known.

Worries of insufficient evidence and the confession not being enough immediately began to fill her thoughts, overtaking the second of relief. Inadequacy had always haunted her, eventually becoming her constant companion. It had been her mission for over half her life to prove Owen's guilt, and the idea that she couldn't control the outcome is ripping her up internally. This time, the damage may be irreparable.

Seeming to read her mind, the detective said, "I got the impression after his arrest that he wasn't interested in retracting the confession. He was eager to tell 'his side of the story,'" he said with air quotes.

Sanchez looked uncomfortable again and cleared his throat. "I'm going to let you get some rest. Once you're released, we'd like to meet with you again. Nurse Cathy is going to make sure she keeps me updated." He looked at the nurse to confirm, and she nodded and smiled good-naturedly.

Cara closed her eyes in resignation and as a dismissal. She heard low whispering and some papers shuffling before the air in the room changed, signaling the emptiness they left behind.

Then, Cara slept. But it wasn't restful. The night was filled with dreams that were too colorful and loud. She awoke often, her pulse pounding her to consciousness. Dread surrounded her like the blanket tucked tightly at her sides. A hospital stay, motherly nurses, a watchful detective, a psychotic brother. All of this was familiar and frightening.

The overcast gloom hanging in the sky the morning Cara returned to the station a few days later, matched her mood perfectly. She was escorted into the building by the officer who had picked her up. He'd attempted to chat casually with her in the car, but she was still having difficulty doing a lot of talking, so she figured she'd save her breath for what was sure to be a longer conversation with the detectives.

Would they believe her? Would they even want to hear what she had to say? The pounding in her ears made her doubtful, but the trembling in her chest reminded her that young Cara, buried deep within the layers of fear and shame, was eager to be set free. Did it matter if they believed her?

Detective Lenderman greeted her first and shook her hand with both of his. It was a gesture that made her feel like he was comforting her, while also expressing his gratitude. After directing her toward a chair across the table, he sat down in his own seat and shuffled a few papers around.

Detective Sanchez had smiled when she entered, but remained seated, arms folded, legs stretched out and crossed at the ankles in casual defiance. He was more guarded than his partner, but his expression today seemed... conflicted. His storm-colored eyes were darker, and instead of the watery gray, two deep, navy orbs blazed into her.

"Thanks for coming in. We wanted to meet with you for a couple of reasons," Detective Lenderman started, and Cara directed her attention back to him.

"One: to turn over Owen's personal belongings that have not proved relevant to our case. And two: to have you confirm your contact info, so we know it's recorded correctly. Once you leave town to go home, we may need to get in touch with you again if we have any questions."

Lenderman smiled pleasantly and picked up his pen, poising it over his notepad.

Sanchez shifted in his seat, sitting up straighter and tucking his feet underneath the chair. He leaned forward to put his elbows on the table, but his eyebrows remained pulled together as he studied his large hands, no longer meeting her eyes.

Cara felt distracted. She nodded in agreement to Lenderman's request and gave the men her new address and phone number, as well as her parent's contact information in case they needed to reach her there.

They turned over Owen's suitcase, and it felt surprisingly empty. She opened it briefly to peek inside and found a toiletry bag containing only a stick of deodorant and contact solution, a Men's Health magazine, a couple rolls of socks, a pair of flip-flops, a few pens, and one mechanical pencil.

As she zipped up the last pocket, Cara asked, "Can you please tell me if you have enough evidence to charge Owen with Liam's murder? Or any of the other men?"

Lenderman looked over to his partner. Sanchez took a deep breath and leaned back in his chair again, this time laying his hands in his lap and looking up at her.

"Well," Sanchez said slowly, "Owen has given us a full statement about the day Liam died, admitting that he killed him, and providing every single detail of his movements before, during, and after the murder."

The detective seemed to hesitate before continuing. She waited.

"We found some additional evidence among his personal belongings and in some of his journals that indicate some connections to Williams and Hoffman. Although, he's continuing to deny that he had anything to do with their deaths."

Cara pondered that in the silence that hung within the lull in conversation. Sitting as still as possible, she focused on the detective's top lip. It was pulled into a straight line. Irritated? Maybe. Skeptical? Definitely. Detective Sanchez needed some convincing of her brother's guilt.

"What led you to believe that Owen killed Warren Williams?" Detective Lenderman finally asked after a minute of the three of them sitting in silence.

"Well, like I've said before, I always thought that Owen killed Liam," she began, "and when I read his first Newsworthy article and learned he was in Mill City, only a short drive from me and my parents, I decided to spy on him a bit."

Her cheeks flushed at the admission. Cara knew she sounded crazy, but she'd already admitted this behavior to them previously, so she continued.

"I followed him out to the crime scene, to the Greenway. I had to hide in the woods to see what he was doing, and he was down at the end of the boat ramp. It was like he was looking for something. He picked something up and when he walked closer to me, I saw that it was his watch. The watch he stole from Liam! Liam had it the day before he died, and Owen had it the day after. Dad never gave him that watch like Owen said he did. Dad gave it to Liam. Then, after Liam died, Mom, or maybe Dad, noticed Owen wearing it and he told a lie about Liam not wanting it, so they just let him keep it. He never took it off after that. Just like Liam never took it off before he died, I guess."

Cara took a breath before continuing. Her throat felt raw and tender.

"Owen went out there to the park, alone, but I overheard him on his phone telling the detective that he was somewhere else and that he wanted to visit the scene again. So, he was lying and covering up the fact that he was already there. But why? I bet he lost that watch when he was there killing Williams, then went back to look for it later."

Sanchez scratched thoughtfully at the stubble on his chin. "How do you think he got Williams out to the park?"

She'd already considered the motives. "Well, he is a journalist. I've read some about Warren Williams, and my understanding is that he loved the spotlight. What if Owen promised to write some feature story on him? Maybe he convinced him to meet at the park? Or it could be that his story idea had some sort of angle about Warren's dad, the mayor. In that case, I would think Warren would want to meet covertly."

Lenderman nodded and took notes. Sanchez continued to rub his chin, then said, "So, in your view, Owen murdered Williams because he was a person who was well-off that would take advantage of those less fortunate. And these things reminded your brother of Liam's entitled behavior? Did Liam also exploit other people?"

Not trusting her expression to remain impassive, she could only nod in agreement.

"What about Hoffman?" Lenderman asked.

"Well, it wasn't until our conversation in the park the other day that I realized Owen had met him before."

"How do you think he convinced Derek to leave his apartment in secret the night of the murder? According to Detective Miller, Ketamine was used to forcefully sedate Hoffman. Do you think that was from your stash?" Sanchez asked.

Interesting and irritating that he'd called it her 'stash.' Terms like that were only meant to blame or intimidate.

"Yeah, I think that he used the K that he'd taken from my parents' house. I've been wondering if maybe he used it on Warren Williams as well? It would have made it easier to sedate him, hit him with the brick, set him up in the car, then rig the car to drive off the end of the boat ramp, don't you think?"

They blinked back at her as if the thought hadn't crossed their minds.

"But to answer your first question, I think he used his sway as a journalist again to convince Derrek that he had some other info about a story that could finally get him arrested. I mean, think about it. Here you've got a guy who's just been doing whatever he wants, with whoever he wants. Forcefully getting what he wanted and forcing people to help him cover it all up and avoid the consequences. What would happen if someone were to say that they had a story that could break it all open and expose him for who he really is? I think he'd try to do whatever it took to stop that person. Maybe Derrek was going to pay Owen off but didn't get a chance."

All of this was circumstantial and didn't amount to real evidence, but it felt so good to share it with someone.

"Did Liam act like that, too?"

361

Looking down at her hands clasped on the table, Cara took a deep breath to keep the tears at bay. It was difficult for her to reminisce about her middle brother's penchant for violence.

"Yes, he did," she whispered. "I was a witness on several occasions to how Liam didn't have any problem hurting someone to get what he wanted. A few times it seemed as if he hurt them or took things from them just for fun. Maybe to get back at them for something they didn't even know they'd done wrong. I think Owen was Liam's favorite target, but not his only victim."

Silent tears ran down her face, clinging to her jaw. She swiped at them with her sleeve and sniffed loudly. It was impossible to remain a mask of neutrality with these memories surfacing. Resentment burned beneath her skin, heating her up.

This wasn't an excuse for Owen's actions, but she wanted the chance to explain to herself and the rest of the world how her oldest brother had revealed himself to be a monster.

"I know this must be difficult," Lenderman said kindly, "we're almost done."

Later, at her hotel, while repacking bags preparing for the trip back to Georgia, Cara pulled out the last of Owen's abandoned items to finish emptying his suitcase. She planned on leaving it behind. The hotel would throw it out.

Instead of paying attention to what was left of his belongings, she focused on what was missing. What could the journals say that connected him to the murders? Hopefully, it was enough. Maybe now her life could begin, and she'd be free of both of her brothers.

It was true, Liam had revealed himself to be a terrible person before he died, taking on the abusive qualities of their dad. But finding him dead, being blamed and vilified, disrupted Cara's life in inexplicable ways. She angrily tossed Owen's belongings in the trash can one at a time, her rage slowly subsiding with every item that landed in the receptacle.

The Men's Health magazine was rolled up and tucked into the mesh pocket on the underside of the lid. As she yanked it loose, a piece of the bag's lining caught on the corner of the curled magazine cover and seemed to pull it back in a strange way. Thinking she'd ripped something, Cara reached into the pocket to push the fabric back into place and felt a hard lump underneath her fingers.

Investigating, she pulled the fabric back up and discovered a small, rectangular object nestled underneath the lining, camouflaged black on black. The flash drive had almost escaped Cara's notice, and most certainly had gone undetected by the police hidden within the lining of the suitcase. It wasn't remarkable in any way. There wasn't a label on the front or back.

Curious, and more than a little excited to have a piece of Owen, maybe a bargaining chip, or a damning bit of evidence, Cara powered up her laptop hoping to view the files. The flash drive had one folder, untitled. Nervously, she opened it.

The strongest sense of déjà vu came over her as soon as she caught sight of the contents. *How could this be, after all this time?* It contained only one document, titled "A Newsworthy Life, Forgotten in Death". The title was similar to Owen's lost article from long ago, but with an ominous tone to it. Trembling fingers moved the pointer to hover over the document. Its last edit was the day Owen was arrested, one hour before they met at the park.

Cara's breath quickened and became loud in her own ears, heart pounding like a bass drum as she opened it. It seemed to be a book he'd written. Scrolling past the title page, she came to the dedication page.

"Written for my little sister, Cara. He was guilty, I was guilty, and now you're guilty. May our surrendering bring us the freedom we deserve."

The metallic taste of blood-filled Cara's mouth. She hadn't realized she was biting the inside of her cheek. It felt like the room was closing in on her. The walls were crumbling, and she needed air.

Desperately, Cara bolted into the bathroom and vomited blood and acid into the toilet. Her weakened legs gave way, dumping her onto the floor in a heap, but the cool tiles were comforting on her burning cheeks.

Unwilling to move and face whatever was going to come next, her emotions exhausted, Cara drifted into a dream.

Owen walked in front of her, never turning. She ran as hard as she could to catch him but couldn't get any closer. Her breathing was deep and ragged. She held a brick in one hand and a needle in the other.

Running, praying he wouldn't turn around. The needle was for her, though, wasn't it? Feeling confused, she slowed to look down at what she carried. It wasn't a brick after all, it was a stone. *Good.* She'd throw the stone at Owen. He deserved it.

But when she looked up to find him, he was no longer walking away from her. He'd come as close as a breath, near enough to easily hit him with her weapon. Owen didn't look scared or nervous or even angry. He was smiling at her. She glanced down at his hands to see that he was also holding a stone and thick, crimson blood dripped from its edges onto the pavement.

Owen's grin deepened as he watched the recognition dawn on her face. He looked pointedly down at Cara's hands, raising his eyebrows, questioning. She imagined swinging her arm quickly through the air at his face, so fast that she'd smash him in the teeth and hopefully shatter them before he could make a move to get out of the way.

But at some point, she'd become sluggish, her limbs heavy and uncooperative. As she pushed her arm forward, her wrist caught and stopped short, like it had reached the end of a tether. Looking down, she saw that her hand was empty, bloody, and handcuffed. Following the path of the cuff's chain with her eyes, she realized that the other end was attached to a large, concrete headstone.

Here lies Liam Joshua Walsh
Son, brother, athlete, friend

When Cara looked up again, Owen was gone, and she was alone.

Chapter 30

" *I*'m sorry, babe, but I'll have to give you a call back a little later. I really don't know how much longer I'll be here." Roberto squeezed the bridge of his nose and closed his heavy eyelids as he listened to his wife's anxious response.

Generally, she had a lot of patience and understanding when it came to him working long hours during a case, but Sophia seemed to be at the end of her rope with this one. He couldn't blame her. He'd only been home to sleep for a few hours twice in the last four days.

More than his absence, she fretted about his health. Recently, so has he. The headaches were becoming more frequent, his stomach was constantly upset, his body ached, and he didn't even want to hazard a guess about how high his blood pressure most likely was. But, like a plane crashing toward the ground, Roberto knew that eventually it would end, and he knew from experience that it would probably feel a lot like a crash. He was hoping to avoid the fiery death part.

Once they'd loaded Cara Walsh into the ambulance at the park, he and John searched Owen's hotel room, confiscating all his belongings. Back at the station, Roberto and John listened to the recording of the siblings' conversation.

It was always a different experience to play back the taped words of someone after hearing them in real-time. There were valuable nuggets of information tucked in the kinds of phrases people used. Of course, what matters most are their exact words. He was pleased to find that Owen's confession of killing Liam Walsh was clear and easy to understand. They had filmed the conversation in the park and had video evidence of him assaulting Cara, as well.

It was a shame that Cara had gotten hurt, but the fact that Owen attacked her did strengthen their case. It was also a shame that he hadn't admitted to killing Johnny Rowe, or the other victims, for that matter.

When they'd tackled and handcuffed Owen after he tried to choke his sister, he didn't seem that surprised. Before being shut away in the back of the cruiser, he said, "You only know half of it. There're always two sides to every story. You need to hear my side." He spoke calmly, angrily perhaps, there was a definite edge to his voice, but he wasn't riled up like Roberto had thought he would be.

It was hard not to rush down to the station to speak to this man that he'd gotten to know over the last several weeks, who was now an admitted murderer. But first, he needed to go visit Cara at the hospital. He didn't particularly like the woman, mostly because he didn't trust her. But John said he could tell that Cara didn't particularly care for Roberto either, so it would be better if he went alone to keep the visit short.

Of course, it turned out that his partner was correct, he wasn't at the hospital for very long, and he'd been able to join John at the station to talk to Owen.

Owen's demeanor had changed drastically from the last time they'd met for an interview the night before. He still seemed to possess that self-confident swagger, but it was no longer charming and had morphed into something sinister and egotistical.

Owen sat across the table from the detectives smirking, body relaxed, legs crossed, sipping the coffee they'd offered him as if he was being interviewed by The Today Show. There was no indication beyond the smear of dirt across his fore-head and the scrape along his cheek and neck, that he'd been tackled roughly to the ground and arrested for assault and attempted murder.

John had begun the interrogation, but it quickly became clear that it would be more of a narration because Owen was eager to speak to them about what happened. He talked as if he was retelling a movie plot or explaining an exciting book to friends, seeming to grow more empowered the longer he spoke about killing his brother. Roberto sat enthralled the entire two hours. He and John didn't have to ask many ques-tions or prompt Owen to continue.

As the topic shifted to the death of Johnny Rowe, Owen seemed to shut down. His enjoyment turned quickly into annoyance.

"I mean, I never met the guy, but I could tell he was a prick. Couldn't you?" he challenged them.

"Anyway," he continued, "I've already told you that I found him lying there, already dead." He paused to smile again, and his eyes drifted to a far-off memory. "It was somewhat of a surprise to find him in such a similar way to how I left my brother...".

He leaned forward conspiratorially and added, "Now, I'm not saying that if he'd still been alive when I walked up that I'd have helped him. That bastard deserved to die from what I've been reading and hearing about him." Leaning back in the chair again, he crossed his arms on his chest in a huff and said, "But, that doesn't matter since he was already dead."

"That was such a short amount of time between seeing him in the parking lot at the trailhead to finding him dead on the trail. Can you explain that? Or have any theories about how it might've happened?" John asked.

Satisfaction bloomed on Owen's face, and he nodded like an encouraging teacher, proud of a student who's found the right answer.

"Well, there was the other car in the lot. Have you questioned that person?"

"What car? You were the only witness that we knew of, and you never mentioned another car in your statement. In fact, in your article, didn't you say that there were no other vehicles?" Roberto was irritated. It had all been going so smoothly up to this point.

"Oh, if I said that, then it was just for dramatic effect," he waved away the issue with his hand as he spoke. "There was a small green car parked off to the side. When Rowe pulled in, he parked close to it, which is why I noticed it. But it really wasn't until this morning that I realized the importance of that car, or even remembered its existence."

"I see," John said. "And who do you think drove that car?"

"I'm assuming it's my sister's car, although I've never known what she drives."

"And why do you assume it's Cara's car?"

Roberto's mouth had gone dry and his mind was spinning. All the thoughts and memories that had been cataloged in his brain related to this case were racing to put themselves in order and catch up to this moment.

Owen dropped the smile and stared, astonished back at the two men as he said, "Because she killed Johnny Rowe, of course."

John's jaw dropped at the same second Roberto's thoughts finally clicked into place.

"I'm sure as a detective, you've observed a person or an object in various situations, but you don't recognize it as being the same as what you've already seen because the change in scenery always adds a layer of ambiguity. The repetition of a certain memory is easily explained away just by putting the object, or person, or situation within a different timeframe or scenario." Roberto found himself nodding in agreement. The human mind was easily influenced, and memories are not always trustworthy.

"Well," he continued, "I've seen that same car at some point during each case I've reported on. Exactly that car. Not just one that looks similar. It has a Southeastern College parking sticker in the top left corner of the windshield. My sister went to Southeastern."

"Are you saying that Cara is responsible for killing Johnny Rowe, Derek Hoffman, and Warren Williams?"

"Yes!" Owen responded enthusiastically, slapping his hand loudly down on the tabletop, but not in frustration, in excitement. He was grinning from ear to ear now.

"Yes!" he repeated, "That's it exactly. My sister has always suspected me. I'm not sure how long she's known that I killed Liam, but she has followed me, and snooped, and harassed me for years. I think she murdered these men that I'd come in contact with, knowing I'd end up reporting on their deaths, hoping to connect me to them and frame me." Owen leaned back, crossing his arms again, still smiling, glad that they were following along.

"So, your sister, in an attempt to bring you to justice for the murder of your brother twelve years ago, killed these men hoping to frame you so you'd finally be arrested...even if it wasn't for the person you actually killed... Which means she is also a murderer." Disbelief dripped from John's tone.

"Bingo." Owen sipped his coffee.

"How do you think she got these men to meet her?"

"I cannot begin to imagine the power of the wiles of a woman." Owen waggled his eyebrows and laughed like he hadn't a care in the world. Roberto shivered.

When the detectives continued to stare at him, he rolled his eyes and said, "I'm sure she probably lured Trés to the boat ramp with the promise of sex. I met him a few times and we had some drinks together the week before he died. If she was spying on me, she knew that. And she would've seen that any-time he was out in that town, women practically threw them-selves at him. Probably for his money, or maybe he's good looking, I really don't know, but it was sickening. She's my sister, but I know she's an attractive woman, she wouldn't have had any trouble. I would bet she met him somewhere else, he took her to his house, and then she convinced him to drive out there to the park. She must've waited until they were at the boat ramp to sedate him, hit him with the brick or maybe a rock that she threw in the river, and position everything else."

"How did she know that you were in Mill City?" John interjected.

Owen seemed to consider that a minute. "I tried to keep that information from my family, but my fiancé knew where I was. Maybe Mom or Dad spoke to her at some point. Cara's always kept up with me from a distance, getting whatever morsel she can out of our parents."

Their conversation was of course being recorded, but John was furiously taking notes. Roberto knew it was his way of sorting through the new information. Owen stared down at the pen scribbling across the page while he continued to sip the coffee. He appeared to be waiting patiently, but the set of his jaw and the white knuckles of his free hand told a dif-ferent story.

"Owen," Roberto decided to break his trance and keep him talking, "what about Derek? Tell us how you think Cara pulled that off."

After a deep sigh, Owen set the cup down and folded his hands together in his lap. Superiority and annoyance emanated from his change in posture.

"First, can I ask you a question?" Without waiting for a response, he continued, "If any of my personal items aren't official evidence, will you be turning them over to Cara or my parents?"

Roberto regarded Owen carefully. "Most likely. Why?"

"Just curious."

Owen unfolded his hands, picked up his coffee cup and took a small sip. After a long look at the detectives, he nodded his head in satisfaction then responded to the question.

"I saw Cara outside a coffee shop in Evanston. At the time, I thought I'd imagined seeing her, but when I mentioned it to her this morning her reaction told me everything I needed to know." He chuckled lightly, shaking his head.

He's nuts. They both are. Roberto's thoughts swirled chaotically, fed by adrenaline, excitement, and fear. *But this man is a master manipulator. Maybe this is all a fantasy in his head.*

Owen continued, "So, it's now clear to me that she was there the day I first heard of Derreck Hoffman. Now, after that..." he swiped his arm through the air, his voice trailing off.

Another sip of coffee. He adjusted the cup's position on the table, scooting it back and forth between his fingers. John and Roberto waited for him to finish his thought. Owen wanted to talk, and they knew he wasn't done.

"... Well, after that, I can only speculate. Has she told you that she uses Ketamine? Of course, she says she's clean." Owen shrugged his shoulders.

Before either detective could answer, he asked, "Have you spoken with Detective Miller?"

They nodded in confirmation.

"Then you know that her theory of the crime would explain how Cara was able to pull that one off. My guess is that she again talked him into getting in the car before she sedated him." Owen glanced down at his hands, rubbing them together nonchalantly.

Roberto, unable to entertain this nonsense any longer, stood abruptly, saying, "Owen, excuse us for a minute."

He felt like both siblings were giving them the run-around, blaming each other. They needed some evidence. He caught John's eye and gestured toward the door with his chin. Without skipping a beat, his partner gathered his notepad and pen, and they quickly exited.

In the next room, they stood staring at the monitor where the video feed for the interrogation room was showing. The journalist just sat there calmly, moving the now empty cup between his fingers on the table. After a few seconds, he picked it up and moved it around in the air above his head, looking straight at the camera, and said, "Another refill, please!"

After Owen was arrested and booked for Liam Walsh's murder, Roberto and John combed through his belongings, dusting for fingerprints, collecting DNA, cataloging items. There were three spiral notebooks in his suitcase that contained notes. Some of the writings read like grocery lists, bulleted and brief. Some of the entries were more like narratives, reflections in a journal.

There were well-organized, logical notes that formed a story, intertwined with notes that sounded paranoid and angry. Owen spoke often of his sister and his fiancé, but he fixated most on the backgrounds and lives of the men that were killed. Roberto read pages and pages of rage-filled rants, blaming everything that's wrong with the world on people like Rowe, Hoffman, and Williams.

John requested access to the evidence reports from Mill City and Evanston, and it took their team a day and a half to carefully comb through it all. They had contacted Detectives Miller and Abernathy earlier in the week after formulating the plan to have Cara tape her conversation with Owen. They needed the other detectives' help in reinterviewing witnesses to find out more about Owen's possible involvement.

In Mill City, several people confirmed seeing Owen and Trés together on at least two occasions. That was an interesting conversation for Roberto, and not just because the detective was from Georgia and had a thick accent. Abernathy spoke about Owen as if he was frightened of him. When Roberto told him of the arrest, the detective's mood shifted, becoming angry.

"Damn it!... I mean, I'm glad he's confessed and that it's solved, but I can't believe I didn't see it back then. I just thought he was weird and messed up because of the whole crazy situation with his family and seeing his dead brother. Damn it. I'll try to get in touch with Mac, he'd want to know."

Abernathy remembered that Owen was not wearing a watch when he first approached him at the crime scene, but then he had it on a few days later during one of their interviews. He said it stuck out in his mind because it was the same watch that he'd worn the first time they'd interviewed teenage Owen after Liam died.

Of course, the physical evidence on Warren William's body and car had long since been washed away, but Roberto asked if Abernathy's team had fingerprinted Williams' house. He confirmed that they had, but none of the prints had matched any of their suspects. That report should arrive in John's inbox sometime today so their analysts can compare the prints lifted from Warren's home to the set they'd collected from Owen. Now, they would also compare them to Cara's.

As for Evanston, Detective Miller hadn't been able to track down the two girls that Owen mentioned speaking with outside of the coffee shop, but the manager of the shop remembered him. She said that he had spent many hours, sometimes entire days, sitting in the corner working on a laptop. She gave a description of him, but no one remembered seeing Cara. They checked Cara's financial records, and she hadn't spent any money in Illinois and there were no cell phone records indicating that she'd traveled there during that time.

Roberto figured she could easily carry and use cash and turn her phone off. He still wasn't sure why he was suspicious of her, just going on the word of a confessed murderer wasn't really evidence. Something about her didn't sit right with him, but there was nothing to say that she was guilty of anything except growing up with, apparently not just one, but two deranged brothers.

With their own case, John and Roberto had hoped to find Rowe's phone, or some additional footprints or evidence at the scene, or anything that could lead them to the murderer. Unfortunately, they'd arrested Motney Bride last week, but they really had no other choice.

After they interviewed first Owen, then Cara, Roberto felt more confused than before they'd had any leads at all. Each was blaming the murders on the other. One, a self-professed killer, who boldly claimed murdering his own brother, yet categorically denied harming these strangers. The other, a victim of her brother's past deceit, who was willing to put herself in harm's way to prove that he's a monster. Neither are believable, except they both are.

The tired detective slammed the phone face down on his desk in exasperation after finally calming his wife's agitated pleas to come home soon.

"Rob? You good?" John rolled his chair to the side of Roberto's desk and peeked around his laptop.

In response, Roberto dropped his head into his hands once again and used his thumbs to massage his temples.

His partner rolled the chair closer and put a hand on Roberto's shoulder.

"Yeah, me too, man," John sighed as he patted him on the back.

"Look, I think... Let's just focus on the next step. We've got both of their prints. We'll hear back about their DNA, uh, soon, hopefully. And we've got the Shanta County team searching Owen's house and car tonight. And if we need them to, the Fulton County team can do the same with Cara's car and apartment at some point. I've got a good feeling about this."

He listened to his friend try to reason with him, but Roberto could hear the hesitation in John's voice. The only certainty that he felt at that moment was that a Walsh had killed at least four people. But which one? Or was it both? Were they both guilty of murder?

Chapter 31

DECEMBER 11, 2019

As her eyes blurred and obliterated her vision of the words dancing across the screen, Cara leaned closer and perched on the edge of the couch, the end of the story finally emerging.

> *Alejandro Gonzalez Iñárritu once said, "Life and death are illusions. We are in a constant state of transformation."*
>
> *As my little brother's last breath left his lips, I felt the beginnings of that transformation within my soul. I felt the fissures in my heart begin to pull together, healing and repairing, while the dark, thick blood drained from the opening in his skull. It was the type of sensation one feels sitting at the base of a fountain, watching the life-giving liquid pour from each tier, cascading downward in a relaxing, peaceful path, settling any angst left within your mind.*
>
> *Liam's death brought me life. I knew being rid of him would make me feel better. I had no idea that*

it would bring me power, confidence, and joy. Joy is not an emotion I'd ever identified in myself before. But I understood in that moment of him dying what it would feel like to begin living, filtering each new day through a lens of happiness.

My brother was a taker, a leech, but more than that, he was a tyrant and a predator. Likewise, our father knew nothing except violence and fear, and he dealt them out like tossing beads off a parade float. That's where I've witnessed someone else's joy. It brought Dad great pleasure to be the creator of our injuries and our depression. Like an artist, the bruises and tears that he splashed onto the canvas of our bodies and hearts, brought him happiness, and I felt it with every blow.

I will say one thing for Dad, though, he inadvertently taught me to overcome obstacles. I learned not to let anyone get in my way on my path to success. Liam joined him to fight against me, but I emerged victorious, a phoenix rising from the ashes.

As Joseph Stalin said, "Death is the solution to all problems. No man- no problem." If I hadn't killed Liam that day, eventually he would've killed me. Perhaps not physically, but I was already dying to his dreams, Mom's neglect, and Dad's disgust, and I wouldn't have survived much longer.

Mostly, I blame my mother. I know it's cliché for a killer to blame his mother, but if my mom had refused to marry Frank, or maybe just stood up to him the first time his calm facade slipped and the violent monster reared its ugly head, then many lives would have been saved.

When she was young, my sister was a lot like our mother: quick to cower and give-in, fearful and anxious, a people-pleaser to a fault. I tried to protect her and help her even though no one provided that for me. I thought I could be a redeemer, nothing like my father.

Cara leaned toward me for a while, and I think I needed that, tried to make that my identity. Unfortunately, I discovered that I didn't respect her for it, and I could never love someone so weak. Perhaps that was another lesson I learned from Frank Walsh.

Transformation does not discriminate, and I watched as it worked through Cara as well, after Liam's death. First, she grew weaker, a ridiculous, soggy mess of a human. It was often amusing, the way she clung to the idea of loving a dead person that she hated when they were alive. I didn't feel sorry for her at all, she brought it on herself.

Cara's discovery of Liam's true persona was quite fortuitous for me. I was pleased with the destruction of their relationship, as it provided the fuel and motivation I needed to finally envision a way to escape. Initially I was irritated with her for being

381

in the woods that day and unknowingly inserting herself into the center of my vindication.

But I quickly realized that it meant I could lay the blame at her feet, that I didn't have to anchor my own demise to his death. Prior to that, I was fully prepared to go down with the ship.

Thankfully, Cara provided a better distraction than I could've planned for. I was able to free myself of my family, and every burden they'd ever pressed upon me. I was free to pursue my dream of writing. I was free to let Liam go and never look back.

Except that I wasn't. Cara surprised me. I'm unable to say that about most people. Humans are predictable, easily manipulated, ready to believe whatever they're hoping is true.

My sister figured me out and saw through my attempt to distance myself from my crime. At some point, she decided that I was in the way of her own happiness. My respect for her has grown over the years, alongside my disdain for her.

Cara must've been paying attention to Dad's lessons as well and she transformed from a soggy mess into a callous manipulator. At first, it seemed as if she'd decided to emulate him instead of our mother.

I realized recently that I was wrong about that. It's not Dad's or Mom's characteristics that I've seen in her, it's Liam's. Perhaps as she watched his blood drain from the gaping head wound my stone left behind, her humanity drained as well. If I was a spiritual person, I might wonder if his demonic soul left his body and latched onto hers because it would be an easier explanation for the sudden explosion of her hatred.

Cara has been stalking me, stealing from me, and tormenting me for twelve years. She took over what Liam started. I thought I could outrun her, outlive her. Turns out, she's more like me than I thought. Turns out, she's worse than I am.

I'm not exactly sure when her switch flipped from victim to victimizer, but I suspect that it began with that first note she left for me to find. Or it might've been when she stole the file that I kept about Liam's death from my room. I guess you could say that story was the precursor to this one, before I was willing to explain my reasons for killing him, and long before I was willing to accept responsibility.

I'd been writing about her for some time, not the reality of who she was, but who I imagined her to be. I was creating a fictional Cara, basing my stories on pieces of my lived experiences and my imagination. It was amazing to watch her become exactly who I described her to be, unexpected certainly, but amazing, nonetheless.

I recognized the potential for evil in my little sister and her metamorphosis into that person confirmed my power as a writer and creator. My stories can

383

bring life and clarity, as well as destruction. I've dedicated this book to her because without Cara, my life might've ended when Liam's did.

Instead, my life has skyrocketed toward fame, and with this final story, most likely infamy. Cara brought me the subject of each of my articles this past year and laid their dead bodies at my doorstep like a kitten trying to please its master. I am grateful to her, in a way, even though her intention was to implicate and ultimately frame me for murders I didn't commit, in the name of the one that I did.

The most satisfying realization, the one that reaches deep into the marrow of who I am and fills me with more joy than I've ever known, is that my father will always be remembered as the monster who raised murderers. I can live with what I've done, and I can even say that I'm proud of what Cara did, because I know without a doubt that this will destroy Frank Walsh.

His children have thoroughly and completely ruined him. It's better than any violent end I've ever dreamed for him. Now, he will live broken and bruised and alone.

My only regret is that my mother will live on with little to no consequences and will continue to cower to my dad, hating us alongside him to save herself, just as she's always done.

Dad, if you're reading this, I hope death takes its time coming for you. I hope that you live a long life and that regret and sorrow eat away at your soul until there's nothing left but your rotten core. No one will pity you. No one will grieve for you. You created me, then you destroyed me, but I became greater than you could've ever planned or imagined. You are a simple, desperate, terrible person whose only achievement is loss and heartache.

Mom, if you're reading this, pray that I'm never released. You fueled the monster that tortured me. You were too weak to fight back. You have lived a worthless life, but I will end it for you if we ever meet again.

Cara, little Care Bear, I have no doubt that you will have a chance to read this. I'm glad that you finally decided to stand up for yourself. Of course, you've only reacted out of weakness and fear, but it's more than Mom was ever capable of. You've been clever and resourceful. However, there are no awards for murdering more people than someone else. You have surpassed me in the only way that doesn't matter, you're more psychotic than I am.

So, Cara, this is a better conclusion than I could've ever hoped for. I thought killing Liam brought me freedom, and it did, somewhat. But I was wrong. I've finally found freedom in embracing my actions.

There is a lightness in my heart that I've never felt before.

At some point, you are going to be arrested and held accountable for murdering Warren Williams, Derreck Hoffman, and Johnny Rowe. But I know that you will not feel the freedom that I've described right away. It will kill you to think that I've won. This is how you die. This is what you deserve.

And after you finally die to your selfish motives, accepting the consequences of your actions, you'll be reborn. You will be ready to live, free from this burden of hatred. The most powerful conclusion to a story is when the villain finds redemption. It's time to confess and live again, to get what you really deserve.

Cara vomited into the small trash can that she'd pulled next to the coffee table for what must've been the fortieth time. There was nothing left in her stomach contents, and it was all empty retching and saliva. It had taken her several days to finish reading Owen's story.

At first, she decided to avoid it, just delete it immediately. The flash drive had been buried at the bottom of her purse as she traveled back to Georgia from New York. It stayed there, present and heavy, for the last few days, but curiosity burned within her, and she had to find out what he knew.

It was always Owen's words that found a way to destroy her, to worm their way into her mind, leaving hollowed trails of doubt and fear. She shouldn't have read it. Standing up from the couch, she slammed the lid of the laptop closed and began to pace around her small apartment living room.

They had no proof. There was more evidence that Owen was responsible for these murders. She knew that. She'd covered her tracks obsessively and collected any trace that would point to her. Maybe she should've destroyed the items currently tucked safely into the box stored at her parents' house.

Anxiously, Cara paced back across the living room, stopping in front of the laptop. No, she couldn't have gotten rid of the syringes. The exchange program she used was a one for one exchange, so she'd have to take the used needles with her to get some new ones. There was no way to tell when she might need some again, so she couldn't risk going completely without until then.

Rowe's phone shouldn't pose a problem. Once it was safe to do so, she'd smash it, burn it, and scatter the pieces in the Chickasaw River a few counties away.

Cara took a deep breath, calming herself with the plan. Opening the laptop, she stared at the typed print until the letters blurred and swam together again, her fingers hesitating over the mouse pad, debating.

How had he figured out it was her? And when? It was clear that Owen was oblivious to her presence in Mill City. Luckily, she was so familiar with the city, she had no difficulties following him. Trés was the easiest victim, and she also had no problem with seducing him and convincing him to meet her at the park.

The rest of the plan solidified without much forethought. She read online about how much of the ketamine it would take to knock out a man his size, so she was ready with the drug but only found the brick on the edge of the parking lot once she and Trés had arrived at the park.

The idea to smash his skull was a last-minute addition because she wasn't entirely sure how long the ketamine would incapacitate him. She wanted to be sure that he drowned.

That first murder scared her. *What had she become?* It was hard to remember the driving force behind such unforgivable actions as she brought the brick down on an unconscious man's face. Repositioning the car to where it needed to be on the edge of the parking lot had been helpful to take her mind away from the violence and regret. But while watching the electric-blue car sink beneath the surface, her heart lifted. It wasn't Trés drowning in the metal coffin, it was Owen.

Cara returned to the town a few days later after reading his first article about the death. The excitement and satisfaction were covered in a thick blanket of uncertainty, because she wanted to be sure that Owen was as connected to the victim as possible. It seemed to be dumb luck when she spotted him covertly hunting around at the crime scene.

A few weeks prior, she followed Owen and Trés from the restaurant where they'd met for lunch down to the Chickasaw River Greenway, which is when she formulated her plan to drown him there. The two men had downed several drinks during their meal, but continued to drink from a bottle of bourbon once they reached the park.

It was busier on the Greenway that afternoon, but Cara still had to hide in the shadows of the woods and couldn't get close enough to hear their conversation. They didn't seem to be bonding or having a good time. There was no loud laughter or animated conversation. Their expressions were serious, but calm, even as they barreled through half the bottle.

There was no reason for her to stick around the entire time because she wasn't going to kill Trés until the next day. It must've been during their conversation that Owen's watch fell off. However it happened, it was pleasing to see how much it ruffled her brother. The drive back home was much smoother. Happiness fueled her, confirming the belief that this was the right thing to do and that she'd gladly do it again.

Derrick Hoffman was much trickier. For one, it was so much harder to track Owen in the large, unfamiliar city. For another, she had to become someone that Derrick would see as an easy prey, to accentuate her naiveté and play down her intelligence. It would've been humiliating except she could tell that pulling off the "bimbo" persona would immediately catch his attention.

Owen had met Derrick a few days after hearing about him from the girls outside the coffee shop. It was clear from his expressions as the girls described the monster, that he was going to seek Derrick out. All she had to do was follow Owen a few times to learn which bars Derrick frequented and where he lived.

Cara was much more prepared the second time she ended someone's life. There was less anxiety and fear because she

already knew what it would be like. She also had a lot of fait
in the amount of heroin and fentanyl that she'd brought. He
college roommate's longtime boyfriend had always been
good source for any drugs that the two friends wanted to tr
in their mission to become numb to the perils of life.

She met both Trés and Derrick just by walking up an
starting a conversation. Men are so needy and predictabl
They think they have all the power and control, but Car
would never allow anyone of the male gender to manipulat
her or degrade her again.

Trés had at least hesitated when she approached him a
the Starbucks. He stood sipping his coffee, looking her u
and down as he considered her reasoning. Cara told him tha
she'd met him a few months before, out at a local bar, but a
the time she'd been with her boyfriend. He invited her bac
to his house before she even finished sharing her sob stor
of betrayal.

Conversely, Derrick hadn't hesitated at all even thoug]
Cara just showed up on his doorstep, wearing a short, blac
cocktail dress with a pair of pink Converse on and explaine
that one of his frat brothers had suggested that she mee
Derrick at this apartment to escort him to the Spring Forma
At the time, she was worried he already had a date, but h
made it clear within five minutes of setting eyes on her tha
he was eager and ready to take her to the dance.

Trés had taken his time trying to seduce Cara, whic]
played into her being able to convince him to take her to th

boat ramp because she said being near the water and in his car would be both "romantic and risky."

Derrick hadn't wasted any time trying to convince her. She'd only managed a little bit of conversation before he began making his moves. Luckily, she was able to escape to the bathroom before anything went beyond making out, giving her some time to prepare the ketamine. Killing him was easier, but way more dangerous. She was relieved everything worked the way she'd planned it. It could've easily gone completely wrong.

Once Derrick was dead, she began to doubt whether she'd done enough to connect her brother to the crimes. It wasn't sufficient that he'd met these men and showed up to report on their deaths. Owen needed to be present for the next murder.

Investigating Owen's next moves through questioning their parents would be difficult since he told them very little about his life, but it was probably Cara's only option. Instead of asking about him directly, her tactic was to ask when the last time either of them had spoken to Chelsey and if they knew how she'd been doing since the move to Redmore. That got her mom's gears turning and she ended up texting Chelsey that same evening.

Chelsey was quick to respond, complaining about the move, ranting about the heat and how lonely she'd been. Cara watched the conversation over her mother's shoulder, hoping that it would steer in the right direction. Sure enough, her next question was if Owen would be returning home to see

Chelsey anytime soon and if he knew how lonely his fiancé had become.

Even without the benefit of hearing Chelsey's voice, Cara could tell the change in tone in the messages. Everyone else could see that Owen's fiancé was more interested in his success and growing popularity than in the idea of being his partner in life, but it didn't seem like he was aware. Or maybe he just didn't care. Maybe Owen wasn't capable of loving anyone.

Chelsey sent back a series of rapid-fire responses, packed with exclamation points and smiley emojis, explaining that Owen was home, but that he'd be leaving for New York in the morning, and he'd promised to scout out a location for a future weekend getaway with her. Surely, New York could provide the luxury and adventure that would knock her out of her slump.

That evening, Cara started researching hikes near New York city. The idea of creating a scenario to mimic the way Liam died snowballed in her mind. The excitement built and as she plotted and planned, she felt closer than ever to catching Owen.

It was risky to choose someone as high-profile as Johnny Rowe, but his legal situation provided some ideas for leverage to use in luring him to meet. Then, all that was needed was to plant the idea of Hudson Highlands State Park, and specifically the quarry off the Bull Hill trail.

That was simple enough to accomplish, mostly because her mother was always eager to have something to say to Chelsey. Owen had been hateful for so many years, their mother longed to stay connected to him in some way and to come across as helpful.

Cara left the article about the hikes open on their computer. Seeing the pictures of the field surrounded by the colorful, rocky hillsides of the quarry prompted her mom to stop and read.

"Cara?"

"Yeah?" It was difficult to disguise the grin in her voice. Some people are so easily manipulated.

"What's this all about? This place looks so pretty! Isn't that the area Chelsey mentioned?"

"Yeah, I think so," she said as she walked in and stood next to her mom. "I got curious and looked it up. It is beautiful. I wonder if Owen knows about it. Chelsey likes hikes and stuff, right? That's not far outside the city, so it might be just her style."

Then she walked back down the hall toward the living room, leaving behind the suggestions like breadcrumbs.

"I think she would..."

As her mom walked through the living room past Cara on the couch, she added, "I'll mention it to her." Cara could tell she was smiling, proud of having a good idea to share.

These memories of how well everything had played out calmed Cara's stomach and she no longer felt so shaky, her fingers steady now as they continued to hover over the mouse pad.

Deciding, she moved the file across the screen to the trash can, emptied the trash, and erased her history. Cara knew she would have to seek out Owen's laptop, which the police were probably already in possession of, or maybe go through the computer at her parents' house to find the original file.

Even if it was created online through Google docs or Word, maybe she would have time to delete it before anyone else knew of its existence. And if they didn't know of its existence, then why would they even go looking for it? Yes, this had to work. There was a good chance that Owen was still logged in to the word processing software at their parents' house.

After removing the flash drive, Cara placed it in a plastic bag, took it to the back porch, and smashed it into tiny pieces with a hammer. After dumping the pieces into an old flowerpot, she placed a newspaper scrap on top and set the contents on fire.

Eventually, the blaze burned itself out. Then, Cara dumped in fresh dirt and a packet of seeds, until finally sprinkling it with water. It was symbolic, just as she'd set fire to her old way of living and grown something new in its place. This wasn't the end, it couldn't be. Just a few more steps to take until she was free. This had to work, Cara's life depended on it

Chapter 32

THE REST OF HER LIFE

"*C*ara? We weren't expecting you today..."

Looking concerned, her mother glanced over her shoulder at something she'd heard. Cara knew it was her father complaining about the interruption to something on TV, most likely a football game.

Everyone in the family always had to tiptoe around the house anytime Frank Walsh was settled into his armchair watching a game. Her mother had earned a sprained wrist two years ago because she'd forgotten to replace the tortilla chips that were part of his chips and salsa ritual for March Madness after Cara had finished them off the day before.

Already fuming about having a client late in the day, which delayed him from arriving home in time to down a few beers before the start of the second round of the tournament, his discovery of a bag full of crumbs had been the straw that broke the proverbial camel's back.

Her mom had immediately started backpedaling and groveling, which only ever added fuel to his fire. When he reached out to remove the bag from his hands, offering to throw it away and get him something else, her husband grabbed her roughly by the wrist and twisted it in a quick movement, sending Rita Walsh to her knees where he left her in a heap on the floor, crying in pain.

The mostly empty bag drifted down to land on top of her writhing body, as he stepped over her to reenter the living room before the game started. The volume on the TV was turned up to its max to drown out her sobbing.

But Cara didn't have time for any timidity today. It was essential that she get to her things.

"I know, Mom, I'm sorry to just drop in," she said with a sigh while pushing past her mother and entering the house. "I won't be long, and I won't be loud," she whispered, "I just have to pick up some more things that I left over here."

Her mother looked worried, wringing her hands, and nodding while following Cara down the hall toward the bedrooms.

"Rita!" His voice boomed from across the house. "Who's at the door?"

She winced, hunching her shoulders up to her ears like a turtle trying to hide. Normally, Cara shared her mom's trepidation of Dad's reactions. Over the years, they'd all perfectly honed their routines to mold themselves around his needs to minimize any interruptions or surprises.

But, despite the disruption Cara was now causing, she continued on her mission, shamefully less concerned about her mother for the time being.

"Oh, it's just Cara stopping by to pick up a box or two from her room. She'll just be a minute!"

Cara darted into her old bedroom, closing the door quickly, but quietly in her mother's face, knowing she wouldn't knock or say anything that would signal a problem to the belligerent man down the hall.

Now a guest room, it was almost emptied of personal belongings and only had a few pieces of furniture left behind. Cara moved straight to the computer, waking it up and watching the screensaver come to life. She'd been right in thinking Owen would still be logged into the various programs and websites.

A copy of the book he'd written was in Word. Following the trail of the document and pushing the "delete forever" button did ease some of the vice that was squeezing at Cara's chest, but she wasn't done.

Opening the door a crack, she peeked down the hall to listen for when it would be safe to sneak out. Sensing it was all clear, she dashed into Liam's room, again softly closing the door behind her. His bedroom hadn't changed in the last twelve years. She'd walked into a shrine. Frank and Rita both refused to take anything down or give even the smallest items away, which had worked out well for Cara's purposes.

Heart pounding in her chest, Cara moved swiftly to the closet. She was much taller than she'd been the first time she discovered the box of stolen items, and it was easy now in adulthood to stand on tiptoes and pull it from its spot high on the shelf. Each time she'd opened it in the last several months, the memories of spite and anger would flood back into her body in a familiar wave of heat and tingling.

Trembling hands pushed aside the forgotten items, digging toward the bottom where she'd stashed Johnny's phone, the embroidered pouch that held the rest of her K and two needles, and the wadded-up Aerosmith T-shirt that she'd worn to meet up with Trés and Johnny, which now had two layers of blood splashed across it mixed in amongst its paint-splatter design. Cara pulled each object from its hiding place and stuffed them into the large purse draped across her body.

Suddenly, there was a loud banging at the front door. It was the sound of a fist slamming into the old wood repeatedly, echoing through the house, and with each blow her heart stuttered and threatened to stop. Cara froze, poised over the box, arms clutching the purse to her body like a lifeline. Footsteps hurried down the hallway toward the bedroom.

Amidst some shouting, several police officers burst into the room, one with his gun drawn and trained on her, yelling for Cara to put her hands on her head. The next few minutes were a blur of activity and Cara felt like she was underwater. Someone snatched the purse, and pushed her forcefully to the carpet, handcuffing her hands behind her back, while reciting the Miranda Rights.

Cara glimpsed her mom in the doorway, shocked into silence. Her dad stood in the background, glaring at Cara as if he'd set her on fire if he could. Turning her head away from the melting stare, she kept her eyes on her own footsteps as the officers led her outside. Each step echoed the beat of the death march, marking the seconds ticking towards her doom. Detective Abernathy stood solemnly next to the cruiser, his glower throwing daggers where her father had left off.

Detective Lenderman was waiting at the station and Cara was glad he was her escort back to New York. There was no pressure to talk, but she didn't even try to restrain the tears from flowing freely. Fear was a visible companion during the hours of traveling, but the detective's kind eyes comforted some of the anxiety.

By that night, Cara sat shaking, alone in an empty interview room. Was it the same one she'd sat in just a week ago? She was shivering, although the temperature in the room was probably not the cause. How long did they intend to make her wait? Her heart rate galloped out of control and sweat rolled down her spine, even as she tucked her fingers into her pockets to keep them warm.

When they'd brought her here, they hadn't given Cara much information and she'd kept her lips squeezed shut, refusing to speak. They would return soon for questioning, what would she say? *What did they know?*

She had to talk to Owen. Would that be possible? If she could only speak to him, Cara might be able to convince her brother to take the blame. He had already confessed to one murder, after all. But how had the police known about the hidden items? Owen? Did he know about them?

Questions bounced around Cara's mind like a pinball machine, leaving her feeling like she was arguing with herself. She felt truly crazy.

The door opened and Detective Sanchez strolled confidently in, by himself this time. A slight smile on his lips, he looked at Cara knowingly. She didn't like how clear and bright his eyes were, very different from the guarded, serious detective she'd spoken with previously.

"Are you ready to talk to us, Ms. Walsh?" He pulled out the chair across the table to sit down.

"No."

Detective Sanchez paused with his hand on the back of the chair but didn't sit. He must've been expecting a different answer. Putting both hands on the chair and leaning forward he said, "Well, we've got some things to talk to you about and then maybe you'll change your mind. Would you like me to call your lawyer?"

"No. I want to talk to my brother. I'll only talk to Owen."

The detective regarded her solemnly for a moment, deciding how much weight to give her declaration. Each of Cara's breaths was heavy and reverberated around the silent room.

Turning to leave, he said, "Let me see what I can do."

What seemed like hours later, after she'd fallen asleep with her head on her arms, she was woken by the door opening again. Cara looked up to find Owen standing just inside the doorway. He looked disheveled, but calm. His hands were cuffed in front of him. As he shuffled into the room, she saw that his ankles were also linked together.

"Hello, Care Bear," he grinned.

Detective Lenderman guided Owen to the table and attached the cuffs to the side of it. A tall, older gentleman, bald, with a large white mustache and wearing a dark, gray suit stood behind Owen. As they sat down, the man settled an expensive looking, but worn, leather briefcase on the table.

"Good evening, Ms. Walsh, my name is Dennis Ramsey, your brother's lawyer. He has asked me to accompany him to speak with you."

Surprised didn't accurately describe Cara's reaction. It felt more like shock, horror, helplessness, and a heavy dose of indignation. A feeling of dread settled across her shoulders like a weighted blanket. Surely her mouth had dropped open, and she hastily did a self-inventory to reset her expression and body language. *He brought a lawyer?*

Owen grinned from ear to ear like a cat who'd swallowed a canary. A shiver ran down Cara's spine and, although it seemed impossible, her brother's smile grew wider. Even though Owen was chained to the table, it felt as if his hands were squeezing her throat closed again and she couldn't breathe.

Owen watched as she placed her hand to her neck in defense and his expression turned quizzical. If Cara hadn't been terrified, she would've laughed at the way he tilted his head like a curious puppy.

"You seem tense," he quipped. "I thought you wanted to talk to me."

Cara pointedly glanced at the lawyer sitting rigidly to Owen's right and then up at the camera in the corner of the room. There didn't seem to be a good way to say what she needed to say.

Owen said, "Oh, don't worry about the audience. They already know everything."

His smile was back then, as he continued, "You've been such a naughty girl."

"What're you talking about?" Cara squeaked, almost choking on her words. It had been so long since she'd uttered anything that her throat was as dry as a desert.

"Let's not make this last any longer than it must, huh? I'll do the talking."

Cara gulped. It felt like she was witnessing the impact of a car crash and couldn't look away.

"You might as well come clean about what you did since you've literally handed the proof of your killing spree to the police. Plus, they now have your fingerprints and DNA to compare to the evidence found at the crime scenes."

Finding her voice again, Cara shouted vehemently, "None of that stuff at Mom and Dad's house was mine! I was just getting it to hand over and prove that you're guilty of killing those men!"

Even though she'd risen to her feet, both men continued to sit calmly, unruffled.

"Well, that doesn't make any sense, does it?" Owen shook his head lightly, clicking his tongue against his teeth.

"Don't waste your time trying to come up with the perfect lie. I've told them everything that I suspected. The detectives weren't sure about my tips, but after ruling me out as the murderer, and finding your fingerprints at some of the scenes, they were willing enough to listen and investigate further." Owen shifted in his seat, sitting up straighter as a thought occurred to him.

"You know, despite what you may think, I'm grateful to you. I'll admit, trying to strangle you probably wasn't my finest hour, but I've had some time to think while I waited for this moment. After years of hard work, your murders are what finally brought me into the spotlight that I deserved. I mean, at first, I was resentful because I didn't want anyone to get the idea that I wouldn't have risen to success without your depravity, but then I realized that it's my talent that has gotten me to this point. It's true you played your role in my advancement, but it would've happened for me regardless of which psychopath I reported on."

Owen took a deep breath, leaning back in the chair as far as the cuffs would allow. Not relaxed, exactly, but satisfied.

"Once I realized what you'd done, how it all came together, I was grateful." He clapped his hands together. "You really have provided me with the perfect ending to my story."

"You haven't got a story!" The retort left Cara's lips before she could stop it. On her feet again, fists balled up at her sides, she wanted to hurt him, to destroy him. *How had she lost control of everything?*

"You need to remain seated, Ms. Walsh, otherwise I'll ask the officers to come back in here and restrain you," Mr. Ramsey said firmly.

Cara turned to look at the lawyer and felt a new wave of hatred wash through her. She hated him, she hated Owen, she hated herself. There was a short standoff during which she wasn't sure if she wanted to sit back down or launch herself across the table at her brother. If this was the end, she would go down fighting.

After a long moment of indecision, Cara slowly lowered herself back in the cold, plastic chair, newly exhausted by hesitation, feeling defeated and run over. Owen remained unmoved and unaffected. Tears began to forge trails down her cheek, dripping from her chin and nose onto the table.

Owen

Death is a waterfall, an enormous volume of water, erupting from the earth, sometimes beginning as a slow trickle, and other times as forceful as a firehose. A trickle can soothe, relaxing you into a peaceful state of mind, or it can feel like a slow, torturous villain.

On the other hand, standing beneath the force of a firehose can drown you, or tear you apart. But stepping back for a different perspective, you'll see a shocking beauty. Either type of waterfall brings life to its surroundings without regard for how it's perceived.

I don't regret killing Liam. His death brought nourishment to my worn-down soul. I thought taking responsibility for his murder would ruin my life further, but what choice did I have?

Stepping back to view the bigger picture, now I realize the beauty of his demise. My days before Liam died were spent living in fear of my tyrannical father, running from shadow to shadow, hiding and hoping not to be harmed. My brother's rise to popularity increased the frequency and intensity of my punishments. He performed perfectly in everything he did, and I could do nothing right.

What a relief to find out that it doesn't have to be that way! Abuse at the hands of my father ended the day Liam's life ended, but my revelations came upon me as a slow trickle, leaving behind a trail of new growth and vibrancy. No, I don't regret killing Liam.

Looking at Cara, half-crazed, sitting across the table from me in the police interview room, it's clear that my sister drowned a long time ago. She's no longer the little girl who needed my companionship and protection. I suppose she never needed either one. She always had a talent for staying out of the way, or if that was impossible, allowing the pain without complaint. I imagine that we are both a product of our broken home, but I'd like to think that I, too, inspired her in some way.

The people in my life have enhanced every element of my story, just like strong characters in a successful piece of writing. Cara and I would, of course, be the protagonists, while my villainous father and brother are the antagonists.

We've all been on separate quests to come out as the victor in this power struggle. For Dad, power was found through causing pain. For me, I harness power through words, creating, teaching, destroying, reviving. Liam used possessions to hold power over others, and Cara sought to control her life and the lives of others to feel powerful. My story has all the elements that matter to make it meaningful and compelling, although there is no moral.

"My story is finished," I told her when she sat back down, "and it's perfect."

Cara's eyes continued their unrelenting weeping, and her voice was thick and shaky with emotion when she spoke again. "Bu-but... I d-destroyed it..."

Poor girl. Why couldn't she just accept the inevitable, just embrace the results of her own actions? I reached across the table to touch her hand. She recoiled from my touch, but I snatched her fingers before she could move them away and held on tightly as I explained.

"Cara, nothing created online is ever really gone. I sent a copy to my publisher, as well as my editor, before meeting you in the park that morning. I suspected what you'd been up to, but I didn't anticipate that you'd wear a wire. I actually thought that you were trying to get more information for your next set-up. But once I was arrested, I began hoping you'd be the one that the police would turn over my belongings to. With your history of snooping, I assumed that you'd be able to find my hidden flash drive. Luckily, that all worked in my favor, and you were able to read my story and, well, here we are." I smiled at her indulgently, hoping to sound encouraging.

"How did you know?" she whispered.

"I didn't *know* until our conversation. Until then it was just a strong hunch and a knowledge centered more in my gut than my head. When you asked me about my watch, I remembered that day I found you snooping in Liam's room. A couple of years ago, I discovered that same box in his closet that I caught you rummaging in not long before he died."

Cara snatched her hand out of my grasp and slapped it down on the table causing Mr. Ramsey to jump in his seat. "You mean before you killed him!" she shouted.

I waved one of my cuffed hands through the air dismissively at her, "Yes, yes. We've already established that. Are you ready to confess to *your* crimes yet?"

Cara sniffed and folded her arms protectively across her body, turning away from me like a child who's been scolded.

I continued, "Anyway, because you've chosen to murder men who embody Liam's fatalistic flaws in a failed attempt to frame me, I figured you would probably hold tightly to that symbolic storyline and use his box of stolen treasures to hide your own trophies of power."

Her shoulders twitched in a slight wince at hearing my words, but Cara remained angled away from me, not meeting my eyes.

I could feel the difference in the air in the room now. My heart pounded in my chest, but not in fear, with excitement. My sister, the murderer, was close to admitting it, to herself and to me, and her confession was essential to my story. The tears were still gathering along her jaw and dripping silently. For a moment I saw a small girl, scared and defenseless, unable to get away from a terrifying older brother who thrived on torturing her.

Now I'm that brother. But Cara's no longer the victim. She deserves this. *I* deserve this.

"I meant what I said, Cara. I'm grateful to you. And I'm proud of you."

I let the smile weave through my words, reassuring and calm. She looked over her shoulder slightly, still not meeting my eyes, but obviously listening.

"You've been loyal, you've been brave, and you've been clever, more than I could've been. Other people..." I swept a cuffed hand in a small gesture through the air indicating anyone outside the room, as well as the rest of the world, "don't understand your loyalty. They'll never get why a sister would be so devoted to an abusive brother, with the purpose of destroying the other brother."

Cara shifted in her seat until she was mostly facing the table, staring down at its surface. She swiped her sleeve across her face, trying to dry her eyes.

"It doesn't matter how you justify it to anyone else, they won't understand," I said softly, speaking only to her. "It's time to be honest with yourself. It's time to embrace what you've done."

The air between us filled with Cara's shallow, gasping breaths, as she struggled to break the surface of the despair that was drowning her. As they slowed, she finally looked up and met my eyes. I could tell she was hollowed out, an empty shell waiting to be refilled. The realization that she couldn't fight anymore was a new dawn rising in her expression, and her gaze burned into mine, pleading. It wouldn't be long now. I was close to the ending.

"Do you want to know how the story ends?"

Nodding solemnly, Cara scooted to the edge of her chair in anticipation.

"You're going to confess and then your life will really begin. Once you are free of this burden, this hatred, that you've carried for twelve years, or maybe forever, you will grow and thrive in ways that you've never imagined. And you will be happy."

A small smile tilted her lips.

"Then, my story will have the perfect ending. And Cara, it's truly glorious. I couldn't have done it without you." I returned her smile.

"My publisher is ready and eager to get my book into the hands of readers as soon as possible. But first, my editor at the newspaper will be publishing the first four chapters of the story, one per week, over the next month in place of my article, enticing the readers, getting them interested, then getting them hooked. They'll have to know what happens next, but to find out, they'll have to wait and buy the book! Our arrests and the Newsworthy articles are the perfect publicity!"

Now, Cara's smile widened into a broad, surprised grin. I paused to appreciate once again the brilliance of the plan. We were going to be rich and, more importantly, famous. And, ironically, it was all thanks to Liam.

"Be brave one more time, Cara. Write your confession. I've written the end of the story, but it's in your hands now. You have the power to make it happen. Finally, *you* have the power. This is your chance to be happy." I sat back, pleased with myself, happier than I've ever been.

I could see the difference in my little sister. She sat up straighter, determined.

"I'm ready," Cara said in a strong, steady voice.

My lawyer, who'd been sitting silently as I had requested, pulled a large, white legal pad from his briefcase, uncapped a pen, and slid both across the table to Cara. She closed her eyes and took a deep breath in through her nose and blew it out of her mouth slowly. Her eyes snapped open and in one smooth movement, Cara licked her lips and pulled the pad closer, picked up the pen and positioned the tip on the first line. Then, she began to write.

Every beginning comes from an ending. What a beautiful conclusion.